"What I'm trying to tell you is we've still got unfinished business."

"What do you mean?" Erica asked. "Dinner last night? Because it was just pizza and—"

"No," Mark interrupted. "It's more than that and you know it. You like me. You think I'm sexy. It's written all over your face."

"And tell me, Senator, what's written all over yours?"

"I'm actually something of a catch. Half the women on the Hill are in love with me."

"Really?"

"Yes, really. I could have any woman I want. It's just . . . well, I seem to have some kind of bee in my bonnet about you at the moment."

Go, go, go! The Marines in his head urged him and he acted, moving closer, close enough to gather her into his arms.

"I don't like unfinished business, Erica Johnson."

By Karyn Langhorne

UNFINISHED BUSINESS
DIARY OF AN UGLY DUCKLING
STREET LEVEL
A PERSONAL MATTER

KARYN LANGHORNE

Unfinished BUSINESS

AVON BOOKS
An Imprint of HarperCollins*Publishers*

This is a work of fiction. Names, characters, places, and incidents are products of the author's imagination or are used fictitiously and are not to be construed as real. Any resemblance to actual events, locales, organizations, or persons, living or dead, is entirely coincidental.

AVON BOOKS
An Imprint of HarperCollins*Publishers*
10 East 53rd Street
New York, New York 10022–5299

Copyright © 2007 by Karyn Wynn Folan
ISBN: 978–0–06–084789–0
ISBN–10: 0–06–084789–1
www.avonbooks.com

First Avon Books paperback printing: June 2007

Avon Trademark Reg. U.S. Pat. Off. and in Other Countries, Marca Registrada, Hecho en U.S.A.
HarperCollins® is a registered trademark of HarperCollins Publishers.

Printed in the U.S.A.

10 9 8 7 6 5 4 3 2 1

For Jill Richburg and John Canary—
who first gave these characters life!

◇◇

Acknowledgments

This book is based on an idea for a novel I had almost seven years ago. It's been through a lot of versions, formats and revisions since then—most notably as a play that ran off-Broadway in early 2001. That play was called *Primary Loyalties*. Before it was a play, though, these characters were presented in a television script that was selected by Lou Viola, then director of a program called "PSNBC." PSNBC gives fresh voices the chance to perform their work in front of NBC television execs, in the hopes of getting a TV deal.

I got to perform a version of this story for PSNBC in May 2000. My good friend Jill Richburg, a sometimes actress and sometimes lawyer (as well as a host of other titles and roles she plays well), played the part of Erica and directed the reading for me. She cast a wonderful actor name John Canary in the part of Mark.

Well, I didn't get a contract with NBC, but I did make a friend in Lou Viola—and in John Canary. Both Jill and John reprised their roles as Mark and Erica in the play I wrote a year later. I can never thank them enough for giving these characters life!

Without Mona Washington (who urged me to turn these characters into a play in the first place) and Lou Viola, who encouraged my writing efforts, I probably never would have finished those early versions of this story. Much love and thanks to you both!

There are plenty of people involved in helping me to tell you these stories, Dear Reader. Most important is my family: Kevin, Sierra and Sommer. They are my "street team": They travel with me to events, listen to me complain about this deadline or that and make dozens of sacrifices for "Mom's career." I love them dearly!

Then there's my mom and dad, Thomas and Evelyn; my sisters, Michele and Ellyn; my brother, Tom. I'm lucky to have you guys. I also want to shout out props to Kevin's family: his mom, Teresa; sisters, Mary and Eileen; brothers, Jimmy, John and Brian. Thanks, guys!

This book would never have been finished without the input of Linda Kenyon, a radio journalist and dear friend who covers Capitol Hill. Linda was willing to share her knowledge of the Senate to give this book a basis in reality.

Tamra Dyson entertained baby Sommer so I could think, and the staff at Ronald McNair Elementary School's BAR-T after-school program entertained Sierra for the same reason. Both deserve awards for their patience and kindness.

Rachel Swartz-Hartje, my personal trainer, made me get on the treadmill and lift some weights while she provided an ear for plot twists and dialogue.

Deep and sincere thanks go to the "dream team": my editor, Esi Sogah; my agent, Audra Barrett; and my publicist, Gabrielle Faulcon. You ladies are beyond fabulous!

And as always, thanks go to you, the reader. I always love hearing from you and getting your thoughts on my work. Republican or Democrat, red state or blue, you're the best!

Put your money where your mouth is.
—American idiom

Chapter 1

〰〰〰〰〰〰〰〰〰〰〰〰〰〰〰〰〰〰〰〰〰〰〰〰〰〰〰〰〰〰〰

"Have you got the money?" Erica muttered, glancing around the lobby, orienting herself for the task ahead.

They had just cleared security—without incident, thank God. Now, all they had to do was get upstairs and into the room. If Angelique had the money, it would all be as simple as Mom's home-baked apple pie.

"Money?" Angelique responded from somewhere over Erica's shoulder. "What money?"

Every nerve in Erica's body flared red alert. She stopped short, turning slowly toward her friend. The money was critical. If Angelique didn't have the money . . .

"You don't have the money? Why not?"

Angelique rolled her eyes and shook her head until her long braids danced on her shoulders like marionettes. "Don't freak out. I have it. But I won't need it," she corrected, waving her finger under Erica's nose. "I won't need it, because you're not actually going to do this."

Erica sighed, relief flooding through her body. Angelique wasn't funny—hadn't ever been—but as long as she still had the money . . .

"We're here, aren't we? I'm wearing it, aren't I?" Erica reminded her, keeping her voice low. It felt like every security guard in the place was checking her out as they hurried along the corridor. But that was silly. They didn't have X-ray vision. *And*, Erica reminded herself, *last time I checked, wearing a T-shirt wasn't against the law.*

Yet.

Another flutter of nervousness winged itself from her throat to her heart, and Erica inhaled deeply and swallowed hard, forcing it down. When she focused on her friend again, Angelique was staring at her.

"If you actually do this, you're flat-out crazy," she pronounced. "Crazy."

"I'm *not* crazy, I'm committed," Erica reminded her.

"Yeah, committed. Committed is exactly what you ought to be, if you ask me." Angelique eyed the light blue blouse Erica had borrowed from her closet of tailored shirts that morning, knowing that the starched cotton was the only thing standing between the world and Erica's offensive T-shirt. "Trust me, girl. If you actually do this, you've lost it. Big-time."

"Oh, I'm going to do it, don't you worry about that," Erica said firmly, and she knew in her heart that no matter how nervous or scared she felt, the words were true. "Now, one more time: Have you got the money?"

Angelique sighed another put-upon-girlfriend sigh, and then nodded. "I've got the thousand you gave me, plus another thousand of my own in cash." She patted the supple leather of her school bag. "If it's more than that, you're SOL."

"It'll be enough," Erica asserted with more confidence than she felt. Angelique opened her mouth for yet another comment, but when Erica cut her mahogany eyes sharply toward the corridor behind them, Angelique folded her lips. They both concentrated on looking innocent and inconsequential for the uniformed Capitol police officer stationed by the elevator doors. He was big, one of those thick-chested brothers with biceps like a normal man's thighs. The thick brother stared them up and down like he suspected something. It wasn't until a big, cheese-eating grin spread across his face that Erica understood that the brother wasn't hating, he was appreciating.

And why not? Erica thought. She was pretty sure it wasn't every day he saw two young, nice-looking sisters exercising their rights as citizens by attending a congressional hearing.

When the elevator doors opened, the dude turned a bit to take in their rear views, but he didn't stop them.

Fortunately, they had the ancient elevator car to themselves.

"Two thousand should be more than enough," Erica repeated as soon as the door closed them into the old metal box.

"Are you sure?" Angelique's voice rose and Erica heard concern mingled with annoyance. "Because I don't have any more money to invest in this venture, Erica, and I have a feeling you won't like jail."

"It'll be enough!" Erica told her and pretended to be fascinated by watching the floor numbers light up over the lift's doorway, so Angelique wouldn't know just how scared she was. *Oh Lord, please let it be enough,* she prayed quickly. *I know it's been a long time since I had a man . . . but I'm sure not ready for a woman.*

"You're not going to do it."

Erica's eyes snapped to her friend's face. They were

her best feature, Erica's eyes. Not that there was anything wrong with the rest of her. Even though she was smack in the middle of her thirties, she had a good figure and the hours logged at the gym to account for it. True, God had been a little generous on the top and the bottom, but any extra weight was certainly in the right places. And her skin was another blessing: creamy and smooth as an exotic coffee drink. She'd stopped processing her hair years ago and now wore it either wrapped like the women in Africa, or in long natural twists that sprang from her head like curly wires. But everyone always came back to the eyes—big and brown and deep-set in the warm oval of her face. And Erica knew how to use them, too. "Girl, you could sell ice to Eskimos with those eyes," her Gram had always said. Erica fixed her face for maximum appeal as she stared down her longtime friend, roommate and general partner in crime.

"I'm going to do it."

They had once been so much alike, but these days even their clothes bespoke the widening gap. In spite of the braids, Angelique was buttoned up and conservative in a nice suit and white blouse. In her long granny-style skirt and leather-free Birkenstock clogs, Erica looked and felt like a gypsy. Angelique must have been thinking something very similar, because she shook her head again.

"Do you have any idea how serious this is?"

"I know exactly how serious it is. That's why I'm doing it, thank you very much. Sometimes you have to put your money where your mouth is." Erica shrugged her sloppy canvas bag a little higher up her shoulders, feeling constricted by the neat lines of Angelique's blouse. Clothing wasn't meant to feel like this—itchy and scratchy and tight. She rubbed at the overprocessed fabric and continued. "I mean, for the love of Jesus, Angie! Haven't you ever been committed to anything in your whole life?" Erica demanded. "I mean, really, truly, deeply committed?"

Angelique gave her another eye roll and pouted her lips into that martyred-sister girl thing Erica hated.

"Don't you start with me, Erica," she warned. "I'm as committed to education as you are. With my credentials, I could be working for a Big Six accounting firm, making a ton of cash, instead of teaching elementary-school math." She frowned again, and Erica knew her friend was thinking—thinking hard—about that ton of cash. "And I'm committed to this friendship, aren't I?" she said after a few moments' pause. "Or else I sure as hell wouldn't be here," she grumbled. "When they commit you, they might as well lock me up, too."

And since there was nothing much she could say to refute that, Erica sighed.

"You're right. Thank you for coming with me. You're the best."

"And you're my girl. You're stone-cold crazy, but you're my girl," Angelique said, trying not to smile.

The elevator doors slid open, depositing them on the fourth floor. Bubbles of nervousness discoed from her heart to her stomach again, but Erica took a few deep, cleansing breaths and focused her attention on their destination.

She knew they had reached the correct door by the two burly Capitol police officers stationed on either side of it. There were probably a half dozen more officers waiting inside, Erica reasoned, stationed strategically around the room and on the watch for people just like her.

God help me, Erica thought, and then centered her courage for the task ahead.

* * *

The Senate hearing room was packed as usual, mostly with print reporters and hired lobbyists who seemed more interested in their PDAs than the proceedings. A single camera, labeled "C-SPAN," was parked at the front of the room where the TV audience could get an unobstructed view of both the witnesses and the panel. A lone technician stood near it, thick black wires draped over his shoulder. Erica followed the camera's aim and found the lens trained on the droning testimony of a middle-aged sister whom Erica recognized as the undersecretary for Elementary School Programs for the Department of Education. Erica searched her memory to find the woman's name: Henrietta Davies.

"We're too late. There's nowhere to sit," Angelique whispered. "Okay. You tried. Now, let's go home."

"No . . ." Erica craned her neck and spied a few seats in the very front row. "Up there."

"But that's right up front!" Angelique complained. She nudged Erica's arm, pointing to the dais at the front of the room. "It's already started, Erica. Are you sure. . . ?"

"Come on," Erica said, pushing her way through the room, muttering her apologies as she jostled against arms and stepped on toes. Angelique would follow, Erica was certain of it. After all, she had on those three-inch black pointy-toe pumps made from the hide of some unfortunate living thing. Girlfriend was going to be in need of a seat.

After a few uncomfortable seconds—and more than few uncomfortable glares—Erica slid into a chair not far from the long table where today's witnesses sat, well within the view of the senators on the panel in front of them. Erica knew most of their faces from watching CNN and C-SPAN, and could have named every member of the Senate's Health, Education, Labor and Pensions Committee, even if their identities weren't emblazoned in white on black placards in front of them. They were from all different states, but they were all men and all white. They were also all over fifty . . . with one notable exception.

He was a young senator from one of those backwater Southern states the rest of the Union didn't pay much attention to—and by far the most handsome member of the committee. Erica studied him, taking in the breadth of his shoulders concealed beneath a neat dark blue suit. He had dark hair, cut too short, like he'd recently been to a U.S. Marine barber for a scalping, but the hair took nothing from the crystal clear of his bright blue eyes . . .

Or the harsh, brooding line of distrust he was frowning right into Erica's face.

She'd seen that look before. In every TV appearance he'd made, this man had one of two looks on his face: a condescending smirk, or this same steely-eyed high-noon stare-down he was giving her now. Those sharp eyes seemed to take her in, digest her and then linger on Erica like he could read the words on the T-shirt concealed beneath the borrowed blouse.

Or like he could see down to her bare skin.

Or like he wanted to.

Or . . . something . . .

And worse, even though he was staring at her with that smug, superior, know-it-all look on his handsome face Erica couldn't tear her eyes away from him—him and that condescending smirk and those flashing blue eyes.

You think you're bad, huh? she thought, giving the man her best "mad dog" mug. *You think you're smart? Welcome to your worst nightmare, Senator. I'm just as bad as you are and twice as smart. So you bring it on, okay? You just bring it on—*

And then, as she was staring at him, challenging him in her mind, the man leaned back a little in his chair and let a slow grin spread slowly across his features. The harsh lines around his lips broke, changing his expression into a gentle playfulness that seemed to penetrate the very core of her being. A strange shot of heat fired through Erica's body, igniting her from nose to toes and every spot in between, and the next thing she knew, she was sitting there, grinning up at him like the whole thing was some kind of game and not as serious as life and death.

"Why is that man smiling at you?" Angelique hissed hot spit into her ear. "Who is he?"

With difficulty, Erica tore her eyes away from the man and turned to her friend.

"That's Senator Mark Newman," she whispered. "Everybody knows him. Even you. He's at the end of his first term—but he's their heir apparent. The one the 'forces of evil' are grooming to run for president in ten or twelve years. If he survives reelection, which I hope he doesn't."

Angelique stared at her blankly. "And I would know that how?"

Erica sighed. "He's the Gulf War hero. The first one. Gulf War One."

Recognition flooded Angelique's face. "Right, right! I *have* heard about him." She nodded, assessing as much of the man's physique as she could with the table in the way. "Well, well. You always hear about his handicap. They don't tell you that he's a cute little war hero, do they?"

"Cute?" Erica stole another glance at the man, who was still staring her down with that little smile on his face—that little smile that said, *I know you*—then rolled her eyes back to her friend, vowing not to look at him anymore. "Sure he's cute, if all you care about is outward appearance. But just below those cool blue eyes and pretty-boy exterior, you'll find a warmongering *hawk*. A conservative nut job. A Right Wing weirdo with pretensions of grandeur. He might be cute, but he's the last thing this country needs."

"Down, girl." Angelique patted Erica's knee, but kept her eyes on Newman. "Mmmm. There are times when I can *almost* see myself with a white man. . . ." She shook her head. "This is one of those times."

The young senator was still staring and smiling like he knew they were talking about him. Angelique was right: He was definitely on the right side of "cute": maybe thirty-seven or -eight, broad-shouldered and vital compared to the grayish and balding heads of the other members of the Committee. With his dark hair, strong, square jaw and crystal blue eyes, he had that look: the look of a man every woman wanted to be with; the look of a man every man would want to be like.

The problem was, he knew it. In addition to being wrong on every issue from air pollution to Afghanistan, he was so damned full of himself, Erica was pretty sure there wasn't room for a single new idea inside him.

You're not that cute, she thought, staring back at him with her most serious expression. *You—are—not— cute—*

Yes, I am. Newman grinned back at her. *Oh yes, I am. And you want me, you know you want me . . . every woman wants me . . .*

And sure enough, a moment later, the warmth of his grin deteriorated into the smug, self-satisfied smirk she'd seen on his face in a dozen television interviews. Erica kept scowling at him and just like that, the spotlight of his attention moved away from her and focused itself on the politics at hand.

"Hold up!" He interrupted the witness, making every head in the room swivel toward him. "Say that again!"

His words were lightly dipped and Southern fried, with just a bit of a drawl, refined so that the word "again" was pronounced as two separate ones, "a" and "gain." He sounded less like a backwater bumpkin than a courtly gentleman of another time.

His tone, on the other hand, was another matter.

Authoritative, self-assured, commanding. It was the voice of a man who had grown a little too used to having people listen to what he said and do what he wanted.

"Wow," Angelique muttered. "He's very . . ."

"Bossy," Erica concluded. "See, that's the trouble with these politicians," she continued in a voice low enough for Angelique's ear only as she stared up at Senator Newman's smirking, bossy, commandingly good-looking self. "They start out as average people . . . but give them a little money and power, and in no time they need to be backed down in a major way."

"And I suppose that's why you're here?" Angelique sounded doubtful.

"Exactly," Erica asserted, nodding. "Now be quiet. I want to hear this."

The undersecretary for Elementary School Programs was a smoothly coiffed, paper-bag-skinned woman who looked up from her reading and focused her attention on the man's cool, blue eyes.

"Which part, Senator?" she practically purred into the microphone.

There were a few snickers around the room: Apparently the deference in the woman's tone wasn't lost on the press corps.

"The part about the budget allocations for the Urban School Lunch Program," Newman barked, rifling through the thick binder. "I can't find the section justifying the allocation."

"It's on page forty-five of my remarks, Senator," Madam Undersecretary murmured, and Erica thought the older woman fluttered her eyelashes a little as she spoke.

Senator Newman fluttered a few more sheets in the thick binder in front of him before coming to rest on the appropriate page. Erica leaned toward the long-legged blonde in the seat beside her, who was flipping the pages of her own binder and, reading sideways on the page, saw a table, its columns filled with numbers ranging from the low millions to double-digit billions.

Newman read the numbers quickly, and then those cerulean eyes pinioned the undersecretary again.

"I notice that the increases in the Urban Lunch Program seem to have come directly out of the Rural Schoolchildren's Initiative," he snapped, running his fingers along the columns of his report.

There was a long pause, and when Erica glanced in her direction, Madam Undersecretary looked a little nervous.

"Well, yes, Senator. That's true."

Those piercing blue eyes seemed to slice the woman into tiny bite-sized bits. The room grew quiet. Erica could almost hear the concentration, as if everyone present were measuring the man against some kind of leadership standard. Erica felt it herself. He had a certain power, an irresistible self-assurance . . . even if he was as wrong as pearl earrings on a potbellied pig.

"Why?" he demanded.

The single-word question sliced the air, hard and razor sharp.

"W—we had a mandate," the woman replied after

a long silence in which the expression she fixed on Newman's face shifted from adoration to fear. "Under the Maxwell-Chortley Act, to trim our budget by ten percent for fiscal—"

Newman waved the explanation away.

"I know all about the requirements of Maxwell-Chortley. I was one of the original cosponsors," he said. "That's not what I asked you. I asked why money was taken from the rural program and added to the urban program."

"There's higher need in the urban program, Senator."

"That's not what my constituents report to me." Newman thrust aside the binder to consult his own notepad. "In fact, my figures show that the rural program was used extensively in my state."

"Yes, Senator, but over all the states, the rural program was substantially overfunded."

"That may be true," Senator Newman interrupted with a nasty edge in his voice, "but does that mean that the rural children in my state go hungry?"

She glanced around the room. The reporters had all come to attention, following this exchange with interest. Apparently Newman's criticisms had put some life into some otherwise dull proceedings.

"We've been asked to make cuts according to Chortley-Maxwell," Madam Undersecretary persisted. "In order to satisfy our federal mandate, something's got to go—"

Erica popped out of her seat, ripping at the buttons of her oxford blouse and revealing the words on her T-shirt: *Books, not bombs!*

"The war is what has to go!" she shouted at the top of her lungs. "If we weren't spending billions in Iraq, we wouldn't have to debate on cuts that take food from the mouths of our schoolchildren!"

The room stirred a little, and Erica heard the sounds

of cameras popping, felt the television lights swinging in her direction. This was the kind of disturbance, the kind of action the cameras lived for.

"Miss, you're out of order!" Erica heard one of the older senators shout as a gavel sounded. Erica had watched enough C-SPAN to know what would happen next. She took a quick glance around the room and saw she was right: the Capitol police were already moving in her direction.

"I'm a teacher!" she shouted quickly toward the panel, finding Senator Newman's eyes with her own. "I teach in an urban school here in the District of Columbia. Every day I spend my own money on food for kids too hungry to learn, too hungry to think. Urban programs desperately need more money for the food-service programs, it's true. Children can't learn if they're hungry—whether they come from city tenements or rural farms. It's time to stop putting taxpayer money into bullets and munitions and center it on our children."

"Order!" The old senator barked again. "Order!"

"Senators," Erica continued, speaking as fast and as loudly as she could. "Why do we kill people to teach people that killing is wrong? How can I explain to my fourth graders that it's wrong to fight when our policies support fighting all over the world? Why do we spend more money to fight wars than to feed our own kids, gentlemen? Why—*Yowch!*"

Two Capitol police officers appeared at either side, yanking her arms so hard behind her back they felt like they were being pulled out of their sockets. She reeled a bit with the shock of the pain.

Then, as suddenly as the sensation began, it ceased. The officers released her and Erica rubbed at one shoulder, nursing a spot that throbbed like it had been touched by a match. An angry voice crested the others in the room.

"This absolutely unnecessary and unacceptable use of force—"

Erica looked up in time to see Mark Newman rise slowly from his chair. And now she could see it: the cane curled in his left hand, supporting his leg and reminding everyone in the room that the man was 100 percent American hero.

"This is still America," he was saying in the voice of a teacher's tirade against a particularly unruly crop of students, "and dissent is not punished with man-handlin'."

"This forum has rules, Mr. Newman," interrupted the Committee's chairman. "And as you are well aware, without order, this deliberative body—"

"I understand all that," Newman snapped, dismissing the corrective influence of the older man with a wave of his fingers. "But as much as I disagree with our young disrupter's sentiments on the war"—and here his eyes shot toward Erica and pinioned her with a gaze that went through her like a laser—"I respect her right to say it without being harmed. Even here. In spite of our rules," he added pointedly.

He paused for a second, holding Erica's eyes with his own. Erica was on the verge of letting out a breathy little "thank you" like some kind of damsel in distress; but before the words could come out, Newman's lips curved upward again, into that knowing, self-satisfied you-want-me smirk. One look at his face and instead of gratitude, a wave of fury swept through Erica, erasing every positive feeling she'd had toward the man in an instant.

He's waiting for me to thank him! He wants the reporters to write about how gallant and wonderful he was, even when interrupted by some disruptive protester—

"Thank you, Senator," Erica hissed in a voice that shook with indignation. "But the chairman is right."

Newman blinked at her in surprise. "But—"

"In schools—both urban and rural—we try to teach students about personal responsibility, Senator Newman. I understood the penalties of breaking the rules when I came here and it's important for all of us to accept the consequence of our actions. After all, I don't want to live in a society without any rules, any more than you do. So if you're done with *your* civil liberties lesson"—she put her hands behind her back and assumed the position for arrest—"I'll continue with *mine*. These officers have a job to do."

A moment later, she was snapped into handcuffs and led from the room. She paused to give the senator a final glance: He was still standing up, leaning hard on the cane and staring after her. She didn't have to be an expert on the man's moods to read that he was angry—angry as he could be without screaming or hollering and completely blowing his cool in front of a few dozen reporters. But it was pretty evident that if his face got any redder, he'd have to explode.

"And Senator?" she called back at him. "I'm issuing you an invitation. Come to my school. Explain your policies—your war—to my kids. Erica Johnson's fourth-grade classroom. Any time you want. Door's open." Erica tossed her curls. *Take that, Mr. Know-it-all*, she thought, and then allowed herself to be removed from the room, Angelique following demurely behind them with the all-important bail money.

God only knows why Peter Malloy, an upstart state congressman with a very small following and an even smaller budget, has challenged veteran Mark Newman for his Senate seat. Newman, a war hero and successful attorney, is as beloved in his home state as any public figure could ever hope to be. Indeed, the only thing that can stop Newman's reelection might be Newman himself, with his sometimes abrasive personality. Otherwise, his seat in the Senate is as sure a thing as the flag, love of country and Mom's homemade apple pie.

—*Conservative Nation*

Chapter 2

◇◇

"She made an ass out of me!"

Mark Newman stumped around the perimeter of his massive desk, tossing today's papers onto yesterday's, adding to the ever-growing pile that covered its surface.

"It wasn't that bad." Chase Alexander, Mark's oldest friend and his chief of staff, eased himself into a chair across from him and loosened his tie. "In fact, I thought you handled it well."

"And thanks to her, you made the evening news," Bitsi Barr added, clicking into the room in those high-heeled loafers she always wore. Her title was media director, but Mark sometimes felt like she was the reincarnation of his mother, from the way she hovered over his every sniffle and fretted over his every move. "Now, sit down before you fall down," she admonished, moving into the space between Mark and his desk to brush against him. "You've spent too much time on that leg already today."

"I've been on my butt all day, Bitsi," Mark reminded her. "I need to move around a bit."

"Save it for therapy tonight. Sit."

"In a minute," Mark muttered, limping away from her to pace between his desk and the window. "I knew she was up to something as soon as she came into the hearing room." The image of the protester, her black hair brushing wild in her face surfaced in his mind again. "Something about the look on her face . . ."

"But you made the evening news," Chase repeated in an easy drawl. Like that was supposed to erase the woman's outrageous T-shirt and even more outrageous remarks. "That's good."

"Good? For whom? The media?" Mark grumbled. "'Man puts head up own ass' is a terrific headline. Did you see her T-shirt? *Books not bombs*. I bet CNN got a good shot of *that*." He sighed, raked his fingers through his hair and grimaced. "It was my own damned fault. I had to open my big mouth when the Capitol police stepped in to do their job. It's just . . . she looked so . . ."

Small . . . helpless . . . determined . . . beautiful . . . the words rotated in his mind, but his lips couldn't choose one. Or at least not one he wanted to say aloud. Erica Johnson's image surged to the front of his mind again. Even in that outrageous getup, with that militant scowl on her face, there was something about her. From the second she'd walked into the room he'd noticed it: something as wild and untamed as the mossy wildernesses of his home state, something uncharted and vast as the dark expanse of a night sky. He'd stared her down and she'd stared back and he could almost read her, cussing him out in her mind.

A worthy adversary, he remembered thinking. And so when she let out that screech of pain, he knew he had to say something, had to do something. After all, even in war, an honorable soldier treats his opponent with dignity.

"Mark? You listening?"

Mark snapped himself back into the moment. "No," he admitted. "Say again?"

"I said—" Chase began.

"Sit down!" Bitsi chided, taking him by the arm and practically shoving him into the expansive leather of his chair. She pried his cane from his fingers and hung it over the back of the credenza, poured him a glass a water, set it within easy reach and perched on the edge of his desk. "Drink. I can tell you're dehydrated. Drink!" And then she waited, clearly planning to supervise every drop of the water's consumption.

"I'm not dehydrated, Bitsi. I had about a gallon of water during the hearing. If I have any more I'll float away," Mark insisted, suppressing his exasperation. "Now stop fussing and let me hear what Chase has to say."

Chase rubbed the top of his head before opening his mouth. Over the years, Mark had watched the spot pass from thin to balding and proceed onward to bald, though Mark couldn't say with certainty this rubbing habit or the passage of time was the cause. "I was saying that before you get your tighty whities in knots about her getting the better of you, let's just think about this a minute." Chase flicked his eyes over Bitsi, Mark and the glass of still untasted water before giving the spot another rub. "See, I'm thinking Bitsi might be able to get you a segment on the Sunday politics shows. A little free campaign advertising—"

"I think that's a wonderful idea!" Bitsi interjected. She slid off her perch at Mark's elbow and paced the room, talking a mile a minute. "I've been cultivating all of our national media contacts, trying to get you more well-known across the country. And this is the perfect thing to pitch to them. And as for the folks back home, you have a decisive lead going into the primary next month. But you can never have too much media exposure, so doing the Sunday shows wouldn't hurt."

"There you go," Chase continued, feeding off the woman's excitement. "It's a natural platform. You talk about education, budget priorities, the progress of the war—"

"How not to handle protesters," Mark added caustically. "Knock it off, you two. Those Sunday show hosts will eat me alive."

"No, they won't." Bitsi tossed her sleek, white-blonde hair so that the ends caressed her sharp chin for an instant. The hair was one of her best features: thick and shiny, cut and curled toward her chin so that it softened the hard edges of her face. "They *love* you, and you know it." She laughed. "The camera loves you. The hosts love you. You're clever and witty and well-informed, too," she gushed. "What's not to love?" She nodded toward the glass. "You just drink your water. I'll take care of everything."

Mark sighed. "I told you, Bitsi. I'm not thirsty."

"Drink it anyway," she said quickly, and before he could respond, she'd crossed the room and was showing them her too-slim figure, concealed in a pantsuit of dark, conservative fabric. "As for the Sunday shows, I'll get on the phone now."

"But the woman, the protester—" Mark began.

"Don't worry about her." Chase fluttered his fingers, dismissing the encounter. "You came out smelling like a rose. Defending the rights of children, smaller, more-efficient government and the right to free speech."

"Couldn't have scripted anything better," Bitsi chimed in, wetting her lips with her tongue. She always wore the same red, red lipstick shade and a generous dose of the same dusky perfume to cover the side effects of her cigarette habit. Smoking in this federal building was strictly prohibited, but Mark knew the second Bitsi hit the open air there would be a Light 100 in her hand. He'd seen her chain smoke a whole pack in the course of single hour's debate when she was nervous. Come to think of it, he'd seen Chase eat a foot-long submarine sandwich in about the same amount of time.

His friends. Mark studied them dispassionately. He'd known Chase since childhood and Bitsi since law school and neither of them had changed much. Chase was always so laid back and relaxed it was easy to ignore the razor-sharp brain at work behind his calm exterior. You underestimated him at your peril, Mark knew. And Bitsi could best be described by a single word: intense. Chase liked to say the woman was missing a critical on/off switch. Mark would have liked to see the man alive who could excite Bitsi as much as a discussion about Mark's career.

They were absolutely dedicated to him. Sometimes a little too dedicated.

"You didn't script it, did you?" he asked, pinioning Bitsi with his firmest no-nonsense glare. "Because that would be—"

"Of course not, Mark!" A hurt look appeared in her blue eyes, as her blonde head bobbled in the negative. "I want you to get as much exposure as you can, I want people to already know who you are when you get ready to make the 'big run.' But I would never *script* anything like that . . ."

Mark shook his head, his thoughts snagged for a moment.

The big run.

President.

President Newman.

He had to admit, he liked the sound of it. He liked the idea of it. But it wasn't time to allow it to pervade his every waking thought. Like that woman with her tight "Bomb" T-shirt and her shouted arguments seemed to be doing.

He zeroed in on Bitsi again. The woman was a lawyer, too. She knew the difference a single word could make.

"So you didn't *script* it. But you didn't *hire* her, did you?"

"Who?"

"Erica Johnson." When the name didn't appear to register in the woman's short-term memory, he added, "'Madam T-shirt.' The black woman who stood up in the hearing. You didn't hire her just to 'craft my image' or anything foolish like that? 'Cause I've told you two—"

"No." Chase shook his round head. "No. Wish we had, though. That was a good exchange. Like Bitsi said, you couldn't write better stuff than that. You two had real chemistry."

"Chemistry?" Bitsi laughed. "Don't you think that's a little . . . strong? You use the word *chemistry* and people start thinking romance or something!"

Mark blinked. *Romance? Where the hell was that coming from?*

"Don't be stupid," he muttered. "There's nothing romantic about it."

Romance? It wasn't even a word in Mark's vocabulary anymore, not since Katharine had died. True, he couldn't deny he'd registered how attractive the protester was—he was still a man, after all. He'd noticed her perfect cinnamon-colored skin, those big, dark eyes flashing with passion, the delicate curve of her neck and the feminine swell of skin where the fabric of her tight T-shirt cupped her breasts. He'd taken in the tight inward curve of her waist and the outward flare of her hips, even concealed as they were by that funny-looking, shapeless skirt. He remembered the black hair, swirled and knotted into a thousand ringlets. He'd even wondered what it might feel like, curling against his fingers.

Yep, she was gorgeous . . . until she opened her mouth.

Irritation burned in Mark's stomach. She'd totally gotten the better of him—and then had the nerve to insist on being escorted out of the building before he'd had a chance to make his point. The sense of being cheated out of winning an argument rankled in his throat.

"Romance? Don't be stupid," he repeated.

"Not like *that*," Chase corrected. "I mean like competitively. Like a couple of racehorses, chomping at the bit. Good stuff."

"Yeah," Mark agreed, thinking over the encounter. "I suppose. Where is she now?" he asked.

"Who?" Chase stood, stretching his hands behind his head and twisting his torso. Mark couldn't help but notice his friend's expanding midsection. Too many lunches with lobbyists, too many after-hours receptions and too many late-night dinners at his desk were turning Chase into a paunchy old man.

He needs a woman, Mark thought. *A good lady to take care of him—without nagging the hell out of him.*

He kept that thought in his brain and said instead, "The woman from the hearing! Is she still in jail?"

Chase rubbed his bald spot and shrugged. "I don't know. That's usually what these protesters want. To make their noises, get arrested and get some coverage on the evening news."

Mark felt around the desk for a remote control and a moment later the television on the credenza at the other end of the room sprang to life. With another click, Mark's preprogrammed channels surfed quickly on their schedule: the local news stations, and then the national ones, and then the C-SPAN networks, and then back again.

"That's going to take some time." Chase stretched again. "Most of the TV reporters haven't filed their stories yet and it's not exactly breaking news." He unfolded himself from his chair. "Long day. Let's go get something to eat."

"How will she get out?" Mark demanded, frowning at the television screen.

"Who?"

Mark rolled his eyes. "Who else? Aren't you listening?"

Chase's eyes zapped onto him, searching. He opened his mouth to voice the query written in them, but was usurped by Bitsi's harsh, "Who cares?"

Both men turned toward her in surprise.

"I mean," she continued in a somewhat softer tone, "she wanted to go to jail, she went to jail and that's that. Usually those people have a whole organization behind them, ready with the bail money the second the charge is processed. You saw the woman in the suit that left with her? Probably her lawyer. She's probably already home eating tofu or garbanzo-bean salad or whatever the Left Wing is serving these days." She clapped her hands as though she had fully disposed of the matter. "Mark, you don't have an event, so you should do your therapy and hit the whirlpool tonight. It'll help with the stiffness."

"For about ten minutes," Mark retorted.

"Still," Bitsi insisted, like she knew the details of his knee joint intimately. "And don't forget to take something for pain when it hurts."

"It always hurts, Bitsi," Mark snapped, hoping

his tone would tell her how close she was to really making him angry. "I'd be a zombie if I took something every time it hurts. I've told you that. I've told the docs, too. They actually agree with me. The pain meds are for extremes, not for every little twinge, okay?" Mark grumbled. "Sometimes you act like it's *your* leg, not mine."

"Don't be silly," she said in that tone that meant she'd decided to ignore him and his annoyance for her own point of view. "You run along with Chase and get some dinner. I'm going to go make some calls, see what's lined up for Sunday already and how we rate for coverage." She turned toward the door. "And—I almost forgot—you've got another one of those packages. From home. That awful little bar you like so much."

"Dickey Joe's?"

Bitsi grimaced. "The same. I don't understand why you like that place. So dark and dank. No ambiance whatsoever."

A grin spread across Mark's face. "It's a guy's place. So of course you don't understand," he teased, winking at Chase.

"Don't be too sure," Chase shot back, adding his own grin to the mix. "I've heard that Bitsi's got a set of brass ones down there."

Bitsi rolled her eyes. "Don't be crude," she said primly and moved toward a corner of the room. Mark noticed for the first time a three-foot-square box, pushed close to the wall. "I'm a little surprised you got one of these this month. Considering what happened with Mary," she muttered.

Mary.

The image of the shy, young woman filled Mark's brain. Since she was the daughter of one of his oldest friends and fellow Marines, he'd wanted to help, offering her a job in his office after graduation. But it turned out she'd had neither the skills nor the temperament for work in the nation's capital. Or around Bitsi.

"I told them to put it here . . . so you wouldn't fall over it," Bitsi was saying.

"Let me have one," he commanded. "After that hearing, Dickey Joe's home brew is exactly what I need."

Bitsi frowned at him but, for once, kept her mouth shut. With a sigh of resignation, she bent over the box, opened the flaps and pulled up a long, dark goose-necked bottle. "I can't believe they actually bottle up some of that nasty home brew they serve and send it to you," she said, delivering the bottle into his waiting hand.

"Man, oh, man . . ." Mark murmured, twisting the cap. The faint aroma of malt and hops mixed with a nuttier, almondlike smell filled the room. "Say what you want, Dickey Joe is the salt of the earth, and his daughter's definitely going to heaven." He saluted his friends with the bottle before taking a swig. "Cheers."

"Ugh." Chase rolled his eyes. "Don't see how you can stand it warm."

"I don't see how you can stand it all." Bitsi grimaced in distaste. "Wouldn't you rather have your water and one of those pills? I'm sure they'd do more for you than *this* stuff. I ought to just throw it out."

"You'll do no such thing." Mark grabbed his cane and stood, hobbling toward the box. Even knowing how much they reminded him of home and happier times, it would be just like Bitsi to dump every last one of the beers down the drain. Mark had no intention of allowing that to happen. "Bitsi, I swear—"

"Okay, okay," Bitsi murmured quickly. "Relax."

She lifted a couple more bottles out of the box and slid them into the little refrigerator hidden in one of the drawers of the large bookcase covering the wall behind her. "I won't destroy your precious home-brewed beer. Just don't drink too many of those, Mark," she cautioned. "Warm or cold. I can't have you wandering the halls of the Capitol intoxicated."

The last restraint on his temper snapped like a dry twig. *Intoxicated?* She was making him sound like some kind of lecherous lush!

"That's enough Bitsi," Mark snapped.

"Enough?" She lifted her brows in wide-eyed innocence. "What do you mean?"

"You know what I mean," Mark growled. "How many years have you known me?"

"Feels like forever," Bitsi said in her worst mother-hen tone. "Ten? No. First year of law school. That makes it thirteen. Thirteen years. Why?"

"You ever—*ever*—seen me drunk?"

Bitsi's lips and forehead crunched toward each other. She shook her head. "I don't think I've ever seen you drink more than one or two, now that you mention it."

"Then stop treating me like a soft-headed teenager who needs his mother to pick up his beer cans!" Mark hissed, stumping back to his chair and lowering himself into it again, glaring at Bitsi all the while. "When I drink, I drink two. Just two, that's it."

Two spots of color appeared on Bitsi's cheeks and her faded blue eyes misted over, but her lips stayed in a firm, determined line.

"I'm sorry," she said crisply, turning away from them and marching toward the door. "If you'll excuse me, gentlemen, I've got calls to make." And she strode out of the room, letting the door close a little too loudly behind her.

"She's *pissed*," Chase muttered.

"Well, so am I. I don't like being treated like a baby, and she knows it," Mark grumbled. "If I didn't back her down from time to time, she'd steamroll all of us, and you know it. Wandering the halls intoxicated? What does she think I am? An alcoholic? She knows me better than that!" He frowned, staring into the dark contents of the bottle. The taste was a little off, a little bitter compared to the stuff Dickey served on tap at his little establishment in Billingham, but Mark chalked it up to the effects of bottling and the lack of refrigeration. Even warm, even with the aftertaste, it was still good stuff. Mark could almost hear his friend's laughter in the dim bar, could almost feel the camaraderie of men who stopped in after a hard day's work to swap stories or shoot an hour's worth of pool. And at the end of the hour, he'd go home. Home to where Katharine would be waiting.

Only now, Katharine was gone and no one was waiting.

For some strange reason, he thought of the woman and her T-shirt again, the way her full breasts strained against the cotton, begging for release . . .

"She can't help it," Chase said genially, pulling him out his reverie just as he felt a knotting in his groin. "She'll do anything to keep your name in the news. And for what it's worth, you *are* her baby. There would be no Senator Newman—and there sure as hell won't be a President Newman—without her. And you know it."

"She wants more than that . . . and *you* know it," Mark said quietly.

Chase sighed. "She's always going to hope, Mark. Until she sees you've . . . moved on," he concluded diplomatically, and Mark knew he was trying to spare him the pain of hearing Katharine's name spoken aloud. "Now," the other man continued briskly, "you want to get something to eat?" He nodded at Mark's cane. "Or are you doing therapy tonight, like Bitsi told you to?"

"No therapy." Mark sighed. The thing with Bitsi bothered him: Chase might be right. She meant well and he'd responded harshly, but then that meddlesome quality about the woman always worked his nerves and his stomach. He rubbed at his midsection, feeling the bubbles of upset churning almost immediately. "My stomach's in knots," he admitted to Chase.

"Probably because you need to eat. It's Tuesday. Chinese on Tuesdays, right? We could go to Oh's Place—"

Mark frowned, his mind elsewhere. "She challenged me to explain the war to her fourth graders, didn't she?" he asked himself out loud. "To explain why we have money for war and not for school lunches or something like that, right?"

Confusion. And more than a little surprise. That's what he read in Chase's face when he finally focused his attention back on the man.

"Yeah," his friend began slowly. "But heck, school lunches are great, but lunches aren't going to matter much when our nation is under attack. We gotta defend the cause of freedom or—"

Mark waved Chase's justification away. "Yeah, I know. I woulda said that if I'd had time before they carted her out of there. Bet you ten bucks that school invitation thing's the sound bite on the late news. And that's *her* point, not mine." He sighed, took another swig of Dickey Joe's warm home brew and pinned his oldest friend with his most determined look.

"So, what do you want?" Chase chuckled a little. "A rematch?"

He imagined her standing in front of him in that crazy earth-goddess outfit, wild ringlets dancing around her head as she moved. He saw her lips curve up into a smile and down into that irked grimace and felt the same fire knotting inside him that he'd felt the first second their eyes had met.

"Yeah," Mark said. "That's exactly what I want. A rematch. You know how I hate to lose, Chase. Even to a beautiful woman."

A smile crept slowly across Chase's face. "Beautiful woman, huh?" he repeated like the phrase had special significance. "Is that right?"

"Well, you saw her," Mark sputtered, heat crawling up his neck. He clawed at his tie, popped open the top button of his white dress shirt, but the heat didn't stop, not even after another swift gulp of beer. "She was gorgeous. For a liberal, I mean. Even you had to notice *that*."

"Sure, I noticed it," Chase agreed, still smiling that annoying little smile. "Just surprised that you did. You haven't noticed much about any woman. Not since"—he paused but could find no way to avoid the words—"since Katharine died."

Even though Chase said his late wife's name with the same gentle reverence Mark himself always used, the pain of her loss always returned to him with the same hard slap. Mark blinked against the wave of grief that washed over him. People kept telling him that the emptiness would fade in time, but somehow, even three years later, his grief still seemed as fresh as yesterday.

"I only noticed her," Mark managed to say, even though the mention of Katharine had submerged him in feelings he'd rather have left undisturbed, "because she made me so damned mad with all that wrongheaded talk. See, what we got here is unfinished business, Chase." He washed the words down with a last, long, slow chug of beer, but kept his eyes fixed on Chase's face. "And you know how I feel about unfinished business."

Chase's gaze was calm and quiet, steady and sure. It was more annoying than any of Bitsi's hovering and mothering, and Mark felt himself about two seconds from barking out something—anything—just to keep his old friend from looking at him another second in that odd, knowing way. But it was Chase himself who broke the stare, bending for the box of warm beer bottles.

"You're right," he said at last, giving Mark another easygoing smile, as he twisted off the bottle's cap and lifted the beer in toast. "She *was* pretty. And so was her friend. It's been a long time since you and I have admired pretty women, my friend." He took a long pull, grimaced at the bitter taste, shrugged off the jacket of his sober gray suit and tossed it onto his chair. "To unfinished business with a very pretty, very African-American, very liberal woman," he said, lifting the beer again. Then, before Mark could object, he leaned forward and grabbed the phone off Mark's desk. "Bits," he said into the receiver. "Come on back in here. Looks like Mark's going back to the fourth grade."

The War in Iraq is the Republican Party's Achilles' heel. There weren't any weapons of mass destruction, there's no exit strategy and the whole world knows it. And as for terrorism, Osama bin Forgotten, and the real terror is the current administration, which has spent billions of dollars that would have been better used on domestic priorities like education and social security.

They don't want to talk about that. It makes them look bad. Our job is to make sure they talk about it. Every day.

—Letter to the Editor, *The Education Protester*

Chapter 3

"How much longer are you going to hold on to this hunk of junk?" Angelique asked as Erica's decade-old import gasped its way into the school parking lot, shaking and wheezing as though on the verge of collapse.

"You know how much money I make, don't you?" Erica yanked on the parking brake and turned to pull her canvas school bag out of the backseat.

"Pennies, just like me," Angelique muttered, sliding out of the vehicle and staring at it in disgust.

"Then you know why I can't buy a new car," Erica snapped. "Be grateful we have wheels at all, considering you don't have a car."

"I'm saving, though—" Angelique began.

"Can you grab the coffees?" Erica interrupted. "My hands are full." She didn't feel like hearing the story again of how Angie's part-time accounting work was going to buy a brand-new Mercedes by 2010.

Angelique leaned back in and grabbed the two Styrofoam cups. "You don't have to take it out on me," she murmured, slamming the door with her hip. "I'm on your side, remember?"

Erica sighed. At times like these, it was tough to have a best friend that you lived with, worked with, commuted with. You had to listen to them talk, even when your mind was busy elsewhere—thinking of broad, blue-suited shoulders wrapped around the most asinine politics in the history of mankind. She tried hard to keep her face straight, hoping Angelique couldn't read her thoughts. "I'm sorry," she said. "It was a tough night. I was in jail—which was no picnic. And then all those reporters calling."

"We took the phone off the hook," Angelique admonished, shaking her head and smiling an irritatingly knowing smile. "Remember? So don't bother trying to blame your agitation on them."

"Whatever." Erica shrugged. The look on her friend's face was getting under her skin, stirring up a bunch of stuff she didn't care to admit to just now. "It was stressful. Even after doing my yoga routine it was hard to relax enough to get to sleep . . ."

Angelique's laughter sounded loud and wrong in the quiet darkness of the parking lot. "That's not it, and you know it," she teased. "Oh come, Erica. Get real with yourself, why don't you?"

"What do you mean?" Erica tried to sound casual, but even she could hear how her voice had risen a full octave.

"What do you mean?" Angelique mimicked. "I mean, we both know you stayed up all night long watching the tape of you and Mr. Handsome Senator from Down South on C-SPAN, uncut and unedited, that's what. And that's why you're tired. Oh no"—she lifted a hand, silencing Erica's intended interruption—"don't bother to deny it. I have to say, I watched it a few times myself. He's a cutie. Definitely a cutie."

"Oh him," Erica muttered with sigh, as if she hadn't

given the man another thought since the hearing yesterday. As if he hadn't been imprinted on her eyelids, wearing that irritating smirk every time she closed them and tried to sleep. "Well," she continued nonchalantly. "He might be cute, but he's also the Antichrist."

"He's not the Antichrist. He just disagrees with you, that's all." Angelique started through the dusty gravel parking lot toward the school's front doors. "Don't be so dramatic."

"I'm not being dramatic," Erica snapped. "I'm just telling you in no uncertain terms, I haven't given that sad, morally misguided man another thought."

"Mmm-hmm," Angelique replied and walked on without another word, leaving Erica to contemplate her backside as she tiptoed toward the school's main entrance in another crisp pantsuit and those high heels. Like she didn't know she'd be on her feet all day, chasing elementary school kids around. Erica glanced down at her own jeans and "Go Solar, Not Ballistic" T-shirt. On the surface of it, Angelique looked more like the kind of woman who would attract the attention of a senator. And yet . . .

The image of a handsome white man with piercing blue eyes and dark hair sashayed through her mind, using that old brown cane not for support but as a Fred Astaire-style prop.

Go away, you blue-eyed devil, Erica told the dancing man, and then struck out after her friend, lugging her heavy bag of textbooks, workbooks, graded papers and treats.

The school building was old—ancient, really. A compilation of aging bricks, and even older plumbing, Bramble Heights had all the problems of many D.C. schools. There were too many stairs and no ramps, too much concrete and not enough grass, too many windows and not enough heat. The children had so much potential and so little resources. Staring at the building's decrepit backside, thinking of the billions spent for killing and the paltry sum spent on children by comparison, Erica felt her anger toward the Mark Newmans of the world hardening again.

If I ever see him again, he's got some explaining to do, she thought, as she and Angelique turned the corner toward the entrance.

Be careful what you wish for. The words rose in Erica's mind the second her brain could comprehend what her eyes were seeing. *Be careful what you wish for: . . . You just might get it.*

She'd gotten it.

Because as soon as they rounded the curve toward the main entrance, she saw them: the big white commercial vans with the satellite dishes on top that the television stations used. Erica faltered and then stopped. Her book bag slid from her shoulders and spilled on the sidewalk.

"Shit," she breathed, staring around in surprise.

"You can say that again," Angelique agreed. "And this shit has your name all over it."

A young-looking white man bounded out of one of the trucks. He wore a pair of headphones and appeared to be listening intently to something. He glanced at Erica as she bent to scoop her books off the ground, and then proceeded at a gallop into the building. As the old double doors swung wide, the sounds of children cavorting loudly in the hallways roared toward her and then were muted as the steel latch reconnected with the bolt.

Erica locked eyes with Angelique.

"Newman," they said simultaneously. Erica set her jaw for battle and hurried toward the door.

About twenty kids, some with parents, most with-

out, played in the large foyer. The doors to the multipurpose room were closed, but the smell of a hot
breakfast floated out into the lobby, tempting the assembly with the promise of a meal.

"What's going on?" Erica asked, turning to an adult
she recognized, the grandmother of a little girl who'd
been in her class two years ago. The little girl's name
was Shauntay Jiles, but the grandmother's name escaped Erica's memory completely.

"They's setting up for some interview here," the
older woman said, her eyebrows arching toward
her graying hair. "Said the children can come in and
get their breakfes' as soon as they get the cameras
ready."

"What interview?"

"Senator somebody-I-never-heard-of." She rolled
her eyes. "They better hurry, tho'. I gotta catch that
seven-forty bus."

"Newman? Senator Mark Newman? Tall, dark hair,
shaved close to his head in military style, deep blue
eyes? Walks with a cane?"

The woman lifted a weary shoulder in a shrug. "I
didn't see all that. Just a bunch of camera folks." She
glanced at her wrist. "And if they make me miss that
seven-forty bus, there's gonna be some serious hell
up in here."

With a feeling of annoyance she hardly knew how
to explain or contain, Erica thanked the woman and
strode to the closed cafeteria door.

"Tall, dark hair, cut military style, deep blue
eyes . . ." Angelique repeated at her heels.

"Shut up, Angelique," Erica snapped and yanked
open the cafeteria door.

The large room was a chaos of lights and cables.
Two large chairs, dragged from Principal Mayes' office, sat facing three cameras arranged about ten yards

away. Erica peered toward the long rows of benches where the children sat to eat.

Mark Newman sat on a bench toward the back of the room near the closed doors to the serving line. He was talking amiably to a small crowd of television technicians as a pretty young white girl, her face bright with attraction, patted his face with powder. He clutched a Styrofoam cup in his hand, wooden cane hooked over the table's edge. Bramble Heights' principal, John Mayes, stood near him, also cradling a Styrofoam cup, his graying hair slick with pomade, his moon-round face consumed by a hearty grin as though he were a part of the story the senator was telling. A tiny woman in a tailored gray suit stood in the space between the men and the camera talking animatedly into a cell phone, swinging a blunt cut of white-blonde hair as she spoke. Her skin was very pale; indeed, the only splash of color in her appearance was the bright red lipstick smeared across her mouth. She reminded Erica of a little sparrow with a worm in its beak, hopping around the room with deliberate purpose.

"What the . . . ?" Erica muttered in amazement.

The birdlike woman holstered her cell phone and was at Erica's elbow in the speed of light.

"There you are," she said, pulling Erica away from Angelique's side and yanking her school bag off her shoulder. "We've been trying to reach you!" She put her hand on her hip and shook her hair at Erica. "Don't you *ever* answer your phone? Sit down, sit down. . . ." She practically shoved Erica into a waiting folding chair. "We're on national TV in less than five minutes!" She waved impatiently at the young makeup girl. "Over here! Quick!"

Erica blinked at her. "Who the heck are you? What the heck is going on here?"

"I'm Bitsi Barr, the senator's media-relations direc-

tor," the woman said, and a flush of pride colored
her white face. "As for the rest, it's pretty obvious,
isn't it? You challenged the senator to explain the
war to your fourth graders during your doomed
little protest yesterday"—she flicked her eyes over
Erica measuringly, taking in every minute detail of
her, right down to the number of millimeters of arch
in her brow—"and since he's not the kind of man to
back down from a challenge, he's here."

"Apparently he's not the kind of man to pass up
an opportunity for a little free publicity, either," Erica
retorted, making no effort to conceal the sarcasm in
her tone.

Bitsi Barr's red lips curved into a small smile that
told Erica exactly how much the other woman disliked her and everything she stood for. "The morning shows took *us* up on our offer to cover it," she
replied, nodding to the room around them. "We'll
be talking with Donna on *Good Morning Nation* in"
—she glanced at her watch—"less than four minutes. Be sure to get some powder on your forehead,
right *there*," she instructed, peering disapprovingly at
Erica's face. "That's going to howl like a siren when
the light hits it." She read the slogan on Erica's chest,
frowned and shrugged. "Could be worse, I guess,"
she mumbled to no one in particular. Then her phone
rang and she hopped away.

The young makeup artist approached Erica's face
with a large powder brush, but Erica slapped her
hand away and slid out of the chair. "Excuse me,"
she said, aiming her eyes and her feet toward the men
at the back of the room.

John Mayes, a smallish black man with very fair
skin, saw her first.

"Ms. Johnson," he began, "I was afraid you
wouldn't make it!"

Erica barely glanced at him. "Oh, I made it okay," she replied and watched Mark Newman's head swivel in her direction.

The girl's makeup had done its work: concealer and a bit of bronze powder gave him a handsome, cover-boy look that would have made him irresistibly sexy if Erica hadn't been too mad to notice. He rose somewhat unsteadily, grabbing the cane for support, while an irritatingly condescending smile immediately covered his face.

"We meet again," he drawled in that totally fake, old-style Southern-gentleman voice. All he needed was a goatee, a white suit and a mint julep, and he could have been Colonel Sanders.

"What the hell are you doing here?" Erica demanded.

Newman's eyebrows rose in false surprise.

"My dear Ms. Johnson, you *invited* me!"

Erica frowned. She would have loved to tell him she had no idea what he was talking about, but that wasn't true. The news stations had been replaying her shouted invitation all night, and unfortunately, she knew it. She wasn't exactly surprised to see him here. This was just the kind of thing she would have expected him to do . . . if she hadn't spent the night having hot dreams about covering every inch of his body with her lips and her tongue and—

"You ought to be ashamed of yourself, Senator. This is a disruption at best," she sputtered at him. "And at worst, you're trying to catch me off guard, just so you can win. Well, it's not going to work, so you can just take your staff and your cameras and go back to Capitol Hill!"

And there it was. The smirk. Deepening on his handsome face, while those sky blue eyes sparkled deliberate mischief at her and killed any attraction toward him she might have felt. In an instant, she saw him as he was a child—about the age of one of her fourth graders—and knew he was up to something, something no damn good. She frowned up at the man, her mind racing, guessing at the plot behind that smirk of a smile. And while she was staring, it was impossible not to notice that he was ridiculously tall, ridiculously broad shouldered . . . and ridiculously full of himself.

"I'm glad to see you, too," he said. He had the nerve to chuckle at her while she sputtered her discomfiture for a number of agonizing seconds.

"You—you—you really take the cake, you know that?" Erica managed when she'd fought down the feeling of heat those eyes had sent soaring through her. "You pretend to be so concerned about education and children, but all the while you're only thinking of how much time you can get in front of the camera. Otherwise, you could have just—just—"

The smirk widened to a grin. Erica opened her mouth to lower the boom, but to her surprise, he lay a long, strong-looking finger against her lips and leaned close.

"I know you have plenty more to say, Ms. Johnson. And I'm sure I deserve it," he murmured in a low voice. "But save it for the cameras, okay?"

Erica stared up at him, speechless at his touch, at his nearness. She'd expected him to reek of some perfume-y men's cologne, but instead he smelled of soap and something else, too vague to name. There was a callus on the tip of the finger that caressed her lips so gently, and in the instant before he moved his hand aside, Erica had almost kissed it. She raised her eyes to his face. The grin was gone and so was its cousin, that arrogant little smirk. Instead, the man was staring at her with a stricken expression on his face, like he, too, had forgotten where he was and what he was supposed to be doing.

"You're going to regret saying that," Erica said, managing to sound irritated and sassy, even though there was no way to ignore the magnetic pull of the man. "I'm going to let you have it, Senator. And in the future"—she inhaled deeply, drawing the last bits of her composure back to her consciousness—"keep your hands to yourself, please."

"Why? Don't trust yourself?" he rumbled in that low for-your-ears-only voice.

"*Excuse* me?" Erica began but there was no time to contemplate it any further, because a voice rang out of the surrounding tangle of cameras and wires,

"Live with New York in one minute!"

An instant later, someone shut off the nearest set of fluorescent lights and plunged the room into near darkness. Only the high beams of the studio lights set around the chairs illuminated the area.

Bitsi Barr hopped up to Erica from out of nowhere. "We're gonna need another chair," she said in quick, clipped and decidedly un-Southern tones. By contrast, Newman's voice dripped out as slow as honey. She gave the senator a gentle shove into the chair waiting behind him. "Sit," she commanded, and then frowned. "You all right? You look a little . . . sweaty." She snapped her fingers and called out into the darkness, "The senator needs some more powder!" Then, "Where's the sound guy? Check the senator's mike and earpiece, will ya?" Her faded blue eyes assessed Erica critically. "I told you to get some makeup on that," she said, jabbing a finger toward Erica's forehead. "Too late now, I guess. Oh well. Hey." She snagged a man in headphones who was hovering over Newman and snapped her fingers in Erica's direction. "Quick. She's got nothing."

Out of the darkness came an older man with a la-
valiere microphone, which he pinned quickly and
professionally to Erica's T-shirt like she were a man-
nequin instead of a live person. He then parked her
in a chair to the senator's left.

She glanced at her adversary. His eyes were closed,
and for a second, Erica thought he was praying to
whatever gods he believed in for the strength to get
through the encounter unscathed. . . . Then she noticed the hand pressed against his stomach, and the
wince crimping his lips and the corners of his eyes.

"Are you all right?" Erica began, distracted from
her anger by the pain etched into the man's face.

His eyes flew open, centering on her with calm certainty. The smirk reappeared on his lips with a vengeance.

"I'm fine. Breakfast didn't agree with me, I guess.
Don't worry your pretty little head about me," he
said, nodding toward the cameras aimed at them like
a firing squad. "Worry about *them*."

Erica shrugged. "All I have to do is tell the truth."

Newman threw back his head and laughed. "Ms.
Johnson," he drawled, "the truth depends on who's
doing the tellin'."

"That's a politician's answer if I ever heard one,"
Erica shot back, her curls bobbing around her head
in a wave.

"Obviously," he agreed.

Erica opened her mouth to respond, but he
wasn't looking at her now. His face was fixed on the
camera.

The makeup girl gave Erica's forehead a quick
swipe, shaking her head as though she, too, believed
far more was needed to keep it from shining like new
money. The sound man stuffed the earpiece into her
ear just as a voice in the darkness surrounding them
shouted, "Donna in New York in five . . . four . . ."

* * *

"Why did you go to the Senate's hearing on elementary education, Ms. Johnson?"

It was going to be fine, Erica thought, grateful that the fluffy morning network anchor had handed her an opportunity to talk about everything that needed to change. She said a quick thank-you to God for the opportunity and said,

"Because I'm sick of funding being cut from education while we're spending billions on an unnecessary war, so—"

"And," the perky morning show host interrupted, as though the pause had been a period and not a comma. "And is that when you challenged Senator Newman to explain the war to your class?"

"I barely remember that part, if you want to know the truth. I was too busy being escorted out of the hearing room in handcuffs," Erica retorted.

"Well, I remember it quite clearly. That's why I'm here," Newman interjected in that fake sing-a-song drawl, and then chuckled a little.

"And what do you intend to tell the children, sir?" the interviewer continued. Erica couldn't see her— could only hear her voice in her ear, but she sounded so courteous and deferential that Erica knew she was sucking up to the man.

She cast a quick glance at Newman's profile: The man was cheesing and grinning and completely eating it up.

It made her want to wretch. The man was arrogant enough, he certainly didn't need any encouragement from Donna Dale of the *Good Morning Nation Show*.

"I intend to—" he began, but Erica grabbed the sentence away from him.

"He intends to load my kids up with the usual gar-

bage about terrorism and September eleventh. And
he intends to ignore the truth: that Iraq has nothing to do with Osama Bin Laden—or should I say,
Osama Bin Forgotten, at least by the senator and his
cronies."

Newman's dark head swung toward hers, his face
clamped into his trademark smirk, tempered with
more than a little annoyance.

"Iraq is a haven for terrorists. And Saddam Hussein—"

"Had nothing to do with 9/11."

Newman frowned. "Not directly, but—"

"But nothing," Erica scoffed. "And now you're taking food out of the mouths of the children of your
own state, for a war that is unnecessary, irrelevant
and none of our business! And the young people
of your state are coming home in body bags by the
dozens!"

Two red spots of ire appeared on the patches of
pale skin on Newman's cheekbones. When he spoke,
there was nothing fake about his voice. It was only
slightly Southern and far more furious.

"You don't know anything about my state, Ms.
Johnson," he said, forgetting about the television
cameras, turning toward her and jabbing the same
finger at her that only a few minutes ago had caressed
her lips. "And you don't know anything about what
it means to serve this country. You and your kind are
free to sit around and complain about what's wrong
with this country thanks to people like the men and
women in my state."

"Me and *my kind*?" Erica's voice rose with her anger. "And just what is that supposed to mean?"

"It means you ultra-Left, I-don't-eat-anything-that-
has-a-face, sandal-wearing, flag-burning—"

"Hold up!" Erica's hand shot up. "Me and my *kind*
love this country, too. Enough to start hollering when

it gets off track. We don't just accept every decision that our leaders make with blind obedience. We ask *questions*, Senator. We don't just pat our children on the head and send them off to be cannon fodder in a conflict that doesn't have any purpose—"

"Defending this country against its enemies is the most important purpose there is!" he snapped.

"Educating the populace of this country is the most important purpose there is! Or least it would be if the federal government and states like yours would spend some money on it!"

Newman scowled at her. "I told you before, you don't know anything about my state, so stop talking about it like—"

"I know it's got the second-highest military enlistment rate in the country."

"We're patriots."

"No, you just haven't provided any better opportunities for your young people."

"They choose to enlist."

"Choose!" Erica spat back at him. "Why on earth would anyone choose to go out and get themselves killed?"

"Some things are *worth* dying for!" Newman's body straightened and there was neither smirk nor smile on his handsome face. The room went suddenly soundless and still, with the weight of his sincerity. A lifetime of commitment and honor in service to the country he loved resonated in the man's voice.

He really believes in that. Honor, duty, country. My country, right or wrong . . . . Erica sighed. His loyalty would have been beautiful . . . if it weren't so dangerous.

The cameras were still rolling, but she forgot them in the intensity of the moment. Instead, she reacted on her instincts, reaching out to grab his hand, curling her fingers around his.

"I'm sorry," she said gently. "You're right, of course. But," she stared into those deep blue eyes, reading in them the twin vipers of his absolute courage and absolute certainty. "Are you sure this is one of them?"

He hesitated only a second, answering simply, "Yes," and then leaned toward her suddenly. "And if you don't know why, it's nothing I can explain to you. But maybe I can show you. The people of my state are the backbone of this country. They know about sacrifice, about believing in something bigger than themselves. They know the meanings of honor and courage. Maybe if you stopped thinking of my state as 'flyover territory,' maybe if you stopped making all kinds of judgments and assumptions about people from states like mine, you'd understand it better," he said in an earnest voice. "You've never even been to my state, have you? Forget the little towns and family farms, you've never even been to Billingham, our capital city, have you? Have you?"

Erica hesitated. "No, but—"

"Then you shouldn't talk." And now that annoying little smirk was back and his eyes gleamed with satisfaction. He settled himself back in his chair as though he had carried the point, and directed his attention to the third eye of the camera again. "See," he drawled in that made-for-television bullshit voice Erica had come to hate with a passion. "You don't know anything about what it means to live in a rural state, about the way my constituents feel about this country and what we're doing in Iraq. What you need to do is come on down South with me."

Erica quirked an eyebrow at him. "Sounds like an ambush to me."

"You mean, kinda like your invitation to come

here?" Newman swung his face away from the camera and the smirk deepened into a maddeningly smug expression as he continued, "I've been willing to come here, but you're not willing to spend even an hour in Billingham, actually talking to the people— actually *listening* to the people. You liberals are all the same. You talk about listening, but you never actually do it. You never leave your safe little enclaves. You never—"

"Oh, cut it out," Erica interrupted. "You want me to go to Billingham? You think it's going to change my mind?"

Another self-satisfied smirk. "I know it will."

Before she could think better of it, Erica had thrust out her hand. "Invitation accepted. You're on, Senator. And I'll spend more than an hour—more than a day, if you want. I'll come to Billingham. I'll come to Billingham for as long as you want."

"Think you can last a whole week?"

"Of course I can."

He stared at her hand for a long second. Then a slow, genuine grin curved over his features. He suddenly looked about ten years younger—and more handsome than ever before. Erica felt her heart do a nervous little side skitter in her chest as he enclosed her brown palm with his pale one.

"You got yourself a deal," he drawled, just as Erica heard a voice in her ear, frantically insisting they were out of time. She came to herself at last, pulled her hand out of the senator's and turned back toward the camera. Donna Dale chattered in her ear about the spirited discussion and her hopes they would both join her again, to tell the nation about Erica's trip down South.

Tell the nation . . .

"Oh shit," Erica muttered, realizing what she'd

just done. But thankfully, the microphone was dead and no one heard it but Mark Newman, who simply threw back his head and laughed like he'd intended to capture her under this barrel all along.

Education is important—we all understand that. But education means nothing if our children's basic freedoms are threatened. Without security, without safety from the threats of terrorism, there can't be any education. All you have to do is look at places where there is war, bloodshed, tyranny and strife, and you'll see I'm right. Children only have the opportunity to learn when there is safety and peace. And that's what we're trying to secure, both for children in the United States and the children in Iraq.

—Senator Mark Newman

Chapter 4

He was the only white person in the room.

Or at least the only all-white person, since a few of the kids had the light bright skin of children of mixed parents. At the talk he'd given earlier, he'd noticed the same thing: kids of every shade of brown, but not one lighter than tan. It was as though the segregation his state had struggled so hard against a generation before had been reinstated by silent consensus. Mark filed the observation away for further consideration, placing it in the growing drawer in his mind labeled "Erica Johnson."

She'd done him the courtesy of keeping her mouth shut during the hastily arranged "special assembly" with the fourth and fifth graders after breakfast and before the start of their school day. And he'd met her challenge: He'd explained to them about the requirements of freedom and the necessities of liberty.

The kids hadn't seemed that impressed. Several of them, he noticed, spent more time watching Erica Johnson than listening to him. And when it was time to ask questions, most of them had seemed far more interested in his cane than any issue of war or peace.

"I got hurt in a war," he had explained. *Before any of you were born*, he thought, looking out at their nine-, ten- and eleven-year-old faces.

"Can't they get you one of them fake legs?" A little boy with cocoa-colored skin raised his hand. "I saw this guy on TV, he had one. He was running a marathon!"

"No." Mark chuckled. "I've still got a leg, thank God. There's still some shrapnel in it, and some pieces of the bones are fused together—that's why I limp. But I don't need a fake one."

"Too bad." The little boy seemed genuinely disheartened. "That fake leg was way cooler than that old cane. You might coulda run a marathon, too."

Kids, Mark thought, smiling a little at the memory. On balance they could have cared less about either war or peace, especially when there were such things as fake legs to discuss and discover.

Erica Johnson wasn't a kid.

And now she had that look on her face—the look that meant he'd won today's battle, but the war itself was very much in question. He was about to make a comment to that effect when she said, "Too bad it's not raining," and stationed him in a chair in the corner near the window. "Sometimes we get a leak right here. You're such a hothead, it would probably feel good to you."

Mark let that one slide. He eased himself into the low student chair with a sigh of gratitude. He felt a little tired, a little lower energy than usual. The damaged cartilage in his knee burned like fire and he closed his eyes for a few seconds, forgetting the day's mission to finger the pill rolling loose in his trouser pocket. He didn't want to take it, didn't want to give in to the pain today, but he didn't want to be hobbling around cursing, either.

When he opened his eyes, she was staring at him like she'd read him, chapter and verse. It was annoying, really. The way this woman insisted on looking at him like she knew something about him, when she clearly didn't. If she weren't so blasted pretty, he might have really gotten p.o.'d about it.

"Do you always wear those damned T-shirts?" he asked, jabbing a finger at the slogan on her chest. "Don't you own any real clothes? Clothes that make you look like a woman?"

Bull's-eye.

Those brown eyes flashed "Drop dead" just as sure as if she'd said it aloud. Mark allowed himself a chuckle as he watched her comeback forming in her eyes, and found himself practically holding his breath in anticipation. He couldn't wait to hear what she was going to say to that one.

But instead of picking up with the T-shirt and running with that ball, she took him somewhere else altogether. Somewhere he hadn't intended on going.

"Why are you still here? You had your morning show and gave your speech to the children and a dozen reporters. You're sure to get all the news coverage you want. Why don't you go back to your office and do whatever it is that you people do. Plot your wars. Dream up conspiracies to oppress the rest of us. Chase your secretaries around your desks. Whatever. Why don't you just go away?"

Mark's smile went sharkish. "Why?" he replied in his nicest, nastiest voice. "You up to something you don't want me to see?"

She opened her mouth, but a rustle of interested noise from the children behind them distracted her from coming back at him with her list of objections and corrections. Angry as she made him, Mark couldn't resist watching her hips sway in those jeans as she marched away from him. He could just imagine them in a nice skirt, maybe a pair of sassy high heels . . .

Get a grip on yourself, a voice in his head that sounded suspiciously like Bitsi reminded him. *She might be gorgeous, but she's the most annoying woman on the planet.*

"Settle down, young people," Erica told them in a voice that walked a narrow line between sternness and encouragement. She turned back to him. "Are you going to be all right here?" she asked coolly. "Do you need anything? A glass of water, maybe? So you can take that pill you've been fingering for the past half hour?"

Crap. How the hell did she know about that?

But all he said was, "Saw that, huh?" pulling on the deepest and most disarming of his Southern accents to let her know she wasn't bothering him in the slightest. He opened his palm to show her the white pill. "I enjoyed the school tour, but there are a lot of stairs, your principal's a bit long-winded and my leg's not what it once was. Hate to take these things, though." He tapped the side of his head. "Dulls the brain."

"Really? Is the entire Republican party taking them?" Before he could reply, she fixed those big eyes at him and shook her head. "All you had to do was say you were hurting and Principal Mayes would have cut the tour short. But you'd rather tough it out. War heroes aren't like the rest of us, I guess."

Mark frowned, his feelings of attraction evaporating. Everything was either an insult or an argument with this woman—absolutely everything. He opened his mouth, but she was already directing her class like he didn't exist.

"Anthony!" she called, summoning a cute little boy with cocoa-colored skin and huge black eyes. He wore a stained white uniform shirt and pair of dark blue pants that looked like they'd seen better days, but his eyes were bright with intelligence.

"Yo?"

Mark recognized the voice as the loud kid who'd been asking questions about his cane.

"Anthony!" Erica repeated as though the kid hadn't responded and Mark heard the authority in her voice. The kid must have heard it, too, because when he spoke again, his voice was cordial and polite.

"Yes, ma'am?"

"Take one of the plastic cups from the bottom drawer of my desk and go down to the water fountain. Our guest would like a glass of water."

"Yes, ma'am." Anthony shot Mark a glance before moving toward his teacher's desk to find the cup and do as he was told. In a flash, he was at Mark's side, nursing a cup that would have overflowed if so much as another drop of liquid were added to its content. As it was, it slopped over Mark's hand as he took it from the boy.

"Thank you, Anthony," he said, smiling into the boy's inquisitive black eyes.

To his surprise, the child executed a nearly perfect military salute and then turned on his heel and marched to his seat as though he'd been living at boot camp for the past several months.

"Morning journals, please," Erica commanded, taking her place at the front of the room. Almost immediately, black composition books were produced from desks and backpacks. "All right, young people," Erica continued, "let's not let our having a guest disrupt our regular routine. Please clear your desks for the daily language worksheet. Keisha and Shawna, you're classroom helpers this week, so please pass these out." She handed two little girls in dark blue jumpers a sheaf of papers.

A sea of hands rose almost immediately.

"Miz Johnson, can I sharpen my pencil?"

"Me, too!"

"I don't have a pencil. Can I borrow one?"

Erica's mouth folded into a grim line.

"I see we're going to have to talk about personal responsibility again. As young learners, you're responsible for your supplies. You all know that you're supposed to check your pencils when you come to the classroom in the morning, and have them ready before we begin the day's work."

"But Miz Johnson," a little girl with long braids interrupted, her hand waving frantically in the air. "We would have, but they made us go to that assembly as soon as we got here. To listen to *him*." She jerked her thumb in Mark's direction. "And that's why we didn't have time to . . ."

From his seat at the back of the room, Mark watched Erica's lips turn downward like she was swallowing a particularly nasty medicine. Mark suspected she was biting back something she desperately wanted to say and he couldn't stop a smile from curving his lips.

She glanced in his direction just in time to see the smile. Immediately, her eyebrows knit together and her dark eyes flashed.

"I had hoped that we would be able to carry on our lessons today as usual," she began slowly in a voice that barely concealed her irritation. "But that clearly isn't going to be the case, so I say we take advantage of the senator's presence and skip ahead to our civics lesson. We've been studying the Constitution. Perhaps Senator Newman can give us some insight beyond what our textbooks can offer?"

"I'd welcome the chance to try." Mark stood and crossed the room in a few uneven strides until he was at the front of the room beside her. He leaned against the edge of her desk and winked at her. "What do you want me to do, Teacher?"

Go straight to hell.

If he read it right, that was what the look on her face said, but the words that came out of her mouth were a quietly controlled, "Get your butt off my desk."

The children laughed.

"Don't nobody touch Miz Johnson's desk. Everybody knows that!" he heard called out from the young voices in the room.

"It's rickety," she said quickly. "I don't want anyone to get hurt."

"Of course it is," Mark agreed, giving the desk a shake and pretending not to notice that it hadn't moved an inch. "Very rickety." He laughed at the way the children's eyes fixed on him, sparkling with interest. He felt movement at his elbow and realized that Erica had placed a chair in the center of the room for him.

"They're too young to vote," she murmured in a voice for his ear's only. "And I'm immune, so you can bump the charm down a few volts, okay?"

"Hey, if you've got it, flaunt it, that's what I always say," he muttered back and watched those big brown eyes roll contempt in his direction before she addressed the class again.

"Who wants to give Senator Newman an overview of what we've studied so far?"

All over the room, little brown hands shot into the air, waving with enthusiasm. Mark stole a glance at Erica: her lovely face was suffused with pride.

"Damon. Rise and present."

At this command, a little boy with a round head shaved bald like an old man, stood up and placed his hand over his heart as if reciting the Pledge of Allegiance.

"We've studied the three branches of government," he began seriously. "There's the executive—that's the president and the cabinet and their agencies. And then the judicial—that's the court system. And then there's the legislative. That's the House of Representatives and the Senate." His eyes found Mark's. "That's where you work."

"Right," Mark said, grinning. "Very good. In the Senate, we—"

"We haven't talked about them yet," Damon interrupted. "We've been talking about the House of Representatives and how they're elected and how the Constitution says there have to be a certain number from each state."

"That's right," Mark nodded, impressed by the little boy's memory and delivery. Whatever Erica didn't understand about the political realities he dealt with every day, it was pretty clear the woman wâs a good teacher. "But the Senate is different."

"Wait!" Damon's tone grew suddenly commanding. "I'm not finished with the House of Representatives!"

Mark chuckled. "By all means, young man. Go on."

The kid hesitated, his hand fluttering from his chest to his side. He looked around uncertainly as though he expected to receive the derision of his classmates, and Mark realized that the boy had misinterpreted his chuckle. After all, the kid was just ten. "I'm not laughing at you, Damon," he said in as gentle a voice as he knew how to use. "About the House of Representatives. Go on."

Damon's eyes flitted to his teacher's for a moment, questioning.

"Go on, Damon," Erica Johnson said in a voice more soothing than he'd ever heard her use before.

"It's all right. I'm sure Senator Newman would like to hear the rest."

The little boy's hand went back to his chest. "The House of Representatives," he continued, "is composed by p—p—population. States with more people have more representatives. States with fewer people have fewer representatives. That's to be sure it looks like America—or at least that the states with the most people get to be heard." Damon frowned. "Only it doesn't look like America really. And the founding fathers didn't intend for it to. Because when they wrote the Constitution, they didn't count the black people. They called them three fifths of a white person because they were slaves and they had no votes at all." His eyes found Mark's. "Why did they do that? Why do white people always think black and brown people are worth less than they are?"

Twenty-five pairs of childish eyes focused on him, waiting for an answer, and Mark knew he'd been set up. He longed to grimace in Erica Johnson's direction, but refused to give her the satisfaction. Instead, he brought himself slowly to his feet and paced toward the child. When he stood in front of him, he bent over as far as he could, so that he look into the boy's dark brown eyes.

"The men who founded our country made a mistake. A serious one, but they were—as all of us are— shaped by their experiences and the beliefs of their time," he said in a voice loud enough for the rest of the class to hear. "At that time—and at many other times in the history of the world—slavery was a reality. And with very few exceptions, in the history of the world, slaves did not have the right to vote. I'm not saying three fifths is right, but in many cultures, slaves would have been counted as zero persons. Nonexistent." He paused. "But the mistake was corrected by the Civil War. A lot of men—white and black—died to fix that great wrong. But it was necessary. Sometimes fighting is the only way." He glanced over his shoulder. "I'm sure Erica—Ms. Johnson—will teach you about that later."

"She did," another voice, slightly familiar, added. Mark turned to find the kid who'd brought him the water, Anthony, on his feet beside his desk. "But the war wasn't enough. It took the Fourteenth and Fifteenth Amendments, which abolished slavery and gave African Americans the right to vote. And those amendments didn't take. We still needed Dr. King."

Mark blinked, impressed. These kids were clearly carefully and thoroughly taught.

"We still need the Voting Rights Act of 1964. And we're still three-fifths persons in lots of ways." The kid was running through American history like he was talking about the latest video game. "Look at what happened after that hurricane in New Orleans."

"I agree. That was a national disgrace," Mark said. "And there's plenty of blame to go around. But let's stick to the Constitution and the laws that support it for now. In our government and our laws, the language of racism is gone. True, in the days after slavery in the South, there were some issues. Some abuses. But all of that—slavery, and Jim Crow and segregation—that was a long time ago." He smiled, trying to turn the tide in a new direction. "You kids live in a much better, much different world, where any of us can accomplish anything, if we're willing to work hard enough for it. Ms. Johnson and I disagree on a million things, but that's one thing we can agree on, right?"

Their eyes locked and he read conflict on her face. There was a part of her that wanted to disagree, he was sure of it, he could read it in the tightness in her face. He could almost hear the words—"legacy of slavery," "reparations," "lingering discrimination"—hovering on her lips. But there was another part, one that couldn't bring itself to tell a room full of ten-year-olds to put limits on their dreams.

She sighed a tiny little sigh before allowing a slow smile to spread across her face. "Yes. If you're willing to work hard enough, if you refuse to take 'no' for an answer, if you're willing to fight for it, then yes," she said. "You can do anything."

Mark grinned at her, patted Damon on the back and stumped back up to the chair at the front of the room.

"Even if you're poor?" Anthony launched the words at him like a missile.

Mark nodded. "I come from one of the poorest states in the Union," he told the boy. "My family was very poor. We didn't have running water in the house until I was twelve. You know what that means?"'

A murmur of curious no's went up around him.

"It means nothing happens when you turn on the faucet. It means there aren't any faucets, or sinks or bathtubs. You take a bath in a metal tin filled with water from the rain barrel or the nearby lake. And when you have to go to the bathroom, you go outside. In a hole in the ground."

A chorus of "ews" and "ughs" filled the room.

"My cousin's water got cut off 'cause they couldn't pay the bill," a little girl explained loudly, waving her hand as though trying to get called on. "They had to buy water from the grocery store to make the toilets flush."

"That happened to my godmother—"

"Once we had to take baths at my grandmother's house because there weren't no water—"

Erica threw her hand in the air, her fingers splayed

into what looked like a peace sign. "Settle down, young people. Settle down! Senator Newman was just trying to make a point—"

"No, I was just telling them about my life," Mark corrected. "I've been as poor as anybody in this room. Poor in a way people don't believe still happens in this country. But I always liked school, and I was always willing to work hard, and the military taught me self-discipline. Those three things, more than anything, are the reasons I was able to escape from that poverty." He turned toward the doorway, half wishing he could have convinced Erica Johnson to allow at least one reporter in the room. The press would have loved this exchange, would have eaten it up with a spoon. He could almost hear the violins as the movie of his life came to its rushing crescendo, and made a quick mental note to ask Bitsi if there might be a way to schedule some kind of "kids' town meeting" when he went back to Billingham next week. Then he refocused his attention on these children and the words he was saying. "And if I can do it, you can, too."

"Yeah, but you're white," Anthony announced.

"So?"

"My brother say white people can do things black people can't." Anthony offered as though this changed the equation considerably.

Mark hesitated, the feeling of ambush creeping along the tender skin at the back of his neck again. The kid's brother was right: Racism was alive and well. But he couldn't very well tell this little boy not to try, just because he was black, could he?

Mark sighed. "There are still obstacles, Anthony, but in the end, I gotta say your brother is more wrong than right. Maybe once upon a time in America, that was true ... but it's not anymore. Maybe I'm just optimistic, but I gotta believe that, white, black, brown, yellow, you can do anything you want in this great country of ours if you're willing to work hard for it. There are still problems, there's still discrimination, but you and your brother have a better chance of success here in America than in any other nation in the world. I believe that," he concluded firmly. "Now, you're right about the House of Representatives being composed by population, but the Senate is different. Two from every state—"

"Thank you, Senator Newman."

He turned to find Erica Johnson's brows furrowed and that tight line around her mouth again. Clearly, the woman was pissed. Again.

"Look, before you give me all the lingering effects of slavery stuff, just let me point out—"

"No, it's not that," She frowned and shook her head. "It's the other part. We don't lecture the kids here at Bramble Heights."

"I wasn't lecturing," Mark asserted. "I was just telling them—"

"I mean," Erica Johnson smiled a little half smile that wasn't a smile at all. "That we don't *tell* the children things. They may be young, and some of them may be disadvantaged, but every kid in this room has a good brain, and I intend for them to become good at using them. I don't want them to become adults who are content with being 'told' things by others. I want them to become adults who are adept at finding out the truth for themselves."

Mark frowned. "This is history, Ms. Johnson. Not some touchy-feely—"

"There's nothing touchy-feely about critical thinking, Senator Newman," she said firmly. "It requires a high degree of intelligence, resourcefulness and analytical thinking to discover the answers for oneself."

"And just how will they make these discoveries?"

No sooner than the words left his lips than the woman's smile changed, blossoming from that strained crimp of tolerance to something warm and full and alive. As Mark watched the love in that smile stretch over her face, something inside him stretched as well, filling him with fire from his neck to his toes. When she locked her glimmering eyes on his, pinned him with that smile—that glorious smile!—he forgot his irritation, forgot she was on the wrong side, forgot all the reasons that had brought him to this place.

Katharine. That was the last time he'd had this feeling. This crazy out-of-his-mind, head-over-heels, burning-with-desire feeling.

"They're going to get into their Discovery Groups and answer these questions," she was saying. She brandished a stack of papers and the same two little girls jumped from their seats to distribute them right on cue. "They can use any sources they like. Their textbooks, of course." She pointed to the computer station and the bookshelves. "The Internet. Our collection of resource books."

Mark swallowed hard, forcing down the feelings consuming him. "Why make it so complicated?" he heard himself saying in a voice that registered on the border of obnoxious, even to his own ears. "I can explain it in two minutes and—"

I've forgotten how to talk to a woman, he realized when the smile drained from her face. *I've forgotten.* And suddenly it mattered to him, mattered enough for him to send up a prayer: *Help me remember, Katharine. Help me.*

"If you just explain it, they will have learned nothing," she finished, her dark eyes flashing. "I don't understand you, Senator. Why are you on the Education Committee? Is it just a springboard to better things? If your expectations for the nation's children are so low, just what kind of electorate are you going to have when it's time for your presidential bid?"

He blinked at her, realizing just how angry his arrogance had made her.

"I didn't mean—"

She waved a slender brown hand at him, dismissing his denial. "I know, I know. I've heard. You're not a candidate. Yet. But you'll have your eye on it in—what—six more years, right?"

Mark opened his mouth, but at the moment, he wasn't entirely sure what his answer should be. He found himself on the fence between wanting to hash through the details of his political career with her—if only to hear what kind of outlandish, ultra-liberal, Left Wing debate she'd launch—and suddenly needing to apologize.

She didn't give him the opportunity to do either.

"Here's hoping you don't get the chance," she muttered under her breath, and then turned to the class. "Young people," she began, silencing them with only her attention. Mark watched her profile as the tense little half smile he'd been getting melted into the softer smile of absolute approval. "Get to work. Show the senator how glorious you are. Show him what money spent on minds can do."

Two dozen heads bent to the task without question or complaint. Mark watched as children eagerly flipped through textbooks or rose to take a seat at the computer. The room seemed charged with a new energy. She was right to call it "discovery": that's exactly what it felt like.

"You can quiz them in a few minutes," she told him and he didn't have to look at her to see her pride. "Education isn't just about school lunches or buildings, Senator. It's about believing in someone. Believing in them more than they believe in themselves,

and watching them blossom. I believe in these kids.
All of us at Bramble Heights do. We're here because
we want to be, and no other reason. There's nothing I
wouldn't do for these kids, including fight with you
and the whole damn Congress if necessary."

And she smiled again, a ray of something pure and
good and wonderful. She stood there, beaming her
pride and love for her students at him with a brightness that pierced some long-dormant corner of his
heart. Unexpected emotions caught him by surprise,
once again: The same strange feeling that had swept
over him when their eyes met in the Senate hearing
room coursed through him. The same thing he'd felt
during the TV interview when her big brown eyes
had locked on his and he'd held those slender fingers
in his own. The same thing that had struck him dumb
here in her classroom only moments ago.

He hadn't felt anything close to this since Katharine died. Mark swallowed, his mind racing, his heart
thumping too hard and too fast in his chest.

There was definitely unfinished business between
them, and for the first time Mark realized it was
deeper and more serious than getting the last word
in a political debate. Because here he was, in front of
God and two dozen fourth graders, gripping his cane
tightly to keep from leaning over right there and capturing the woman's smile with his lips and holding it
for his very own.

Waging war to stop terrorism is like using gasoline to put out a fire.

—Antiwar slogan

Chapter 5

"No." Erica turned on her heel and walked away from him, even though she knew it would be useless. Mark Newman was certainly one of the most arrogant, self-aggrandizing men she'd ever met, but he was also one of the most tenacious. And Angelique had had the nerve to back out on her. Stood in the doorway of her classroom, with that stupid little grin on her face and insisted she had other plans for the evening. Which Erica knew fully well was a bald-faced lie. Angelique never had any plans, any evening.

"Come on . . ." his voice had shifted from a commanding to a wheedling tone. "Why not?"

"Don't you have somewhere else to be?" she asked him in exasperation. "Isn't there a vote on the Hill or a cocktail party with a bunch of lobbyists or something that desperately needs your attention?"

That quirky little grin covered the lower half of his face. "Nope. Turns out my schedule is clear."

"It's been clear all day," Erica muttered. "I'm beginning to wonder just what the taxpayers pay you for." She turned away from him again, trudging quickly toward her car, her head down.

"I cleared the day for you and your class," he said and she heard the cane crunching the gravel of the parking lot as he followed her. "Most women would be flattered."

Erica whirled on him. "In case you hadn't noticed, Senator. I'm *not* most women. I really wish you'd just—just—"

"Was I that bad at teaching?" he asked.

No, you're actually rather it good at it, she almost admitted, but she swallowed the words knowing full well they'd swell his head to unmanageable proportions if she spoke them aloud. The kids had actually seemed to enjoy having him around after she'd allowed him to become a "resource" for their assignments. And, if she wanted to be honest about it, once he'd stripped off that suit jacket that looked like it had cost a couple of million dollars at some custom men's store, loosened his tie and rolled up his sleeves and started bending over desks, helping her students with the nuances of civics and language arts, math and science, he'd been maddeningly sexy.

"You were . . . okay," she said grudgingly.

"Okay?" His voice rose in mock insult as he smirked down at her. "I was better than okay. I was *good*." He sighed a little and rubbed his forehead. "But I gotta admit, I don't know how you do it every day. Those kids are exhausting." His eyes swept over her body, taking in more than muscle and bone, but he confined his remarks on it to, "You must be tougher than you look."

Erica rolled her eyes. "Gee, thanks. I think."

"Seriously," he asked in a tone to match the word. "It's hard work, but you do it well. Those kids adore you."

There was something more than the compliment in his eyes and in his tone. Something, suddenly intimate, suddenly real. It made that warm, fluttery feeling kick up again in the pit of Erica's stomach—and she wasn't about to have it.

"Go home, Senator," she said, turning her back on him again.

"Can't," he said. "No car.'"

Erica rolled her eyes. "Fine. Call your driver. One of the perks of office, I'm guessing."

"Can't," he said in the same easy way and still just a step behind her. For a tired man with a cane, he moved surprisingly fast when he wanted to be annoying. "No driver."

"Then get a cab!" Erica shouted over her shoulder.

"Ms. Johnson—Erica—may I call you Erica?"

"No."

"Erica," he continued as though she had given him permission, "I don't understand why this is such a big deal. It's been a long day for both of us. You've got to eat, I've got to eat—"

"But we don't have to eat together," Erica reminded him. "And to be honest, Mark Newman, I've had just about enough of you for one day, so—"

His face changed so abruptly Erica let the rest of the sentence die unspoken. The characteristic smirk that usually graced the man's features slid into an expression Erica had rarely seen on any person's face. An extreme tenderness and an extreme pain mingled in his eyes as his lips froze in a strained smile.

"What is it?" Erica asked urgently, registering his expression in confusion. "Are you all right?"

He shook his head, focusing his attention fully on her face again, and in that very instant that smug little smile reappeared on his face. "Of course," he said, gathering himself to his full height and beaming down at her as though nothing unusual had happened in that half second. "My wife used to say that to me, that's all," he said in the most casual of tones, like he was talking about the weather. "'I've had just about enough of you, Mark.' Katharine said that a million times if she said it once. In that exact tone of voice you just used. Said I was enough to try the patience of a saint." He limped past her, indicating her little import. "Let me guess. Yours?" he gestured toward the bumper stickers on the rear fender: MAKE LOVE, NOT WAR, and IT TAKES A VILLAGE TO RAISE A CHILD. And Erica's favorite: DON'T BLAME ME, I VOTED FOR THE OTHER GUY.

Erica ignored him. "I can see why your wife would say that. What happened? She finally had enough and left?"

He shook his head.

"No. She died. Shot in a holdup at a grocery store." He tapped on the passenger side door with his cane, and to Erica's surprise the lock popped open as though it had been jimmied. A moment later, the senator had folded his long, lean length into her car.

"I—I'm sorry," Erica stammered. "I didn't—"

"Wednesday. Pizza," he told her in that confident, Mr. Untouchable voice, and then slammed the car door and sat there, staring at her like she was his hired driver. "I usually have pizza on Wednesday."

Nerve. That's what the man had. Pure, unadulterated nerve. It was almost funny.

Almost.

"Well, bully for you," Erica muttered.

He reached across to the driver's side and rolled down the old car's old-fashioned hand crank window. "What?" he demanded, like he was the King of the Parking Lot.

"Nothing," Erica said calmly. "Except this 'take charge' bullshit you're running on me is not going to work. Good night, Senator."

"Come to dinner with me, Erica," he said, dropping drawl and drama for an earnest tone. "I need to know a few things to set up your visit to Billingham, and" —he hesitated a moment—"I'd like to tell you about my Katharine . . . if you feel like listening."

My Katharine. He spoke the name with such gentleness it was clear he'd cherished the woman as much when she was alive as he did her memory. Erica felt a lump of jealousy rise in her throat. It must be wonderful to feel cherished. If her own experiences and the experiences of her girlfriends were any measure, it was as rare as plutonium to find a man who knew the meaning of the word.

Erica stared at him harder. He was smiling that little smirk-smile again, but this time she tried to see beyond that unfortunate habitual quirk of his lips to the man within. There had to be something beneath it, something deeper . . .

But if there was any depth to him it all, it certainly wasn't readily apparent. Erica hesitated. The last thing she wanted to do was spend another minute in the company of a man who irritated her as much as Mark Newman could, just by breathing.

"Oh, come on," he urged. "I won't bite, if you won't."

Erica sighed, tossed her books into the backseat and slid into the driver's seat, firing up the tiny engine with a quick turn of her key. "You're buying," she grumbled without looking at him, but she knew that smile had widened to cover his whole face.

"A gentleman always does," he purred at her, and Erica had to grip the steering wheel hard to keep from calling him everything but a gentleman, and to remind herself that she was, indeed, a lady.

He was quiet in the car, except for when he barked out directions like a general on the battlefield. Erica expected they were headed to some upscale Italian eatery, with a charming brick oven and booth seats, where they made pizzas with exotic ingredients most normal folk wouldn't eat. But instead, he directed her into a neighborhood she knew well, where little mom-and-pop takeouts dotted a busy street in the shadow of Union Station.

"Here," he said, pointing to a small storefront in the middle of the block on the other side of the street. "Mama Tia's."

Erica flipped a quick U-turn and whipped the little car into a curbside parking space without a word. As she set the parking brake, she felt the man's eyes on her.

"That was some pretty good driving, for a woman."

"What kind of chauvinistic B.S. is that?" Erica rolled her eyes. "Honestly, Newman, what planet are you from?"

"I meant it as a compliment!" he said, smiling slyly, like he knew he'd pressed every one of her buttons and had done so deliberately. "Of course, it helps when you drive one of these itty-bitty clown cars. Back home I got a dual-cab pickup that's probably three times the size of this thing."

"And drinks six times more gas," Erica retorted angrily. "Increasing the demand for limited resources and depleting our environment."

The smirk widened on his face. "Exactly," he said joyfully. "But it's a helluva a lot more comfortable, I guarantee it."

Erica slung her purse over her shoulder and opened the car door. "Let's get this straight, Senator. I agreed to go home with you to East Bumfuck, or wherever it is that you're from. But if you think I'm participating in some big primary-election publicity stunt, you can forget about it. I'm not going to let you humiliate me, or belittle my point of view. And most of all, I can absolutely assure you that I am not riding around in any gas-guzzling, dual-cab, pickup truck with a gun rack and the Confederate flag on the rear windshield!"

"So the answer is no?"

"Absolutely no," Erica asserted, shaking her head until the loose curls brushed her cheeks. "Unequivocally no. No. No. NO."

He grinned, looking deliciously boyishly handsome in a buzz-cut John Travolta-ish sort of way.

"That's what you said about dinner," he said and limped his way ahead of her into the restaurant.

Mama Tia was behind the bulletproof glass at the order window—a precaution Erica hated but knew the area required. But when the older woman saw them, she hopped off her stool and opened the steel door separating them from herself and the cash drawer. A moment later, her plump form, squeezed into too-tight blue jeans and a large cook's apron, appeared in the restaurant's lobby.

"Well, aren't you both a sight for sore eyes!" she cried, in a voice without the slightest hint of Italian heritage in it. That was no surprise: The woman was just as clearly African American as Erica herself. She opened her arms and just as Erica was about to move forward to receive her hug, Mark Newman stepped into them. "Mark!" Mama Tia was saying, joy carved into the smile on her face. "It's been a long time."

"Too long, Mama," Newman was saying his voice muffled by the woman's plump shoulder. "Way too long."

"I been seein' you on the news, tho'," the woman continued as she released him. "You been lookin' kinda tired to me. Working too hard."

Erica glanced up at the man, searching for signs of

fatigue. For the first time she noticed the puffy smudges of gray beneath his eyes and fine, tight wrinkles crimping the corners of those clear blue eyes.

"Tryin' to do the right thing by the people who sent me here," he replied, and for the first time since she'd met him, he put aside the "aw shucks" routine long enough to sound almost sincere. "They sent me here to work for the common good, not goof off."

Mama Tia patted his arm. "Killing yourself won't do no one no good, Mark. You know that, same as I do."

The woman's laser-sharp black eyes swung in Erica's direction.

"Erica Marie Johnson!" She cried, and enveloped Erica in a bone-crushing hug. "Girl, I'm so proud of *you*! Saw you on the news this morning. You were so quick and smart and right dead on the money. I couldn't help but think to myself, 'Now *there's* a combination that might just be able to do some good in this world. Mark Newman and Erica Johnson.' And now here you two are in my restaurant."

"Mama." Newman sounded puzzled. "You know Erica?"

Mama chuckled. "Know her? I changed this child's diapers."

Erica felt a flush of embarrassment rise to her cheeks. "Well, not quite," she said quickly.

"Yes, I'm sure I did," Mama Tia insisted. "At least once. Back when your Grandma owned a dress shop down the block."

"I grew up in this neighborhood," Erica explained. "Two streets over. I used to work here after school in high school."

"Best worker we ever had, bar none," Mama Tia asserted, shaking her head.

Mark Newman's face seemed to crumple. "Then, I

guess," he said lamely, "You've had the pizza."

"Had it!" Mama Tia's hands went to her hips. "If you weren't with her, I bet she'd go back there with me and make her pizza her own damn self."

"Oh," Mark murmured. "I see."

Erica grinned. It was obvious he'd selected the place to impress her with his knowledge of delicious but little-known D.C. eateries and was now completely discomfited that his plans had been foiled. Erica felt suddenly glad she'd allowed herself to be manipulated into coming; the look on his face right now was worth all the garbage he'd been spouting all day.

"I'm sorry I haven't been around to visit you in a while," she said to the older woman.

"It's all right. I know you don't live right around the corner anymore. Sometimes I think about picking up and moving myself."

"How's business, Mama?" Mark asked, and again, he sounded genuine, like he was truly concerned.

Mama Tia sighed. "We got the business. Mama Tia's as popular as ever with those who *know*." She shook her head. "Problem is the crime. Seems like every other week I'm replacing a lock some desperate soul bashed up trying to break in here. Or cleaning up graffiti, or investing in some new security thingamabob." She glanced over her head at a small camera mounted on the ceiling above them. "But it don't seem to make much difference. Just last week, Tony—you remember my husband, Tony?"

"Of course." There was no forgetting Tia or Tony. In Erica's childhood, they were the only interracial couple she'd ever known: Tia, an African-American goddess, and Tony, a stocky bronze Italian with a thick flip of dark hair. Whatever their differences, their marriage must have worked: They'd been at it for at least twenty-five years, Erica guessed.

"Got mugged," Mama Tia finished. "Trying to make a deposit. He's all right," she continued quickly in response to their noises of concern. "But it makes the two of us say—"

A bell jangled behind them and the three of them turned toward the sound.

A person—Erica couldn't be sure if it were a man or woman—in sunglasses, a ball cap and a broad-striped flannel shirt, stepped into the store, paused long enough to take them all in and muttered, "Too crowded," in a voice that sounded completely phony, before turning for the sidewalk again.

"Crowded? If he calls this crowded he must be used to some *serious* backwater joints. You know, population: one. Or something," Mama Tia quipped. She threw back her head and laughed at herself like it was Amateur Night at the Apollo.

Mark frowned, staring toward the door, even though the person was by now long gone.

"What's the matter?"

"I'm not sure . . ." He shook his head. "Something familiar about that guy." He sighed, turning back to them. "Can't place it."

"Too much stuff up there," Mama Tia said, tapping the side of Mark's head. "You need a break and I intend to provide it. For two of my favorite customers, I'll make a special exception. You two can eat in" —she pointed to a single wobbly-looking metal table with a chair at either side, set at the end of the room not far from the bar-covered windows— "if you want to. This ain't The Palm, but you're welcome."

Erica studied the lonely little table in dismay. "What happened to your eat-in business, Mama?"

Mama Tia shook her round head. "Had to stop it. Them hoods would come in here and tear everything up. Had a couple of serious fights—bad enough for the police to be called. So finally, Tony and me, we just took all the tables and chairs but that one. It's for people to sit while's they wait for their carry-out. But, like I said, tonight, it's all yours. I'll even wait the table. It'll be like the old days, if you want."

Erica forgot about the unpleasantness of sitting down across from Newman and embraced the woman. "Of course we want," she said.

"Thanks for makin' an exception." Newman grinned and started toward the little table. He pulled out the battered aluminum chair closest to him and held it. "Ms. Johnson?"

For a second, she just stared at him, wondering why he was calling her name. Then in the next instant, she understood the old-school, chivalrous gesture. She hesitated, flustered by conflicting feelings: flattery, appreciation, annoyance and embarrassment.

But it didn't matter. She never got a chance to actually sit, anyway, because the door chime clanged again, and once again, the three of them turned. This time, two young men entered the tiny store.

Erica knew instantly what was about to happen, and before she could stop herself, she glanced toward the steel doors separating the lobby from the rear of the store, protecting the other employees and the night's cash. The door was hanging wide open. Mama Tia, in her happiness to see them, had forgotten about store security.

Both of the men were dressed in dark jackets, their collars high toward their ears, baseball caps jammed tight over faces concealed by ski masks. Erica could just barely make out a pair of black eyes on one of them, when his companion pulled a small handgun out of his pocket and pointed it at Erica.

"Yo!" he said in a voice of menacing authority.

"Throw that pocketbook on the floor. Right here in front of me."

There was mace on her key ring, but as a matter of course, she'd stowed her keys almost immediately after they'd stepped into the restaurant. Erica loosened her purse from her shoulder.

"Don't." Mark Newman's voice cut the air with deliberate and certain command. "Don't give him anything."

Erica stopped. The young gun's eyes swung away from Erica and onto Mark Newman. His weapon swung with them.

"Don't start none, won't be none, old man." The kid sneered at him, nodding the other robber toward the steel doors and the cash register.

"You don't want to do this, young man," Newman hissed. His voice shook, not with fear, but with pure anger. Erica glanced at him: she could only see his profile, but his jaw was tight and his eyes hard. His fingers were curled so tightly around his stick that his knuckles popped whitely beneath his skin.

"Oh no, you don't," Mama Tia hollered and Erica suspected the cry was more of a warning to the kitchen staff than any serious attempt to thwart the robbers as she threw herself in front of the steel doors. "Don't!"

The crack of a bullet split the silence and both Erica and Mama Tia cowered, their hands over their ears. Only Mark Newman hadn't flinched: He stood stock still in the center of the room, leaning on his stick and scowling like he was a second from committing murder.

"Throw me the damn pocketbook, bitch!" the young thug screamed.

Erica glanced at Mark again. This time he said nothing, but there was a glimmer of something in his eyes as he nodded just the slightest bit, communicating. *Resist*, those eyes said. *Resist*.

Erica slid the bag off her shoulder . . . and threw it hard into the young criminal's face.

"Take it!" she shouted at the top of her lungs, just as Mark jabbed the kid in the solar plexus with his cane. The gun barked again, wild and loose as it flew out of the kid's hand and upward into the air. Erica heard the bullet streak past her ear with a hot, loud, *zinging* sound and flinched, ducking away from it.

When she looked up again, a full-blown melee had erupted in the small diner. Mama Tia had grabbed a baseball bat from some out-of-nowhere hiding place and was beating the hell out of the kid who had the nerve to approach her cash drawer, while her husband and two scared-looking employees huddled in a corner of the kitchen. Erica's eyes flicked over Papa Tony: his swarthy face was nearly as pale as his apron, which, stained with pizza sauce as it was, made him look almost bloody. A cordless phone was pressed to his ear and over the din of Mama Tia's fury, Erica could just make out the beginnings of his conversation with an emergency operator.

"Yeah, we got 'em both," Tony told the phone. "My wife's got one and the senator, he's got the other."

"I oughta knock you out," the outraged Mama Tia was saying, brandishing the bat over the now-bare head of the kid on the floor beneath her.

"Please, don't hit me again, lady. That shit hurts." He cowered, raising his arm slightly to protect himself from the expected blow.

"You think it don't hurt nobody to come in here and try to steal from me? And what did you think that gun was for? You think that first lick hurt," Mama Tia grumbled. "I'll show you *hurt*." She waved the bat like the kid's head was a baseball and she was aiming for a grand slam. "I'll show you *hurt*."

She didn't strike, though. The danger was over, the kid was scared and, Erica knew, Mama Tia wouldn't do any more than fuss and threaten now.

Erica turned toward Mark Newman.

She didn't know what she had been expecting to see—only that it wasn't what she was seeing.

Newman's face had gone into a hard mask of controlled violence. He held his cane like a sword in front of him, pointing the end of it at the chest of the young criminal like he intended to stab the man with it. And when Erica looked more closely it was clear he had the means to do it: the soft rubber bottom of the cane was gone. Instead, a six-inch blade, sharp as death, protruded from the wooden cylinder like a bayonet.

"The police are on the way!" Papa Tony called.

The young man under Newman's makeshift bayonet made a sudden lunge. With surprising agility, Newman lunged with him, pointing the tip of the knife at the kid's jugular with an expression on his face that seemed to boil the man down to his naked essence: equal parts protector, violator, hero and killer.

"Erica," he commanded, and Erica felt her muscles snap to attention as though she'd been taking his orders all her life. "His gun's on the floor." He nodded toward the ground, but never took his eyes off his opponent. "By your foot. Pick it up."

Erica hesitated. She disliked guns, had never held one in her life and didn't want to start today.

"I'll just kick it over—"

"No! Pick it up!" Newman shouted at her, and there was an edge of something desperate in his voice. Erica glanced at him: his face was very pale, very sweaty and there were tight lines around his lips and mouth as though he were in great pain.

His leg, Erica realized with a flash of understanding. *He's standing on the bad leg.*

Reluctantly, Erica stooped, but the kid must have realized he had only one chance. He dove for the floor, just as Newman lost his balance. Erica felt the cool metal come into her fingers as she scooped up the weapon. She held it in front of her, clasped tight in both her shaking hands.

"Don't!" she hollered at the kid. "Don't or I'll— I'll—I'll . . ."

But the kid didn't hear her. He read her fear of the weapon in her eyes and knew she wouldn't— couldn't—use it. Before Erica could even muster the courage to threaten to fire, the young thug had already bolted out the door.

Erica let her hands fall to her sides. Her whole body was trembling, shaking with the thoughts of what could have happened, what didn't happen, what she'd let happen . . .

"Done good," Newman murmured, touching a lever along the cane's curved handle. The blade sprang back into the staff and disappeared. "Done good," he repeated gently, and she realized he was standing right beside her, leaning harder than ever on his old wooden stick. He gently pried the weapon from her fingers, cracked open the barrel and counted the shells in the chamber. "This thing was ready for business. One less gun in the hands of an unprincipled idiot," he pronounced. "Done good."

"But . . . he . . . " Erica heard her own voice, high and distant, as though someone very young and very far away was speaking. "He . . . he . . . got away . . . "

"But you got the gun," Newman said calmly.

"I . . . got . . . " Erica repeated blankly. She'd held

a gun. A weapon. Her stomach churned with the thought.

"I wish I could have kept him under my knife a few minutes longer, but . . . " He sighed, patting his leg. "I'm not what I used to be."

Erica stared at him, hearing him but not hearing him, seeing him but not seeing him. The room went kind of fuzzy and there was a tinny, whining noise, like a mosquito had taken up residence in her eardrum. Erica rubbed at the side of her face, feeling warm and wet on her fingertips.

A loaded gun . . .

Those bright blue eyes met hers, searching her, and his frown deepened.

"You're bleeding," he said. A large pale hand caught the side of her face, stroking at her right ear with an unexpected gentleness. Then it was gone. He showed her his fingers, smeared with bright red blood. "The bullet must have grazed . . . "

Erica didn't hear the rest. A strange sensation of heat climbed from her stomach to her brain. She touched the warm, wet spot at the side of her neck again and stared at her red-stained fingers.

Blood . . . her own blood . . .

"Whoa, there." The voice sounded disembodied and far away. "I got you . . . " and Erica felt herself sink against something warm and solid. "I got you."

She shook her head, clearing away the fuzzy heat, but her legs still felt like jelly and her stomach inside out. Erica looked around: Mark Newman's face was suspiciously close to hers, bright blue eyes only inches away.

"Better?" he asked.

"Than what?" Erica heard herself mutter. Her voice sounded like a distant echo. She reached for the side of her neck again, but Newman grabbed her fingers and pushed them down.

"A second ago, woman." The smirk was back on his face, but it didn't look so aggravating while there was such concern in his eyes. "You nearly blacked out on me."

"I . . . nearly . . . " Erica repeated, struggling to make the room stop swimming. The chair she'd somehow come to be seated on moved a little and she looked down to see a dark blue stretch of pants leg where her chair should have been, but it took her foggy brain a while to work out why.

"Nothing like the sight of that much of your own blood to make you weak-kneed," he drawled at her, and Erica slowly became aware of the man's fingers around her wrist and his arm wrapped around her waist. "I've seen seasoned soldiers go down like rotten trees." He inspected the side of her neck. "Looks like it's just a scratch. A pretty *good* scratch—but just a scratch."

"I—I heard the bullet," Erica stammered.

"Thank God you weren't a millimeter closer," the man growled into her ear and the arm around her seemed to tighten. "This story could have had a very bad ending. A very, very bad ending."

Erica took a deep, shaky breath. He was right. That wild shot had whizzed past her ear close enough to draw blood. A few tenths of an inch closer and . . .

Erica gulped for air, fighting down an inexplicable panic. "I hate guns . . . " she tried to say. "I hate violence . . . I hate . . . blood . . . "

Then everything went sort of dark and murky again, then bounced back to brightness. She focused her mind on what was right on in front of her.

That really *wasn't* a chair beneath her bottom was it? She glanced down again, the room snapping back into sharp focus as quickly as it had slid out of it.

Mark Newman sat on the chair, his cane lying on the scuffed linoleum beside him. His right leg was stretched out stiff in front of him, his left leg bent beside it . . . and on that leg—

"Oh my God," she murmured in a shaky, weak voice. "I'm sitting on a Conservative's lap."

Mark Newman's lips curled upward into the biggest, happiest, devilishly handsome grin Erica could ever remember seeing on any man.

"Safest place in the room," he drawled in a voice gone Gomer Pyle and Jed Clampett again.

But for some reason, with her head all light and fuzzy and weird, the sing-songy drawl didn't bother her that much. She lay her head against his shoulder, felt his warmth and closed her eyes, breathing in his strength until her own returned.

"I was looking forward to gettin' the chance to talk." The words rumbled warm in her ear. "But it's not to be. A little more unfinished business, I guess."

"Unfinished business?" Erica asked when her head finally started to clear. She lifted her head, meeting those clear blue eyes again in query.

"Yeah," he rumbled on, and for the first time she noticed his lips—how pink and soft and kissable . . .

Their eyes met and she realized he had been considering her own lips with equal attention.

But then the sound of nearing sirens filled the room. In a matter of seconds, Erica knew, the red and blue lights of a half dozen police cars would be flashing outside and the tiny storefront would be crowded with EMTs and officers.

Shaky as she was, the knowledge brought her back to herself. Erica slid quickly off the man's lap just as she saw the lights appear outside the wide front windows.

"Unfinished business," she repeated, though she wasn't sure why. The only thing she was sure of was that, at that moment, finishing any business with this man would be by far the most dangerous of the evening's events.

If we don't stand up for something, we'll fall for anything.

—War slogan

Chapter 6

◇◇◇

"Thanks for coming," Mark murmured, sliding into the rear of Chase's dark sedan with what felt like the last of his strength.

It was late—nearly ten. The police had taken the captured would-be robber away, gathered information from Mark, Erica, Tia and Tony, and begun their search for the one that got away. Mark had managed to keep it together while the officers did their duty and until he'd seen Erica safely bundled into her car with a patch of white gauze taped to her freshly stitched ear.

"Do you need a lift?" she'd asked him and he might have taken her up on it, had it not been for the exhaustion in her face and her voice. That and the throbbing in his knee that he knew wouldn't withstand the effort of bending to slide into that tiny car.

"I'll be fine," he'd told her even though he knew from the way the pain spiked that he wasn't. "Go home. Get some sleep."

The evening had drained her, too. All the "fight" had left those smoky eyes of hers as she mumbled, "Good night," cranked up the engine and pulled off into the night. He watched, leaning hard on the cane, trying hard to keep the weight off his bad leg. When her brake lights disappeared from view, he lifted the cane and turned, hopping on his one good leg back toward the pizzeria to wait for Chase.

"You know, we could get you a driver," Chase muttered, pulling Mark out of his thoughts.

"She said the same thing," Mark muttered, biting his lip. It had been a long while since he'd hurt this bad. A long, long while.

Chase's eyes found his in the rearview mirror.

"Who?"

"Erica."

"Of course." Chase nodded. "And she's right, too. Heck, there's still half a dozen police cars lined up out there. Any one of them could have run you home."

"No." Mark shook his head. "First of all, I wouldn't ask them to do that. They're law-enforcement officers, not taxi services. And second . . . " He let the sentence die unfinished, knowing Chase could finish it in his own mind. They both knew it wasn't good for too many people to see him in these moments of weakness. Especially not a mere two weeks before an election.

"That bad, huh?" the other man asked.

Mark nodded.

"Worse than little white pills?"

Mark nodded.

"Do we need to make a stop?"

Mark nodded once again. "Sorry, Chase."

Chase shook his head. "No problem. I'll call ahead. Let the doc know we're coming."

"Thanks." Mark stretched his throbbing leg out on the leather seat, rubbing the kneecap like that might help.

It didn't.

He closed his eyes and shifted his focus toward anything that might distract him from the pain. Erica Johnson's face immediately stepped into the void, right at the moment when she'd realized she was sitting on his lap. If he hadn't been hurting so much, he might have laughed aloud just remembering the stricken expression that had crossed her face. It was almost worth the whole encounter with those hoodlums—the sudden wrenching shift of his weight as he lunged at the one with the gun and the unfortunate prolonged pressure on the damaged cartilage of his knee joint that had brought him to this moment of exquisite agony.

She was lovely, but that didn't explain the feeling that had swept over him when he'd held her in his arms. Why did his heart keep telling him that she belonged there? Why did his body react like he couldn't bear for her to leave his side ever again—even though he knew in his brain that the whole thing was absolutely preposterous? He couldn't possibly be falling for a woman so irritatingly granola, could he? He couldn't possibly be losing his head to a twenty-first-century flower child who actually believed all the conflicts in the world could be solved if everyone would just lay down their weapons and make love, not war?

Ridiculous.

Mark grimaced, rubbing his hands over his face. *I'm just tired*, he told himself. *I'm tired and hurting, and the looming election is starting to get to me. I'm tired and she's pretty and that's that. That's all there is.*

"Yeah, ten minutes," he heard Chase say, then the sound of his cell phone as the connection was severed. "Doc was on her way to the hospital, so she's going to meet us at your condo," he said, finding Mark in the rearview mirror, concern in his eyes. "Hang in there, buddy, okay?"

* * *

"This is going to hurt like hell."

Dr. Marian Salter had the bedside manner of an Old West sheriff: straight shooting, with no sugarcoating whatsoever.

"What else is new?" Mark tried to grin, offering up the dregs of his charm through gritted teeth, as though tonight might be the night she finally gave in and smiled at him. Winning the bet he and Chase had made six years ago when they'd first come to Washington and this woman had first entered their lives as Mark's physician would be some small consolation for tonight's suffering.

"You're never going to get that woman to smile," Chase had asserted on the first of these sessions with Dr. Salter—a cortisone shot under the cover of darkness. "She plays for the 'all girl' team, if you get my drift. She's immune to your masculine charms. Not only that, I'm pretty sure she's a Democrat."

"Doesn't matter. She'll smile at me," Mark had promised him, taking the woman on as a project right there on the spot. "One day. You'll see."

But so far it was no dice, and today was no exception. The woman's expression stayed just as flat as her iron gray hair, which she always wore cut in a short, boyish style that looked just as wash-and-wear as the rest of her. Mark couldn't recall her ever wearing so much as a swipe of lipstick or a hint of perfume. Right now, he could have cared less if the woman was straight or gay, if she ever smiled at him or anyone else: She was one of the best orthopedists in the United States and happened to be on the faculty at nearby Georgetown Medical Center. She could have dressed like a peg-legged pirate for all Mark cared at that moment, as long as she did her job.

"It's full of fluid again. I'm going to have to drain

it before I can give you the cortisone shot," she murmured, manipulating the scarred flesh around his kneecap. "I'll numb it a little first, but you're still going to have some discomfort," she said more to the knee than to Mark. "Might help to have a distraction."

"Consider it done!" Chase exclaimed appearing from the kitchen as if on cue, one of Dickey Joe's beers in each of his hands. "I snagged a six-pack from the office. They're even cold this time."

Mark tried to grin, but he knew the effort was a sad imitation of the real thing. Right now, even Dickey Joe's beer couldn't tear his attention from the burning pain in his leg. "That's great," he managed, closing his hand around the bottle. "You think of everything." His eyes swept over the good doctor, already preparing the needles for the procedure ahead. "Doc, will you join us?"

She shook her head without looking up. "Enjoy," she muttered. "Ready?"

Mark took a quick pull at the beer and nodded. "Fire away."

The needle was long and thin and cut through his skin and muscle with agonizing purpose. Mark heard a long, loud shout, but it took him a moment to recognize himself as the sound's source.

"Shit," he muttered. "Shit . . . shit . . ."

"Half way." The doctor's voice was detached and calm.

Only half way? Mark wanted to scream. She was killing him with this damn thing and talking about half way? What the—

"Done," she said softly, and Mark realized he'd had his eyes closed only when he opened them and saw her disposing of the needle with a quick flip of her gloved hand. "That was the painkiller. We'll start removing the fluid next."

"That was the painkiller?" Mark sputtered, his voice shaky even to his own ear. He rubbed his sweaty forehead with an even sweatier palm. "The cure's worse than the disease, huh, Doc?"

Nothing. Not a quiver of the lip, one way or the other. She eyed him dispassionately and said flatly, "The next two shouldn't hurt as much. Ready?"

"No," Mark answered truthfully. He wasn't ready. He'd never be ready. For the millionth time, he swore an oath to put an end to the embedded shrapnel and the fused bones and just have the entire leg amputated mid-thigh. Then he could get one of those fake legs that little boy—Anthony, he recalled effortlessly—found so fascinating.

"He's got a real leg, Anthony. And that's much better than anything artificial," Erica Johnson said softly in his memory. "Now stop asking that question."

Mark sighed, took another swig of beer and glanced at Chase, who hovered near the black leather sofa that had become a makeshift emergency room, looking like he'd rather have been just about anywhere else. "Talk about something," he told his friend. "Talk to me."

"About what?" Chase took the seat farthest from Dr. Salter and her bag of needles and instruments and rubbed his bald spot. "The campaign?"

"No," Mark shook his head. "I hear about that all the time. No politics. Talk about something interesting. Tell me some gossip. Something. Anything . . . distracting."

"Anything?" Chase sounded dubious.

"Anything," Mark repeated. "Anything. Just talk. Don't think I can get through this on Dickey Joe's alone." And as if to prove the point, he took another deep swallow and frowned.

Chase hesitated, and Mark knew he was searching

the extensive vault of information stored in his brain for an appropriate topic. He opened his mouth, appearing on the verge of saying something and then stopped short. Mischief dawned in his eyes and a smile curved over his face.

"Have you—?" Mark stopped him with a finger and pointed at the next needle, this one attached to a larger syringe to extract the fluid surrounding his inflamed cartilage, ready in the doctor's hand.

"Fire when ready," he told the woman and nodded at Chase to signal simultaneous conversation.

Without an instant's pause, Dr. Salter complied, searing his flesh with the second assault. Mark gritted his teeth. *This is better? This is numb?* He thought, but aloud he hissed in Chase's direction, "Talk! Talk!"

"The topic is 'women,'" Chase said quickly.

"Go 'head," Mark urged, grimacing, barely hearing the words.

"You ever dated a woman of another race?"

"No," Mark shook his head, struggling not to cry out. "Not yet."

"Not yet? Does that mean you're planning on it?"

Not yet? Is that what I just said? This Erica woman is like a virus. Mark shook his head again. "Nothing is imminent. I just don't rule it out."

"Does that mean you rule it *in*?" Chase asked, with all the doggedness of the lawyer he was.

Mark rolled his eyes. "It means," he managed, while the needle seemed to scrape against his very bones. "Life is long and the world is full of possibilities."

"So dating Erica Johnson is a possibility for you."

Mark swung his head in his friend's direction, a query on his face.

"Erica Johnson?" he asked. "I'm not dating Erica Johnson."

"Oh really?" Chase's round face broke into a beaming smile. "And what do we call dinner at Mama Tia's tonight?"

"We call it working," Mark grunted, shaking his head. "We were just—"

"Oh come on, Mark!" Chase exclaimed, chuckling a little as though there were really something funny about Mark's reply. "You don't honestly expect anyone to believe that, do you? Not after that TV interview today!"

"Look," Mark grumbled, forgetting about the doctor and her instruments of torture long enough to fix his friend with his most serious gaze. "I don't know where you're going with this, Chase, but—"

"There's only one place *to* go, Mark. It's pretty clear you two like each other. Even though your politics are on different planets, you definitely like each other."

"I respect Erica—Ms. Johnson," Mark declared, uncomfortable with the direction the conversation had taken. "And I certainly don't *dislike* her."

"It's more than that." Chase took a long pull of beer, grimaced and murmured, "This stuff is just nasty, Mark," before repeating, "It's more than that. And you know it."

And Chase had the nerve to stare at him like he'd read Mark's mind. Or even worse, like he'd read Mark's groin.

"Well," Mark muttered, heat rising in his ears and cheeks. "I confess I had noticed a couple of moments when . . . I don't know. She looked at me funny. Like she might have had a crush on me or something. But that's got nothing to do with me. You know how it is with me and women, Chase," Mark sighed. "They love me. God knows why."

For some reason, that made his friend laugh so hard the room vibrated with his guffaws. "I'm sorry," he sputtered before breaking out in another fit. "I'm sorry. It's just, that's such bullshit, Mark."

Mark swiveled on the sofa, almost jerking himself out of the doctor's grasp. "What's so funny?" he demanded. "You know what I'm talking about! Bitsi, for example. And you've seen the way the little interns in the office go all gushy when I'm around! If Erica Johnson wants to make eyes at me, then—"

"That's just it." Chase managed to stop laughing, but he was still grinning like he might start again at any second. "I'm not talking about her, Mark. I'm talking about *you*, my friend." He rubbed the spot on his head and continued before Mark could interrupt. "You can't stop talking about this woman, Mark. And for all your bullshit about how the women *love* you, you've never taken any of them up on it. You've had all kinds of opportunities . . ."—Chase shook his head—"and done nothing. Nada. Some ladies' man, you are. Own your shit, man. You're a one-woman man. For a long time, even after she died, that woman was Katharine. And now, it's Erica Johnson. I knew it from the moment you stood up in that hearing yesterday." Another mischievous glint lit his eyes. "You want to talk about goo-goo eyes, you should take a look at your own face."

Mark opened his mouth to protest, but before he could speak, Erica Johnson's face rose in his mind and the feeling swept over him again—the same feeling he'd had standing next to her in the classroom, when she'd had that happy, proud smile on her face and every nerve in his body had wanted nothing more than to gather her into his arms and kiss her until neither one of them could breathe.

Own your shit. Is that what Chase had said? "I don't know if it's all that," he said slowly. "But I'll admit there's something there." Mark raised his eyes to his friend's face and sighed, almost grateful to have the weird feelings churning inside him out on the table. "Let's just assume," he continued tentatively, "for the sake of argument, that you're right. That there's more between me and Erica than just politics." He skewered his longtime friend with his gaze. "Is it going to be a problem?"

Chase shook his head. "Not for me. I'm pretty sure Bitsi's going to hate it, though. Probably already does. For reasons both personal and professional. After that"—he shrugged his shoulders and rubbed the spot—"I don't know. Does it matter?"

"Of course it matters," Mark grumbled. "We've just started our work here in Washington. I don't want to lose my seat with the job half done."

"Forget the politics." Chase swept the campaign, the election and all of Capitol Hill aside with a brush of his hand. He leaned close to Mark, close enough that Mark could smell the bitter malt of Dickey Joe's on his breath. "Does it matter?"

Mark considered the man carefully, analyzing his meaning in every sense of the phrase.

"No, it doesn't matter," he replied. "It doesn't matter except," he said, sighing, "it's been so long, Chase. I'm out of practice with this kind of thing. I mean, I know how to flirt, to work the angles when I need to, but . . ." He shook his head. "I'm not sure I know how to talk to a woman anymore." He looked into his friend's eyes again. "Not when it matters. Not about things that matter."

Chase nodded. "I know what you mean. But it's got to be like riding a bicycle. Or at least like falling off one, right?" He chortled a little at his joke and rubbed the spot. "Don't worry about it, Mark. Think before you open that big trap of yours and you'll find the words."

Mark quirked an eyebrow at him. "And the politics?"

"That might be tough. Especially given the race differences. But that's a cheap target, and I got to think
even Malloy's too sophisticated for that. And then
there's the fact that you can count on Erica to disagree with every word you say." He shrugged. "But
there are other couples in Washington who belong to
different parties. There are definitely a few negative
scenarios, but it's still a good thing, in my opinion."

"How so?"

"Because, at the end of the day, you're still a *man*,
Mark. Politics and government offices aside, if it's a
good thing for *you*, it's good." His friend's muddy
brown eyes flickered over him. "You've been alone
too long, Mark."

Mark nodded, feeling the truth of the words. "I can
say the same for you, buddy."

Chase grinned. "Don't worry about me. I'm working on it."

Working on it? This was news. Mark lifted an eyebrow for the follow-up, but was interrupted by Dr.
Salter's brusque, "All done."

He looked down at her and was surprised to find
his knee wrapped tight in bandages and bolstered by
a couple of ice packs.

"Stay off it," the woman barked, barely looking at
him as she put her implements away. "Crutches tomorrow. You should be able to put some weight on it
again by Friday. But take it easy."

Mark opened his mouth to thank her, but the woman waved her hand to silence him. "And for what it's
worth, speaking strictly as your physician, if you like
this woman, you should go for it, and to hell with
what anyone says," she continued, her dark eyes
flashing with sudden tumultuous emotion. "Studies

have shown that people in solid relationships experience less pain from chronic conditions like yours than their unattached counterparts, Senator. And if I may be so bold"—she hesitated—"I think a woman like Johnson is *exactly* what you need."

And then the impossible happened: The grim Dr. Salter's lips curved upward and parted into the sunniest smile Mark had every seen.

"Good night," she murmured, and gathered her things and let herself out before Mark could decipher the meaning of either the words or the smile.

I'm not trying to advance a political agenda. Senator Newman disagrees, of course, but I don't think of myself as particularly political, if you want to know the truth. I think I'm following the teachings of Jesus. He did say, "Love your enemies," right? He didn't say love some of your enemies and bomb the hell out of the rest of them.

—Erica Johnson, on *Good Morning Nation*

Chapter 7

"How's the ear?" Angelique looked up from her laptop and squinted in Erica's direction.

Automatically Erica reached up to caress the few stitches notched into her lobe. "Fine," she mumbled, padding into the kitchen to pour herself a cup of coffee. "You're up early."

"Yep." Angelique nodded. "You've inspired me."

Erica had gotten back to the row house she and Angelique shared under her own power and in her own car, in spite of Newman's offers of everything from a cab to a personal escort. The house clung to the edges of the newly gentrified Capitol Hill by a thread, but was without a doubt the worst house on the block. Left to Angelique by her elderly parents when they passed away a few years before, the place had been in serious disrepair. Now, except for the political signs littering the postage stamp of a lawn, the place was looking downright uninhabitable.

Erica focused her attention on her friend. She wore a purple silk do-rag on her head, and her braids hung long and loose beneath it. She'd taken out her contacts, and with her glasses and lack of makeup, she looked every one of her thirty-four years. Erica sighed, remembering what she'd read somewhere about the high number of single black professional women, looking for a brother who could fill all the boxes on their checklist—and finding the pickings to be extremely thin.

"Yep, you've inspired me," Angelique repeated, giving her mouse a final click and pushing the laptop off her knees. "Watching you and that white boy has worn down the last of my resistance," she continued as if Erica had asked. "Last night, I made me a profile on one of those interracial dating sites. Then I went into their chat room and I already made a friend. His screen name is Mr. Politics D.C., only it's all consonants. MRPLTKSDC. I almost didn't get it, at first."

"You what?" Erica stared at her, her mouth open in shock.

"You heard me!" Angelique grinned a big, happy grin that seemed a little much for 4:30 A.M. "Shoot, if *you* can get you a white man, I know I can, too! Maybe one with a little *money* . . . "

Erica shook her head. There were so many things wrong with that statement, she hardly knew where to begin. "For the millionth time," she muttered, "he's not my man. I don't even like him."

"Mmm-hmm." Angelique watched as Erica unplugged the toaster before plugging in the coffeepot, to keep the home's old electric wires from shorting. Erica handed her the empty carafe and made sure she abandoned the computer long enough to add some water to it before turning away to pull fresh Fair Trade beans from the refrigerator. The things were outrageously expensive—she could have bought a two-gallon drum of regular ground coffee from the grocery store for the same price—but it felt good to know that the farmers in Africa and South America were paid a living wage.

Even if she and Angelique were about to go broke.

"You look like you haven't slept at all," Angelique said over the running water. "Bad dreams?"

Erica shrugged. "Sort of."

"About the robbery, or about Newman?" Angelique's tone was sly, like she knew the remark would get something going.

"Neither," Erica lied. "It's hot back there," she said, gesturing with her head toward the short corridor where the bedrooms lay. "Don't you think it's hot back there?"

"Oh, it's hot all right." Angelique's lips curved into that little smile she'd been giving Erica every other minute since they'd first encountered one Senator Mark Newman. Erica knew what was coming next. "Or at least, I believe you're hot," she teased. "Hot for a certain somebody."

"For the last time, I am not," Erica grumbled, feeling irritated by the mere mention of the man, and even more irritated by the fact that he had indeed been dancing in her dreams again. And worse, now she had the feeling like she had made a critical error. Like in a moment of weakness—after all, she'd sat on his lap and clung to him like a life raft, for Heaven's sake—she might have given him the impression that she might like him a tiny bit.

"Tell the truth, girl," Angelique was saying, as though she'd read Erica's mind. "He's not as bad as you thought he'd be. Admit it!"

Erica considered.

"Okay," she said at last. "You're right."

"I knew it!" Angelique exclaimed. "I knew it!"

"He's not the Antichrist. He's more like the man possessed by legions of demons. You remember that Bible story?"

Angelique frowned. "I don't get you, Erica," she said, sliding the carafe full of water across the counter and seating herself on the small kitchen's lone stool. She popped her laptop open and Erica heard her start clicking away again, at least until the roar of the coffee grinder drowned her out.

"I think you should take a look at this," she said, sliding the computer across the counter.

"And this, and this . . . "

"I get it," Erica muttered rubbing her forehead. "The robbery is all over the news. Newman's a hero. Again. Whoopee. I'm sure he and that awful media person of his are thrilled."

Angelique eyed her. "What do you know about him, really?" she asked in the slow, considering voice that meant she'd been thinking. Again. "Look, I know you know how he voted on education policy. And I know you know his stance on the war. But what do you know about *him*? As a man."

Erica frowned. "He told my class he grew up poor. Really poor," she said, considering his background. "And he told me that his wife died."

"When?" Angelique asked. "How?"

"She was shot," Erica answered. "But I don't know when."

Angelique had already bent her neck to the computer again and was typing furiously. "Okay . . . of course there's the Senate bio. It's not going to give us the kind of information we really want, but I'll save it, anyway. You can look it over later. And there's a bunch of newspaper articles—hundreds of them, it looks like." She frowned. "But a lot of them are about the same things: his war injury, his Senate bid . . ."

Erica crept around the small counter until she could see the screen over Angelique's shoulder. The search engine had revealed a long list of "hits": mostly newspaper articles, a few dating back over a decade.

"Wait a minute," Angelique muttered, scrolling down to an entry halfway down the list. "Here."

With a single click of her mouse, they were directed to an archived newspaper story with the headline FRESHMAN SENATOR'S WIFE KILLED IN ROBBERY ATTEMPT.

Erica and Angelique read silently. The article chronicled the life of Katharine Miltke Newman, who had died only three years earlier. She and her husband of twelve years, said the story, had been high-school sweethearts. She'd been killed intervening when three teenagers had tried to rob an old man leaving a grocery store. Accompanying the words was a picture of a woman with a gentle smile and a headful of dark, 1980s-style big hair.

"That must be an old picture," Angelique observed, closing the file and selecting another article. This one featured photos of a very young Mark Newman in a crisp military uniform, both legs strong and whole, standing alongside the big-haired woman. He was grinning from ear to ear and looking annoyingly pleased with himself.

"Before Gulf One, I guess," Erica murmured.

"Yeah," Angelique said quietly. "You can really see the difference, can't you?"

"Well, it's pretty obvious," Erica agreed. "Now he has to use that cane."

Angelique's face swung toward her in astonishment. "Is that the only difference you see?" she asked with a frown. "Nothing else?"

"Well, he's older of course," Erica added quickly. "But we're all older."

"Older? That's *it*?" Angelique sounded mildly disgusted. She turned to the computer again and with a few strokes had located a more recent photo of Newman. She created a split-screen effect so that the two versions of the man appeared side by side. She gestured toward the screen again. "You don't see it?" She brushed a finger over the on-screen image, touching the mouth and eyes. "Here and here?"

Erica studied the photographs carefully.

"I don't know what you want me to see," she said at last. "He looks older. He's got a cane . . . What?" she stared at Angelique, waiting for enlightenment. "What do you see?"

Angelique shook her head. "Man, this is incredible," she muttered under her breath. Then, without a word, she stood up, the stool scraping against the old linoleum. "I don't understand you, Erica."

"What?" Erica repeated in genuine confusion.

"You fight so hard for everyone else's pain: the Sudanese refugees, migrant workers in El Salvador, Indonesian children working in sweatshops—the list of your causes goes on and on." She shook her head again. "But you've got this guy cast in such a narrow little role, you won't even let him have his own pain."

"The Mark Newmans of the world don't feel that kind of pain, Angelique," Erica scoffed. "They don't feel anything. They're too full of themselves."

Angelique stared at her in sad resignation. "I guess you have to see it that way. Because if you could see his pain, then he'd be human, and you'd have to feel bad for him, too—even though he supports the war, voted for the Other Guy, and is a card-carrying whack job, right?" But before Erica could answer, she continued with, "I'm going to get a shower and get dressed. Thank God tomorrow's Friday, right?" She shuffled toward the door. "And don't forget to clean your mail out of the bowl," she added over her shoulder, referring to the wide decorative bowl they kept on the little table in the foyer for this purpose. "It's overflowing." Then she was gone.

Erica frowned after her and then slid onto the vacant stool, staring down at the man's images on the computer screen. She studied Mark Newman's handsome face, both now and then. He was obviously extremely happy in the earlier photo, while the second looked like some kind of official shot and his face was set into an unsmiling mask. There was more gray in the hair, there were more lines in the face and, of course, a different expression crimped those thin lips. Erica couldn't be sure she saw anything in Mark Newman's face. Anything beyond his own certainty that he was the center of the universe.

But last night . . .

She recalled the man's expression in an instant. Sure, she'd seen that smug smirk and this grim empty look—more times than she cared to count. But twice, his face had done something she hadn't expected. The first when he'd referenced his late wife. "My Katharine," he'd called her, with a look of such sudden gentleness the woman's loss seemed almost overwhelmingly fresh.

And again, when she'd found himself in his arms after the robbery. The way he seemed to be contemplating her lips at the very instant she was considering tasting his.

I'm losing it, Erica thought, touching her ear. *That bullet must have done more damage than I thought.*

Bugged by Angelique's words, she turned her attention to Katharine Newman's face instead. *What must it have been like for this woman to be married to this annoying, obnoxious man?* she wondered, staring at the woman's contented smile. Was she as phony and plastic and full of herself as he was? Was she some kind of female version of the same whack-job reasoning that Newman espoused? As his wife, did she walk two steps behind him and defer to him in all matters, like Erica had heard of women doing in some places?

Or maybe . . .

Maybe she'd liked the protected feeling of being in his arms.

Maybe she'd liked the sound of his laughter or the challenge of matching wits with him?

Maybe he made her silly and giddy and happy and frustrated and annoyed and . . .

"Tell me," Erica demanded, staring hard at Katharine Newman's smiling face.

But of course the old photograph remained silent, and the two of them just kept grinning up at her, frozen in their happiness.

Erica turned her attention to the grim, unsmiling photograph from the senator's official bio. "Tell me," she demanded again. But instead of an answer, she got ice blue eyes and the silent treatment. She read in the face the iron will of a man who either knew no pain or wasn't about to admit to it.

"This is stupid," she said aloud to the empty kitchen and pushed the computer away. Instead of contemplating Newman, she grabbed a mug from the cabinet and poured herself a cup of coffee, doctored it up with a splash of hazelnut-flavored cream and carried it with her through the house to the foyer.

The bowl was indeed full—only not just with Erica's stuff as Angelique's comments had led her to believe.

"Bamboozled again," Erica muttered, beginning the job of sorting through whose mail was whose and what mail was what. She had a pretty decent pile with Angelique's name on it when she heard the sound of the mail slot and the *whoosh* of an envelope as it sailed through the opening.

Erica turned. A little shot of the cool morning air penetrated the space around her, giving the moment an ominous creepiness.

Especially since a solitary plain white envelope now lay on the old hardwood floor.

"I know the post office isn't delivering this early," Erica muttered, bending to pick it up. It was probably from Newman—had to be. This was just the kind of thing he'd do, she was sure of it. He was probably standing somewhere in the near-dark dawn, accompanied by this aide or that, waiting to jump out at her like some kind of Ed McMahon gone wrong, just as soon as she'd read the missive he'd sent.

Think again, bucko!

Erica grabbed the door handle, flipped the lock and opened it wide.

But there wasn't anyone there. No one. Well, not exactly no one: A lady stood at the edge of the fence in her bathrobe, holding a leash. She looked guilty as hell when Erica frowned at her, calling quickly to the fluffy white pooch buried somewhere in the high grass of Erica and Angelique's front lawn.

"I . . . uh . . . wasn't sure anyone lived here," she stammered, yanking the dog out of the grass. "Sorry."

Erica closed the front door slowly. It was definitely a good news/bad news situation: The bad news was that there was a fresh load of dog poop somewhere on the front lawn . . . but the good news was that load of crap wasn't personified by Senator Mark Newman.

Erica smiled at her little joke, and imagined the senator's face when—no, if—he ever got to hear it. He would probably give her that lopsided little smirk, the look that meant the barb had bounced off that super-inflated ego of his and that his laser-sharp brain had already processed a rebuttal. He was definitely clever, she admitted only slightly grudgingly. And strong.

The feeling of being in his arms surfaced once again, the sound of his voice rumbling in his chest beneath her ear.

Whoa, she thought. *Down, girl.* But then it occurred to her that *whoa* was exactly the sort of word the senator would have used.

"He's like slow poison," she muttered to herself, turning the white envelope over in her hands. "Slow, deadly poison."

The envelope wasn't heavy, wasn't thick. It seemed like there was only one sheet of paper inside. No longer able to contain her curiosity, Erica slid a finger under the adhesive flap and ripped it open.

It was a photograph, printed not on the glossy thick stock of a professional, but on plain white computer paper as though on a home printer. The image was completely familiar and totally disconcerting: herself, sitting on Mark Newman's lap with her head against his chest like she belonged there; Newman looking smug and tender at the same time.

Erica couldn't figure out when or how it could have been taken. There had been photographers at the school, but that was earlier, before the robbery, and the bullet and the gun—before any moment as intimate as this.

He's just trying to embarrass me, she'd thought, turning the shot over to decipher some red writing scrawled across the back.

"Stay in Washington, nigger bitch," it read.

Dread swept over Erica in an icy black wave. She

was about to crumple the thing in her fist, to rip it into tiny pieces and burn it to ashes until another calmer voice whispered direction from the back of her brain. She hurried back to the kitchen, found her school bag and stuffed the nasty-gram inside.

Somehow, she'd have to find the time to deliver it to its rightful owner today. Even if it meant finding a substitute teacher to take her place at Bramble Heights Elementary.

Except for ending slavery, fascism, communism, and Nazism, war has never solved anything!
—War slogan

Chapter 8

"This one says, 'Senator foils pizzeria holdup.' And here: 'Robber's case cracked by Senator's cane.' And this one: 'Newman gets tough on D.C. crime.'"

Bitsi tossed the newspapers onto Mark's desk like she was disgusted.

"Hey, I'm a local hero," Mark quipped. "Thought you'd be happy!"

But instead of smiling, Bitsi's frown deepened. A conversation was brewing between them, Mark could feel it. Bitsi wasn't stupid: She knew something was up between Mark and Erica. But instead of shooting straight at the target, she was choosing to skim around it—picking off the corners before going for the kill. Mark cut a glance at Chase, but the man kept his eyes on his coffee mug as though it held the power to predict the future.

Mark suppressed a sigh and pulled the newspapers toward him. He scanned the first story quickly, observing that there was nothing damning in the account. If anything, it was a little heavy on the praise, making him sound like the only quick-thinking patron, when in fact Erica, Mama Tia, and Papa Tony had played important roles in the arrest. He grabbed the second newspaper and then the third, skimming through the stories quickly before looking up at his two staffers. "Seriously, I don't see a problem here."

Chase pushed his glasses higher up his nose, grabbed the top paper and shuffled through it until he found the section dedicated to gossip. He folded the paper with a sharp crease and tossed it back at Mark without a word, while Bitsi paced the office with her white-blonde head down and her arms folded tight across her chest.

With a quick flick of the eye, Mark understood he was reading the gossip column in the Lifestyle section. Someone had outlined the offending blurb in bright yellow highlighter.

Not that there was any way he was likely to miss it, with the headline THE SENATOR'S NEW WOMAN in bold black letters.

It wasn't long—just a few sentences, really, all conjecture and guesswork. An "available" U.S. senator currently up for reelection in his home state seemed to be choosing to spend time in the company of a certain D.C. public-school teacher and antiwar protester. Perhaps there was a little more going on than debate and policy?

When he looked up, Bitsi was studying him as if he were a Sudoku puzzle.

"Aw c'mon," Mark slipped into the easy, country-boy style he often used to joke her out of a bad humor. "It's a *gossip* column. These folks make a living out of trying to get something out of nothing." He gestured toward the story. "They're just trying to justify their existence. They have to talk about somebody. Heck, last year they had me linked to that supermodel who came to Capitol Hill to testify about health care. We all know how untrue that one was," he said, rolling his eyes.

"Dead wrong," Chase seconded, but he had that silly little, I've-got-a-secret look on his broad face. Mark felt himself on the verge of a smile, too, and struggled to hold it back. When the time was right, he'd bring Bitsi in on the things they'd spent the early hours of the day talking about. For now, it was a discussion about women best left between men.

As if she sensed the exclusion, Bitsi darted a glance between them and cleared her throat. "It's just, we've been getting some phone calls," she announced.

"Must be a slow news day for the Washington press corps."

Bitsi shook her head until her hair swung in two blonde sheets toward her face. "They weren't calls from *Washington*, Mark. They were from *constituents*. From the folks back home. They saw *Good Morning Nation*. They've also noticed the . . . uh"—her lips crunched into a frown of distaste—"chemistry . . . between you and the Johnson woman." Her head wobbled some more. "And they don't much like it."

Mark stole a glance at Chase, but the other man was typing something into his PDA as fast as his thumbs could move. Mark sighed. Last night they'd hashed through the whole thing as though dating a woman were a complex piece of legislation. Chase had seemed like the original answer man. This morning, he was too lost in his electronics to even look up.

"Show me," Mark commanded his media director. He watched Bitsi lift her notebook off the edge of his desk and produce a series of pink phone messages and white e-mail printouts. These she shuffled through quickly until she found the ones she wanted. "This one calls it chemistry. These say, 'romantic interest' and 'attraction,' respectively. This one"—she shook a piece of white paper free of the pile—"says you spent the whole interview making 'goo-goo eyes' at her." She laid them on the desk in front of him. "And all of them are very specific about one thing: She's black. And that's no good."

"No good, huh?" he muttered, grabbing the pink sheets and skimming them quickly. "This one really does say 'Goo-goo eyes!'" Mark exploded, choking back a guffaw. "Chase, did you hear that? Your favorite phrase!"

"Yeah, sure," Chase murmured, looking up with a confused expression that meant he hadn't heard a word. "Yeah," he repeated, returning to his device.

"Favorite phrase?" Bitsi asked. "'Goo-goo eyes?'" She frowned. "Why?"

"Never mind," Mark said, deflecting her. The last thing he needed was Bitsi's input. Not when it was entirely possible that he'd mess it up on his own. "Not important." And to prove it, he turned his attention back to the dozen or so messages, skimming them quickly. He looked up, expecting to find her staring at him, but instead Bitsi was wearing a tread in the middle of his rug, pacing steadily back and forth.

"Two questions," Mark began, pushing the pink slips away and holding up two fingers. "Question one: You don't *really* think these few oddballs and bigots are a problem, do you, Bits?"

She looked up, a frown still marring her red lips.

"They could be."

"Could be," Mark repeated dubiously. "Okay then. Two: How many favorable responses have we gotten from yesterday's interview?"

Bitsi's eyebrows rose. "Favorable?"

"Yeah, favorable," Mark repeated. "That means good."

A pink flush of anger appeared on each of Bitsi's cheeks. "You know," she said in a carefully controlled tone that failed to disguise how very annoyed she was. "That's not helpful, Mark. I'm doing my best to protect you here, but you're really pushing my buttons now, so—"

Mark sighed. He was always snapping at Bitsi lately, especially since Erica Johnson had entered his life and started rearranging his emotional furniture.

I'll sit down with Bitsi. Later, he told himself. *After this election is behind us. When there's more time and we're all not on edge.*

But just thinking of that conversation filled him with dread. He knew he didn't have the words to explain to Bitsi where his feelings for her ended. She'd get all emotional and he'd lose his way. *Women*, he added mentally. *Almost all of them were impossible to talk to.* Especially when emotions were involved. And Bitsi, for all her intelligence and logic, had emotions a-plenty.

"I know, I know," he said more gently. "I'm sorry. But you get my point. How'm I supposed to keep this in perspective if all you'll tell me about is the Confederate whackos and the redneck rebs?"

Bitsi sighed. She approached the desk again, reached for a fat folder beneath her notebook and slid it toward him. Inside were dozens of messages and e-mails expressing interest and appreciation for the "Newman/Johnson Project."

The Newman/Johnson Project, Mark thought, a smile curving his lips. Leave it to Bitsi to come up with the perfect phrase for the whole affair.

He made a note to run that one up the flagpole with Erica and see if she saluted. She'd probably hate it simply because he liked it, he realized, but instead of irritating him, the thought made him want to laugh out loud. He didn't realize he was sitting there grinning like a goofball until Bitsi cleared her throat a little more forcefully than was strictly necessary. He focused his attention back on the two staffers.

"Seems to me the positives far outweigh the negatives here, Bitsi," he said, closing the folder. "I don't think we can let a little gossip and some angry assholes derail us, do you? And if Malloy's desperate enough to try to play some kind of race card, I say let him. He can't actually hurt me, and he'll end up looking like a bigot, right?"

"Right," Chase muttered absently to his PDA.

"Wrong," Bitsi asserted firmly. "I don't know what you're up to, Mark, but I'll tell you this: I will not stand idly by and allow you to alienate your supporters on the eve of an election, just because you're horny or you've got jungle fever or whatever. You've decided to get back into the dating game and that's fine. But I really think you'd be better off with a white woman."

Anger overtook his body in an instant and before he knew it he'd grabbed the crutches from the credenza behind him and swung himself toward Bitsi to hiss his fury into her face.

"What?" Mark glowered at her. "What did you say?"

She whirled at him, eyes flashing. "I said, I really think—"

The buzz of the intercom interrupted her.

"Senator?" The voice of the intern *du jour*—a coed who giggled nervously every time Mark entered the room and whose name he couldn't remember for the life of him—filled the room. "There's a Ms. Erica Johnson here to see you."

Bitsi stopped, her mouth still open, her finger still

aimed in a point in midair. Chase finally pulled his face out of his PDA, a startled, deer-in-the-headlights look on his face.

"Send her in," Mark replied, immediately pushing the blowup brewing with Bitsi to the back of his mind. Cursing the unwieldy crutches, he maneuvered himself toward the door, averting his face from his colleagues long enough to get his expression under control. But there was no way of checking the way his heart skipped in anticipation.

He didn't remember thrusting the crutches behind him, as though he could somehow hide them, and he didn't feel the customary twinge of pain as he tested his weight on his bad leg. All he remembered was that within seconds of the young intern's announcement of Erica's presence, he was standing in front of her, staring down into her lovely face.

She was wearing a pair of dark slacks and an odd capelike thing, made of a fabric that looked like fur but, he suspected, given her convictions, was more likely to be some kind of synthetic. Over her shoulder was draped the strap of her duffel bag. Mark peered closer. The bandage the paramedics had taped to her earlobe was still securely in place.

She glanced around the room with an expression that made his smile of welcome freeze on his face.

He'd never seen her eyes so uncertain or her forehead so drawn. Her lips were held tight together, like she was biting back a scream. He didn't know her well enough to be sure, but she looked scared.

"I'm sorry to interrupt you," she began.

"You're not interrupting me," he said quickly, limping as close to her as could, the better to search her face for an explanation for that frightened, worried look marring her features. "What's wrong?"

Her eyes darted away from his, taking in Chase and Bitsi with apprehension.

"Oh, forgive my lack of manners," he said. "This is Chase Alexander, my chief of staff and one of my oldest friends. And I think you know Bitsi Barr, my media director?"

Chase crossed the room quickly, offering Erica his hand and a nimble smile, but Mark knew his friend's quick mind had absorbed every detail about her, from the Birkenstock clogs to the colorful African tie she wore around her unruly hair like a headband. "Nice to meet you at last," he said, pumping her fingers with his own. "The senator speaks very highly of you . . . and very often of you," he added with a chuckle.

"Nice to meet you," Erica Johnson murmured graciously enough, but she let the remark pass without a response. Mark could tell she'd barely heard the man. Even Chase quirked a puzzled eyebrow in Mark's direction.

"Hello," Bitsi said in a brittle voice, without moving an inch in Erica's direction. The disrespect in her tone was palpable, and Mark felt his anger re-ignite in the pit of his stomach. He made a mental note to finish their conversation and to back Bitsi up—way up this time—but for now he satisfied himself with shooting an evil glare in her direction.

"Hello," Erica replied, not seeming to notice Bitsi's brush-off any more than Chase's attempts at charm. In fact, her eyes had barely left Mark's face. "If you have a moment," she said in a low voice. "I need to speak to you. Alone."

"Alone?" Bitsi hacked into the conversation like a buzz saw. "I'm sure that's not necessary. We're both Mark's closest advisors. Anything you say to him, he's only going to tell us later, anyway, so—"

"That may be," Erica interjected in a no-nonsense voice that sounded more like the woman Mark thought he knew. "Who *he* talks to is his business. Who *I* talk to is mine."

"Of course," Chase said, taking Bitsi by the arm and giving her a not-so-subtle yank. "But don't sneak off without saying good-bye. We need to talk to you a bit about what to expect during your visit to Billingham. Mark's campaigning for reelection, you know. Primary voting is in a week, so we're down to the wire. Got a busy few days planned. We'll be sure to get you a rough itinerary, so you'll know what to expect. Right, Bitsi?"

Bitsi folded her lips and glared at Erica like she was the most hated of enemies.

"Right, Bitsi?" Chase repeated even more forcefully.

"Sure," Bitsi muttered through gritted teeth. "Absolutely. Unless" —Bitsi managed an ugly, red-lipped smile—"you've decided not to go, for some reason."

Erica's eyes left Mark's face. She surveyed Bitsi for a long, silent moment, and for the first time, Mark noticed the envelope she held tightly in her fingers.

"If I decide not to go," she said deliberately. "It'll be because *I* decided that was the right decision and not because of anything anyone *else*"—she emphasized the word so strongly that Chase cut a glance of query toward Mark—"said or did. Do you understand me, Ms. Barr?"

Bitsi shot her another nasty little smile.

"Of course," she said patronizingly. "What other reason could there be?"

What the . . . ?

Mark's gaze swung between the two women. They'd clearly drawn some kind of battle line between them . . . but when? And over what? He glanced at Chase, but the man's raised eyebrows indicated a confusion that mirrored his own.

"Thanks, Chase, Bits," Mark said when the female stare-down continued without any apparent end in sight.

Chase smiled a smile that didn't reach the concern in his eyes. "Don't mind her." He tossed the words lightly at Erica like they were a joke she was supposed to catch. "We never do." He clapped Mark hard on the back, took Bitsi firmly by the arm and guided her toward the door. "Come on, Bitsi. We've got work to do."

As soon as the door closed firmly behind them, Mark opened his mouth.

"What can I do for—"

"Here," she said, thrusting the envelope toward him. "It came this morning. Early. Did you get anything like it?"

Mark opened the envelope and was surprised to see himself with Erica perched on his knee. More surprising was his expression: even to his own eyes, he looked very comfortable, very content.

"Where'd you get this?" he asked, looking up at her. "I don't remember any photographers."

"Read the back," she insisted, practically yanking the photo out of his hands and turning it over. "Read it."

Mark read, and then his eyes locked on her face.

"Where'd you get this?" he repeated.

"Someone brought it to my door. Dropped it in the mail slot. Early this morning. I thought it was from you. Until I opened it," she explained in a quick rush of breath. "She wants to scare me."

Mark stared down at her, watching the lines tightening on her face as she spoke. "Who?"

"That Bitsi woman. I'd bet you my salary she's responsible for this. You heard what she said just now. About my deciding not to go, 'for some reason.'"

Mark shook his head. "I think I'd know if I saw Bitsi Barr last night at Mama Tia's Pizza. She was nowhere near there. And if she was nowhere near there, there's no way she could have taken that picture."

"She hired someone!" Erica snapped. "Maybe that guy who came in and left. Only he didn't leave. He must have hung around. Then, when the robbery and everything happened—"

"Okay, here comes the whole Right Wing conspiracy thing, right?"

"Well, it's *possible!*" she snapped.

"No, Erica. It's not." Mark gently nudged her toward the chair Chase had just vacated and hopped toward the one beside it. "First of all, I don't think that guy had a camera. And even if he did, he could only have gotten a picture this good from *inside* Mama's place. And I'm certain he didn't come back in."

"You don't think Mama Tia or Papa Tony—"

"Of course not. They're an interracial couple, too," he began, and it wasn't until the words were out that he realized the implication of what he'd just said. "Or at least," he backpedaled, "they don't have any reason to keep you from going home with me—I mean," he corrected again, "home to Billingham with me."

She was hearing him but not hearing him, for which Mark found himself very grateful. Everything that came out of his mouth seemed to suggest something more than a professional relationship; every move he made seemed to suggest more intimate possibilities.

I don't know how to do this. I don't know how to dance around this, he thought with sudden panic. He took a breath, focused on the matter at hand, and reached for the phone. "We should let the authorities handle this," he said.

Her hand whipped out, covering his and stopping him cold.

"That's it!" she cried, conspiracy dancing in her eyes. "That's what she wants. She wants a lot of press and attention. She wants to stir up enough controversy to keep you in the news for the next two decades."

Mark stared at her for a long second before bursting into laugher, but burst he did. And once he did, he couldn't stop, even when she frowned at him like she was strongly considering slapping his face. "Forgive me," he said when the laughter mellowed down to a chuckle. "But if you'd been in this room just two minutes ago, you'd know that comment is, as your students would say, the most whack thing I've ever heard."

"Why? Because it's Bitsi? She's awful. I can't believe you can stand to have her around."

"She doesn't like you much, either," Mark replied, thinking over the "white woman" comment and the daggers the women had just shot at each other. What was it about strong women? Why was it so many of them seemed to hate each other? "Bitsi's got her faults, and she's very protective of me, I admit it. But she'd never do anything like this."

"But—"

"Never." Mark shook his head and reached for the phone again. "A threat involving a member of the Senate sounds all kinds of alarms around here." He pried the letter from her fingers again. "I'll turn that over to the Capitol police and let them handle it. They'll send a security detail back home with us, just to be sure. Until then, I've got nothing to offer you in terms of protection beyond myself." He considered that a moment. "Now, I really think we should call in the police."

"And I really think we should call off the whole thing. I've got a bad feeling now."

Mark felt the smile curving his lips long before she shot him that irritated glance that let him know she'd seen it, too, and didn't appreciate it.

"What?" she snapped. "*You* didn't get a nasty-gram delivered to your house. I'm telling you, you might call Billingham home, but it's beginning to sound like you've got a state full of closed-minded bigots. And that sounds like my idea of hell." She squinted down at the photo printout. "Not to mention hazardous to my health."

"Maybe," Mark drawled, "but you're still going."

She glared daggers at him. "Oh, really? And who died and crowned you king?"

"You did," he replied, watching her eyes flash. She was definitely getting pissed, but he liked the firefight brewing in her eyes much more than the frighten gaze she'd entered the office with. "I can read you like a book, you know that?"

She folded her arms over her chest and glared at him. "Okay, Mr. Know-it-all. What makes you think I'm going with you even around the block, let alone out of Washington?"

"Three things," Mark said, leaning close to her and turning his Southern charm on high even though it was clearly annoying the hell out of her. "First, we're getting national coverage of this visit. You know *exactly* how it will look if you back down now—and I don't believe you want to hand me that victory. In fact, I *know* you don't." He grabbed the nasty message and danced it under her nose. "Second, you're not the kind of woman to let some ignorant, misguided person stop you from doing anything you're committed to and . . ." He hesitated. His next words had serious implications, but considering the lecture he was giving the woman on commitment and character, he couldn't very well just sweep it under the rug. "And finally"—he paused, cleared his throat and began again. "Finally, like I told you yesterday . . ."

No, that wasn't it. He cleared his throat again and started once more. "This photo eloquently captures . . ." He rolled his eyes. "What I'm trying to tell you is, we've still got unfinished business, you and me."

He stopped, hoping she would catch his drift and spare him the necessity of going into confusing and mushy details, but she was staring at him like he'd grown a third eye.

"Unfinished business?" she asked, her brow crimping in confusion. "What do you mean? You mean dinner last night? Because it was just a pizza and—"

"No," Mark interrupted, annoyed by her refusal to play along. She knew exactly what he was talking about and was going to make him work for every bit of it. "It's more than that, and you know it."

"I don't know what you mean."

"I mean," Mark waved the photo at her. "Look at your face, woman. Look at your face and tell me you don't know what I mean," he growled. "You like me. You think I'm sexy. Look! It's written all over your face."

She didn't even glance at the photo.

"And tell me, Senator," she said in that irritatingly cool voice of hers. "What's written all over yours?"

Mark felt color rising to his cheeks yet again. A few days ago, he couldn't have remembered the last time that happened in his adult life. But since he'd met this woman, it was getting to be an hourly occurrence.

"W—well," he stammered. "I said we had unfinished business, didn't I? I mean"—his brain froze, gave up, shut down, but his lips kept moving, making sounds—"I don't have any trouble with women. Hell, I could have any woman I want—"

"Really?" she said, though for some reason she chose that moment to stand up and give herself a quick tour of his office, turning so he couldn't see her face.

"Really," he continued, still feeling the fire in his face. "I'm, uh, I'm actually something of a catch—or so they tell me," he heard himself saying, even while another part of him was hollering *Abandon ship*! like he was taking on water. "Half the women on the Hill are in love with me. You don't know how many interns we've had to send back to school because they were too infatuated with me to do their jobs."

"Really?" she said again, in the exact same tone of voice as she assessed the walls, taking in the pictures of Mark with this person and that, the books lining the shelves, every little object on the credenza.

"Yes, really," Mark continued, even though he felt the hole getting deeper and bigger and wider around him. "I could have any woman I want. It's just, well, I—I seem to have some kind of bee in my bonnet about you at the moment, so—"

"What's this?" she asked, bending toward the box containing Dickey Joe's home brew.

"Beer. A friend of mine brews it and bottles it for me. You're welcome to try it," he said impatiently, rising to limp toward her, putting as little weight on his bad leg as he could without reaching for the crutches to hold him up. To work this right, he'd need both hands free. When he'd made his way painfully across the room to where she stood, he leaned against the bookcase like he was posing—not like a man afraid he'd fall over. "Did you hear what I said?"

She lifted a bottle out of the box, frowned at it with

a deliberation Bitsi would have been proud of, and then placed it back in the box. She lifted her eyes toward him again, and he realized that she was every bit as uncomfortable as he was. "I heard it," she said flatly. "I just don't know what you mean."

He inhaled and the smell of her perfume filled his nostrils: something gently floral that reminded him of wild sunflowers bowing under a summer sun. He leaned closer to her and watched her lift her chin and latch her eyes on his face.

Go, go, go! The Marines in his head urged him and he acted, moving another step closer, close enough to gather her into his arms. "I mean," he heard himself saying in a voice he didn't quite recognize. "I don't like unfinished business, Erica."

He read "yes" in her eyes and made his move. He leaned the last inch closer and captured her lips with his own.

Her lips were soft and full, and she tasted of something fruity and spicy at the same time. After that first second of surprise, when her mouth was still against his, Mark felt her leaning into him, kissing him back with a curiosity equal to his own. Mark wished he could let go and pull her closer to him as the desire for something more than a kiss crested inside him. But he if let go he'd fall, and he knew it, so he kept one hand firmly locked on a ledge of the bookcase.

Finally she pulled away, and when he opened his eyes she was staring at him with an annoyingly knowing smile on her face.

"Unfinished business, huh?" she said in a brisk businesslike tone that made him want to grab her and bend her to his will. "Why can't you just admit you like me?"

"Because I'm not sure I do," Mark quipped back, as his brain went AWOL once again. "For all I know," he continued, hoping that he hadn't just blown it again, "this is some kind of fatal attraction or something. I mean, I'm not crazy about the idea of being attracted to someone who's as wrong as you are."

"And I'm not crazy about walking into a hostile environment," she shot back.

"Don't let the images of the bad old days of the Civil Rights Movement fool you. That was then. This is fifty years later." He nodded toward his desk, where the picture with its ugly, red, racist writing lay. "And that's just the babbling of a nutcase." He positioned himself against the bookcase like he couldn't have cared less one way or the other, even though his heart was thumping loud in his ears. It was the same jittery feeling he remembered from his years in the military, right before an important mission or maneuver. An edgy sense of excitement, shellacked with masculine calm. "So, you goin', or what?"

He tried not to look at her, but when his curiosity got the better of him, he found her staring up at him with that same little smile on her face.

"You know," she began slowly, "I usually get dinner or something before a kiss like that."

"I tried. We were interrupted by a couple of would-be thieves, remember?"

"Try again. I mean, I don't know anything about you. As a man. As a person. I want to know who you are. Really. Who you are, other than"—she frowned as though the words complicated the matter—"a self-absorbed jerk."

Mark laughed. She was right, of course. He was sounding like a jerk. But he was a jerk with a dinner date. "Done. Tonight, seven P.M. It's Thursday. I have fish on Thursdays, so I know a place that—"

She shook her head. "Not tonight, I have plans. Tomorrow. Seven P.M."

"You don't have any plans."

"I do. PTA meeting. It's been scheduled for months."

He frowned, not sure if she was telling the truth or playing hard to get. "I'll have to check the schedule, but I think that will work."

"Good." She glanced over her shoulder at the crutches. "And you aren't fooling anybody with all this posturing and posing. I know you hurt yourself last night, so use those things if you need to."

Mark frowned. "I'm all right. Just a little sore, that's all," he told her, and sidestepped any further discussion by saying, "Tomorrow's Friday. On Friday I have steak. We'll go to Brighton's. Might have to meet you at the restaurant instead of picking you up like a proper gentleman caller, though."

"Thursday, steak? Friday fish? Is this some kind of religious thing?"

"Not exactly." He chuckled. "Just a personal habit. And it's the other way around: steak on Friday, fish on Thursday. Sundays and Fridays I have steak—or at least red meat. Tuesdays I like Hunan pork. Wednesday Italian and on Saturdays and Monday, chicken of some kind."

She stared at him, again like he had lost his mind. "Don't you ever try anything different? Just because it's there?"

He shook his head. "When it comes to food, I'm not one for adventure. My staff knows the schedule and when I go to dinners, people just work with it. Friday, we'll go to Brighton's." He nodded toward her oddball collection of colorful clothes. "And none of that. Leave the political slogans at home. I assume you have a nice dress."

A flicker of something skittered across her face. Doubt? Fear? He wasn't sure. It was there for just a fraction of a second. Then it was gone. "Yes, I have a dress," she said, raising her chin at him as though these, too, were fighting words.

"Good. Now, that leaves only one thing." He skewered her with his gaze again. "You goin' with me back to Billingham, or what?"

Another flicker and this time he was sure.

Fear.

She opened her mouth and he knew he was about to hear a lot of bravado and bluster. But deep inside, she was scared to death.

She was gorgeous, spirited and sexy. And she was right: he wanted her like crazy. Something about her made every hair on his body stand straight up, and certain other parts, too. He wanted her, wanted to find out what would happen after a kiss, wanted to feel her body wrapped around his and hear his name as a scream of pleasure on her lips.

He wanted her, whether her views on life and politics were right or wrong or indifferent. But he liked her a little better for those two little flickers of absolutely human, absolutely justifiable terror, and the way she mastered them with a single blink. *Gorgeous, spirited, sexy and brave,* he thought adding the word to the growing list of her virtues. She was irritating as all hell, but he liked her. A hell of a lot.

"I'll go," she said, "on two conditions." She showed him her fingers. "First"—she nodded toward the picture—"you call the cops about *that*—but discreetly. I don't want anyone in this office to know. I don't want to give that woman the satisfaction of thinking she's scaring me. But maybe they can get me a full contingent of bodyguards if I'm making this trip."

"What else do you want? Bulletproof vest? An armored car?"

That was funny, wasn't it? At least clever? But she

was looking at him again like she'd just as soon slap him as answer.

"You got any of that stuff?" she demanded.

Mark shook his head. "No, but—"

"The second thing is," she interrupted, and those luminous eyes locked on him again and he knew, short of permission to mine uranium, he'd give her just about anything she asked for. "I want my friend Angelique to come with us."

"What for? Protection?" he chuckled. "From what I saw of her, Angelique's not much of a bodyguard."

"Not protection." She tossed her head, sending those wild curls flying. "For moral support. I'm entering hostile territory, going to your Billingham. You brought a full contingent of aides to my school. If I'm going to get booed and heckled on your turf, seems like I should have one friend who loves me to turn to."

For a second, he thought he saw a tear, shimmering just a blink away from being shed, shining in her eyes. But he must have been mistaken, because when he reached for her, she shrugged away from him with a "No more of that, Senator" that sounded about as far from tears as east from west.

"All right," he agreed. "Angelique gets a ticket, too."

She exhaled as though a weight had fallen from her shoulders. "Fine. Then gas up the jet, or saddle up the horses or whatever it is you country people do." She sighed. "I'm ready to visit the backwater and get this whole thing over with. Now, honor your bargain," she said, reaching for the phone and delivering it into his hand.

When her skin brushed against his and Mark felt his body react from heart to groin, he wondered if any of this was a good idea. They could talk politics and argue and fuss until the cows came home, but the business between them wasn't going to be finished until he'd possessed her body with his own, and he had the feeling she knew it, too.

People ask me, "Why are you running for Senate, Pete? Don't you know you can't beat Mark Newman?" Well, I'll tell you why: I think Mark Newman has lost sight of what's important. I think he's spending too much time up there in Washington, chasing after the media spotlight and his own ambitions for the White House. I don't think he cares about you or me or any of the folks in our great state. Yessir, I think Mark Newman can be beat. And I think I'm just the guy to do it.

—Peter Malloy

Chapter 9

∞∞

Erica sat at a small table in the center of the room, her legs crossed beneath her blue silk dress, leg swinging with impatience as the minute hand on her watch crept past 8:36 to 8:37. One more minute, she told herself, as she had for the past seven minutes, fury setting her jaw.

She was the only black person in the crowded but posh palace of a place. Even the waiters were all white. She imagined the kitchen, suspecting that there, too, was a monochrome of whiteness. Except for the dishwasher. He might be black. Or Hispanic. Or both. The thought made her even angrier. This would be the kind of place he would pick: a place that was a throwback to an earlier America where white people held privilege and the rest of the people were invisible.

"Black people built this country!" she wanted to shout. "*Si se puede!*" Either that, or run back to the kitchen and start banging pots to the tune of "El Liberte!"

No one else seemed to find anything wrong in the room, even her solitary self. Erica pulled at the fabric of the borrowed silk dress and surveyed the room again.

The place really was an "old boys' club": dark décor, club chairs, low lighting. The customers were mostly men, though a few women peppered the room. Almost all, male and female, wore suits, as though their dinner was nothing more than an extension of the workday. Erica got the sense of deals being made over the proverbial handshake.

She sighed.

Here I am, cooling my heels in the sort of place I hate by the very nature of its existence, all because . . .

Because . . .

Because of that man and his damned kiss, she admitted, feeling even angrier with herself than with the restaurant. That kiss had turned the world upside down. For an instant she'd have turned in her ACLU card, signed up for the John Birch Society, allowed the clock to be turned back to 1950—anything, anything at all—just to keep that man's lips locked on her own.

Just when, she wondered, had she gotten so weak?

Maybe I shouldn't go with him down to Billingham, she thought. *Either that or I should just sleep with him and be done with it—*

A burst of raucous male laughter, as loud and raw as anything out of a locker room, exploded in the air. Erica caught a snippet of conversation that ended in the words, "And that's why *we're* the real America!"

Erica frowned, not liking the sound of that one bit. She turned a little, making sure her face expressed her disapproval, just as Mark Newman strode into the room.

Well, not strode, exactly. More like limped or something. But he did it with such authority that one hardly noticed the awkwardness of his gait. He had the cane with him again, and in a weird way it was like a part of him. He'd integrated it into his identity without allowing it to hinder his seeming strength or masculinity a single bit.

"Look who it is . . ." she heard one of the men at the nearby table murmur, just loud enough for the others to hear. Erica cut her eyes in that direction, taking in a white-haired man with a big beak of a nose as the apparent speaker.

"Senator Newman," one of the white-haired man's companions offered. Erica took him in, too, without his noticing: a red-faced dude with a bald head. "Insufferable, isn't he?"

"But I guess we must make nice with the future presidential candidate," the white-haired man continued, as though the very idea made him want to hurl. "He's the leadership's darling. And the media seems to find him absolutely charming. God only knows why."

"You know why!" The bald man chuckled. "Look at him!"

"Oh, I don't know." A third man added his comments to the conversation. "He might just get plucked in the primary."

"Malloy will need something pretty explosive to manage that," the white-haired man disagreed. "Don't see Newman being that stupid."

"Well, it's not over yet," the third man added. "And either way, he's got at least five or six more years of dues to pay." He shrugged. "Anything can happen."

"Here he comes," the white-haired man muttered. "Mark!"

Mark nodded at them and Erica saw the slight shift from smile to smirk as he turned his face toward them.

He doesn't like them, either, Erica realized, watching

these men who'd just run him down within her earshot seconds before, now hail him, urging him to join
them.

"Sorry," she heard him say in that demandingly
certain tone he was master of. "Got my eye on far
more attractive company." Then without another
word, he passed them and within seconds stood over
her with that beaming, full-of-himself, boyish grin on
his face.

"Hey," he drawled, all slow and Southern and dripping with syrupy sweetness.

And just like that, her anger melted away and
her brain froze and her heart started acting stupid again. Erica stared up him for a moment, too
tongue-tied by the larger-than-life quality of the
man to say anything. His dark hair was growing
out a bit, and his ears looked a little less prominent,
sticking out of the whiteness of his head. He wore
his gray suit easily, with the casual demeanor of a
working man, even if that work had consisted of sitting on his rump, running his mouth. But mostly, it
was his eyes and lips that made words flee from her
brain: the first, blue and clear and fixed on her with
what looked like genuine pleasure, the second soft
and fine and, she knew for a fact, almost perfected
fitted to her own.

Unfinished business.

His words for this insane attraction. Angelique
started talking in her brain about "humanity" and
"personal pain."

And now, here he was again, looking at her with that
sort of look that could melt a woman's heart, dissolve her
into a useless puddle of mushy emotion, make her vul-
nerable to the worse treatment in the world, and Erica felt
herself slipping into its spell. Even the fact that he was a
Republican didn't matter—not while he was looking at

her with those eyes and speaking to her with those lips.

Then he started talking, and ruined everything. ". . . Don't like that dress much," he was muttering, analyzing her like a frustrating bit of legislation. "Probably suits your girlfriend Angelique, but it doesn't do anything for you." He reached toward the dress's neckline, pulling. "Bet you got one of them T-shirts on under there somewhere . . ."

"Hey!" Erica snapped, shoving his hand away. And just like that the moment of infatuation went as fast as it came, leaving her with only one feeling for the man: irritation. "That's my body you're messing with. Keep your paws to yourself!"

He leaned forward, devilment in his eyes, and she could smell the faint aroma of alcohol on his breath. "You didn't say that the other day."

"Shut up," Erica snapped, half rising. "Or I'm leaving. I swear I will."

"All right, all right," he conceded, chuckling a little. "Couldn't resist. But seriously, that's not your dress, is it?"

Erica felt a flush of embarrassment color her cheeks. "What difference does it make?" she demanded. "I thought you'd like it. It's . . . blue . . . and silk . . . covers everything and isn't printed with anything you might find objectionable."

"Which is exactly what's wrong with it. It doesn't suit you." He frowned. "I saw you in something more . . . more . . ." He shrugged and flashed her that up-to-no-good grin again. "Unusual."

Erica rolled her eyes. "Well, I'm glad to disappoint you. In fact," she made to rise again. "I'm thinking this whole thing was one big mistake. What happened between us in your office—"

"You mean the kiss?" he interrupted, the grin crimping into its distant cousin the smirk.

"Y—yes," Erica stammered, feeling suddenly nervous and quaky again. "That."

"That," he agreed. "I guess you're right: it was probably just a mistake. You couldn't keep your hands off me, but it could have been a mistake. Still"—he lifted another shoulder—"shouldn't stop us from having a nice dinner. Besides we still have things to discuss." He leaned back a little, reaching deep into his breast pocket to produce several sheets of folded paper and tossed them across the table at her.

"What's this?" Erica asked.

"First one's your copy of the police report. Right now, since I didn't receive any kind of threat, the Capitol police consider it a matter for the D.C. police. Which, my dear, means—"

"No one's going to do anything," Erica finished with a sigh.

"Well, there's not a lot they *can* do. There's not much to go on. And a woman like you has plenty of enemies."

"I do not."

"You must," he responded. "Saying the things you say, doing the things you do, wearing the things you wear. I say and do all the *right* things." His eyes strayed to the nearby table of men, and Erica was surprised to find them staring back at him with interest. "And people still hate me for it," he muttered. He pasted the phoniest smile she'd ever seen on his face and nodded pleasantly in their direction. Before Erica could comment, he turned back to her and continued briskly. "The Capitol police will intervene if I receive any kind of similar threat. They'll assess its gravity, perhaps assign some kind of security detail, if they think it's necessary. But for now"—he shrugged—"don't worry. It's probably nothing. Just a crackpot who saw you on TV. You're in the phone book,

right?" Erica nodded. "Then you were easy enough
to find. And besides, you don't have anything to worry about." He gave her another one of those bullshit
grins. "I'll protect you."

Erica rolled her eyes and shook her head, but instead of going there with him, she focused her attention on the second piece of paper.

"The next two are your tickets and our itinerary.
Session finishes on Wednesday, so we'll leave on
Thursday. Got a lot on the schedule. A few are op-
tional for you, but . . . you've stirred up a lot of interest among Billingham's citizens. Seems from the mail
I'm getting that people want to talk to you. Try to set
you straight on a few things, probably." He paused
and when Erica looked up, he was rubbing his forehead.

"What's the matter?"

"I don't know," he murmured. "Felt a little queasy
all of the sudden." He reached for the glass of ice water on the table and Erica noticed his hand shook a
little before closing around it. He drank it all down
without stopping. The B.S. smile showed itself again
in spite of the sudden pallor of his face. "That's better," he lied. "I was at a cocktail party. Let the server
talk me into some kind of munchy thing I shouldn't
have eaten." He grimaced. "I'd have done better with
one of Dickey Joe's home brews."

They were interrupted by a waiter who made a
great show of presenting the menus and explaining
the specials before disappearing to some unseen re-
cess with the promise to return for their decisions.

Erica studied her companion. The tight lines were
back in his face—the same tight lines Angelique had
pointed out when they searched his photographs on-
line. As much as she hated to admit it, Angelique was
right: he was hurting. Hurting pretty bad.

"We can go, if you're not feeling well—"

"I feel fine," he snapped, sounding truly irritated. "Stop trying to find ways to get out of this. That's the point, isn't it? For us to spend time together, realize no matter how much sparking goes on between us, we can't stand each other and in so doing completely detonate this . . . this . . ."

"Crime growing between us?" Erica offered.

His features twisted into a slight wince of pain at the word *crime* and she wished she'd chosen another. "I was going to call it an attraction, but crime might be right."

"I'm sorry," she mumbled. "Bad word choice."

He shook his head. "No. Good word choice. Criminals are sneaky, insidious, and aggressive. Sometimes love is the same way."

Love? Had he actually used that word? Erica let out a shaky little laugh. "I don't think we need to go that far. We both just love a good fight. That, and maybe you need to find one of those silly women chasing you and take her up on her offer."

"Oh yeah?" he smirked at her. "And what's your excuse, Ms. Johnson? You need to take someone up on *his* offer—"

"Have you made your decision?"

The waiter stood over them, supercilious in his black-and-white uniform.

"We have. We'll have the prime rib, medium-rare," Mark muttered without really looking at him at all. "Side of mashed potatoes and whatever the vegetable is."

"Broccoli."

"Whatever it is," Mark repeated. "Just water for me. No, maybe a little Pellegrino—"

"Excuse me," Erica interrupted, glaring at him. "I can order for myself and I don't want prime rib."

"Trust me, the prime rib is excellent here."

"I don't care if it's encrusted with diamonds, I don't want it. I don't eat meat."

Mark let out a short bark of annoyed laughter. "Why aren't I surprised?" he muttered. "Honestly woman, if I say white, you say black just to spite me, don't you?"

Erica smiled at him sweetly. "That's oddly appropriate, given the differences between us, isn't it?"

Mark rolled his eyes and shook his head, and Erica felt his annoyance rolling off him in waves.

It's your own damn fault, Mr. Steak-on-Friday, Erica thought. *I didn't pick the restaurant. If you'd just asked me—*

"We have a lovely Atlantic lobster," the waiter offered. Erica glanced up at the man: the frozen smile on his face suggested that he wanted to be far away from the fight that was brewing. "We usually serve it with our surf and turf, but I can get it for you without the turf," he finished, offering an anemic chuckle.

Erica gave him a small smile for the effort.

"Uh, no. I try not to eat fish, either. I'll just have a salad, no dressing."

"Very good, ma'am. Sir."

The waiter gathered the menus and beat his retreat, just as Mark leaned toward Erica with that irritating little smirk on his face and said, "What are you? One of those people who believes she can fuel her body on the energy of the sun?"

"No," Erica said defensively. "I'm a vegan."

"You're a nutcase."

"Just because I don't believe in eating our fellow creatures doesn't mean I'm a nutcase."

"Yes, it does," Mark insisted, his voice rising. He leaned across the table, eyes hard, cheeks flushed with annoyance. "Look, God made man and gave him dominion over the Earth and all the creatures in it."

"That doesn't mean He intended for man to *eat* them!"

Mark's smirk flattened to a hard line.

"The early humans were carnivores."

"The early humans ate a lot more nuts and berries and grains than they did meat. It was too hard to catch and kill!"

"Well, it's easy enough now."

"And that's the problem. Have you ever been to your typical factory farm? Have you seen how the animals are fed, treated, slaughtered?"

"I know all about it," he countered. "Meat processing is federally regulated. I'm on the Senate Agricultural Committee."

"Well, Mr. Senate Agricultural Committee," Erica shot back, becoming more heated with every sentence the man uttered. "I don't see how you can know about it and still willingly eat it."

Mark snorted. "There might be some room for improvement in the process, but that's no reason to eschew it completely—"

"It's inhumane."

"And this conversation is inane," Mark announced as though he were the sole arbiter of inanity on the planet. "I can't believe this. You're sitting in a five-star steakhouse, planning to eat nothing but lettuce. I could have taken you to a corner deli if I'd known that was all you were gonna eat. It's the stupidest thing I've ever heard of."

Erica folded her lips, sealing in a dozen pungent responses.

"Well, I guess that finished our business. I hate your guts and I'd never sleep with you in a million, billion years. Good night," she said calmly,

got to her feet and started moving for the exit with
what she hoped would pass for cool and imperial
grace, at a speed just a little too fast for a man with
a cane.

But damn if the man couldn't move fast when he
wanted to—cane or no.

He caught her in the lobby, out of the sight of the
main dining room but still in the audience of the
same slender hostess who had escorted Erica to her
table an hour ago, a half dozen black-jacketed valets,
and a few arriving patrons.

"Where the hell do you think you're going?" He
growled into her ear, taking her arm.

"Home. You can eat the salad." She surveyed him
quickly. He still didn't look quite well, but he didn't
look bad, either. Erica had the feeling he had to be
pretty darn sick before he ever looked anything but
handsome. "I'm sure you could use it. Might help to
get that stick out of your butt."

She struggled away from him, but his grasp on her
arm tightened.

"You are *not* leaving."

"Watch me."

"You are *not* leaving."

"Fine." Erica pulled away from him again. "I'll just
go in the ladies' room."

"Fine," Mark agreed. "I'll just go with you."

His face was set in seriousness. Erica dug in for
battle. If he wanted a war, by God, she was prepared
to fight.

"Okay. Fine, Mr. Pervert," she said and started
moving, almost pulling him along since he hadn't released her. When they stood right outside the door,
Erica felt like a 200-pound weight had been attached
to her arm.

"Aw, Erica. C'mon. I didn't mean—"

She pushed on the swinging door marked LADIES and dragged him reluctantly inside.

"Happy now?" she asked.

It was huge, marbled and formal, including a separate room lined with mirrors and several boudoir chairs for the comfortable freshening of faces. Further inside, in the lavatory area, a real live human attendant stood near a clutch of towels, soaps, perfumes and cosmetics. The woman was elderly, round and Hispanic. *Figures*, Erica thought. That was the unspoken mantra of places like this. Keep the brown people out of sight.

"Uh, ma'am, sir," the attendant stuttered in halting English. "This is de *ladies'* room."

"I know that! And so does he!" Erica exclaimed, fumbling for her purse. "Is there anyone else in here?"

The attendant shook her carefully hennaed dye job. "Not at the moment, but—"

"Here," Erica thrust a ten-dollar bill into the woman's hand. "This *gentleman* and I need to have a few *words* with each other in private. Go! And keep everyone else out, too!"

"But ma'am—"

"Five minutes."

The woman looked at Erica and then the money. She shrugged and exited.

"You really are a prize, you know that?" Mark sputtered, his face red with embarrassed anger. "I'm a United States senator and I'm standing in the fucking ladies' room—"

"Don't curse at me, Mark Newman—"

"I'm in the ladies' room of one of the most exclusive restaurants in this town, for Christ sakes!" he roared. "Do you know who's out there? Lobbyists. Power players. Half the *Congress*—"

"Then you should have let me leave like I wanted

to! But no, you have to manhandle people. You have to assert yourself. Big important *senator* that you are!"

"Aw, cut it out. You know I'm not like that. I just meant—"

"I don't know anything but what you keep showing me. And that's that you're pretty damned impressed with yourself. That you think you're right about everything and when you're not, you just steamroll over any objections. Or objectors. Well, let's get this straight, for once and for all. I'm not at all impressed with you and I'm not going to be steamrolled and I'm not going to fawn all over you because you're a senator or a hero or anything more than a man!" Erica turned away from him. "Now, if you'll excuse me, this ugly dress that you don't like needs to be returned to Angelique."

And once again, she marched away from him.

I don't need this infuriating asshole. The words bubbled in her brain, hot with the passion of her anger. *He may be a great kisser and he may be smart and good-looking and clever, but I don't need him or his bullshit—*

She had reached the door of the ladies' room when he stopped her with, "Erica, wait."

His tone was soft, almost sad. As much as she wanted to ignore it, as much as she wanted to pretend like there was no making up, no going back, no way he could apologize or make it right, she stopped and turned slowly toward him.

"I . . ." he began, his eyes on one of the glossy Italianate ceramic floor tiles between them. "I didn't mean the dress was ugly. I just meant . . ." He cast around the room as though he were looking for the right words to finish the sentence, the words to erase the impact of what he'd said before. Finally, he just sighed. "What I meant was you'd look beautiful in a paper sack," he said gruffly, his eyes finding hers at last.

Erica paused, weighing the sincerity of his words in her mind.

"Look, Mark," she said, taking a step away from the door. A step closer to him. "We can't just fight all the time." She sighed. "And that's not what I came here for tonight. I came here to . . ." she paused, searching for the words. "I don't know. Find out who you are. Try to see you differently. Or maybe just to prove that what happened in your office was some kind of weird accident. But one thing I know"—she made her voice firm and held his eyes with her own just so he'd understand how serious this was, how she'd expect to be treated before they took another step deeper into territories unknown—"I *believe* in this stuff—whether you call it crap or not. I've dedicated my life to this stuff you call crap. I may not have been in a war, and I may not know how to use a gun, and I may even be scared of blood, but that doesn't mean I don't consider what I believe in worth fighting for. Worth dying for, as much as anything you believe in. I don't need to spend my mealtimes—or any time—having the very essence of who I am insulted. And if you can't stop yourself from doing that, then—"

"Okay, okay." He sighed, rubbing his face. Again, Erica thought she noticed a slight tick of pain in his smirk as he took a halting step closer to her, bridging the distance between them. "I'm sorry, okay?" He reached out a hand in a gesture of peace. "I've never been good with this sort of stuff, and I'm way out of practice," he offered. "Gimme a little time to get back in the game, okay?"

Erica glanced at the ladies' room door again, but there was no reason to leave now, not when the man was standing there with his hand outstretched, just waiting for her to take it, just waiting for another chance.

"I guess," she murmured, taking the last step toward him and entwining her fingers in his. His hand was warm and steady and strong. "I suppose we're both trying to figure out this business between us."

With one hand—the other was locked around the cane—he pulled her against him so quickly, Erica gasped in surprise. An instant later his mouth descended on hers with a force so sudden, she felt as though he were trying to crush the words back down her throat. Thrown, surprised, she resisted at first, and then responded, winding her arms around his neck with a shuddering passion that made her knees weak and her resolve weaker. Every part of her body from her breasts to her crotch turned to liquid as she strained against him. His good hand squeezed the globes of her behind, lifting the subdued blue silk to caress the bare skin beneath.

Oh my God. Erica shuddered, probing his mouth with her tongue, teasing him with the promise of what her lips could do. She let her hand slip to the bulge in his trousers and felt his manhood jump in response, insistent under her touch, while his marauding hand maneuvered its way downward until a finger brushed against her tenderest nub. Erica jumped with the power of her body's response. *Oh my God*, she thought again, as her insides sucked at his finger in quivering excitement. *It's been way too long.*

"That's what you wanted all along," he murmured along the side of her neck, as she let out a ragged moan of suppressed desire.

Erica stroked his erection through his pants. "What about you? Your soldier's standing at attention. You want me much more than I want you. Admit it."

He nuzzled the side of her face, while another finger slipped deeper into the vise of her thighs. "Admit you want me, first," he breathed into her ear. "Admit it, or else."

She wanted to deny it, but it was hard, now that her whole body had come alive. She clung to him for fear her shaking knees would give out and she'd end up on the bathroom floor.

"Or else what?" she purred, while a quiver of nervousness swept over her. The only thing he could do that would annoy her at that moment was stop the steady thrumming of those fingers between her legs. And to assure he wouldn't, Erica moved herself against them, reaching up to caress his face with her palm, watching the hard line of resolve on his forehead grow smooth under her touch. She brushed his mouth gently with a fingertip and he closed his eyes. She could feel his chest rise slowly in a deep inhale. She drew him forward, taking his lips in a gentle exploration of their softness, and then gave him another excruciatingly slow butterfly tease, and another, before giving him more, the deeper one, the one that made him groan with an urgency neither of them could contain. In a flash Erica imagined them entwined together in a big, soft bed somewhere. A shiver of anticipation swept through her body.

"I need to be inside you," he whispered. "Let's just skip all this 'get to know you' stuff and—"

Great. Erica yanked herself away from him, breaking the connection of fingers on skin at every level as she pulled Angelique's dress back down over her hips. *He thinks I'm easy.* She pushed aside the fact that she'd been imagining just how it would feel to make love to this man only seconds ago. After all, it was one thing to think about it herself, and another thing for the man to simply assume it was going to happen.

"What?" he asked, a stricken look on his face. "What did I do?"

"You ruin everything, Mark," she hissed in a tone that made it clear she was highly offended. "You just have to ruin everything."

"Why? You're a liberated woman, right? I thought your kind didn't blush at the idea of premarital sex. You bra-burning girls practically invented it, for heaven's sake."

Erica sighed.

"Did you hear what I just said to you?"

His eyebrows shot up in genuine confusion. "Was that wrong?"

"This could never work," Erica shook her head and stepped away from him. "Forget the white-black thing, you're just too—too—"

But once again he caught her in his arms and pulled her close, kissing her again, long and hard. Erica felt herself melting against him, meeting him.

"Too?" he asked, and when he finally released her, she was too woozy and confused to consider him "too" anything.

"I—I don't understand this," she murmured. "I absolutely loathe you."

"Yes, I know."

"And yet . . ."

"Yet . . ."

Erica shook her head. "It doesn't make any sense. The more we're around each other the more clear it becomes: We could never make this work. Even when you're trying, everything you say is wrong. Everything you do . . ."

"Well, not everything," he reminded her, showing her his fingers, still damp with her juice. Erica wasn't amused.

"Okay. There's something physical there, I'll admit

it. But that's not enough. And we both know it."

His face got that look: considering, calculating. "Look, I'm not willing to give up what I believe in—any more than you are. But you said you'd give me a chance to learn the game. Let's let it ride a little longer. At least until we get back from Billingham. Not sure why," he continued when she cocked a questioning eyebrow at him. "But since you're going, anyway, we might as well keep trying to figure this thing out." He sighed with regret for what the evening might have been and then nodded toward the doors and the restaurant beyond them. "Now, come on. Let's get something to eat."

"I *told* you—"

"And I heard you," he said, waving the rest of the sentence away. "We'll cancel the order and do something else. Something you want to do."

Erica eyed him skeptically. "On one condition. No politics. I don't know what we're gonna talk about . . . but no politics. Let's see if there's anything we agree on. Anything at all."

That smile, the real one, the one that made him look like a handsome man and not like some all-knowing asshole covered his face. "Like that. Wish I'd said it myself," he agreed readily. "All right. Take me where you want to go."

Polling suggests that Mark Newman's recent debates with antiwar protester Erica Johnson have hurt his reelection bid, but only slightly. While Newman still enjoys a substantial lead, challenger Peter Malloy seems to have narrowed the gap slightly. The question is whether that gap comes from the now quite famous debates between Newman and Johnson . . . or from the rumors of the growing personal relationship between them.

—The *Billingham News*

Chapter 10

"So why did you run for office in the first place?"

He glanced over at her, or what he could see of her in the low light. Her idea of dinner had turned out to be a vegetarian restaurant in the left-of-center neighborhood of Takoma Park, where she'd asked him questions about his family, about his childhood, about the funny and sad and crazy things that had happened to him when he was a fraction of the man he was now—all with that inquisitive look on her face—like he was a puzzle she couldn't quite figure out.

And the food hadn't been half bad either, he hesitated to admit. He'd had a burger of something plant-like that tasted amazingly like real food. Had he not been fully aware that he wasn't eating meat, he might have been completely deceived.

Then a very slow stroll with ice-cream cones in hand along the Mall, the grassy stretch between the Capitol Building and the Jefferson Memorial.

He'd rather the evening had ended entirely differently. The beast they'd ignited in the ladies' room was still howling within him, threatening to break its chain and force her to his will. Years of lust, years of passion he'd kept buried inside him since Katharine's death had sprung to life. Every time she spoke, he felt her tongue in his mouth. Every time she looked at him, he imagined the feel of her breasts against his chest and her ass beneath his hand. The air between them was heavy with the mossy scent of her most private parts and Mark wanted nothing more than to bury his nose and mouth in that smell.

I lived years without sex, he thought, walking beside her in the cool September air. *And now, in a matter of minutes, I'm busted back to being a sex-starved eighteen-year-old.* He kept telling himself to be cool, but he knew full well he'd have got down on his one good knee and begged her for it, if he'd thought it would do him any good.

But it wouldn't and he knew it, so he contented himself with limping along beside her, talking about himself and watching her listen. Just when Mark's leg was starting to smart from the exertion, she pointed to one of the many benches along the way and said, "Let's sit."

For a while they had sat in silence, taking in the oddly romantic view. The Capitol was lit up like a national jewel, spotlights hitting its dome and running along the Italianate marble, illuminating its architecture in brilliant relief against the night sky.

So why did you run for office in the first place? Her question hung in the air.

"That might be a political question." He chuckled. "Remember our deal?"

"I remember it," she said, all smart-edged and certain, awakening in him dual emotions of attraction and irritation. "But I'm not asking it that way. I'm asking it as a question of character. What kind of person runs for office? What kind of person becomes a public servant—given all the crap you have to go through and put up with?"

"It's not crap," he replied. "You like that word. Anything you dislike or disagree with is 'crap.' Well, democracy is not 'crap.' Government is not 'crap.' It's important."

She rolled her eyes at him. "Of course it's not," she said. "And I'm not going there with you, remember? So why don't you just answer the question. What kind of person runs for office?"

Mark frowned. She was speaking sweetly—a little too sweetly, maybe—and she still made his whole life sound like a disease. He sighed. It wasn't going to be easy, finding any common ground with this woman outside of searing kisses and grinding body parts.

"I don't know what kind of person runs for office," Mark answered slowly, "but I'll tell you why I did. It's simple really: Dr. Mabry made me do it." And seeing the frown of query on her face, he continued. "Dr. Mabry taught English 101 at State College. 'Bloody Mary Mabry' they called her. Because if she graded your paper and found it lacking, you'd get back one big red mess." He chuckled with the memory and watched as Erica smiled along with him, her head inclined toward him with interest. Even in the near darkness, there was no way to ignore her beauty: the long curve of her neck, the sculpted outlines of her cheekbones, and the pert pucker of her lips. Looking at her stirred that tightness in his groin again, but talking to her like this stirred something, too. Something higher in his anatomy. After its long absence, his brain suddenly sprang to life again.

"So Dr. Mabry?" she prompted. "She made you run for public office? How?"

"Just something she said once," Mark continued, picking up the skein of the story where he'd left off.

"See, she was more than just an English teacher. She was like . . ."—he hesitated—"Introduction to Life 101. No, Introduction to Adulthood 101. I can still remember reading some great work of classic literature— *Sister Carrie* or *Tale of Two Cities*—and hearing her incorporate the novel into a discussion of modern issues, modern problems. 'You have a responsibility as educated members of this society to serve it,'" he said, doing his best to imitate the voice of his old mentor. "And if you don't do it, some less-qualified jerk will. Someone like Peter Malloy. And trust me, if you think I'm bad, you ain't seen nothing yet. At least I'm not stupid. And at least, I'm not so narrow-minded I can't listen to another point of you—I mean *view*," he finished quickly. "Too many Pete Malloys get elected and we'll all have to suffer the consequences."

Those deep brown eyes of hers were riveted to his face. She had pulled some kind of shawl from out of that sloppy handbag she carried and now her shoulders were draped in brilliant colors: orange, reds and yellows. It suited her so much better than the staid blue dress. He opened his mouth to try to find the words to tell her so, but before he got the chance, she asked, "Pete Malloy is the guy challenging you for your Senate seat?"

Mark nodded. "One of 'em. He's the other Republican I'm going to beat in the primary next week. Then there's Duncan Dukes. He's the Democrat I'm going to beat in November."

He waited, sure she would jump all over his certainty of victory, but she just wrinkled her nose and asked, "Is Malloy that bad? Is he *really* worse than *you*?"

Mark couldn't help but chuckle.

"*I* think so," he replied. "But I guess he's not that bad. It's just he's never been anywhere. Never seen anything. Never really been out of his one little corner of the state. Which is fine when you're a state representative and that's your job—to represent that one little corner of the state to the best of your ability. But it's something else when you're talking about the United States Senate, where you have to be able to deal with people from all over the country, all over the ideological spectrum." He shook his head. "I can't imagine how Malloy would deal with Bob Nanke. You know who he is, right?"

"Of course. He's a Democrat." Erica nodded. "And he's gay, isn't he?"

"Very." Mark laughed. "I can't see Malloy being willing to so much as shake his hand. Forget about partner with him on a campaign reform initiative, like I did."

"You did?" She frowned. "I don't remember reading about that."

"It's going to be introduced next month. After the primaries. But we've been working together on it for months. It's going to be—" He stopped himself. "Sorry. I was talking politics, wasn't I? I can hear Dr. Mabry now: 'Mr. Newman, could you stick to the subject, please?'"

She laughed—not that hard, nasty sound that he'd heard a little too often, but a genuine sound of amusement that brought something he'd thought was dead alive inside him.

"Did she really sound like that?"

"What?" Mark grinned beside her.

"Like that. Nasal. High-pitched. Old-lady Southern?"

Mark nodded. He held up two fingers in an oath. "Boy Scouts' honor."

She cut her eyes at him. "I bet you *were* a Boy Scout."

He shook his head. "Naw, not me. We didn't have money for uniforms or dues or any of that." His head wagged again with the memory of hard times, before he raised his eyes to her face. "Who's the worst kid in your class?"

"None of them," she answered promptly. "Some are more challenging than others," she added quickly. "But none are 'bad.'"

"Okay, the 'most challenging,'" Mark repeated the politically correct phrase and tried hard to keep the sarcasm out of his voice, even though he wasn't certain he had succeeded. The moment was magical—he had the sense of really connecting to this woman at last—but *most challenging*? He wanted to roll his eyes and curse political correctness back to hell where it belonged. "I miss the days when you could call a kid 'bad' and not get a lecture about how you're damaging their tender psyches," he couldn't stop himself from saying, and grimaced against her expected response.

But she simply ignored him, pulling that colorful shawl a little tighter around her shoulders as though she were still cold. Mark swept off the jacket of his conservative blue suit and draped it over her shoulders.

"Thanks," she murmured, and once again he got those laser eyes, parsing him down to atoms. "I guess it would have to be Anthony," she said at last, returning the conversation to their last avenue. "You met him. The one fascinated with fake legs?"

Mark grinned, nodded and let her continue.

"He's a very smart boy, but . . . " She hesitated, and he felt her editing out less than flattering responses before she selected, "He has some behavior issues."

"Well, I was an Anthony. And I didn't have any behavior issues. I was just plain ol' *bad*."

Again she erupted in that musical laughter and Mark's heart soared.

"How bad?" she asked.

"Bad," he repeated, warming to the reminiscence. "Tacks in the teacher's chair, graffiti, cutting up . . . You name it, I probably did it."

"Somehow, I believe that."

"I thought you might. Might have ended up as just another beer-drinking, carousing good ol' boy, if it hadn't been for the U.S. Marine Corps. The Marine Corps . . . and my Katharine." He shook his head against the sting the memory of her always brought him. "The two of them probably saved my life." He considered the statement for a moment, and then corrected himself. "On second thought, I know they did."

"Tell me about her. About you . . . and her."

The words were simple, straightforward almost journalistic in their inquiry, but when he looked over at her, there was something almost wistful in her eyes.

He inhaled, focusing his eyes on the twilight of the mall and searching himself for the words to explain his feelings; but all that came out was a quiet and unoriginal, "I miss her."

She did it again. Wordlessly, soundlessly, curled those fingers over his, warm and soft and filled with such comfort he couldn't explain the sudden sense of peace that surrounded him like a blanket.

He had been about to tell her about it: how he'd enlisted after a brush with the law when he was 19 after Katharine had demanded he either make something of himself or leave her alone. About how the training had taught him about discipline, order, teamwork and pride—and Katharine had taught him to compromise, to listen, to attempt the hard job of a walk in the other man's shoes. But instead he fell silent, staring out at the grassy walk in front of them.

A shadowy figure was walking slowly across the Mall, on a dead even course toward the bench where they sat. All he could make out was a jacket and a ball cap. It was impossible to tell gender, between the androgyny of the clothing and the dimness and distance.

He wasn't sure if it was the figure's disheveled appearance or the lingering effects of that oddball photograph she'd gotten, but Erica Johnson's fingers tightened on his. Beside him on the bench, she'd come to attention so quickly his jacket had slipped from her shoulders. The figure continued its slow march toward them.

"Mark," she began, and he heard her fear plainly. "What . . . ?"

"I don't know," Mark said, already pulling himself to his feet. "But I intend to find out."

"Let's just go," she said, rising, too. "Let's just—"

"No one's running me off this Mall," he told her softly. "If things get dicey, you run, you hear me? You run for help. Scream your head off, too. That always helps." Then he stepped off toward the figure.

She caught him by the arm. "What are you going to do?"

"Find out what he—or she—wants," he said, popping the spring on the old cane, testing the blade before concealing it again.

"Where did you get that thing?" she asked, and he heard an unmistakable edge of revulsion in her voice.

"It was made for me by a buddy from the Corps," he replied. "Something to beat back the chicks with," he added, knowing it would irritate her just enough to distract her from her fears. Before she could request elaboration, he stumped away from her with a low-toned, "Stay here."

The figure was within twenty feet of him, still moving slowly and deliberately. Mark realized the baggy, nondescript jacket and hat were set at angles to best conceal the figure's identity. Even the hands were crammed into the pockets, giving the person a hunched-over appearance.

Mark set his face in a hard line and notched his voice to match.

"Hey!" he shouted, making it clear with just his words that there would be a fight, if one was wanted. "What do you want?"

The figure stopped. It stood still in the dim grass, backlit by a streetlamp across the Mall, its details still all but indistinguishable. And in response to Mark's demand, it answered not a word.

"You heard me," Mark growled, taking another halting step toward the shadowy figure. "What do you want?"

"Jes' gonna ask if you got a cig'rette, man," a bewildered-sounding voice wheezed out of the darkness. "Saw you sitting there and I was jes' gonna ask if you got cig'rettes." The figure raised its hands and he saw they were gnarled and matted with dirt.

Homeless guy, Mark concluded, relaxing a little. Probably one of the dozens that lived on the benches lining the Mall. "Sorry." He lowered the cane and shook his head. "No cigarettes."

"Oh," the skeletal man sounded genuinely crestfallen. "Well, you got some spare change?"

Mark shook his head. "Sorry. No change."

"Here."

Mark turned to find Erica at his elbow. Before he could stop her, she was stretching a dollar toward the man.

The spectral man moved much faster now that money was on offer. He covered the ground between them in twice the time of the slow, deliberate step that he had used to cross the grass.

"Thanks." He breathed alcohol and filth at them. "Thanks," he repeated, and then turned on his heel with an almost military precision and hurried back into the dark shadows of the other side of the Mall.

"What did you do that for?" Mark snapped, frowning down at Erica.

Her eyes flashed. "What do you mean, 'what did I do that for'? The guy is homeless. He needs that money for food!"

"Yeah, he *needs* it for food," Mark grumbled. "But he's going to use it for beer. You just contributed to his slow suicide."

He wished he hadn't said it, because a sort of pained expression dawned in her eyes before she retorted, "Maybe. But what were *you* going to do for him?" She barely paused long enough for him to open his mouth. "Nothing," she finished. "Your kind never do anything for anyone who can't help themselves."

Your kind. The words registered like a nasty punch to the gut.

"He's not my responsibility," Mark said, feeling the argument gearing up between them. "He's his own."

"No, he's *our* responsibility. All of us. He's another soul fallen through the cracks. You don't know his story, you don't know what happened to him that made him the way he is."

"I know enough," Mark said, turning away from her to begin the slow limp back to the bench.

"And what do you know? What's enough?"

"I know that whatever happened in his life, instead of beating it, he let it beat him. And that makes him weak."

"I don't see how you can say that!"

"Easy," Mark continued, and suddenly he was angry—angry at her, angry at the man, angry at the whole conversation. "You think he's the only one who's had hard times? The only one who's felt pain or sorrow or loss?" Mark shook his head. "I've felt all of those things . . . and so have you. And neither one of us is sneaking up to people, begging for a dollar on the street. We've felt those things and we've managed to find a way to pull ourselves through it without a handout."

"You're strong, Mark," she reminded him. "Don't you have even a little compassion for those weaker than you?"

He had a flash, a series of ugly memories crowding in on him in quick succession. He saw himself as a younger man, lost and directionless, as likely to embark on a path of alcohol and drug abuse as anything. He saw himself again, struggling against the lure of painkillers, grieving the loss of himself even as the nation hailed him a hero. And he saw himself again, in the depth of his mind's eye, a widower, alone without his life partner and best friend. His two-beer-a-day habit, drunk whether in company or alone, buzzed around him. Two a day and no more. A habit. A reminder of the ongoing need to ease both physical and emotional pain. But all he could manage to say was a terse, "I *am* that guy. But for the grace of God."

She looked at him, her eyes bright with some emotion, and once again Mark found himself struggling with the competing desires to lash out in irritation, rejecting her and her pity—and to pull her toward him, binding her to his side forever.

"Give your money to a shelter, Erica," Mark muttered, looking away from her again before she could say anything that would tip the balance within him in either direction. "It's getting late."

She must have read the war within him in his eyes, because this time she offered no protest. She shivered a little under her colorful shawl as they reached the bench they had so suddenly vacated.

"What's that?" she asked, pointing toward something gleaming white in the darkness. "Did you leave something?"

Mark shook his head. "I don't think so." He touched the spring and stabbed at the white thing with the cane, spearing it. "But let's see."

It was a plain white envelope bearing the name ERICA JOHNSON typed in block letters on the surface. Inside, he could tell, there appeared to be a single piece of paper. Even in the low light, Mark could see red writing scrawled across the white sheet inside. He glanced at Erica and saw her face tighten.

"It's another one," she said, and he noticed her voice was surprisingly steady, surprisingly calm, considering that someone—some person or people unknown—had been near enough to leave this missive on the very bench they had been sitting on. And might still be near.

She looked away from him, taking in the still silences of the night, searching the nearby benches for someone—anyone—who might be responsible for the envelope. But there was no one. Not even the homeless man who had approached them moments ago was in sight. From all appearances, they were alone on the Mall.

"Open it," she said in a voice he barely recognized. Commanding. Determined. Tough.

On the reflex of his military training, Mark obeyed immediately, slitting the envelope and pulling out the contents.

"This isn't possible . . ." he breathed as the image registered in his brain. "How is this possible?"

Erica took the sheet of paper from his hands, processed the image in a glance and turned it over, reading the red writing with every outward appearance of absolute calm.

"'Stay out of Billingham, nigger bitch. This is your last warning.'" Her eyes searched his. "Who's doing this? How are they doing this?"

Mark slid the picture out of her hands. It was another grainy copy, printed out on plain white paper instead of glossy photo stock.

"I don't know," he answered. "No one knew we were going in there. The bathroom was empty, you sent the attendant out. We were completely alone."

"Apparently not," Erica said with that same grim determination. She took the photo from him and frowned at it so severely, Mark felt an unanticipated sense of dismay.

Was it that bad? he wondered, to have been captured in his arms, in the ladies' room of a pricey downtown restaurant, captured looking like she was kissing him with all the love and passion her body possessed?

Of course, there was the fact that her dress was up to her waist and his hand was somewhere best left to the imagination . . . but they were both single, both unencumbered, both of legal age. It was embarrassing, certainly, for both of them. But he didn't regret it. Did she?

He stared down into her face as she studied the picture, trying hard to decipher her expression. When she looked up at him with a frown etched into her face, he felt his heart sink.

She's going to say the party's over. She's going to say she doesn't want to see me again.

"I have plenty of reservations about you . . . and

about me and you," she said, an expression in her lovely brown eyes that foretold a war he didn't want to fight. "But apparently someone has even more serious ones," she murmured. "And my gut tells me that Bitsi woman is at the bottom of this."

Mark relaxed. Not good-bye. Just this again. "Erica. I told you—"

"I know what you told me. But that's what my gut says."

Bitsi.

She was protective as all hell—and she'd made it more than clear, she didn't like Erica Johnson. Not one bit. But to stoop to this level? He found himself shaking his head. No. Whatever the tensions between himself and Bitsi, he couldn't believe she'd do anything to hurt him or someone he loved.

Mark inhaled sharply. *Love*. The word kept rolling around in his consciousness and tumbling out of his mouth like it intended to take up permanent residence.

"What's wrong?" Erica asked, her brow crinkling with concern.

"Nothing," he answered quickly. "Stomach's still a little off, that's all." And he was glad it wasn't a lie. His tofu burger was turning in his stomach like a top and suddenly his mouth was dry. He pulled the photo from her fingers again and stuffed into his pocket. "I'm going to show this to Sergeant McAfee."

"He's already told you, he can't do anything," she reminded him at the mention of the stiff-lipped Capitol police detective who'd responded to the call about the first photo. "It's addressed to me. It's out of his jurisdiction."

Mark thought for only a moment, but everything within him reached the same conclusion. "I think he should know," he told her. "It's pretty clear now whoever's doing this is following us. And unless I miss my guess, it's pretty clear there's only one way to flush this wannabe stalker out of his—"

"—or her," Erica interrupted.

"Or her hiding place," Mark continued.

"And what's that?"

Mark leaned toward her. He was close enough to feel her breath, warm and steady in his ear, close enough for the curls of her unruly hair to brush against his chin. He wanted to gather her into his arms right then, right there, and dare the unknown photographer to take his next shot. But he settled for running his finger down the length of her cheek.

"We just need to keep doing what we're doing," he whispered. "Whatever the hell that is."

I'm not sure she's an asset, but once the senator has an idea about something, you can't tell him anything. And that's what makes him such a great leader. He doesn't follow polls or trends, and he won't be swayed by public opinion. He follows God and his own heart.

—Bitsi Barr

Chapter 11

"We're sitting way back here? I was sure we would be in first class or something," Angelique griped, as they took seats in the rear of the airplane. "Is he sitting up front? Because if he is—"

"I don't know where he's sitting," Erica replied, watching the travelers boarding the plane around them. She couldn't even see the first class cabin from here. A quip—something along the lines of "I bet he's up there having his feet massaged at taxpayer expense"—bubbled on her lips, but she pressed it back. He might be sitting in first class . . . and he might not. From what she was getting to know about Mark Newman, she couldn't be sure. After all, she'd been surprised to find there wasn't a private jet waiting—they were flying commercial.

"I wanted to sit in first class," Angelique pouted, settling her carry-on luggage into the space beneath the seat in front of her. Really it was just the laptop and her purse. Lately the laptop had been getting a lot of play. A heck of a lot of play.

"You're lucky to have a chair at all," Erica reminded her. "I had to give up some pretty valuable leverage to get you here. Remember that."

"Your personal bodyguard and cheering section." Angelique struggled to cross her legs in the narrow space between the rows. "That's me." She sighed. "Always a bridesmaid. Never a bride."

Erica rolled her eyes. "No one's getting married, Angelique. As weird as this whole thing's getting, marriage is the last thing—"

"Shh." Angelique slapped at her arm, her voice lowering to a hiss. "Here he comes."

And sure enough, there he came, limping down the plane's narrow aisle looking a little tired and a little pale, but in spite of those facts, as handsome as ever. Erica felt her heart give its usual little hiccup of attraction, along with that strong, sudden sexual pull.

"Someone's a little excited," Angelique teased, nodding toward Erica's long-sleeved "America's been Bush-whacked" T-shirt, which suddenly had two nipple-sized peaks right in the center.

"Be quiet." Erica crossed her arms to hide the evidence, just as Newman approached them.

"Hello, Angelique," he said, beaming friendliness at Erica's friend, as though he had been in the habit of seeing her daily. "Thanks for coming."

"Thanks for the ticket." Angelique grinned back at him, like he was old buddy.

But Mark's attention had shifted away from the other woman, and Erica felt herself under its intense heat.

"Hey there," he drawled. "What's the shirt say?"

"Nothing you're going to like," Erica said quickly without lowering her arms.

He grinned at her like he knew exactly why her arms stayed crossed over her chest and leaned even closer.

"Well, you might want to change it," he suggested. "You're heading into hostile territory, remember?"

His gaze shifted toward Angelique again. "Maybe you two can swap in the ladies' room . . ." He winked. "Again."

Angelique opened her mouth to say something that Erica was pretty sure would be highly critical of her roommate's wardrobe, but Erica refused her the opportunity.

"I thought that was the point," she said firmly. "To make my opposition clear—and allow your constituents to rally around you as the defender of the free world?" *Ha! Sank your battleship*, she thought as his grin dimmed to that irritated smirk. He opened his mouth, and Erica steeled herself for his comeback.

"We don't have time for this, Mark," Bitsi's harsh voice interjected. "We hit the ground running, with a Q & A in Billingham. The advance word is, it's going to be tough. We just barely carried that district six years ago, and the folks are even more critical now. You've got to be ready, Mark."

"I know, I know," Mark grumbled, waving her away. "You go on and sit. I'm coming."

Bitsi shot them an evil glare and squeezed past him toward the very last row of seats, about three rows behind where Erica and Angelique sat.

"Need a favor, Angelique," Mark drawled in his honey sweet, up-to-no-good voice. "Chase needs to sit with Erica. Brief her a bit on what to expect. So, my dear lady, if you wouldn't mind moving back a row . . ."

Angelique popped out of her seat like she had springs and moved into the seat behind them, beside a youngish-looking man in a blue baseball cap and sunglasses. His head was turned toward the window and his mouth was half open in the way of one asleep.

"Sure, Mark," Angelique replied in her normal, a-little-loud street voice, oblivious to the man or his evident fatigue. "But you know what I think would be the best thing for Erica?"

"What?"

A sly grin spread across Angelique's face. "If *you* sat there and . . . you know. Briefed her, or debriefed her or—"

"I like the way you think." Mark chuckled.

Who died and made you Cupid, stupid? The words were on the tip of Erica's tongue when Chase huffed down the aisle and tossed his carry-on into the overhead.

"Ready?" he asked, sliding into the seat Angelique had so recently vacated, looking up at Mark and then over at Erica.

To Erica's surprise, Mark leaned over and kissed her on the forehead, leaving the spot burning with the desire for more. Much more.

"Take care of her, Chase," he said. He stumped away from them toward the back of the plane. Erica turned, watching him take his seat, stretching the damaged right leg out into the aisle. He caught her eye, winked and then turned toward Bitsi with a ready-to-work expression.

Bitsi wasn't looking at him. She was staring at Erica with an expression of such determined malevolence, Erica felt almost as though she'd been slapped.

What a ride.

Newman needed a private jet, considering how heated his staff got in their preparations. Although she'd read the itinerary carefully, Chase had gone over it in great detail: Mark was attending black-tie events, mixed in with pancake suppers and church services. Town meetings and closed-door sessions with state leaders. It was clear that Newman was in for a busy week, and so was she. And other than a couple of school visits, she was due to be pretty ignorant and pretty uncomfortable most of the week. Except for when war was the topic, Erica knew very little about the issues of Newman's home state: farm subsidies and coal mining, resource development and smalltown initiatives.

"Who committed me to *that*?" Erica heard Mark ask once from the rows behind her, with more than a little irritation evident in his tone. "You know I'm as useless as a one-armed paper hanger at those things."

And for once, Bitsi's usually strident voice dropped into a low tone Erica couldn't hear. Then Mark's voice, loud and still annoyed, barked out.

"I'd rather just take Erica. Can't we do that?"

There was a sudden silence behind her, and Erica itched to turn her head to see their faces, but Chase was trying to tell her something about this afternoon's event with an earnestness that made her want to at least seem like she was listening to the man. But whatever Mark had proposed he "just take her to" was floating past Bitsi like a lead balloon.

"I'm not sure that's such a good idea," Erica thought she heard the blonde woman saying.

"Why?" Mark asked, sounding genuinely curious. "She's every bit as attractive as that newscaster woman you're always setting me up with. And unlike that woman, she's actually got a brain."

"I doubt she has anything appropriate to wear. The event isn't on her schedule and we don't have a week to make her over enough to be acceptable for this kind of thing, so—"

"Oh come on." Mark's voice cut through her bullshit with the acid of annoyance. "I'm sure we can find her an appropriate dress with a little effort. I want her to go. I think it would be good."

Silence. Erica could almost feel the skinny woman searching for a way to break it to him, but she said nothing.

"Everyone knows she's with me this week. What's the problem?" Mark asked again.

"No problem," Bitsi said in clipped, brusque voice that let everyone in earshot know that she had plenty of problems . . . and most of them started and ended with Erica Johnson.

When the plane touched ground, Erica wished she'd done what the writer of those nasty little letters had wanted and stayed home.

The airport, a long flat space surrounded by trees, looked like it was miles from any kind of civilization. Erica leaned toward the window and was shocked to see cornfields growing on the wide spaces bordering the tarmac. The air-traffic control tower rose out of the dying yellow stalks like a lighthouse in a brown sea. Erica peered across the aisle, staring toward the opposite window, hoping for a city view, but was met with more cornfields.

"Where the heck are we?" she asked, not really expecting an answer.

A few minutes before landing, Bitsi had appeared at Chase's shoulder.

"He wants her to come sit with him," she said, doing her best not to look directly at Erica. "He wants to talk to her."

Erica ignored the looks Chase and Angelique tossed in her direction and moved down the aisle, sliding past Mark into the empty seat beside him without making him get up.

"Welcome to my home," he said in a voice that had lost all the sophistication of Washington and sang with the pride of Dixie. He stared past her out the window, a slight smile softening his features. "Home," he repeated, his fingers finding hers and squeezing, gently. "We're home."

She wanted to snatch her fingers away, but she couldn't. Because it was there again: that weirdo feeling of safety and certainty, as if it were somehow the most natural thing in the world to be sitting here with this unlikely man, holding his hand and staring at cornfields while the jet taxied slowly up to the gate and the passengers started to rise, gather their belongings and press toward the exit. Mark released her hand and felt around the seat, searching for something.

"See you tonight, Mark," Chase called back to them as he headed for the front.

"Seven," Mark answered.

"St. Matthew's Episcopal Church." Bitsi's tone said she expected the words to be forgotten as soon as she spoke them. "Directions are on your date book."

"I know where St. Matthew's is, Bits," Mark gave her that trademark smirk. "I've been to services there a thousand times over the years."

"Well"—Bitsi's eyes flickered over Erica again, this time with something akin to jealousy in them— "don't be late. Nestor will meet you at the Q &A, so—"

"I won't be late for that, either."

Bitsi frowned, and then turned toward Angelique. "Come on," she said in a tone only slightly more pleasant than the one she used with Erica. "I'll take you over to Dickson's Inn. That's where you'll be staying."

For the first time, Angelique looked a little nervous. "I thought I was going to the Q & A," she said, glancing at Erica. "Moral support and all that."

"You're going to the Town Meeting," Bitsi replied. "Not the Q & A. Now come on—"

Angelique refused to budge until Erica nodded at her.

"I think I'll be okay. Go ahead."

Angie frowned, but in the end she, too, made her way up the narrow airplane aisle. As her slender form disappeared onto the jetway, Erica thought she felt other eyes on her, as though she were being stared at. She scanned the passengers, but no eyes were aimed in her direction. None at all. Even the man in the ball cap and sunglasses finally ambled up the aisle, rubbing at his chin and stretching as though he'd slept the entire trip.

Erica gathered up her things and waited, expecting Mark to move. The plane was quickly emptying, only a few others were lingering in their seats, and the aisle was clear. But Mark didn't move at all. He just kept staring out the window, waiting for something. Erica had no clue what until all the other passengers had deplaned.

"Senator?" A flight attendant leaned over them. "It's all clear now."

"Thank you," Mark murmured, but still waited, tapping his cane gently against the carpet until the flight crew had also gathered their things and left the plane.

"I'm sorry to make you wait so long, Erica," he said at last, staring at his shoes.

"Is this some kind of security concern?"

He shook his head.

"I don't really buy into all that security stuff," he said, shaking his head. "I know some of my colleagues hire bodyguards, but for me, it's a waste of money. People in my state didn't send me to Washington to get a big staff and a big head. I did call my friends at the state police about you, though. They'll have both uniformed and plainclothes officers at all our events and one at the inn, just in case. But that's not why we're still sitting here on an empty plane."

Erica nodded, appreciating the precautions. "Okay, then why *are* we still sitting here?"

A self-deprecating smile lifted the corners of his lips and he shot her a quick glance. "It's more . . . personal." He hooked the cane over his arm and braced his weight on the back of the seat in front of him. "You and me—we've already been through a lot together, right?"

Erica hesitated, frowning at him. "Right . . ."

"Well, looks like I'm trusting you with a little more, okay?"

"Trusting me with what, Mark? What's—"

He let out a groan of pain that echoed in the empty plane. "Shit, shit, shit," he cursed in absolute agony as he limped into the aisle, grasping his knee. "Oh shit . . ."

"Are you all right?" Erica stumbled out behind him as he crumpled against the back of the nearest seat, wrapping her arms around him as if she could support him. "What is it? Do you want me to get someone?—"

"No, no." He shook his head. Erica stared up into his face. His eyes were screwed tightly shut and his face was pale and slick with sweat. "It passes," he said in a tight voice. "I just . . . have to . . . work out . . . the stiffness . . . my cane . . ."

Erica bent, retrieving it from where he had dropped it and bending his fingers around it.

Mark took a deep, determined breath and began walking slowly up and back along the narrow airplane aisle, his lips clamped tight with agony. Erica watched him with concern. All of the smugness was gone, eclipsed by pain. The cover-boy handsomeness had also evaporated: His face was all jagged, hard edges as he limped a few feet forward then turned to limp back toward her. Erica watched, helpless, as he gritted his teeth, placing less and less weight on the cane, and more and more on his damaged left knee, until at last he opened his eyes and looked up at her.

"Sorry about that," he drawled, trying hard to smirk, trying to seem like the past five minutes had been nothing more than a little entertainment. "Flying is murder on this bum leg of mine."

"Wouldn't it help to fly first class? You'd have more room."

He ran a hand over his face, wiping away sweat. "Do you know much about Billingham?"

Erica frowned. "What's that got to do with whether you fly first class?"

"Just answer the question. What do you know about Billingham?"

Erica hesitated. Other than its long history of segregation and continuing civil rights struggle, she didn't know much. She wished she'd paid a little bit more attention to the things Chase had been trying to tell her . . . instead of straining to overhear what Bitsi had been saying to Mark.

"Well," she said slowly. "I know it's the capital city of a very poor state."

"Exactly. People here don't pay taxes so their public *servants*"—he emphasized the word—"can be comfortable. They pay taxes so that money can come back around for the public good. And if it's not going to come around for the public good, then we sure as hell ought to be paying a whole lot less taxes than we are."

Erica rolled her eyes. "Look, I know where you're going and I'm not getting into a tax-and-spend argument with you right now. I'm just saying that I don't believe the people want you to suffer like that when a few extra dollars could make the difference."

"I'm more than happy to suffer a bit for these folks," he said earnestly. "Traveling this state, I've seen far worse suffering than anything I'll ever go through." He braced himself on his cane and rolled up the sleeves of his dress shirt. Without his suit jacket and tie, with the sleeves revealing his muscular forearms and his face and hair wet with sweat, he looked less like a senator and more like a farmhand.

A sexy, sweaty, strong farmhand.

A sexy, sweaty, strong farmhand who was now looking at her as though he knew exactly what she was thinking. Erica shook herself out of her contemplation of Mark Newman and bent over to pull her handbag out from the space beneath the seat.

"You could pay the difference out of your own pocket, Mr. High and Mighty," she commented. "But I guess you just get some perverse pleasure out of hurting." She stood up, and stretched herself toward the overhead compartment, popping it open.

Her carry-on bag tumbled out, nearly knocking her over in its race toward the floor. Erica let out a little shriek of surprise and jumped away from the tumbling handle and wheels, backing into the solid weight that was Mark Newman. Automatically, his free hand clamped around her waist, spinning her protectively into his chest.

"All right?" she heard his voice rumble into the top of her head.

She nodded, lifting her head toward his. Those piercing eyes were fixed on hers again with that same annoying little half-smile. "It just startled me, that's all," she said, trying hard to recover her toughness, even though she was wrapped in the crook of the man's arm . . . yet again.

And once again, her whole body trembled and

knotted with passion for the man. Once again, she felt on the verge of wrapping herself fully around him and joining the Mile High Club.

If one could do that in an empty airplane already on the ground.

"Startled, sure," he nodded, smirking all the worse.

"What?" Erica demanded. "You saw that suitcase come flying out of there!"

"Sure, I saw it," he drawled down at her in that soft intimate voice he seemed to reserve just for her. "It's just . . ."—a long, pale index finger stroked the side of her face, intoxicating her with its gentle caress— "I can't help but notice how you'll go to any length to get into my arms. Runaway luggage, nearly getting shot . . . You sure you're not writing threatening letters to yourself, girl?"

"You can let me go," Erica muttered, trying her best to sound annoyed and coming out somewhere between seductive and sensitive. Her throat itched, she tried to clear it. Her lips were dry, she touched them with her tongue. The air in the plane grew heavy and hot, and she could feel the warm wet skin of the man beneath his dress shirt and smell the warm musk of his manliness filling the air between them. *Get the heck away from this dude*, a voice in her head was practically screaming, but it was as if her feet had been rooted to the spot. She couldn't have moved out of this man's arms if her very life had depended on it. Her fingers seemed to move on their own, up his shoulder, around his neck, stroking his dark hair and the bones of his cheek and chin.

I don't know how much longer I can resist him, another voice added. *I don't know how much longer I want to*. And this one seemed to come directly from her heart.

He was staring at her, an expression in those blue eyes that seemed to echo the confusion and attraction Erica felt racing around her own brain. As if there were a part of him that wanted to run for the hills and another part that wanted to taste her lips. The struggle continued in his eyes until at last, he sighed. Erica felt his body relax as he lowered his head. She closed her eyes, lifted her face and—   •

Clang.

The sound separated her from the man's side like a cleaving knife.

"Sorry," a human voice said a moment later, and Erica realized that the sound had come from the slamming of the rear cabin doors. At the same instant, a blue-uniformed man with a trash bag in his gloved hands took his place in the aisle. He was probably in his fifties, with brown eyes and leathery red skin. "Thought ev'rybody was off. Just gotta get up the trash. This bird's going back out in a half hour."

"No problem. We're going," Mark said easily enough. He stretched the hook of his cane toward the handle of Erica's carry-on, snagging it and lifting the bag into the upright position easily.

"I've got it now, thank you," Erica said, and was surprised at how breathless she sounded in her own ears. "Gosh, it's hot in here, isn't it?" she continued waving the still air around her as though it alone could account for her accelerated pulse rate. "It's just . . . too hot."

Fortunately, the jumpsuited man could have cared less about her. His eyes followed the cane, and then traveled slowly up Mark's body.

"You're him, aren't you? You're Mark Newman!"

Mark grinned. "I am."

"Well, I voted for you," the man said, pumping Mark's hand up and down with a frightening energy.

"Yes, sir. You're a real-life American hero."

"I was just doing my patriotic duty. Those kids over there now, they're the heroes, if you ask me."

"My son is over there." The man continued to shake Mark's hand, transfixed. "Not much choices for young folk in these parts. Either the military, or go on welfare with the white trash and the niggers—"

It took just a second for the word to settle in each of their ears. Erica felt herself stiffen. All the air on the plane had gone cold.

"I'm sorry, ma'am," the uniformed man was saying. "It's just my way of speakin'. The boys—African Americans—" he used the correct term carefully as though it felt strange in his mouth. "The African-American boys around here, they hear me say it all the time. Don't mean nothing. Didn't mean no harm."

Erica blinked at him. He seemed to be waiting for her to say something, but she couldn't think of what. "It's okay"? It wasn't. "I accept your apology"? How could she, when he just admitted he used the word with the "boys" all the time?

"Welcome to Billingham," she murmured, certain both men knew *exactly* what she meant.

"It's an unfortunate choice of words... uh... Davy," Newman said, reading the man's name badge. "But I'm glad your son chose to serve his country, and I'll pray for his safe return."

Erica turned away from them, hurrying up the aisle and out onto the jetway ramp, dragging her suitcase behind her on its little casters. It wasn't until she stood in the air conditioning of the airport gate that she felt herself breathe.

She looked around her. It was a small airport but perfectly familiar: the same kind of joined plastic chairs in the sitting areas, the same little counters where the ticket agents stood, the same wide windows so that the waiting passengers could see the planes, familiar concession stands located along the wide concourse. Everything was as it should be except that, here, whites used the pejorative *nigger* in conversation as "just a way of speaking," and . . . she'd been less than a second away from laying a big old lip-lock on a warmongering white man who was proud of calling this place home.

"Erica!" He was behind her, she could feel him, all of her senses hyper-aware, like they always were when he was around. It was like her body had suddenly betrayed her convictions and left her mind alone to fend for itself.

She didn't turn around, but gripped the handle of her suitcase more tightly and took a few steps further into the concourse, staying out of reach of those firm fingers, those muscular arms, that rock-solid chest.

"Erica!"

"I'm going to get something to drink," she told the voice, not turning to look at him or stopping long enough for him to get within grasping distance, or she knew those fingers would be curled around her arm again. She moved as steadily and purposefully as a woman dying of thirst toward the nearest vendor.

"Erica." His voice had that growl of irritation again. "Look, about what happened back on the plane—"

"Nothing happened back on the plane," she assured him. "You can talk with anyone you want, using whatever language you want. I don't have to like it or agree with it. This is America, right?"

But she'd reached the nearest concession and there was nowhere left to move. His hand came down on her shoulder, warm and possessive, but she shrugged it off and stepped away.

"Cut it out. It's not like you've never heard the

word *nigger* before. Your fourth graders toss it around at each other like it was 'hello.' I heard 'em. After the assembly."

"And it makes me cringe. But at least they're all black. And children."

"So it's okay when used heedlessly and innocently by children—"

"They hardly know what it means—"

"Neither does that guy."

"I highly doubt that. White people invented that term and they damn sure know what they mean when they say it!"

"Your little black kids know what it means, too," he hissed, leaning close enough for her to smell him again. "So I guess what you're telling me is, it's okay if you're black but not okay if you're white."

"Yes, that's exactly what I'm telling you, and if you were anywhere near as smart as people keep telling me you are, you'd understand that!" Erica shouted at him. "And at least you could have said something to the guy—"

"What do you want me to *say*?" Mark barked in frustration. "You heard him, you saw him. He was embarrassed enough already. What did you want me to do, kick him?"

"You could have told him it was *wrong*—"

"He already knows it's *wrong*. He's just a good old boy, probably just barely scraped his way out of high school, but he knows it's wrong. It's just the way of talking he's used to, that's all. I can take one look at him and know he honestly didn't mean anything by it."

"Fine." Erica threw her hand up like a shield between them. "You don't get this, and you never will. Every time I start to think there might be something between us, you prove me wrong." She shook her head. "There's no point in talking to you. No point at all." She looked around. "Where's your driver or your aide or whoever's supposed to be meeting us? Call them or summon them or whatever the hell it is you do. I'm ready to go. Get this whole experience over with."

"I thought you wanted a drink."

"I do. But I don't want a soda anymore. I need something much stronger if I'm going to get through a week here with you."

"A drink?" That smirk of a grin creased Newman's face, and Erica had to tighten her hand on her suitcase to keep from slapping him. "I know just the place. But first, we got a Q & A to get to."

"Fine," Erica snapped. "Where's the driver? Where's the car?"

"My driver? My car?" Newman's eyes twinkled blue mischief at her. "Right this way."

He stumped down the concourse two full steps beyond her ability to keep pace. Not that she minded; she was only too glad not have those bright eyes focused on her, only too glad not to have to feel the way she felt looking into them.

As they exited the terminal, Newman paused to fish a coin out of his pocket and flip it into a large fountain spouting water toward the steaming humid sky.

"In thanksgiving for another safe return," he declared just before the coin hit the water. Erica watched it settle, joining thousands of other coins glittering on the fountain's blue bottom. She opened her mouth to ask, but by then he had limped on, nearly reaching a covered parking garage. She swallowed her questions and hurried to catch up, already sweating in the Southern heat.

It took a moment for her eyes to adjust to the comparative darkness of the garage, but the respite from the harsh sun was welcome.

"Erica!"

Erica blinked, turning toward the sound of her name.

A dusty red pickup truck sat in a handicapped space only a few feet from the garage entrance.

To say the car was old would have been an understatement: it was ancient, and not in the "classic" car sense. Its rusted red body suggested years of hard driving, but it was so dirty, it was hard to tell just how many years that might have been, or even what make or model it was. At first glance, Erica thought there was a Confederate flag painted on the back window, but upon second glance she realized it was the state flag, with its suspiciously similar placements of blue stripes and stars.

Mark Newman stood beside it.

"Over here!" he said, waving her toward the old truck. A moment later, he swung open the passenger-side door. "She's a little dirty," he said with a grin, "but she's been sitting in this garage for almost two months. Didn't drive 'er when I was here two weeks ago, so I'll clean her up this afternoon and she'll look good as new."

Erica stared at him.

"You're kidding, right?" she said at last. "This isn't your car. I thought you told me you don't drive—"

"No ma'am," he corrected, smirking for all he was worth. "I told you I couldn't drive a regular car." He patted the truck. "Old Red here isn't a regular car. She's specially outfitted. Custom, I guess you'd call it. To accommodate my . . . uh . . . limitations. Now, are you going to get in, or what?"

Or what. The words were on the tip of her tongue and she was within seconds of saying them out of pure frustration and bad attitude. *It's bad enough that it's a pickup truck, bad enough that he's got that flag on the rear window,* she told herself, as she tightened her grip on her luggage and walked up to the truck's door. *But if he's got a gun rack, I swear I'm getting on the next plane out of here.*

Gingerly, Erica approached the passenger door and leaned inside.

A gun rack.

"There is no way I'm—" she began.

But then he slid the cane into the slots and grinned.

"Not everything is what you think," he teased. "Get in."

She sighed in relief, hopped up on the running board and climbed inside, cranking down the window to let some air inside. He deposited her bag and his briefcase in the truck bed and slid into the driver's seat a moment later. He reached across her to open the glove box and pulled out a silver key ring.

"You keep your keys in the car?" she asked, incredulous.

His chuckle was as relaxed as the rest of him seemed to be. In fact, Erica noticed, ever since he'd deplaned he seemed more centered, more . . . normal, if a guy like Mark Newman could be considered normal in any sense of the word.

"No one's going to steal this truck. And if they did, the state police would have it back to me within the hour."

"You're awfully sure of that."

He nodded. "I am. First of all, it's a heck of a lot safer here than where you come from. And second of all, most of the state knows this truck. I campaign in it, from it, out of it." He patted the dashboard. "Old Red here is a little famous."

Erica sighed. "As long as Old Red has air-conditioning, everything will be fine. This heat is giving me a headache."

The smile slid off Mark's face. "Actually, no," he said apologetically. "But once we get rolling you'll feel better. And I haven't forgotten about that drink. I know just the place. Q & A first, though. Or Bitsi will have my head."

"I don't think it's your head she wants," Erica muttered, as the old truck's engine roared to life. A moment later they were on their way.

What once looked like a slam dunk for Mark Newman now appears to be a race, as challenger Peter Malloy narrows the gap between the two men for incumbent Newman's Senate seat. Asked about his come-from-behind strategy, Malloy said, "Voters are beginning to realize that Mark Newman's mind is more on his love life than the needs of the people of this state. Now the love of a good woman—whatever color she is—is one of the greatest blessings a man can receive. But when we meet to debate this week, I got me a couple of questions for the honorable Mr. Newman. First of all, just who is paying for this courtship—him or the people of this state? And second, how can he date a woman whose views are so repugnant to everything this party holds dear? He's telling everybody his views haven't been affected by her influence, but I ask you, how on Earth can that be true?"

—The *Billingham News*

Chapter 12

"Where is the city? The houses? The buildings?" she asked him when she turned away from the cool breeze of the window to look in his direction.

She had to be hot as hell in that long-sleeved T-shirt. It was perfect for mid-March in Washington, but totally wrong for the climate here, where the temperature was closer to 90 than 60 degrees. He wanted to suggest she change—strip the thing off right here and now, replace it with anything in her suitcase more comfortable. But he was pretty sure that it wouldn't come out right.

Especially with his attraction to her zooming around between them like a bumblebee looking for a flower. She'd think he was trying to get her into bed—which he was.

Not yet, a voice within him cautioned. *Soon, but not yet.*

"City's about fifteen miles," he told her, shouting a little over the rushing air pouring in through the open windows. "We built the airport a ways from where most people live. Less noise pollution."

She nodded her understanding, and then turned away from him again.

Mark cast a sidelong glance at her. She was showing him nothing but profile: the long curve of her neck, the perfect shell of her ear, marred a little by the couple of dark stitches where the bullet had nicked it the other night. A strand of her jet-black hair hung damply against her cheek, looking surprisingly lank and straight compared to the wild waves covering her head. He imagined it spread around her head like a dark halo on a white pillow, imagined himself winding it around his fingers.

Snap out of it, a voice in his brain commanded, and he blinked a couple of times, forcing his attention back to the road. *Snap out of it. We've got work to do.*

And in that uncanny way she had of looking at him like she could read his mind, she turned back to him, locking away his heart with those smoldering eyes.

"Look out!"

Mark jerked the steering wheel hard to the left to avoid a rabbit as it jumped out of the nearby green.

"That bunny was nearly roadkill," he muttered.

"I don't think you hit him, though," she said, turning to stare out the truck's rear window. Her arm brushed his shoulder, setting everything inside him afire again.

"Nope, I didn't hit him," he heard himself saying, like his mind was his own. "If I'd hit him, trust me. We'd know." He cleared his throat, determined to steer himself out of dangerous waters. "Can I ask you a personal question?"

It was like one of those glass partitions that separated driver and passenger in fancy limousines suddenly went up between them. She was still looking at him with those soft brown eyes, but he sensed her wariness.

"You can ask. I might not answer, but you can ask," she said, showing him her profile again.

"Why aren't you married? A beautiful woman like you . . ." he stopped, reigning himself in before he was in too deeply. "A woman should be married. Especially a woman like you."

Her head whipped toward him again, and he knew it had come out wrong. He curled his lips into a smile and watched that irritated look blossom on her face again.

"What's that supposed to mean?" she fumed. "'A woman like me should be married.' I suppose you think all women should be married—that it's a woman's place to be under some man's thumb."

"Here we go." Mark sighed, exasperated. "You know, right when I start to get all mushy about you, you bring me right back to wondering what the hell is wrong with me. I thank you for that."

Amazement shone in her eyes. "You were getting mushy? About me?"

Mark locked his eyes on the road. "Not exactly," he muttered. "You've got me saying things I don't mean to say."

"But that is what you said. That's exactly what you said."

"Well, it's not what I meant."

"Then, please explain what you meant."

A million macho, smart-mouthed quips circled his mind, but he finally rejected them all. "All right. Don't take this wrong way, but . . ."—he practiced the words in his head a moment, before saying calmly— "I'm beginning to like you a little. Even though you're a Left Wing nutcase," he added quickly. "I mean, I knew I was . . . *attracted* to you. But now I realize it's more than that. I'm starting to like you."

She frowned at him. "You like me?"

"A little, yes."

"A little."

A pink tinge crept over her caramel-colored skin. She turned toward the window again.

"You like me," he heard her murmur. "And I . . ." but the words were caught by the wind and he wasn't entirely sure whether she was reciprocating his sentiments or scorning them.

Mark focused his attention on the road. She was right: This was one lonesome stretch of highway. Billingham seemed forever away; the airport, miles behind them; Washington, D.C. a distant memory. Right now, amidst the waving fields of corn, they might have been the only two people in the world.

Silence filled the cab for a while. Mark kept his eyes on the road ahead until, out of the clear blue nothingness, she said, "I was married once. Did I tell you?"

He turned toward her, but she was studying her hands as though the answers to life's riddles were written there.

"What happened?"

She lifted her shoulders in the smallest of shrugs. "It ended." Her eyes found his. "I ended it."

"Why?"

Her sigh was heavy and long. "Well, you might find this a little surprising, coming from me, but . . . I guess I wanted the white-picket-fence thing. You know, a home. A family. Sort of"—she cut her eyes at him like she was expecting to be made fun of—"traditional."

"Nothing wrong with that," Mark said quietly.

"Nothing, except it's unrealistic," she said in a voice that scoffed the idea of domestic happiness. "It takes two incomes to have any hopes of buying any kind of house in D.C. anymore. And for most of our marriage, we only had one: mine. Reggie quit his job to pursue his dream—he wanted to be a writer. Don't get me wrong, he had talent and I was totally in support of him," she added quickly, but Mark noticed the furrow that came to her brow, as if the memory were particularly uncomfortable. "I just didn't know that pursuing his dream would cost so much."

"Financially?"

When her eyes found his, there was a wry sort of pain in them he'd never read before. "Financially, emotionally, physically. See, Reggie was used to making money. And with his new venture, he wasn't making anything. And that made him feel insecure, I guess. I thought that was why he was in such a rush for us to get pregnant, even though I kept telling him the timing wasn't right. And when I refused, he had to build up his self-esteem somehow. And he did that with a string of women. A string of women other than me." He watched as those lovely eyes filled with an unbecoming bitterness. "And that's why a woman like me isn't married. I'm not in the market for heartache, Mark. From you or anyone else. I can do bad all by myself, thank you very much."

I hate Reggie. The thought knotted in the pit of his stomach as soon as he saw the bitterness in her eyes, heard it in her voice. There was a part of him—a big part, if he wanted to be honest—that wanted to pull the truck over right then and wrap her into his arms and remind her that not every man was a Reggie. That a man could be faithful to just one woman until the day he died if he were a man of honor. A man of character. That there were places in the world where there were still white picket fences and Sunday dinners and children playing hide-and-seek by twilight.

But instead, he simply nodded. "I'm not looking for

heartache, either," he told the road. "I've had enough of it to last a lifetime."

He knew she was staring. He knew she was going to ask that painful question that still haunted his nights. He felt the grief welling up inside him, pinching at the edges of his heart. He swallowed, hoping for the grace to tell the story one more time without breaking down.

He piloted the truck around the next bend in the road. A lone car was parked along the side of the road with its trunk open and its hood up.

"Lousy place to be stranded," Erica observed.

"You said it," Mark agreed, taking in the driver, who stood leaning against the vehicle, holding what Mark thought might be a cell phone. "Better see if he needs some help."

The car looked suspiciously shiny, as though it was either new or recently washed and waxed. The driver shifted nervously as Mark slowed Old Red and pulled up behind him.

"That's the guy from the plane!" Erica cried as they got close enough to see a dark baseball cap and sunglasses. "The one who was sitting next to Angelique. He slept the whole way."

Mark studied the man, frowning. His gut told him there was something about this guy . . . something either eerily familiar or eerily strange. He couldn't place it. To all appearances, the dude was just a fellow traveler having a bit of very bad luck.

"This is a terrible place to be stranded. There isn't another car on the road!" Erica popped the door handle and was on the verge of sliding out of the car, when Mark barked, "No."

Her eyes found his, inquisitive, confused. Scared.

"You don't think . . ." she began in a low voice, craning her neck toward the blank stretch of road behind them. "I thought you said there would be state police—"

"I'm sure it's fine," Mark said, struggling to keep his voice calm and reassuring. "I just think . . ." She frowned at him and he knew she wasn't buying his act. Not for a second. "I'll find out what's what," he finished, sliding slowly out of the truck and reaching for his cane.

He tested his weight on the soft dirt of the roadside, then limped toward the man . . . or at least he thought it was a man. It was hard to tell, the way the dude kept pulling his baseball cap down low over his face, which was already concealed by a large pair of aviator glasses. Mark noticed he wore a windbreaker, a dubious fashion choice given the heat of the day.

A flash of memory flickered in Mark's mind, but he couldn't be sure. After all, Erica had said they'd seen the guy on the plane. That might be the only place he knew this guy from. And yet . . .

"Hey," Mark drawled, reverting to the easy, neighborly manner of Southern speech as if he hadn't stepped off a plane from Washington less than half an hour ago. "Looks like you got some trouble."

"Yeah," the man answered and the voice at least was unmistakably male. The stranded motorist shifted the little black device from his hand to his jacket pocket and buried his face deeper into his collar as though avoiding a brisk wind.

Only there wasn't a wind. Not even a breeze. The air was warm and still and the Southern sun beat down on them with its usual relentlessness.

"Need some help? There's a little place up the road there with a telephone, if you need it," Mark offered. "Cell phones don't always work good out here."

But he could tell the man wasn't listening. He was

peering toward the cab of Old Red with more than curious interest.

"No, no," the dude muttered vaguely. "It's a rental. Just picked it up from the airport. I've already called back. My cell's working fine. Told them they gave me a lemon, Senator."

Senator. The dude knew who he was, but he didn't have the accent of a native. Which led to one obvious conclusion.

"All righty," Mark said calmly. "Take care." And he turned on his heel and stumped back to the car.

Erica Johnson had worry etched into the very bones of her face when he hoisted himself back into the cab beside her.

"What is it?"

"Car trouble, or so he says," Mark told her, gunning the truck's engine.

"But you don't believe him?"

Mark shook his head. "That fella's Washington press corps if he's anything."

Relief coursed across her face. "Oh. For a second, I thought . . ."

"Never thought a dull ol' boy like me would be dodging the paparazzi."

She flashed him a smile. "You're plenty interesting," she said. That lovely pink color flushed her skin again. "I mean . . ."

"Yeah," he agreed. "But you're even more interesting."

"Me?"

He nodded. "That's what that dude there wants. A picture of you—or more precisely, a picture of us, if you get my drift."

"You don't think he's the one taking those pictures? The ones of us . . ." she let the sentence die unfinished, knowing he knew what she meant.

"I don't think so. Professional photographers don't hold on to photos that good. That ladies'-room photo definitely would have hit the papers by now if it was shot by a pro." He leaned toward her. "Apparently, though, the Washington gossip columns need some fodder. I'm personally not in the mood to oblige. How 'bout you?"

For an instant, her expression seemed to go blank while she thought it through. Then that light of determination came to her eyes.

"What should we do?"

Mark grinned. "You duck and cover—and Old Red and I'll lose him."

The hum of the engine, the thrill of their mission and the smile she gave him made his heart thump with fresh desire. He cut the wheels of the truck sharply and a moment later, Old Red bounded onto the pavement again, flying past the dude in the rental and leaving him quite literally in the dust.

Nestor Hannegan looked good, considering his age and state of health, Mark thought as he shook the old man's hand. He was Mark's political mentor—sort of a godfather—a legend of state politics. He was also a resident of this district of Billingham and never failed to make an appearance at any event—whether it was a fund-raiser, town meeting or Q & A—Mark held.

"Good to see you, son," Nestor wheezed in a voice that had passed decrepit and headed straight for ancient. "Good to see you." He twisted his torso around until the veins stood blue and sentient in his neck. Mark followed his gaze: This event was in the large auditorium of Westlake High School, and there seemed to be very few chairs unoccupied. Mark noticed that most of the attendees seemed to be clutching white flyers in their hands.

"Good turnout," Nestor pronounced. "But then, under the circumstances . . ." He cut his eyes at Erica.

"Forgive me. My mama taught me manners, but I seem to have forgotten 'em. Nestor Hannegan, I'd like to present Ms.—Erica Johnson." Nestor offered Erica a pale, blue-veined hand.

"Hello," Erica said, giving him a wary smile.

To Mark's surprise the old man paused long enough to read her T-shirt, and then grimaced. He said nothing to Erica—not one single word—just quirked an eyebrow at Mark that communicated doubt as fully as if he'd spoken. The rudeness was so unlike the man's usual courtly charm that Mark felt it like a sharp poke with a stick. When he glanced down at Erica, there was a determined little smile on her face, like she'd taken the man's bad behavior as a challenge.

"Well, I suppose we should get started." Nestor signaled to a heavyset woman, who took her place in front of a microphone and lectern. He lowered himself back into his chair.

"Oh this is going to be so much *fun*," Erica muttered, her voice dripping with sarcasm as she took the seat closest to the end of the stage and the exit. "There's not one friendly face out there," she added, nodding at the sea of waiting voters.

Mark glanced out at the crowd again. It was true, they did seem agitated, as though there had been a fight in the hallway and everyone was still all excited about it. More than once, he caught someone looking down at the white paper and then up at him and over at Erica.

"You're reading it wrong," he told her, though he wasn't entirely sure that she was. "They're friendly enough. Just looks like whatever's on that paper has got them all excited."

"They look like a lynch mob to me," she murmured just as the heavyset woman's voice rang through the room, amplified by the public address system. She introduced Mark and explained how participants could present their questions.

When she was finished, she turned toward Mark and he stood.

He made his usual opening remarks: something about how nice it was to be home, working hard on critical issues in Washington, eager to be reelected and continue to serve, looking forward to answering their questions. He'd said it all many times over the course of the campaign, but every time, he felt a kind of jittery enthusiasm, as though he were gearing up for a marathon.

And this time, he was distracted by the response of his audience. The white paper was pulling their attention away from him and everywhere he looked, instead of interest in him or his words, he saw heads bent toward the paper or leaning toward each other to whisper covertly. Mark mentally dubbed one of the women as "whisperer-in-chief" since she bounced out of her chair while he was talking to whisper with not one, but four different others.

"I'm not sure my guest needs an introduction," Mark finished, turning on the best of his charm as he gestured toward Erica. "Most of you saw her on the news and you already know she's hear to learn a little bit about the other side of the story." He chuckled a bit. "Who knows, maybe a good ol' Billingham welcome could change her mind." Then he added, just in case, "And I know you good people will give her a welcome she won't soon forget. Now, I'm looking forward to taking your questions."

Normally, when he finished this part there was applause. But today, he turned away from them to the sound of silence, except for the squish of the rubber tip of his cane connecting with the wood of the stage floor.

There was a long, weird pause before anyone moved. Then, as though elected by committee, the "whisperer-in-chief" took her place at one of the microphones placed strategically in the aisles.

A stocky, flat block of a person from shoulders to knees without any appreciable curves, she wore a white tank embroidered in red thread with an emblem he couldn't decipher tucked into a longish navy blue skirt. She had a wedge cut of gray hair, a masculine manner, and a surprisingly sexy, feminine voice.

"Hi. I'm Joanne Kimble. I'm president of the Ladies United Services," she said, not sounding hostile at all. "Your speech was . . . very nice, but I think we're all much more interested in what you have to say about the fax."

"Fax?" Mark frowned. "What fax?"

"The fax. Surely you've seen it? Came through late this afternoon. I sure would like to know a little bit more about some of the things it says."

Mark frowned toward Nestor, but the older man suddenly seemed captivated by his hands. Mark glanced toward the wings of the stage, where a couple of junior aides waited like understudies. One of them scrambled off the stage and approached someone in the audience.

"I don't know what you're talking about, Ms. Kimble. I don't think we sent around any faxes," Mark said.

"Oh, you definitely wouldn't have *sent* this, but I'm

sure you were going to address it. We were just talking about that, wondering why you didn't bring it up. Personally, that's the only reason I'm here. I want to hear what you have to say for yourself."

Mark frowned. "Anybody else get this fax?"

All around the room, hands lifted, most bearing the same white paper.

Mark glanced back toward Erica just as a young intern stumbled across the stage to hand him the fax.

The paper had been folded into four tight creases and pressed flat by the pressure of Bill's back pocket. Mark pulled it open slowly, his every gesture commanding the attention of every face in the quiet room. This was it: this was the response he always tried to get from an audience, and now he had it, except that it was of the morbid variety.

At the top of the fax were the words FOUR THINGS MARK NEWMAN DOESN'T WANT YOU TO KNOW, followed by three bullets misrepresenting his stances on three issues: veteran's affairs, abortion and national health care. Following each issue, Mark's vote on a specific senate bill was attributed. Beneath the bullets floated a black-and-white reprint of the photograph of Erica on his lap the night of the holdup. The reproduced image was fuzzy, Erica's skin seeming darker, almost receding into the dark night of the photograph's backdrop. At one edge of the paper, in the tiniest script legible, were the words "Paid for by the Campaign against Political Duplicity."

There was no fourth bullet, and Mark began preparing a mental response that included this oversight as just one indication of why the flyer deserved no more than a trash can's attention. But a flash of a second later, he understood. The picture was the fourth bullet: the shot of Mark and Erica together, looking both shaken and strangely content in black-and-white.

Mark glanced behind him. Nestor Hannegan wouldn't look at him; clearly, he'd known what the fax contained and had chosen to say nothing. Mark processed the betrayal quickly and put it aside for action later. He zeroed his attention on Erica, who gazed back at him, puzzlement deepening on her face. Mark sighed, running his hand over the sparse brush of his hair in annoyance.

"What crap," he muttered, forgetting about the microphone and the packed crowd of avid listeners. "What a piece of cowardly crap . . . Joanne," he drawled. "When'd you say you got this?"

"Late this afternoon. I was at the office doing some paperwork, and it was there."

"Your fax machine the kind that records the number of an incoming call?"

"Yeah, it does that."

Mark nodded. "I think we're gonna have to go check that out."

Nestor rose slowly and interjected, "Well, Senator, you plan on answering the lady's question, or not?"

Every face in the room swung toward him. As Mark gazed out at them, he saw even more copies of the document making their way out of purses, pockets and notebooks and circulating the room to breathe the breath of understanding on the few ignorant and unwashed. Mark winced as the heavy woman who had introduced him passed a copy down to Erica, murmuring something gentle and sympathetic that Mark didn't quite catch.

He watched her face as she read it, its meaning and implications registering only in the deep lift of her chest as she inhaled. Her lashes dropped over her eyes for a moment before she raised her eyes to his face. They expressed a devastating hurt that struck his heart more completely than a million tears.

"Now I understand what was going on in this room as I was speaking a few moments ago," Mark said at last. "I was talking sincerely about elevating political discourse. I was talking about trying to outline a new plan, a new premise and a new reputation for our state. And you were waiting for me to respond to this . . . crap. So here it is."

Mark slid off the stool, limped over to Erica and snatched the flyer from her hand. He frowned at it, and then ripped it deliberately in half, from top to bottom, then again and again until it was a handful of confetti. He tossed the shreds into the air and let them fall around him like rain.

A sole pair of hands came together in slow, deliberate applause. Mark turned.

Erica. She was pounding her palms together, her face a grim mask. A fragment of a second later, someone deep in the crowd joined in, followed by another pair of hands, and then another. A blink later, and the room exploded into assertive applause, punctuated by an occasional whoop of support.

"This is the kind of garbage, the kind of crap," he shouted over the clamor, "that has turned millions of Americans away from participation in the political process. This kind of crap shames us as Americans, degrades our democracy. And I'm sick of it. I'm sick of appeals to our paranoia . . . and our prejudice. I'm sick of faxes full of lies and inaccuracies and misrepresentations calculated to hurt. I'm sick of accusations from organizations too afraid to make their presence known in the light of day. And most of all, I'm sorry. I'm sorry that innocent people—good, caring, sincere people like my friend Ms. Johnson—get caught in the crossfire of what we call our political system."

He shook his head.

"I said to you earlier that I wanted to change that for our state. That I wanted to do something radically different. And as much as I hate everything that piece of paper stands for, I guess I ought be glad for it. And I ought to thank Ms. Kimble there and Nestor Hannegan and all of you for putting it out before us so we can all see—see the kind of garbage that's become politics as usual in this country. We can see it and make a decision. We can engage it, we can fall into the trap of punch and counterpunch. We can go dig up dirt on the other guys and lob it around until we're all smeared with mud. Or we can take the high ground." He paused. "I've already decided what ground I'm taking. But it takes you choosing with me. It takes you being willing to say with me, 'Enough is enough,' and mobilizing with me to make the changes real. And if we don't do this, we're going to end up with the kind of candidate—the kind of senator, the kind of state—that earns the favor of the dubious organization that put out that thing. Or . . . we can stay focused on the issues. We can disagree as people of good conscience sometimes do, but at least we're shooting straight. We're sticking to the task at hand."

The words were met with a smattering of applause.

"Now does anyone have any real questions?" Mark demanded, barely realizing that he'd slipped into a voice of near-military command. "Questions about how we can work together to make this state—and this nation—great?"

Other acclamations and assents scattered the room along with a buzz of satisfied commentary. Heads bent toward each other muttering anew, but this time, the whispers earned him smiles and nods and the suggestion of favor. He was about to continue, to launch an encore of his bid for their support when a rangy-looking man in pair of bib overalls approached one of the microphones.

"Well, I don't disagree with you, Senator." The word was missing the central vowel, coming out "sen'tor," as though the man's tongue refused to be hurried. "Not one bit. An', for what it's worth, I think I could really get behind you. I like what you've got to say, and the way you say it."

"Thank you. Your support is no small thing."

The man nodded, acknowledging the truth of those words with an easiness that contradicted his dress and manner.

"Well, you might can have it. But see"—he lowered his weatherbeaten face to the toes of his dusty black boots— "thing is, much as I don't like that flyer, if I come out for you, folks is gonna ask me about the stuff that's written on it." He looked up at Mark then, penetrating him with a pair of clear blue eyes. "I gotta be able to give them an answer. A better answer than 'politics as usual,' if you know what I mean. You got to give folks credit. Folks is smart enough to think that's just a dodge—to think that you ain't answering because you can't answer." He shuffled his feet slightly, apparently simultaneously shuffling words in his brain. "You gotta give me what I need to respond to 'em," he continued at last. "To persuade 'em that you oughta be their senator again this time around. You get me?"

Mark nodded. He got it. The old farmer wanted to know what was up.

"Fair enough." Mark leaned close to the microphone, making ready for the real work of the night. "Ask me anything you want to know about what's on that paper—anything about my record in the Senate, anything about my background or my experience—

and I'll answer it, fully and truthfully." He paused. "But don't ask me to comment on things that involve Ms. Johnson. I don't think it's right for me to comment on anything that affects her until I've had a chance to talk with her about it. After all"—he looked around the room—"she's not running for Senate. I am. Can we do that?"

In most faces he read eager assent, but more than a few eyes strayed to Erica as though withholding their agreement until receiving a response—no matter how small—from her. He watched her assess the faces—mostly white faces—peering expectantly at her from every corner of the room, her expression kaleidoscoping emotion.

She could sink him, he knew it. She could freak out, or go to that scary "far left" place. She could call them all on the carpet, accuse them of being bigots just for their curiosity. She could do so many things, so many things that would torpedo this event and spill over onto others.

And the worst part would be that they would deserve it. The fax was ugly, indefensible, and racist.

She cleared her throat.

"I'm sorry," she began in a low voice, addressing the room without the aid of the sound system, but it was so quiet, Mark was pretty sure even those in the back heard every word. "I'm more than little upset by all of this." She paused, and when she spoke again, her voice was stronger and more audible. "But it makes it a little easier to have been the target of something so vicious in the company of such supportive and committed people." She managed a smile. "Thank you all for that. You all know I don't agree with Mark—the senator—on very much. But he's right about one thing: you've got to keep this campaign centered on what's really important: the war and the economy and Social Security and the challenges facing our country." She nodded toward the paper still in her hands. "Not some crap like this. So answer the man's questions, Senator," she teased.

There was a twitter of laughter.

"Well," Mark said, sending her a look of gratitude before tearing his attention from her face. "I have my orders. Let's take this stuff point by point."

100% Troop Support
0% War Support
—Anti-war slogan

Chapter 13

◇◇

She wasn't going in there.

He'd promised her a drink, but this place looked like Johnny Reb's favorite hangout: a dull, flat, cinder-block building with a few neon beer signs and no windows. Nothing but dusty pickups and even dustier motorcycles in the dirt parking lot.

"High class," Erica muttered.

"They're good people," was all he offered by way of encouragement, rubbing at his forehead with the back of his hand. "And I could really use a beer."

Erica stared up at him. He did look a little bedraggled. But then considering how a simple Q & A had nearly turned into a forum on interracial relationships, you could hardly blame the guy for looking a little queasy. He looked a little sweaty, too, like the Q & A had worked his Right Guard. But the sweatiness could have just been the result of the sultry drive in un-air-conditioned Old Red, which had the back of his white dress shirt sticking to him like a wet rag.

Her own T-shirt clung to her back, equally damp and uncomfortable—and she knew fully well in her own case it wasn't Old Red.

Right about now, she was sweating everything.

Damned if this isn't a weird spot to be in, she had thought, listening at the Q & A. *I'm almost rooting for a man on the wrong side.* She had the same thought over and over as, one by one, Newman's constituents stood to ask their questions. The war came up time and time again, and Newman was right: The people took a peculiar pride in sending their sons and daughters off to fight. But again and again, they asked the question on every American's lips:

When will this end?

It was the question that Newman most needed to be able to answer, and the only question for which he had no answer at all.

Well, not the only question.

He didn't have a definition for the exact state of their relationship, either, and at some point, soon, Erica knew, they were going to have to have "the talk," and either quit or damn the torpedoes and go full speed ahead.

They hadn't talked during the drive. Not about the fax, or the Q & A or the war or the relationship or anything. The only words spoken were, "I promised you a drink," and something told Erica this wasn't the time to question him about the fax and its possible relationship to the odd pictures she'd been receiving, even though she couldn't have been more certain of a connection if the sender had signed his or her name. Instead, she studied the tight lines of his profile, watching a frown deepen on his face as he sank into a reverie that she sensed had nothing to do with her.

Then they had pulled into the parking lot in front of this place.

Mark stumped around the truck to the passenger side and offered her his hand.

"I think I need a clean shirt," she told him, sliding
out to join him. "I can smell myself."

He leaned toward her, sniffing, and she caught a
whiff of him. It had, indeed, been a long day.

"You're fine," he told her. "Fresh as a daisy."

"Yeah, a dead one," she told him, leaning into the
back of the truck for her bag. "Is there a ladies' room
in there?"

He frowned. "You know . . . I don't know," he said,
as though it were the first time he'd contemplated the
question. "I know there's a men's room . . . but I don't
think I've ever seen a woman in Dickey Joe's, now
that you mention it. At least, other than Mary."

"Who's Mary?"

A troubled expression creased his face for a moment. "Dickey's daughter. She worked in my office
for a while, but it didn't work out. She's a terrific kid,
but terribly shy. I think it was all a little much for her,
the pace, the workload . . . Bitsi." And from the way
he said it, Erica knew instantly there was a whole
story there, waiting to be told. "But you're right," he
continued briskly, as Erica extracted a new top and
zipped the bag closed again. "If Mary's there, there's
got to be somewhere for a woman to do her thing."

"Well, well. Look what the cat dragged in!"

The place was as dim and dank as she would have
expected from its outside, but a good deal cleaner. It
had all the ubiquitous features of a honky-tonk bar:
wooden tables and chairs tucked into dark corners
populated by tattooed men with pink necks and forearms, a long bar complete with stools, a pool table, a
jukebox, and Dickey Joe: a fifty-something, big-bellied
man with a shock of salt-and-pepper hair growing
from his head to the sides of his face, to his chin.

"Hey, there, Dickey. How the hell are you?" Mark

shook the man's hand warmly. "Good to see you."

"It's about time you got here. Your flight got in almost four hours ago. I had Mary check for me. I was beginning to wonder if you weren't coming this time." He nodded toward his daughter, a fresh-faced twenty-something Erica felt old just looking at.

"Bite your tongue." Mark laughed. "Me, come home and not stop at Dickey's?" He shook his head. "Don't think so. I'm a little late today because—"

"Campaigning." The young woman's voice was very soft, and immediately after she spoke she lowered her eyes as though she feared she shouldn't have.

"That's right," Mark said in the calm, gentle voice one might use to talk to a small child. "Had to race to town to talk to some people. It's nice to see you, Mary. How're you getting along?"

Even with her eyes averted and her head bent, it was impossible to miss how the girl turned crimson. Instead of answering the question, she turned away and busied herself with beer glasses.

"She's fine, Mark, just fine. Doin' some volunteer work over at Mercy Hospital. And of course, helpin' me. I don't know what I'd do without her."

Mark followed the girl with his eyes for a long second, before turning his attention back to his old friend. "Well, as you can see, I'm not traveling alone. Dickey, I'd like you to meet—"

"Already know who *you* are! You're the school-teacher!" Dickey said, shaking a finger in Erica's direction. "The one what was on TV with my boy, here, a few days back."

"I am." Erica smiled into Dickey's broad, red face. *In a few more years, he'll be a perfect Santa Claus*, she thought. He'd be good at it, too. He had that bartender's way of making people feel welcome, feel at ease. "Nice to meet you . . . uh . . . Mr.—"

"None of that. Everybody calls me 'Dickey Joe' and you ain't gonna be the exception. Hey Mary!" Dickey called over his shoulder. "We got us a couple of cel-e-brit-ies in 'ere today!"

"Yes sir," Mary agreed in that same soft voice. She turned and Erica saw she'd drawn two beers with huge, foaming heads. She set one down in front of Erica and the other in front of Mark without looking at either one of them.

"Y'all want some food today? Mary does the best barbeque this side of the Mississippi."

Mark glanced at Erica. "You hungry?"

Erica imagined a pile of slaughtered meat slathered with hickory sauce, and her stomach turned. Even though she was starving, something told her Dickey Joe's idea of a salad would be a single leaf of iceberg with a tomato on the side. She conjured as phony a smile as any politician would have been proud to own and shook her head. "Just very, very thirsty."

"You're at the right place. Dickey Joe's is just about the best beer ever brewed." Mark curled his fist appreciatively around the cold glass and lifted it, as though preparing to toast, before stopping short. "Please tell me you drink beer."

"Actually," Erica began, intending to finish with *I hate beer*, until she noticed the pained expression on his face. She glanced at the faces of their hosts. Dickey Joe's eyes were riveted to her face with an expression of eager anticipation, and even Mary had raised her eyes to stare at Erica with interest. "Actually, I don't usually drink at all," she continued, and watched all their face fall until she finished with, "but today, I'll make an exception."

She could see Mark's shoulders relax, and the

smile that lit up his face made the lie worthwhile. "To friends, old and new," he said, nodding first toward Dickey Joe and Mary, and then toward Erica before taking a long pull on the glass.

Erica raised the glass to her face. It smelled awful—like something rotten—but she held her breath and poured a full swallow into her mouth.

My God, it was nasty. Nastier than it smelled. Erica managed to gulp it down without choking, but it was hard to keep herself from grimacing at the awfulness of it all.

Mark Newman and Dickey Joe chuckled like they'd had a joke at her expense.

"You like it?" Mark asked.

"It's . . . uh . . . very good," Erica lied, but they must not have been convinced, because the men laughed again.

"Well, there's plenty of it," Dickey Joe declared. "Drink up!"

Erica stared at the still full glass. There was no way she could stomach even the smallest sip of the stuff.

"I—is there a place where I can . . . um . . . freshen up a little?" she stammered instead.

"Sure thing, little lady. Mary!"

The girl was already wiping her hands on her apron and opening the flap that separated the bar from the tiny restaurant. She scurried away, her head down, and Erica could only assume she was intended to follow.

The girl led her out of the public areas of the bar and through a small kitchen area to a little closet of a room at the very rear of the restaurant.

"There's a restroom out front," she said, daring to cast a quick, interested glance at Erica's face, "But this is the one I use."

"Thanks, Mary," Erica said. "I'll just be a second.

Wait for me? I don't think I can find my way back."

The girl flashed Erica a quick smile and nodded until her lank blonde ponytail swished on her slender shoulders.

It wasn't the Ritz Carlton, but the restroom was serviceable and clean. After using the facilities, Erica stripped off her hot, long-sleeved shirt and splashed some cool water on her face and under her arms. Thanking the god of preparedness, she pulled a tiny trial-size tube of deodorant from her satchel and spritzed on a little body spray to cover the worst of the funk. She put on the sleeveless white tank she'd pulled from her bag and immediately felt appropriately dressed for the weather at last. As for the hair, it was too hot here to keep it loose, so she pulled a scarf from her bag and followed the tradition of her ancestors.

"You look different," Mary said, considering her fully for the first time since they'd met. Her pale blue eyes seemed to dart over every detail of Erica's appearance before she lowered them again and turned to lead the way back into the bar.

"Thanks . . . I think," Erica said, following her once again. "Is that good?"

The girl's ponytail bobbed affirmative. "You don't look like a Washington woman."

Erica laughed. "Depends on what you know about Washington women. What does 'not Washington' look like to you?"

Mary's eyes found Erica's for another brief second. "Not Bitsi Barr," she said in a voice that resonated with deep dislike. But by then they were back with the menfolk, and Mary kept her eyes low and her mouth shut. Erica didn't get the chance to ask her just what had happened between her and Mark's media director that had left her so angry and so bitter.

* * *

"Oh my God," Mark breathed, rising unsteadily as she entered. "It's a miracle. An absolute miracle!" he cried, saluting her with his beer glass. "Your shirt!"

"What?" Erica asked turning around to see what on Earth he could be talking about. "You don't like it?"

"I love it," he said smirking sarcasm and looking like he was desperately in need of being slapped. "It's the most beautiful shirt you own. Why? Because it doesn't have one of those idiotic slogans on it."

Erica rolled her eyes. "Very funny, wise guy. For your information, I have lots of shirts that don't—"

"'Scuse me. Senator?"

Mark turned away from Erica to face the voice.

A wiry man with a bedraggled gray ponytail stood at his elbow. Erica took him in, from his black biker vest to the "Semper Fi" tattoo on his forearm. When the man raised his right arm, she drew back with a little gasp, half expecting him to strike.

But the arm ended in a hand raised in a salute.

"From one veteran to another, thank you, sir," the man said, the heels of his scuffed black cycle boots scraping the floor as he came to full attention.

The smirk slid off Mark's face and his expression grew suddenly grim. "Thank *you*, sir," he said, returning the salute and then clasping the man's hand in a handshake. "Marine Corps?"

The man nodded. "Vietnam."

"Thank you for your service."

"And you for yours, sir." The man shuffled from foot to foot. "I heard about what you did in Gulf One. Hope you can hold the line with the folks in D.C. like that."

"I'll do my best," Mark replied.

The man's eyes left Mark's for a moment and focused on Erica with a peculiar intensity. Was it her imagination, or did the man's expression change, just a little? Erica had the feeling of being x-rayed or Xeroxed by his cool gray eyes. She didn't like the feeling one bit. When she glanced at Mark, he was frowning like he'd seen the change in the man, too. But all the guy said was, "You know what this man did, miss?" in a perfectly calm and rational voice.

"I've read about some of it, but I don't know the whole story," she told the aging veteran, thanking God and Angelique that she'd actually read some of those old war-hero articles on the Internet. "He's never told me the details."

Something like a blush rose in Mark's cheeks, and he mumbled something incomprehensible.

"I can tell you," Dickey Joe volunteered. "I love the story. Tell it every chance I get. It's got everything: drama, mystery, intrigue . . ."

As testament to the story's power, Mary took the barstool next to Erica and leaned her forearms on the counter expectantly.

"Most people don't know much about Gulf One," the veteran added, easing his slender, leather-clad self onto the barstool beside Mark. "Some of these kids don't even know Saddam invaded Kuwait and had to get his butt kicked out."

"Well, it was over in a little over a month," Mark muttered self-deprecatingly.

"The length of the conflict doesn't matter," the other man said, with an air of quiet certainty. "The greatest acts of heroism—of self sacrifice—are made in a matter of minutes."

"True." Dickey Joe set a beer in front of the man and nodded. "On the house. In honor of my boy here." And he gave Mark another of those massive shoulder claps that passed for affection between men.

A grin of genuine affection, tinged with more than

a little embarrassment, covered Mark's face. "Cut it out, Dickey Joe," he muttered.

But Dickey Joe had already leaned toward Erica and stuck a beefy red finger in her face. "See, this is how it happened. We went over there to teach that Saddam a lesson, right? And most of the war was them air strikes. Missiles laying waste to everything."

"Shock and awe," added the veteran with a relish that made Erica more than a little uncomfortable. "We shocked and awed 'em all right."

"But," Dickey Joe continued as though there had been no interruption. "What most people don't realize, is there was also a ground war going on, too."

"Kosijo," interrupted the other man, nodding knowingly.

"Kosijo," Mark repeated. His voice sounded oddly hollow, like he was trying to shake a memory that wasn't entirely pleasant and failing. "Kosijo."

Between Dickey Joe and the old veteran, the story came out: how Mark's reconnaissance unit had found themselves surrounded by Iraqi tanks in the middle of the desert with no communications and no backup. How they'd had no choice but to defend their position from hostile fire. How, at cost of life and limb, they'd managed to beat back the enemy, and in the process, convince Saddam's army that they didn't have a prayer in a ground war with the Coalition forces.

"How did you get hurt?" Erica asked, since the men telling the story seemed to care more for the Iraqi body count than anything else.

"An incoming grenade," Mark muttered. "Didn't dive for cover fast enough."

And Dickey Joe and the veteran picked up that thread and sewed another American flag with it, wrapping Mark from head to toe in glory.

Erica watched Mark's face closely. He hadn't said much while the men narrated his war experiences. Except for the occasional correction or clarification, he let their glowing words stand. But it was funny— he didn't look particularly proud of himself, either.

Which, for the man Erica had come to know, was oddly uncharacteristic.

When the story was done and the memories stopped playing, the bar was strangely silent. Erica looked around to find them all staring at Mark: Dickey Joe and the old veteran with a kind of quiet pride, Mary with eyes full of youthful admiration. Mark himself seemed unaware of them. He was frowning into his beer like it held important information. He looked like he'd gone somewhere else, somewhere he didn't want or need to be.

Erica didn't like that dark look on his face. Didn't like it one bit.

"Thank you." She let her fingers find his again, and when his face turned toward hers with a smirk of surprise, she knew she'd pulled him out of whatever mental hole he'd sunk into. "I appreciate hearing that story. Many men wouldn't have done what you did"—and here the old-timers launched into a chorus of "amens" accompanied by nods of agreement— "but after that Q & A today, I can honestly say I've seen firsthand how you handle pressure, so I'm not surprised."

He grinned at her and Erica felt that odd warmth spread from her heart to her cheeks to certain other regions of her body that shouldn't have had a thing to do with this man or his smile and yet always seemed to. It took her a second to recognize what was shining out of his eyes at her, it was so familiar and so foreign at the same time. But an instant later, she knew. It was the same happy pride she'd seen in her students' faces when, after long effort, they'd won her hard-earned praise.

He stood stiffly. In spite of the libation and the cool of the room, he still looked a little worse for wear. *Maybe he's coming down with something,* Erica thought, staring up at him with concern. *This schedule is enough to make anyone sick.*

"I've got to get Erica to the inn," he was telling them.

"You mean Mrs. Dickson's Bed and Breakfast up on North Street?"

Mark nodded. "The same."

"You'll like it there," Dickey Joe proclaimed. "Beautiful old building, restored and modernized. Much nicer than some stuffy old hotel."

"Sounds lovely," Erica said and rubbed her forehead a little. "I confess I could use a little rest."

"It's been a long day for her," Mark told them and there was no mistaking the possessive tone in his voice. Erica watched as the father and daughter exchanged a quick glance.

"Long morning for you, too. That plane ride didn't do either of us much good," Erica said, touching his shoulder.

"You're right," he agreed. "And we have to be at a town meeting at St. Matthew's tonight at . . . uh . . ."

"Seven," she finished for him.

"You're gonna have to start taking her with you everywhere, son," Dickey Joe laughed. "She's got a mind like a steel trap, that one. Even if she do come from up North."

"Well, we disagree on most things, but"—Mark cut a sly glance at Erica's face and watched her roll her eyes in mock annoyance—"she is a woman of many remarkable qualities."

"I know all about you Southern men and your flattery," she quipped. "And read my lips: It will not work."

I want to taste your lips, not read 'em.

The words were dancing in his eyes. Erica took one look at him and felt her cheeks getting hot, even though not a word had been spoken aloud. When she raised her eyes again, Mary was staring at her and she could have sworn the girl's expression said, "I know your secret."

Mark reached into his wallet and pulled out a bill.

"How many times do I have to tell you, your money is no good here?" Dickey Joe began, but Mark cut him off with, "As many times as I have to tell *you*: I pay my way. And add this gentleman's refreshments to my tab." He turned toward the old vet and offered him his hand. "In thanks for his kind words. And now, good people"—he reached for Erica's hand and caught it easily—"this good lady needs a little rest before our next engagement. She's got a whirlwind tour ahead."

Chapter 14

◇◇◇

"Very, very interesting . . ." Angelique considered the disruptive fax from the Q & A like she'd recently been appointed to Scotland Yard. "But not unexpected," she pronounced, handing it back to Erica and resuming the activity of applying a coat of body lotion to each of her long, slim legs. She had recently showered and her braids were wrapped in a towel. "I mean this is high-stakes politics, not the playground," she told her legs. "And you guys have been sparking some serious chemistry ever since that hearing. My only question is, do you think that thing was sent by the same person? The one who was sending those pictures to you?"

Erica nodded. "I'm sure of it. And I know it's that Bitsi chick."

Angelique squirted out another thick handful of lotion and started in on her arms and shoulders. "How do you know?"

"Well, first because she's that sort. Bitchy. Nasty. Can't stand for anything to be out of her control." She hesitated, not sure if she wanted to fully voice her suppositions. "I think . . . she's in love with him."

Angelique shrugged. "I don't doubt it," she said matter-of-factly. "And I'd buy that she'd send you nasty-grams. But I don't believe she'd jeopardize his reelection by sending that fax. It just doesn't make sense."

"Yeah, well, she's crazy," Erica muttered. "She's crazy, so of course it doesn't make sense. And I'm not the only one who thinks she's off her rocker," Erica continued, quickly filling Angelique in on the visit to Dickey Joe's Tavern and her brief but enlightening conversation with the timid Mary.

"Mary's probably in love with him, too." Angelique laughed. Erica watched her pace the hardwood floor of her spacious, airy bedroom in the lovely bed and breakfast Mark had chosen for them. In the time Erica had experienced her first adventures in Billingham, Angelique had carefully unpacked her suitcase and now pulled a pretty pink sundress from the closet. Apparently, she'd also eaten a nice lunch, as evidenced by the empty dishes on a little cart near the door. Erica's stomach growled in envy. All she'd gotten for her afternoon was a bunch of hard-to-answer questions and a sip of bitter-tasting beer.

And the pleasure of Mark Newman's company—which certainly had value, even if she wasn't exactly sure how much that value was.

"It's probably eating those two white women up that he's totally head-over-heels smitten with you," Angelique said, slipping the dress over her head. "They hate that you're gonna be the one to snuggle up at night with that tall, smart, handsome hunk of something-something!"

"I'm not doing any such thing," Erica said primly.

"Oh really?" Angelique's voice had that doubting-Thomas quality that Erica knew very well. "Do you mean to tell me you're not thinking about jumping his bones just about every time you're together? Because, as they say here in the South, 'that dog don't hunt.'"

Erica opened her mouth to make the token denial, then thought better of it. "Okay, okay. He's got . . . a certain physical appeal."

"Damn straight." Angelique dabbed some perfume behind her knees and on her wrists. "He's F-I-N-E. And smart. And powerful. All together, that's a helluva sexy combination. No woman in her right mind would walk away from that." She frowned. "Except maybe you."

"All right, all right. I admit I'm attracted to him. And sometimes I think . . ." but it was too hard to explain the way she sometimes felt in the man's presence. Like everything was going to be all right. Like there wasn't anything she couldn't do as long as he was near.

"Sometimes you think . . . ?" Angelique prompted, and when Erica looked up, the other woman had paused from the process of applying makeup and was watching her face.

Erica shook those feelings from her mind. "Sometimes I think," she finished quickly, "that we should just sleep together and get it over with. But that's stupid, too, because I'm not interested in just a physical thing! I want to get married again someday, Angelique. I want kids. I want more than just a good time. And when it comes right down to it, Mark Newman just isn't the one for all that." She shook her head. "He's not what I'm looking for in a man. Far from it."

"I see," Angelique said, but it was evident from the sound in her voice that she saw something far different. "And just what are you looking for again?"

"You know!" Erica exclaimed. And surely, as much

as they talked about men, Angelique must have known. Erica had only recited the list a few thousand times. "A politically, socially and globally aware man who honors a Higher Power and respects all human life. He should know what it means to be culturally oppressed and be a crusader against poverty, ignorance and violence," Erica reminded her, going through the litany as smoothly as she had ever done. "And it would be nice if he was a vegan, but I suppose I could deal with him being a vegetarian. Mark Newman is none of those things, trust me," she asserted, pushing aside the memory of how it had felt to be crushed in his strong arms or consumed by his hungry kisses. "Not one."

"Oh, I don't know," Angelique said slowly. "You may not agree with him, but the man is certainly politically, socially and globally aware."

"He is not," Erica insisted.

"All I'm saying is he's got to be just as well-informed as you are. Otherwise you two wouldn't have anything to argue about, right?"

Erica considered a moment. Angelique had a point, sort of.

"And didn't you tell me that he prays before eating? Sounds like a man who honors a Higher Power to me."

"Yes, but he doesn't honor human life. He doesn't honor life at all. He's killed people, for heaven's sake!"

There was a short silence before Angelique offered in a low voice: "It was a war, Erica. I know how you feel about war, and I respect that," she added quickly before Erica could launch into any of a thousand objections and counterpoints. "But once he was in it, what did you want him to do? Lie down and be slaughtered?" She sighed. "He might have killed some people, but he also saved some. Can't you give the man some credit for that?"

The golden ropes of her friend's argument laced around her like restraints. That and the story she'd been told from the old-timers in the bar about Mark's war experiences. "All the more reason for him to be an antiwar crusader now," she asserted after the feelings of pride and sympathy for Newman had dissipated. "All the more reason for him to hate violence of any kind."

"I'm absolutely positive the man doesn't love violence. And so are you, if you'll let go of your precious ideologies for just a minute," Angelique insisted, fastening a pair of small Diamonique earrings to her lobes before padding around the fluffy, be-pillowed bed to look for her shoes. "All in all, he sounds like your perfect match for the whole nine yards: marriage, family and white picket fence."

"Bite your tongue!" Erica heard her voice rising and felt the heat of her denial in her cheeks, but she couldn't stop herself. "First of all, he's still a Republican—and a politician! And besides, he eats meat. And he's white! Don't forget that one!" She shook her head. "This would never work, between us. Never."

"Then just sleep with him," Angelique said lightly. "Lighten up. Have some fun."

Erica frowned. "No."

Angelique sighed. "Okay, Erica. I give up. But I ask you: how many straight men, of any race, have you met who met any of these crazy criteria of yours?"

Erica fell silent, her brain working overtime toward an answer. There had been plenty of first dates with men met at a rally for this or a cause for that. And absolutely no second dates.

"That's what I thought," Angelique observed. "I

think you've got two lists, E. One you admit to and another that you hold in your heart. I mean, maybe what you like in a guy isn't that he believes in the right causes or eats the right food. Maybe what you want is someone passionate, someone honorable, someone who challenges you, who has a sense of humor. And it never hurts if he's sexy as all hell."

"He's not sexy as all hell."

"You just said he was."

"I did not. I just said . . ."

Angelique shook her head. "You know something, Erica? You're a hypocrite."

Hypocrite. The word stung like a slap. Erica opened her mouth, ready to launch into a full manifesto in her defense, but Angelique picked up her purse and headed toward the door, cutting off her retort with a dismissive, "Now go to your own room and think about it. I gotta go."

"Where?" Erica asked. "Where are you going?"

"Out."

"Out where? You don't a soul around here! Do you?"

A wide smile coursed across Angelique's face.

"I've got a meeting," she replied evasively. "And so do you. St. Matthew's Church, remember?"

Thank God for handicapped parking, Erica thought as they pulled into the church's parking lot. They would have been hard-pressed to find another space, as late as they were, and as crowded with cars as the lot was.

And it wasn't Erica's fault.

Mark had been late—almost a half hour late. He arrived smelling wonderful and in a fresh suit and tie—but not looking well. Not looking well at all.

Pale and sweaty. Gray shadows beneath his eyes.

That tightness around the lips that she'd begun to associate with pain. He looked like he was fully in the throes of a bad case of the flu.

"What's the matter?" Erica asked immediately, stepping close to him and swiping her hand across his forehead. It was cool and damp, not feverish as she had expected.

"Nothing," he muttered, and his lips quirked into that smirk she hated so much. "Musta eaten something that disagreed with me, that's all."

"You feel nauseous? What did you eat?"

His only response was an irritated frown. "I'm all right."

"What did you eat?"

He rolled his eyes. "I don't want a lecture, Erica."

"Just tell me, Mark."

He sighed. "It's Saturday."

"Chinese?"

He nodded. "From a takeout place, near my house." He grimaced. "I was starved, so I guess I ate too fast or something."

Erica frowned up at him. "Do you think you should call Bitsi? Cancel the evening?—"

"No." He shook his head. "It's all right. I'm already better." He tried for a smile and failed miserably. "My stomach's a lot less queasy than it was even an hour ago. I'll be all right. Besides"—he rubbed a palm over his lips and chin—"this close to an election, you show up, no matter what. Every appearance can make a difference."

"I thought you were way ahead. I thought—"

Another smirk of a smile. "I thought so, too. But after seeing that fax this afternoon, I'm beginning to wonder what's up."

"Do you know who sent it?"

"I have my suspicions," he muttered darkly. "And

I'll tell you about them, but not now. We need to get to this town meeting before I lose any more support."

"It's about time." The orange embers of a cigarette butt beamed evilly in the darkness of the church's carefully tended garden as Mark grabbed Erica's hand and limped quickly up the stone path toward the woman's dark silhouette. "Where the hell have you been?" Bitsi barked. In the stillness of the courtyard, her tone was irritated and commanding. Erica flinched. She sounded like she was the senator.

Apparently, Mark hadn't cared for her tone, either. "I told you: I wasn't feeling well," he snapped.

Even in the relative darkness, Erica saw the woman's thin lips crimp into a tight scowl. "Well," she drawled in a tone Erica had often used with her fourth graders. "You're gonna have to do better, Mark. These people vote. Last time they voted for you. Take them for granted and they won't do it again."

Mark nodded quickly, but Erica felt his fingers tighten around hers. She looked up into his face, but it was inscrutable in the darkness. "What do I need to know?" he asked.

"About what we expected," Bitsi muttered, tossing her cigarette onto the flagstones and fishing into her handbag to produce a notepad. "The perennial three: jobs, schools, taxes. And the new one." She cut her eyes at Erica. "The war. They still support it, but they want to know there are plans to bring the kids home."

Mark nodded. "Okay. Anything else?"

Bitsi's eyes slashed at Erica again. "They're a little curious about her. Most of them got that little fax, too." She said the word like it was something nasty she'd been forced to eat. "But if I were you, I really wouldn't get too far down that path with this crowd.

Save it for the debate day after tomorrow. Where you can get the most mileage out of her and this whole mess."

It's a good thing for Bitsi he's holding my slapping hand, Erica thought. *Otherwise . . .*

"Gee, Bitsi," Erica said, managing to keep her voice calm and sweet. "You really know how to hurt a girl. How much mileage has he gotten out of you?"

Bitsi ignored her. "We'd better get you in there," she said quickly, smoothing Mark's suit jacket around his shoulders with an almost maternal air. "I don't really care for this suit—it makes you look boxy—but oh well. And if I'd known you were looking this gray, I'd have brought my compact. Too late now." She tsk-tsk'd. "Hope they won't think you're sick. No one wants to vote for a man who looks like death warmed over." And she nodded toward the latticed windows of the sanctuary beyond.

Erica followed her gaze and saw what appeared to be a large multipurpose room, lined with folding chairs filled with people. The room was every bit as crowded as the high school auditorium had been. Apparently the folks of Mark's state took their politics very seriously.

"They're gonna have to take me 'as is' tonight," Mark said grimly. "More substance than form, I hope." And he started past her.

"Yes," Bitsi said slowly, surveying them coolly. "Only . . ."—she paused, milking the moment, before continuing with a demure, "Well, maybe it's not my place to say anything."

"Speak. You know I value your opinion." Mark said, but he was already making his way toward the entrance doors.

"Well . . ." Bitsi continued, and her normally sharp voice had a coy edge to it. "And this is only a suggestion. I wouldn't want anyone to think I'm *racist* or anything, but you might want to let go of Ms. Johnson's hand. I mean, we already have the implications of the fax to deal with, and" —she giggled a snide little giggle that wasn't a giggle at all—"she *can* walk for herself, right?"

There was a split second when Mark's face clamped in on itself and Erica thought Bitsi might get a taste of her boss's anger. As both women watched, Mark's face seemed to undergo half a dozen permutations as he put his aide's words through every possible intended meaning and a few that she might not have intended at all.

"I think I'll hold on to it a while longer, if it's all the same to you, Bits," he said in a low, calm voice, while those penetrating blue eyes seemed to measure the little woman from her tip to her toes.

"You're the boss, Boss," Bitsi said lightly, but her eyes crawled over Erica with a new intensity. "Now let's get a move on. The people are waiting."

The room was packed with white people—more white people than Erica could remember seeing in her life. Back in D.C. there were white people, true, but there were also Hispanic people and Asian people, African people and Jewish people—all kinds of people. Just about everywhere you went you'd see people of all different creeds and colors, mixing together in all kinds of ways.

"We're not in Chocolate City anymore," she murmured under her breath, looking around at the whiteness of this gathering. She craned her neck toward the back of the room and saw Angelique, sitting next to Chase Alexander, looking expectantly at the podium, the lone brown speck in the white sea that was the room.

As they entered, the whole room fell silent. There was none of the murmuring and muttering that had characterized the atmosphere in the high-school gym. It was quiet, reverent, as though she had walked into the church sanctuary in the middle of a service, rather than a political event in its multipurpose room. Erica felt suddenly uncertain, suddenly self-conscious. Every ugly thing she'd ever heard about Southern white folks crossed her mind. For a quick instant, a movie played in her head featuring nooses and lynch mobs, and she was pretty sure she shrank a little closer to Newman until she was able to clear it from her mind.

"I'm sorry I'm late, everyone. I had to retrieve our guest. You men know how our lovely ladies are," he drawled in a voice that exuded charm and he raised his arm to show the assembly their joined hands. "Folks, this is Miss Erica Johnson, the lady you've been readin' about, or maybe you've seen her on TV. She challenged me to answer some hard questions about the war, and accepted my challenge to hear the other side. I know some of you received something on your fax machines and you might have some questions. But we'll talk about that in a minute. For now, I'd like y'all to show her such a thorough dose of Southern hospitality she won't want to go back to Washington ever again."

These words were met with a roar of thunderous applause that filled Erica's ears like a sudden wave of love.

Still holding on to her, Mark limped his way down the aisles toward a little stage at the top of the room, interrupted every few steps by men and women who leaned out of their seats to shake his hand or wrap him in an embrace. To Erica's surprise, some of this welcome was extended to her as well, as men and women both stood to offer her their hands or arms. And it was then, and only then, that Mark Newman released her hand.

At last, when the applause had died and they'd made their way to the little dais, Mark accepted a microphone and parked himself in a chair. He shook hands with a man in a black short-sleeved shirt and white collar who introduced himself to Erica as "Reverend Knull," and with a middle-aged Congress woman who had an abundance of curly hair that looked like it had been last cut in the 1980s. Erica shook both their hands and sat in the metal folding chair they assigned her, smoothing her skirt a little and adjusting the folds of the T-shirt she had selected for the evening: IF THE PEOPLE WILL LEAD, THEIR LEADERS WILL FOLLOW.

Mark made a short speech, sounding stronger and healthier and more alive with every word he spoke. This time, however, he addressed the issue of the fax without taking any questions about it or their relationship, sounding annoyed with the whole thing.

I'm hurting his career, Erica thought. And instead of triumphant, the knowledge made her feel sad on so many levels that she wanted to burst into tears.

Hypocrite, she heard Angelique muttering in her ear. Erica glanced into the audience, but Angelique was giving Mark Newman her full attention and didn't seem to be all that interested in her best friend, who was quietly dying on the podium.

Because, sitting there, in front of all these good, churchgoing voters, Erica realized the woman was absolutely right.

She had fallen completely for Mark Newman, wrongheaded politics and all.

Right when, from all appearances, he'd reached the opposite conclusion about *her*.

"All right, folks," Mark said, settling himself into his chair and leaning toward the crowd. "I know you all have been waiting and you need to get on home in time to tuck in the kids. Some of y'all have livestock to check on, too, so I'll make my updates brief so we can get to your questions. Here's what I've been doing in Washington . . ."

Erica couldn't stop herself from staring at him, listening quietly while his voice gained energy and strength. He talked about farm legislation, conservation, taxes, and once again, she found herself impressed. He was wrong on the substance—and from time to time she had to fold her lips tight and remind herself that this was his show, not hers—but he was certainly knowledgeable and he managed to convey complicated concepts to his audience without talking down to them. When she looked away from him out into the sea of faces, it was obvious that his constituents were eating him up with a spoon. She peered around the room, taking them in. Most were between the ages of thirty and sixty, almost all paired off in couples, though here and there were the stray singles. And in a far corner, she saw a familiar-looking blonde head that she could have sworn belonged to Mary. But regardless of age and hair color, attire or education, all had the look of the middlingly prosperous, and of course they were all white.

Typical Republicans, Erica decided, finding her anger to hide her pain. She made a mental note to send these people a snapshot of the rest of the country just so they'd know there were black and brown, yellow and red people in it.

Then, from somewhere out in the crowd, a woman wailed. Instantly the room went still. Heads turned toward her as she buried her face in a tissue. A red-faced man with salt-and-pepper hair wearing a pair of faded jeans patted her shoulder awkwardly, looking as if he was only seconds from dissolving into tears himself.

"Maude and John Bunter. Their son was killed in Iraq," the Congresswoman whispered in Mark's direction. "They just found out a couple of days ago. Body hasn't even made it home yet."

But Mark was already moving. He moved slowly off the dais and down the aisle toward the couple, the soft *squish* of the tip of his cane countering the woman's anguished sobs.

Erica watched, like everyone else in the room, as he made a wounded soldier's slow progress toward the couple, watched as the people seated nearby yielded their places until Mark was standing right beside Maude and John Bunter.

"I grieve your loss." Mark's voice was soft, but it resonated in the multipurpose room. "All of us in this room, all of America grieves your loss," he continued gently. "Your son's sacrifice was not in vain. His dedication, his patriotism, his commitment to freedom. None of us will ever forget those things."

Maude Bunter nodded, tears rolling down her cheeks. "Thank you," she whispered.

"Yes," John Bunter added in a strained voice, offering Mark his hand. "Thank you, sir."

Mark stared at the bereaved father's hand for a moment. Then to their surprise, he bent down and enveloped the couple in an embrace. "I'm so sorry," Erica thought she heard him say. "He was a good kid."

Erica looked around the room. Many were weeping openly; others had their eyes closed as if in prayer. The others on the dais were staring at Mark, who still held the couple in an embrace, as if waiting. A feeling tugged at Erica's heart, and before she knew it she was standing with the microphone in her hand. From the back of the room, she saw Bitsi's face shift into an expression of horror, but she didn't let that stop her.

She opened her mouth.

She hadn't been sure what she was going to sing, only that she was going to. It was as if the voice of God was speaking directly to her heart right then, joining her hatred of the war with the spirit of grief in the room. And God had a song picked out.

"Be not dismayed, whate'er betide." Erica heard the old song come from a place deep inside her. "God will take care of you."

There was a split second when all of the eyes in the room turned toward her in surprise, and Erica wondered if she'd just made a terrible mistake. Even Mark's head turned toward her with an expression Erica couldn't decipher etched into the strong lines around his forehead and lips.

Then Angelique stood from her place at the back of the room and joined Erica in the old hymn.

"Beneath his wings of love, abide. God will take care of you," she sang, loud and slightly off-key. An instant later, Chase popped up beside her and to her surprise, the man had a lovely tenor that harmonized with Erica's soprano. And when other voices joined hers from the back of the room, the atmosphere in the room changed. And soon the whole room had filled with voices, joined together in the song as one.

Mark made his way back to the dais and Erica heard his voice, singing in a tone-deaf bass, as he took his place again. He cut a glance at her as the song concluded, and Erica saw his lips were curled into that little smile again. But there was something different in his eyes. Something warm and appreciative and . . .

Erica felt her heart do a funny little skipping, dipping thing that couldn't be a good sign.

"Thank you, Erica," he said softly. "I think we needed to be reminded that we're all in God's hands. And I know we all pray for the Bunters, for their son Abel. And we all pray for our fighting men and women, wherever they are."

"Amen," Erica whispered.

"All right," Mark said, briskly transitioning the meeting yet again. "I know y'all got questions and concerns. We've done enough talking from up here. Time to hear from you folks. We're your servants, remember? It's just like my friend Ms. Johnson's shirt says: 'If the people will lead, their leaders will follow.'" He reached into his jacket pocket and produced a small notebook and pen. "Tell me."

I believe all of us are guided by God away from our sorrows and toward our joys. It's just sometimes we're too damn stupid and stubborn to recognize our joys when they find us.

—Mark Newman

Chapter 15

He could have just dropped her off, but something took over his reason and he dragged his bum leg up the five steps into the old Victorian home. And he would have left her after she crossed the threshold of the bedroom reserved for his special guests, a sunny room overlooking North Street with a wide bay window, huge four-poster bed, and a little sitting room off to the side. But he definitely should have left before Erica Johnson opened the door and led him inside.

Unfinished business was banging at the front of his brain, tingling down the back of his spine, brushing at the corners of his consciousness.

Every minute she was near him, the feeling grew stronger, harder to deny, harder to laugh about, harder to dismiss. But tonight, tonight when she'd burst into song and transformed a moment into something so intimate and so beautiful . . .

Mark felt the last of his resistance evaporate. He would have this woman in his arms tonight. He would have this woman's body entwined with his tonight. He would have this woman's essence joined with his tonight or willingly die with the effort.

"Well," she was saying, and he knew she felt it, too, "do you want me to come with you to the rally tomorrow?"

The sound of her voice faded away, and all he could hear was his own heart beating. He watched her lips, full and inviting, making words that evaporated unheard as desire thrilled along every nerve in his body. He closed his eyes and inhaled. Her image was still imprinted on his eyelids, the smell of her perfume filled his nostrils.

"Mark? Did you hear me? Do you want me to—"

I want you. I want you tomorrow, I want you the day after that . . . I want you. Right now.

Words weren't required when actions spoke volumes. Mark let his instinct take over, trusting it was the right act at the right time.

"Yes," he said, letting the cane fall. He reached for her, leaning into her for support as both his arms encircled her. "Yes, Erica. I want you," he murmured, as those bottomless brown eyes rose to his face, full of love, full of pride. "My Erica," he whispered.

"Oh, Mark," she breathed into his ear. "Mark."

It was all the encouragement he needed. He pressed her closer to him, caressing the soft curves of her body as he buried his hungry mouth in hers, unleashing the passion that had lain dormant inside him since a mugger's bullet had taken Katharine from him years before.

Before I met Mark Newman, I'd never have come here. But now that I'm here, I have to say . . . it's a wonderful place.

—Erica Johnson

Chapter 16

✕✕✕

She should have pushed him away, that's what she should have done.

She should have shoved him hard enough to make it perfectly clear how she felt about him—him with his smirking arrogance and his Southern charm.

She should have slapped the teeth out of his warmongering, Dixie-loving, all-wrong Republican mouth.

But that kiss . . .

That kiss . . .

That kiss was a stealth missile all its own, guaranteed to shock and awe all of her resistance away. And under the command of that kiss Erica wrapped her arms around him and kissed him back, her body pressed against his like her life depended on him. Sure, he was wrong about every issue under the sun. But he was smart and kind and generous and heroic and—cane or no, Republican or no, white or no—sexy as all hell.

This is crazy, she thought as the kiss deepened to a second and third, and then so many she lost count, as she felt his lips traveling down the side of her face and neck, along her collarbone and the delicate skin of her shoulders.

This is insanity, she thought, as his fingertips found their way beneath the T-shirt he hated so much to caress her breasts, and then, with the masterful, arrogant certainty that was his way, to dispose of the top all together.

This is wrong, she thought, yanking his shirt off and feeling the smooth, hard skin of his chest, cool under her fingers and lips as she pressed her face against him.

This will never work, she thought as he backed her into the bedroom and onto the thick, white goosedown comforter.

There weren't many opportunities for thinking after that.

"Now," Erica moaned, shivering with urgency as he peeled off her skirt and the lacy panties she'd donned for reasons she wasn't sure she would have admitted only a few hours ago. "Now."

And Mark Newman was nothing if not a man of action. He said nothing, but when she opened her eyes, a naked man stood before her, balanced on one foot, with a grim "Get 'er done" expression on his face and a condom in his hand. Erica glanced down at his manhood rising from a nest of dark hair with relief. What they said about white men really wasn't true . . . at least not about this one.

She noticed he had to hop a little to swing the stiff left leg onto the bed, but after that, she forgot about his impairments because the man didn't have any. As if feeling her own fire, he dispensed with further prelude and took his position between her waiting thighs.

If she hadn't been so wet, so ready for him, it might have hurt, he thrust so confidently, so certainly and so immediately into her warmth.

God help me, Erica thought as her body stretched to accommodate his urgency. *Good, good God . . .*

"Oh yes," he murmured in her ear, like a man returning to a beloved home after years away. "Yes."

And like he'd known her body all his life, he found his stroke and proceeded to work her like he was getting paid. Erica wrapped her legs and arms around him and held on while he pounded into her with single-minded intensity, letting nothing, not her cries or her moans, her sighs or her curses, stop him. Erica lost herself in waves of ecstasy . . . once, twice and was cresting a third time when she heard him whisper, "I'm coming . . . I'm . . ."

Then his body tensed and he let out a groan that sounded like the last gasp of a dying man. Erica gripped him tightly with everything she had: arms, legs, pelvis and privates as he shuddered against her and collapsed, slick with sweat. And still Erica held on, savoring the last of his erection until, a second later, another orgasm shattered and broke and she squirmed beneath him, her insides clenching and unclenching, her mind gone, her eyes closed.

It took a few seconds for consciousness to float back into her body. Erica let out a sigh of pure contentment, opened her eyes . . .

And looked up into Mark Newman's smirking face.

"I knew you wanted me," he drawled, sounding completely self-satisfied and far more annoying than he should have at a moment like this. "I knew it the very first day."

I just slept with the most infuriating man alive, Erica thought. But instead of smacking him, she laughed. "Your post-coital banter needs some work, Newman. Besides, it's *you* who wanted *me*."

"Desperately," he agreed. "Now, admit it," he said

into the skin along her neck, setting Erica ablaze with desire again. "You wanted me." He kissed her again, soft feathery kisses that traveled from her forehead and along the side of her face. "You still want me. Admit it," he whispered. "You want me."

"No," Erica breathed, but it was all getting confusing again. "No."

"Yes." The word was a whisper against her lips. "Say it."

"No." Erica protested again, but now those insistent, demanding lips were on hers again and her resistance was weakening. "No . . ."

"Yes." His lips were still nuzzling hers. "Say it, Erica. I need to hear you."

"Yes." Erica sighed, pulling his face close to hers again. "Yes, yes . . ."

"I knew it." He chuckled. "From the very first day."

Erica rolled her eyes, but she couldn't help smiling at him. "Okay, okay. No need to gloat."

"Oh yes, there is." He rolled to his back and pulled her against him. "It's not every day I convert a liberal to the cause."

"Wait just a minute." Erica bristled. "You haven't converted anyone to anything. Let's just get that straight. I'm not changing my party affiliation just because of a few body fluids."

His laughter rumbled in his chest, filling her ear. "Somehow, I wouldn't have expected any less of you." He sighed. "You know, we're in for it now."

Erica lifted her head to peer into his face. He looked a thousand times better than he had earlier in the afternoon, and Erica wasn't sure if his improvement could be attributed to the successful digestion of bad Chinese food, the close of a long day or a solid orgasm. "What do you mean 'in for it'?"

He quirked her a quick smile that never reached his eyes. "The fax. The letters. The campaign. The whole *ten* yards. And now I can't even deny that there's something going on." He brushed a kiss against the side of her forehead.

"Oh, you could."

He shook his head. "Couldn't. This might come as a shock to you, but I'm a terrible liar."

Erica considered him a moment. His bright eyes were as wide open and clear as September skies, and she read in him the exact depth of his feelings for her.

It was terrifying.

Almost terrifying enough to make her want to wriggle out of his arms, run for the bathroom, lock the door until the next flight back to the District could be arranged. Almost.

What the hell am I doing? she asked herself for what felt like the millionth time. *What the hell am I doing here with this man?*

"You're right. If you're going to keep looking at me like that, it's better if you just tell the truth, Mr. Senator."

"Am I that obvious?"

"Am I that obvious?" Erica mimicked. She pinned his face between her fingers. "Your eyes gave you away from Jump Street, Mark. The way you looked at me . . ."

His muscular chest rose and fell with the weight of his sigh. "Yeah, I know. Katharine always said I was in the wrong business for a man who can't lie worth a damn. She always said it would catch up to me one day. Looks like she was right."

He fell silent for a moment. Erica let him process the memory of his late wife into the moment before asking, "You haven't been with anyone since she died?"

Mark shook his head. "I've had my chances. But . . ." he shrugged away the thought. "I dunno. People tell me I took her loss pretty hard. I guess I did. I was real angry for a real long time, I know that. I still am."

His face clamped down again. Erica watched the tight lines appear in his jaw and his forehead and sighed.

"It isn't right, what happened to Katharine. I know that. But crime is what happens when people feel desperate, Mark. When there aren't better options for them to get what they need."

"No," he interrupted, sliding away from her and out of bed. "There's no justification for murder. There's no justification for killing an innocent person! An innocent woman who just happened to come between some dumbass and a few dollars."

"Mark," Erica insisted, sitting up. "Don't you know anything about the kids who did it? Didn't you hear anything about how they grew up? What they were up against?"

His head swung from side to side and she watched the harsh, remote mask return to his features.

"There is no justification for killing," he repeated. "None."

"Oh really? Then I guess you don't believe in war any more," Erica shot back at him. "Wait a minute. That's right. You're a big *fan* of wars!"

"That's different, Erica, and you know it," he said with a sigh. "Nobody supports war. Least of all anyone who's been in one. But sometimes they're necessary, that's all."

"Why?"

He stood at the end of the bed, naked as the day he was born, glaring at her. "What are you talking about?"

"I'm talking about war, Mark. I'm talking about the

slaughter of innocents with air strikes and 'shock and awe' and all this other bullshit you believe in—"

"For the last time, defending this country is not bullshit!" he roared at her.

"It wouldn't be, if we were actually under attack!"

"What did you call September eleventh, Erica?" he countered, anger making his voice hard and deadly. "What did you call planes flying into the Pentagon, leveling the World Trade Center? What the hell do you call that, other than spilling innocent blood for no goddamned reason?"

"I call that wrong, Mark," Erica agreed, crawling across the bed toward him. "And you're right, we need to protect ourselves. But war spills plenty of innocent blood, too. What about the Iraqi women and children, Mark? Innocent people just trying to go about their business while bombs fall from the sky. In a way they're just like Katharine."

His hand came up like an axe, chopping up her words.

"You don't understand," he argued, limping across the room to retrieve his pants. "You don't understand the reasons for wars, you don't understand the policy decisions that make it necessary, you don't understand the pride I felt—I still feel—in my service."

Erica watched him. His face crunched in pain as he bent to retrieve his pants from the floor. He hopped on his good leg toward the bed and leaned on its corner for support. Erica crept closer to him and for the first time she saw the scars.

They were evil-looking: a twisted devil's railroad of thick, ugly welts that traveled the distance from the middle of his thigh down to his calf. His knee was a misshapen ball in the middle of his leg.

"Oh Mark," she murmured, running her fingertips gently over the scarred flesh. "It's horrible."

He seemed at first not to have any idea what she was talking about. "It's not so bad," he said at last. "At least I still have a leg."

"I know." Erica shook her head. "But it's so unnecessary."

"Freedom isn't unnecessary, Erica," he said in that tight voice that meant they were still arguing. They could either spend the remainder of their time together fighting, or . . .

Erica made a decision, quick as flash. She kissed the kneecap.

"You're wrong," she murmured into his skin. "But just this once, I'll overlook it."

His laughter filled the air above her head.

"You'll overlook it, huh"?" he rumbled.

"Yes." Erica kissed the inside of his thigh and heard the laughter ease into a deep, slow breath. "Just this once. Now, let's make love, not war."

Her lips traveled up his leg toward his groin and when he spoke again, his voice sounded raspy and tortured, and she knew her kisses were finding their mark.

"What are you doing to me, Erica Johnson? You and me. It's just crazy."

"I know," Erica murmured, nuzzling her way toward the most sensitive spot of his anatomy. He shifted slightly, settling himself down on the bed, surrendering to her ministrations.

"I mean," he groaned, "you do something to me . . . something. . . ." He sighed again. "I don't know . . ."

"I know," Erica agreed, moving her mouth closer to his source, fingering his shaft and watching his face change as desire overtook him. "I mean, you're totally wrong for me. In every way. Look at you: You're a white, war-loving, Right Wing, whack-a-doodle."

"Uh huh," he agreed, closing his eyes and pulling

her head closer to him. "And you're a left-of-center hippy chick with the dumbest T-shirts I've ever seen."

"You forgot black."

"I didn't forget," he whispered. "It just didn't seem important at this exact moment."

"Oh . . . that's good of you," Erica murmured, and swallowed him whole.

The ringing woke them both. Erica sat up with a start and was surprised to find herself nestled in the crook of Mark's bare arm, as comfortable and relaxed as if she'd made a practice of being there for the last several decades. As for the man himself, he started awake the second she moved, and she couldn't help but notice that his first instinct was to pull her back into his arms.

"Phone," Erica mumbled, taking in the dark stillness of the room around them as she deciphered the tones of the ring. "Yours?" she asked, not recognizing its melody.

"Yep," he murmured, struggling to right himself on his bad knee.

"Oh cut it out. You're going to fall over. I'll do it," Erica volunteered, diving for the clothing scattered between the two rooms until she found the offending instrument. "Here."

"Yeah?" he groaned into the phone. "What do you want?"

Erica watched his face change from annoyance to concern. "You're kidding," he exclaimed, turning his wrist to reveal the face of his watch. "Oh crap. Okay, okay. I'll be there in . . . no, uh . . . I'm not at home. I need at least thirty minutes." He hung up. "Help me," he barked in Erica's direction. "It's six fifteen. I'm supposed to be on a plane out to Harpersville—"

"Fifteen minutes ago," Erica finished for him, remembering the schedule. She sprang off the bed and scrambled through the suite for the rest of his clothes. "Get in the shower."

He shook his head. Erica noticed that he again looked too pale and he was rubbing at his abdomen as though the stomachache he'd been complaining about was back. She was about to ask him about it when he said, "Can't wear the same clothes. I gotta go home."

"Home?" Erica glanced at the clock on the nightstand. "How far away is that?"

"Just a couple of minutes." He sighed and slid off the bed, testing his knee with a grimace of pain. "Crap, crap, crap . . ." he muttered, hobbling around the room, reacclimating himself to standing upright.

Erica bent, gathering his clothes into a pile. "Boy, are you in the weeds, brother."

"You can say that again. Bitsi's furious." He sighed. "It's going to be a tough day."

"For me too," Erica agreed. "I have to go shopping for a formal dress."

Mark's laughter rang through the room. "Right, sure," he said sarcastically. "Tough."

Erica shook her head. "Laugh if you want. When it comes to clothing, men definitely have it made. You wear a classic tux, you're fine, great. For a woman . . . it's a whole other ball game."

He limped over to her. Erica expected him to grab his clothes from her hands and begin throwing them on, but instead he leaned down to kiss her forehead. "I'm sure whatever you pick will be lovely," he murmured.

It was a moment of intimacy unlike anything Erica had ever experienced in her life. Her heart took a long, slow elevator ride into the pit of her stomach and she felt her body flooding with a fresh wave of desire. If only he didn't have to go.

"Go," she told him, managing a smile in spite of the fact that she wanted to grab him and pull him down on top of her to continue the loving that yesterday had begun. "Bitsi's waiting. From everything I've seen, you don't want to be on Bitsi's bad side."

"Neither do you. You'd better get ready."

Erica frowned. "What do I have to do with it?"

"Bitsi's not going with me. She's spending the day with you. She's going to help you get around town, find a dress."

"Me?" Erica shook her head. "Oh no. Keep that crazy bitch away from me, Mark. I'm not kidding. Take her with you or something. Anything. Just keep her the heck away from me."

He rolled his eyes. "She's not out to get you, Erica. In case you haven't noticed, you haven't got any more of those photos since we got here."

"How convenient," Erica countered. "She knows you've got undercover officers stationed here and there. That's why she switched methodologies. Now she's faxing your constituents."

"Not this again. I told you before: Bitsi would never do that." He spoke the words in flat, closed denial. "Never."

"How can you be so sure?" Erica insisted. "How—"

"Because I am." He leaned against the bed, balancing himself as he stepped into his pants. For a second, Erica forgot her arguments in the lean muscles of his arms and chest, his legs and thighs. "Whoever sent those pictures must still be in Washington." His head wagged from side to side. "She's not out to get you, Erica."

"Was she out to get Mary?"

His eyes snapped to her face.

"What do you know about that?" he demanded.

Erica blinked her surprise. "Nothing, really . . . except what I gleaned from what little Mary said." She quickly related her trip to the ladies' room with the shy young woman.

Mark listened avidly, and then crossed the room and settled himself back on the edge of the bed with a sigh. "Okay, look. I'm going to tell you this, but you've got to promise me you'll treat this with absolute confidentiality."

Erica sank down on the bed beside him. "You have my word, Mark. Anything you have to tell me is strictly between us."

He gave her a quick, grim nod. "All right," he said as though he were still wrestling mightily with the decision. "All right. It's true there's bad blood between Bitsi and Mary. Very bad blood."

"But why?"

Mark fixed those crystal blue marbles on her face with the seriousness of the grave. "Because like most women, they're both desperately in love with me."

All that is needed for evil to triumph, is for good men to do nothing.

—Edmund Burke

Chapter 17

‹◊›

Mark drove the short distance between Dickson's Inn and his house with the windows down, drinking in the cool predawn air, savoring the memory of being with Erica Johnson. He could still smell her perfume on his body, feel the pressure of her touch and the sound of her laughter in his ears . . .

Because laugh is what she did when he told her about Bitsi and Mary. And not in a good way. Powerless to stop it, he'd watched her face harden as soon as the words were out of his mouth.

"Of course they are," she said, her voice dripping with bitter sarcasm. "*All* women are hopelessly in love with you. I should have expected that." And then she laughed that laugh that set Mark's jaw on edge. "Really, Mark, you got me that time." And even worse than the sound of that hardnosed laugh was the fact that she moved her sweet-smelling self off the bed away from him.

"I'm serious, Erica," he insisted.

"Oh, I know," she said lightly, and then to his dismay, she covered her curvaceous brown body with a robe and went about the process of selecting the day's T-shirt from the stack in her suitcase. "Believe me, I know."

"I'm not being arrogant."

"Arrogant? No, not you!" she exclaimed, and there was no mistaking the derision in her voice.

If he'd had a grain of sense, he realized now, he'd have kept his mouth shut. But instead, he dug his hole a little deeper by insisting, "I can't help it if it's true."

"Well." She whirled toward him, clutching a little cosmetics case to her chest. "I guess I'm just another link in your chain then, right?"

Crap.

Too late, he understood that he'd said it all wrong and now she thought . . . she thought . . . well, he wasn't exactly sure what she was thinking. Only that it was something she shouldn't be.

"Erica," he began. "C'mon. I didn't mean it like that. I just meant—"

"I know what you meant, Mark," she said in a calm, chilly voice that shut him out as thoroughly as if she'd slammed a door in his face. "You'd better get moving. I'm going to get a shower." Then she really did slam a door in his face, disappearing into the bathroom without another word.

I'm an idiot, Katharine, Mark confided as he climbed into Old Red and maneuvered through the dark streets. Something about being back in Billingham always brought her near to him. Sometimes when things were quiet and still, like they were now, he could almost feel her presence again.

I'm an idiot with a whole lot of explaining to do. I'm an idiot who's got a lot of changing to do . . . if I'm going to keep this woman near me.

He could almost imagine his wife in the car beside

him. He could almost smell her perfume wafting through the open windows to tickle his nose.

Every woman's in love with you, Mark. He could hear her voice, teasing him in his mind. *But what about you? Who do you love? And if you love her, did you remember to tell her?*

Crap. I knew I was forgetting something.

He heard her laughter in his head: musical, loving and light. In that instant he made his decision.

He'd finish the business in the only way he knew how. When the time was right, he'd make her know how he felt. He'd make her know that he was serious and there wasn't a man or woman alive who'd stop him.

He drove through the quiet suburbs of Billingham to the leafy Victorian he and Katharine had called home. In the driveway, Mark sat for a minute, staring at the house.

For the first time in years seeing the place didn't feel like a punch in the stomach. The garden was as well-tended as when Katharine was alive, thanks to the ministrations of the lawn service he hired. With wisteria climbing up the porch trellis, the porch swing squeaking back and forth in the gentle dawn breeze and light shining from somewhere deep in the house, the place almost looked lived in. But Mark knew better. Inside he'd find weeks of mail stacked up by the housekeeper, and everything perfectly in its place in the way that only an unlived-in home could be. And the silence.

Mark sighed. He opened the door and slid out of the truck, reaching back inside to grab his cane off the gun rack. He fingered his pocket for the key and limped up the curving sidewalk as quickly as he could. The three steps of the front porch felt a little like high hurdles, but he reminded himself of the hot shower to come, gritted his teeth and climbed them. He had opened the screened door and bent toward the lock when he felt it.

The odd but unmistakable feeling of being watched by unseen eyes.

Mark looked around, immediately on his guard. He pressed the lever on the hook of his cane and heard the blade slide into readiness.

The neighborhood was quiet as it should have been at this hour of the morning. Across the street, a sprinkler system swished water on an already green lawn. Mark considered the block, but there was nothing really unusual: homes quiet and still, cars sitting in driveways like they were resting, not a soul moving anywhere on the street.

But the feeling was still with him, and he couldn't stop himself from calling out, "Who's there?"

He got no answer but the rustling leaves and the dancing shadows on his lawn.

Mark took a halting step back to the stairs, craning his neck toward the shadows. He thought of Buddy, the old reliable hound who'd lived with him in this house until it became obvious that Mark's travels would take him too far from home to care for the animal. The dog had the best nose in three counties, there wasn't a lick of doubt about it. If there were someone lurking around the house, Buddy would have known it.

But there was no Buddy to rely upon, just Mark and his own instincts, once honed sharp by military training, but now, in the long years since, he couldn't be sure.

He limped slowly down the porch steps, his cane out in front of him like a bayonet.

"I know you're there," he called into the darkness

in his sternest, most commanding voice. "Show yourself."

The breeze whistled through the leaves of the sycamore tree, but there was no other response.

He wasn't sure how long he stood there, inquiring into the darkness and getting no reply, but when the minutes ticked into the double digits and there was no other sound but the gentle wind, he slowly relaxed his guard, hoisted himself back up the porch stairs and limped into the house.

He knew instantly that the danger hadn't passed.

First of all, there was a brightness at the back of the house that there shouldn't have been, as though all the lights were on at the rear of the house.

And then there was the sound: a low hum of machinery that Mark didn't recognize. It sounded like it was coming from the little room to the left of the kitchen that he and Katharine had converted to an office years ago.

Mark stopped in the foyer, catching the screened door before it could slam behind him, his mind racing through the possibilities. There was a revolver in a metal box in a kitchen cabinet, and his hunting rifle was in an upstairs closet. But neither weapon was easily accessible. Getting either would take time, make noise.

And he didn't want to make noise. He wanted to find out who was in his house and why.

Fifteen years ago, before the injury, he knew he could have taken an intruder with his bare hands, silent as death itself. But these days it would be harder, especially if the person was armed and expecting him. Especially with his knee still tender from the exertion in the pizzeria and the stress of the campaign trail. But he knew he'd have to take his chances. He offered up a prayer to God, and then moved through the foyer toward the bright lights of the kitchen as soundlessly as possible.

He could see nothing but the outline of fluorescent light through the closed swinging door that separated him from the kitchen. He listened hard, but all he could hear was that mechanical sound, buzzing and whining softly and insistently. Mark pushed at the swinging door and stepped into the kitchen, his cane out in front of him like a sword.

There was no one there.

The room was bright with light and completely empty. The back door swung open to the night, sending the gentle aromas of the garden and little else into the room, and the sense of the house being occupied left Mark's consciousness. Someone had been here: that was patently obvious. But that someone was now gone, leaving nothing but the lights on and the door wide open to mark their presence.

And that sound.

Mark moved quickly through the kitchen, following the noise to his office.

He didn't need to turn on any lights here either. The sound was coming from a copy machine: The tiny desktop model he'd bought for this space years ago was working overtime, its little motor squealing with the effort of producing copy after copy. The small machine's output tray was full to overflowing and the floor was littered with the excess. Mark stumped over to the desk and grabbed a copy from the top, the paper still warm from the machine.

It was a copy of a picture.

Or rather, a copy of a copy of a picture, gray and grainy, hard to distinguish at first if you didn't know what you were looking at.

But Mark knew exactly what he was looking at, and a sudden flame of embarrassment lit his cheeks.

Because he was holding in his hands a very blurry, very grainy photograph of himself in the most compromising of positions with a very lovely and very naked Erica Johnson.

Cursing, Mark jammed it deep into his pocket and stumped out of the house, not even bothering to lock the door behind him. As he headed toward Old Red, he heard the sound of a car engine springing to life on his otherwise silent street, saw the headlights as it sped up the street away from him.

He thought he recognized both car and driver: a nondescript rental driven by a man in sunglasses and a baseball cap.

He hopped into Old Red as fast as his damaged body would allow, throwing the cane down onto the seat beside him. He gunned the engine, sending the tires squealing down the driveway as the old truck roared into the street and into the night.

He'd gone about a mile when he realized the guy had too much of a lead. The only way he'd catch up would be to break every traffic law known to man.

Reluctantly, Mark turned the truck around and headed back home, his fury rising with his certainty. He'd lost the guy, but for the first time, he thought he understood exactly what was going on, and he knew exactly what to do about it.

I'm not supposed to want him to win—I mean, he believes in all the wrong things. But I don't want him to lose, either. He's wrong, but if there have to be wars, if there have to be soldiers, I'd like for them all to be as careful, deliberative and as principled as Mark Newman.

—Erica Johnson

Chapter 18

◇◇

She had just stepped out of the shower when some-one knocked on the door.

For a second her heart leaped with the hope that it might be Mark. That he might have thought about himself a minute and come back to apologize.

But there was no way that was possible. By now he was on a plane, on his way to stump for reelection in another town—another town where all the women were as desperately in love with him as all the women here.

Including you?

The question rose in her mind as though asked by a stranger.

Fortunately, there was another, more insistent tap on the door and she chose to answer it.

"Ms. Johnson?" Erica recognized the kindly voice of the B and B owner, Mrs. Dickson. "I have some breakfast for you. May I come in?"

"Sure," Erica hollered, toweling off quickly and reaching for her favorite pair of jeans and the top T-shirt on the pile in her suitcase, a faded old tie-dye that read WAR IS SO LAST CENTURY. "I'll be out in a second."

"I'll just set it here, out in the sitting room," the woman called, the nearness of her voice indicating that she was already in that space. "And you have a phone message from Bitsi Barr. She'll be over to take you dress shopping at seven. Your friend Ms. Dawson is already gone. She said she'd meet you back here in time for the party this evening."

"Thank you," Erica replied.

"Is everything all right?" Mrs. Dickson asked as Erica entered the room.

She had those bright, interested, in-your-business eyes, hidden behind a pair of rimless spectacles, and the habit of pursing her lips when she wasn't using them to speak. She wasn't an old woman by any stretch of the imagination—Erica pegged her as late forties or early fifties—but her old-lady busy-body quality seemed to add ten years to her face.

"Fine, thanks," Erica said, forcing her voice to brightness. For a second, the woman's query seemed to encompass far more than it appeared. Erica took a quick but casual glance around the room, checking to make sure there was neither shoe, nor belt, nor boxer shorts left anywhere visible. "Just fine."

The woman's eyes darted around the room, following her own. "Did you sleep well?"

Erica pushed down the memory of her erotic evening with Mark Newman and replied simply, "Just lovely," with her widest smile.

"That's great," the other woman replied with an equal hardiness, which Erica found just a tad suspicious. "I thought you might have been working late."

Erica frowned. "Working late?"

Mrs. Dickson pursed her lips. "I could have sworn I saw the senator's old red truck out front until very late last night."

Or very early this morning, she might as well have said.

A flush of heat crept up Erica's throat. Exactly what was she supposed to say: No? Yes? Was this some kind of secret dalliance or open affair? What the heck were they doing?

Erica opened her mouth, then thought better of it and simply let the woman reach whatever conclusion silence required her to reach.

"Well," Mrs. Dickson said with one last look around the room. "I guess I better let you eat. I've known Bitsi since high school and she's a lot of things, but she's never late."

"I'll bet," Erica muttered, before remembering that for all she knew, Ellen Dickson and Bitsi Barr were best friends. "Thanks for breakfast."

"No problem. Comes with the room," the woman answered cheerfully and finally turned to go. "Oh. What's this?" she asked, stooping toward the floor.

Erica felt her heart stop. Mark had left something! What was it? His airplane ticket? A copy of that insidious fax? A used condom?

"It's for you," Mrs. Dickson murmured, turning a crisp, white envelope over between her fingers before handing it to Erica. "Gee." She scratched her head and pursed her lips so deliberately her glasses hitched an inch on her nose. "I could have sworn that wasn't there when I came in." She shook away her confusion with a chuckle. "Maybe my husband is right. He swears since we started running this inn, I've started losing my mind. Just leave the dishes there when you're done. I'll get them when I come in to make the bed later."

"Thanks," Erica responded, waiting for the door to close behind the woman before sitting down at the little table. She set the envelope on the tray and poured herself a cup of coffee before reaching for it again.

It was light, and Erica could tell it contained only a single piece of paper. Her name appeared in dark type across the face. It had the look of one of those official communications—so black-and-white, so crisp —that Erica expected a list of the day's itinerary or an outline of the Who's Who of their evening soiree.

Or one of those photographs.

Only Mark was right. There hadn't been a photograph since they'd left Washington.

Erica slid a finger under the flap of the envelope and pulled out its innards, flipping the paper open. A sick feeling rocked her stomach like she'd been sucker punched.

A grainy copy of herself and Mark Newman entangled like longtime lovers on Mrs. Dickson's white four-poster glared at her from inside. With trembling hands, Erica turned the paper over, but this time there was nothing—no words, no threats, no nothing.

"How. . . ?" she murmured in a trembling voice, glancing around the room. "How. . . ?"

Erica frowned in confusion, looking around the room again. The bedroom shades were still tightly drawn, and it was impossible to see in from the outside. She stalked into the sitting room. Mrs. Dickson had raised the shades in this room, letting the already bright light of a new day, but when Erica pulled them again, the room was shuttered and dark. There was no light coming from outside, and no way anyone from the outside could have seen in. In fact, the photos looked like they had to have been taken from inside the bedroom. But that was impossible, wasn't it?

Surely she and Mark would have noticed if someone else was in the room, wouldn't they?

Mark.

His name rose to her lips as automatically as her next breath, and instantly his face, his smell, the feel of him was in her mind.

Did he know? Had he, too, received this—this picture, this warning, this—

Automatically, she reached for the cell phone in its clip on the hip of her jeans, and then thought better of it. If someone were taking pictures, could they also be intercepting calls?

Shaking, nervous where only moments ago she'd felt completely safe, Erica rose and hurried into the bedroom, checking the ceiling and walls, and then the bed itself. Not that she knew for certain she'd recognize the camera that could have caught such an explicit image, but it was the only thing she could think of to do.

But of course, amateur that she was, she found nothing—nothing at all that looked anything like a bug, a camera or anything of the kind.

Calm down, she told herself. *Calm down and think.*

She sank down on the bed and closed her eyes, forcing herself to take some deep breaths as she asked herself over and over again, *Why? Why would she do such a thing? What kind of crazy woman would go so far, and what would she do next?*

There were supposed to be plainclothes police around here somewhere. There was supposed to be protection. Erica hurriedly stuffed the photo back in its envelope and rushed toward the door, just as a tart rapping shook it. Before Erica could reply, Bitsi Barr yanked it open.

"Are you ready?" she barked, flicking out her wrist to consult the time. "They're waiting for us."

"Sure," Erica said, far more casually than she felt. She crammed the photo into the back pocket of her jeans and reached for her purse, wishing that at least Angelique was around to watch her back.

But Angelique had become mysteriously unavailable for a good deal of this trip.

Bitsi's eyes swept over Erica's T-shirt, reading silently. She crimped her tight little lips into a frown of disapproval. "Is that what you're wearing today? Don't you own anything else?"

Erica ignored her questions in favor of one of her own. "Have you seen any of Sergeant McAfee's people? Mark said they were around."

"Sure, they're around," Bitsi said, as though she were completely uninterested in this topic. "Are you ready?"

"Sure," Erica said hesitantly. "Only I was just hoping I could maybe see one of the cops for a minute."

Bitsi's sharp eyes fixed on Erica's face. "Why?" she demanded with such sudden force and nastiness that Erica stepped back a pace. "What do you need a cop for?"

Erica froze. There was something almost threatening in the woman's manner, and for a second, Erica was almost too afraid to push the matter.

This woman's seriously crazy.

The thought popped in and out of her mind like one of those annoying advertisements on the Internet. Erica hesitated for only a second while her backbone snapped back into place. She glared at the woman with her hardest, steeliest I'm-in-charge-of-this-playground gaze.

"I think you know, Bitsi," she said, don't-mess-with-a-sister in her voice.

Now it was Bitsi's turn to step back. Fear glittered in her pale blue eyes, naked and obvious, for an instant before she brought her face under control.

"Our driver is a cop," she said, cool as Christmas. "I'm sure you're perfectly safe, but . . ." She shrugged her shoulders and looked away. "Do what you want to do. Only, I'd think about it first."

"What's that supposed to mean?"

"It means"—Bitsi's voice had the tone of a cat playing with a mouse—"it's already been observed that the truck was here all night. If there's anything the police need to know about—anything that might have happened as a result of the senator's *all-night visit*"—she put a nasty little emphasis on the words—"it has the potential to be seriously embarrassing for him. And for you, though you'll understand if your embarrassment isn't my chief concern."

"I think Mark's safety should be your concern."

Bitsi laughed. "Mark's very well protected. Better than he even knows. We hired a private guard for him two years ago. An ex-CIA spy, in fact. This guy is so good, the senator still hasn't detected him. And that's impressive, considering the senator's military experience with reconnaissance. I wouldn't worry about his safety, and I don't really think anyone is after *you*."

"Except maybe you."

The words were out before she could stop them. Bitsi lifted an eyebrow in only the faintest evidence of surprise.

"Whatever do you mean?"

"You know exactly what I mean," Erica shot back. "Cut it out. I don't know how you did it, but I know you did it. Why you did it—why you'd do something so—so—*sick*—that's another question. Especially since you're supposed to be so . . ."

In love with him. She stopped short, the words hovering on her tongue. Mark's assertions buzzed around her and Erica longed to fling them in Bitsi's face. She longed to call this pale wench out on her little game, longed to smack the woman in the face with the facts: that she loved Mark, and Mark didn't love her back. That driving Erica away wouldn't drive Mark into her arms.

But she'd promised him she wouldn't.

"I'm supposed to be 'so' *what*? In love with him?" she finished, before letting out a whoop of laughter. "Is that what he told you?"

Erica stared at her, speechless and confused, while the woman chuckled until her eyes nearly ran with tears.

"Mark Newman, you're too much," Bitsi murmured as though the man were present. "You're just too full of yourself for words."

"Th—then you aren't—you aren't—" Erica stammered.

"No." Bitsi shook her head emphatically. "No. Maybe I was, once. Years ago, when I first met him. But I've long since gotten over it." She laughed again. "I know Mark would be shocked to hear it, but it *is* possible to get over him." Her pale blue eyes found Erica's. "I guess it's important that you know that, since the better question is, Are *you* in love with him?"

Erica hesitated, watching the changes play over the woman's face. Only moments ago, the woman's expression had been disinterested and dismissive. But now, suddenly, Bitsi Barr was interested in her. A little too interested.

"Because if you are, let me just tell you, you are one of hundreds," Bitsi continued, when Erica didn't answer. "Maybe thousands."

"No," Erica said as straight-faced as she could manage. "No. I'm not in love with Mark Newman."

In love with Mark Newman.

The moment the words escaped her mouth and she heard them, hanging in the air like bubbles, that funny little feeling of heat struck her stomach again. Mark Newman's image seemed to float in each bubble, smiling that quirky little smile he always smiled just before he said something wrongheaded and crazy. Mad as she was at Bitsi Barr and the whole damn situation, Erica had to work hard to keep a silly little smile from curving her lips.

"I don't believe you. You're in love with him," Bitsi asserted, her eyes flashing and her voice rising. "I *know* you are!" She paused, but only long enough to gather steam. "You don't actually think he can love you, do you? You don't actually *expect* anything. Because I'll tell you right now, Mark Newman loves one thing: himself. Himself and his career. That's why I had to . . ."

Erica waited, but the woman closed her lips tightly and suddenly became very interested in the door.

"You had to do what, Bitsi? What did you have to do?"

"Nothing." Even though her pale face had turned the most uncomfortable-looking shade of pink, Bitsi found her chilliest voice again. "You wouldn't understand."

The woman refused to look at her, but that didn't stop Erica from staring her down like she'd stolen something. "I understand plenty, Bitchy—I mean, Bitsi," Erica hissed. "And let me tell you this. I'm not some little shy country girl, like Mary. I don't scare easy. I don't know exactly what you're up to, or exactly what you're trying to prove, but you need to stop it or you're going to end up in jail. I, for one, would love to press charges."

"I'm sure I don't know what you're babbling about. Now, come on," she said, turning abruptly on her stack-heeled loafer, yanking open Erica's door and disappearing down the hallway. "They're opening this boutique early just for you, and I don't think it's right to keep them waiting."

"We need to talk. No more of this intermediary to intermediary bullshit. Man to man."

Peter Malloy blinked at him in surprise. But then, he had reason to: It was still early—not even 7 A.M.—and here was Mark Newman, standing outside his hotel room, snorting war in his face as though the debate were today, at this very hour, only without an audience and without any politics.

He was supposed to be in the air by now, on his way to Malloy's home city. But that would have to wait. Especially since Mark knew that Malloy wasn't in Harpersville but right here in Billingham, preparing for the following day's debate.

He'd get to Harpersville and its good citizens as soon as possible and apologize profusely for his delay.

Later.

Mark stared at him, taking in his opponent. Normally, he saw Pete Malloy in his suit and tie, salt-and-pepper hair carefully coiffed, camera ready. But now, the other man wore a plain white T-shirt and pair of shorts, and had the weak-eyed, tousled look of a man awakened from a deep sleep.

"Can't this wait?" Malloy croaked, scratching at his stubbly chin. "My family is here." He nodded into the room behind him. "They're still asleep."

"Then you need to come out into the hallway," Mark commanded, "unless you want them to know what kind of sleazy, underhanded shit you're willing to do to win an election."

The man hesitated, and for a moment, Mark saw

himself as he must have appeared to the other man: fully dressed in a suit and tie, wide awake and coldly alert. Perhaps even a little menacing.

"All right," Malloy said, and Mark saw a flicker of fear in the man's pasty face. "Just let me get a robe or something."

"Now!" Mark roared.

Malloy hopped into the hallway like a frightened bird.

Good, Mark thought. *I want him to be scared. I want . . .*

"I said 'all right!'" Malloy repeated, his voice an octave higher than it had been when he first opened the door. "What on Earth is wrong with you? Why are you here? What do you want?"

Mark pulled the crumpled paper from his pocket and threw it at Malloy. It bounced off the man's chest before he caught it in an awkward bobble of hands.

"Open it!" Mark demanded, lifting his cane slightly, pointing toward the crumpled paper. "Open it and tell me you didn't have anything to do with that!"

Malloy's hands shook as he pulled the paper ball open and studied it, his face pinkening with embarrassment. "I—I'm sure I don't know what you mean by b—bringing me this kind of thing," he muttered.

"You know exactly why I brought it to you, Malloy," Mark hissed, raising his cane in the other man's direction. "You know, because you hired the photographer who took this picture, you sick fuck."

"M—Mark," Malloy began. "Calm down."

"Calm down!" Mark exploded, losing the battle to control both his voice and his temper. "You send me some shit like this and tell me to 'calm down'?" He stepped closer to the man, backing him against the wall of the corridor, until there were only inches separating them. "Is this how you want to win? With threats and blackmail and innuendo? You want to win by spying on and frightening an innocent woman? By appealing to the worst of the electorate's nature? Or did you just plan to humiliate me with that?" He snatched the photo from Malloy's hands. "You can't beat me any other way, so you're going to drag the most decent thing in my life into the mud? She doesn't deserve that, man. She's a good person! She hasn't done anything cheap or tawdry or—"

"I didn't have anything to do with it."

"For God's sake, man." Mark spat the words at his adversary, glaring at him like he meant to do him physical harm. "Don't lie."

"I'm not," Malloy insisted. "I don't know who did this but it wasn't me. I had nothing to do with it." His eyes locked onto Mark's. "I swear."

Mark hesitated. He'd known Pete Malloy for several years, at least casually, when they'd served in the state house of representatives together. He'd never much liked the man—he was a little *too* conservative, a little *too* religious, and a little too unimaginative— for Mark's tastes. He'd known him to be narrow-minded, stupid and a little shameless in pandering to his own constituency. But he'd never known him to lie straight to another man's face.

"What about the other pictures—in the pizzeria back in Washington and in the ladies' room? And the fax?"

Fear shimmered in Pete Malloy's eyes. "I—I don't know anything about anything that happened in Washington. But the fax . . ." He tried to smile, but he was too scared to pull it off. "I mean, it's politics, right? An attack ad. My campaign director suggested we go negative, and I can't think of anything much more negative than that woman with her crazy T-shirts and the outrageous things she says. So I agreed to the fax to try to sway some voters."

"Where did you get the photo, if you didn't have it taken? The one you used in the fax?"

Malloy shrugged. "I don't know where it came from. My campaign director said he'd gotten a photo. I thought maybe that was a publicity shot or something. From the newspaper services or something—I don't know." He shook his head. "All's I know is, I didn't take it and I didn't have it taken. I don't have funds enough to be sending photographers up to D.C. to take pictures of you and your nigger girlfriend."

Mark's hand was already in a fist and it wasn't until he saw the other man flinch in preparation for impact that he realized how close he'd come to hitting him. He checked himself, pulling the punch at the last moment and stepped out of easy range.

"I hope I beat you, Malloy," he muttered at the other man. "Because you'd set this state back forty years if you go to the Senate." He grimaced, hating the words he knew he'd have to say next. "But I believe you. I don't guess you had these photos taken. I believe you're willing to take the benefits, if somehow whoever's doing this can discredit me with them . . . but I don't believe you're following me, taking pictures."

"Nobody needs to discredit you, Newman. You're doing a good job discrediting yourself." Malloy sounded like he'd found courage from somewhere, though Mark couldn't imagine just where. "Fornicating, gallivanting all over the state with that Left Wing, liberal nig—black woman—like she's as good as a white woman." Malloy scoffed. "Your lead is slipping. Keep doing what you're doing and it's gonna be all gone. The folks of this state don't cotton to all that mess. You'll see."

Mark stared at the man. It was amazing that his attitudes still existed in this century. How many of his constituents shared them, Mark wondered, for the first time understanding Erica's fears, her anger, her unease in Billingham. His anger drained out of him, leaving a heavy weight of sadness and a grim determination not to rest until prejudice was a thing of the past.

"It's going to be a pleasure defeating you, Pete," he told the man in a soft voice. "An absolute pleasure."

It's my understanding that 13 percent of the marriages in our state are between people of different ethnicities—a little more than the national average. Our state is known for being behind the curve on many issues of national concern, but in romantic race relations, it looks like we're ahead.

—Chase Alexander

Chapter 19

◇◇

"Any of these will do."

Erica glanced down at the pile of clothes on the woman's arm. They were all shades of black or purple, all covered with gaudy sequins, all short-sleeved sack-like tops with long, near-the-ankle skirts.

Ugh, Erica thought. *Mother-of-the-bride dresses. Matronly. Ugly.*

Erica had expected as much the moment they walked into the shop. It had the look of old, white womanhood: faded and perfumey, as stuck in a time warp as a blue rinse. But it wasn't the dress shop that had her on edge.

As soon as they'd left the hotel, she'd had the feeling of being watched. Watched leaving. Watched as she got into the car and followed as they drove through the early-morning streets. The feeling had never subsided; not even when Bitsi parked her dark sedan in front of this boutique and hopped out, impatient for Erica to follow. Erica slid out tentatively, all the little hairs at the back of her neck standing at attention. Someone had watched them last night. And took pictures. Erica shuddered. The same sicko might be watching her right now.

She glanced around, taking in the small parking lot and the empty stretch of sidewalk surrounding the little dress shop. Most of the other stores were closed, but there were a few people patronizing a coffeehouse in this freshly gentrified strip of downtown, and there were plenty of cars in the streets. Everyone seemed to be going about their own business, paying one black woman in jeans, a head wrap and a T-shirt no mind at all.

She still couldn't shake the feeling, not even now as they stood safely inside the boutique.

And just where was Angelique?

If this is what you call having my back, Erica told her friend in her mind, *I'd hate to see what would happen if you came at me from the front.*

Something was definitely up with Angie. She'd been almost completely AWOL the entire trip, seeming to only drift in and out of the Dickson B and B to strip out of one summery sundress and change into another. Erica was dying to know the scoop, but at the rate things were going, they'd probably be back at Bramble Heights before the woman could make time in her busy schedule give Erica an update.

Hopefully they'd both make it back to Bramble Heights. Considering the evil glare the little blonde woman in front of her was shooting in Erica's direction—and the latest, most intrusive, white-enveloped picture—Erica was getting nervous. More than a little nervous.

"I think something like this," Bitsi said, pulling out a huge, black muumuu of a gown with a cowl neck and silvery batwing sleeves.

Erica stared at the other woman. She was very

petite—probably could have shopped in the girls' section if she wanted to—and she wore a short, close-tailored red jacket, demure silk camisole and a blue skirt with hose and a pair of stack-heeled loafers. She wasn't exactly stylish, but even she didn't look like she would have worn any of the dresses she was thrusting at Erica like they were the latest thing from the pages of *Vogue*.

"No," Erica told her firmly. "I'm only thirty-three. My great-grandmother wouldn't wear that."

Bitsi's eyes circled her sockets as she replaced the dress. She stalked across the store to another section and pulled out a long, blue figure-skimming thing with a plunging neckline. It looked like what Miss America would wear to the prom.

"I suppose you like this."

"You suppose wrong," Erica replied, taking another glance out the window, hoping against hope to see some kind of police car, some evidence of the "protection" Mark had promised.

Nothing.

"This one's red." Bitsi yanked a halter-styled nightmare from yet another rack and held it against her little body with a lame attempt at dramatic flare. "I hear that's a popular color with black people."

Erica swallowed down the insult with a roll of her eyes. "Do you own your trailer, Bitsi?" she asked sweetly. "Or just rent it?"

The blonde woman's cheeks flamed bright red, and she opened her mouth to say something particularly rude and nasty. But she didn't get the chance.

"Hello, hello!"

A woman emerged from the back of the store. She was probably in her late sixties, but that hadn't stopped her from lining her eyes with thick black eyeliner and mascara and painting her lips a happy pink.

There was probably enough yellow dye in her hair to color a continent, but she had a sincerely pleasant smile on her face as she hurried toward them and caught Erica's hand in her own. "Welcome!" she drawled in a voice as sweet and slow as syrup. "It's so nice to have you here, Ms. Johnson. I've been watching you and our boy Mark on TV! When Bitsi called yesterday to tell me you needed a dress, I was so *honored*!"

Bitsi pasted the phoniest grin Erica had ever seen on her lips and gushed, "Where else would we come? La Belle Dame is still the best place for women's gowns in Billingham!" And when the older lady's eyes sparkled with pride, she continued. "Erica Johnson, meet Fantine Moore, one of the proprietors."

"Hello, Ms. Moore," Erica said, managing a smile.

"Nope, none of that," the woman said taking Erica's arm and looping it through her own. "Call me Fantine. Everyone does. Goodness, what are you two doing over *here*? These dresses are way too large—and if I may say so, too old—for pretty young things like the two of you. Step over here. I've got a couple of *couture* dresses, as well as a few originals from some of our local designers. There's a couple of Vera Wangs and a sweet little Armani, but it's cocktail length, not quite right for tonight." She released Erica suddenly and stepped back. Her eyes skimmed over Erica's T-shirt, processed the slogan with a quick lift of her penciled eyebrow, and then cast her eye over the rest of Erica's torso, assessing her figure. "Hmmm," she murmured, like a doctor considering an interesting case. "With your skin tone, I think you'd carry off a jewel tone really well. And that figure just begs for something strapless." She tapped her lipsticked mouth with a manicured finger. "Do you have any favorite designers?"

Erica hesitated. She didn't know a fashion designer from a *foie gras*. Once again, she wished Angelique were here and called her friend a few choice names in her mind. "No favorites," she said quickly. "But I'm particular about fabrics. Nothing synthetic. I like natural fibers."

"Of course." Fantine nodded as if Erica's criteria were nothing out of the ordinary.

"And I don't like to look like everyone else."

Fantine laughed. "That goes without saying, my dear. Now, just let me show you a few things right over here. They're all one-hundred percent silk, all one of a kind."

Silk? Erica ran through the list of acceptable fabrics in her mind. Was silk one of the fabrics created by young women enslaved in sweatshops in Indonesia? She couldn't remember.

Dresses are the last thing on my mind right now, Erica wanted to shout. *For all I know, this bitch standing next to me wants to kill me. For all I know, that picture of me and Mark is going to be all over the news by nightfall. For all I know, I just became the Monica Lewinsky of Mark Newman's political career.*

But she couldn't say any of that. Instead, Erica allowed herself to be led off the main sales floor and into a smaller room, where dresses swaddled in plastic hung on a few metal racks lining the walls.

"These are for our special customers," Fantine said proudly. "Each of these dresses is an original made with only the highest-quality fabric. If you see one you like, Gladys—that's my partner—and I will fit it for you. That's no small thing. Fitting some of these gowns is like constructing a brand-new dress! But don't worry: We'll get it done and have it delivered to Dickson's in plenty of time for the ball." She pulled out one of the garment bags and unzipped it, showing Erica a swath of the most exquisite shade of purple she had ever seen.

"It's beautiful," she said, unable to stop herself from reaching out to caress the soft fabric. "But I'm sure I could never afford anything like this."

Confusion crumpled Fantine's face as her eyes darted between Erica and Bitsi. "It's all taken care of, dear!" she exclaimed. "Didn't Bitsi tell you?"

Erica shook her head.

"The senator reactivated his personal account yesterday. His late wife used to shop here, you know," Fantine informed her, unzipping the garment bag fully to reveal the rest of the gown. "You're supposed to pick whatever you want, and I have firm instructions not to take a dime from you!"

"No." Erica shook her head. "I can't let him do that."

Fantine's grin widened. "He said you'd say that." She swung her face toward Bitsi. "I can't believe you didn't *tell* her!"

Bitsi folded her lips and glowered at the woman.

"He said to tell you—and this is him talking now, not me—that he can't have you showing up in some crazy hippy outfit and that you should consider the gown a thank-you gift."

Crazy hippy outfit? The words stung like a slap. Erica let the sumptuous purple fabric slip from her fingers.

"Thank-you gift?" she repeated. "For what?"

Fantine blinked. "I don't know. I assumed you would. For coming, I guess."

Coming. Erica's stomach twisted with the multiple meanings of the word. He was thanking his "crazy hippy" for "coming." It would have almost been funny if it hadn't been so sad. Was the picture something of his devising? she wondered. She was a public-school teacher, after all. That X-rated photo was the kind of thing that could get her fired. Was that his way of making sure his "crazy hippy" kept on going after "coming?"

No, she told herself. *I don't believe he'd do that. I don't believe he'd sink that low.*

But she couldn't be sure. Not with Bitsi reminding her that the man's ego and career were at the center of his life. Not with the creepy feeling of being constantly under surveillance and the ugly evidence still stuffed in her jeans pocket. Not with knowing that after everything, he still considered her a "crazy hippy."

And to think she'd actually almost believed that a relationship with the man might work.

"I'll show you a 'crazy hippy,'" Erica muttered to herself.

"What did you say, dear?"

"Nothing. This is lovely," she said aloud, stepping away from the gown. "But it isn't quite what I had in mind."

"Oh?" Fantine looked slightly hurt. "I think the color would suit you very well," she continued, recovering quickly. "But we have plenty of others."

"I don't think any of them will work," Erica said, shaking her head.

Her tone must have registered on Bitsi's radar, because she pounced into the conversation with sudden energy.

"Why? What's wrong with them?"

"They're just a little too conservative."

"But sweetie, I have plenty of racier stuff," Fantine began, but Bitsi overrode her with a strident, "The senator is conservative. Very conservative."

Everywhere but in the bedroom, Erica almost snapped just to watch that smug expression slide off the media director's face.

"I know he is," she heard herself saying, "but I'm

not." She turned back to the elderly proprietress. "Fantine, if I found the right fabric, do you think you and your partner would have time to make me a dress?"

Fantine's eyebrows rose and her mouth stretched wide in surprise. "Gladys is the best seamstress in Billingham," she said, and her bosom seemed to inflate a little with her pride. "She can make anything—anything at all. But . . . " She shook her head. "In one day? Even if we started right now, we'd only have ten or eleven hours. Not much time to build from scratch."

Erica looked around.

"Is she here? Right now?"

"Well . . . yes. She's working on the final alterations for a wedding gown. It has to be finished today."

"I have something really simple in mind, I promise. And I can do some of it myself. I'm pretty decent with the basics."

Fantine hesitated. "I don't know," she said slowly.

"Please? At least let me talk to her—to both of you—about what I have in mind."

The woman patted her golden hair and chewed off a fine smear of lipstick as she considered. "Well," she drawled at last, "I guess so. Gladys!" She yelled like she was calling a farmhand to the dinner table. "Hey Gladys! Come on back to the couture room."

For a moment, the three of them stood in an awkward silence, waiting. Then the curtains of the couture room parted and a woman appeared.

She was dark-skinned, the color of old mahogany with her hair wrapped in a colorful turban high around her head and a pair of glasses on a chain around her neck. An apron stuck through with pins covered a beautiful caftan in an African-inspired print. Erica noticed her hands: thick with the hard work of sewing, with calluses around the pads of her fingers.

"What are you screaming about, Fantine?" Gladys demanded in the voice of an old-school black matron. "Don't you know I'm working on that damn wedding dress? And you come, a-screaming and a-hollerin'—" She stopped short, taking in Erica in a single piercing gaze. "Well, I declare. You're that girl on the TV."

Erica felt the first genuine smile she'd smiled in a long while curve over her face. She'd never met this woman—never laid eyes on her before in her life—and yet she instantly felt she knew her. She was Mama Tia and Gram and so many of the older black women she'd known in her life, just a more Southern version. And even better, Gladys was staring her down like she knew Erica down to her bones. Knew her, and understood her, too.

"She's got to go with Senator Newman to an event tonight," Fantine was saying. "I told her you can sew anything. But I don't know if you have time."

Gladys's face broke into a smile that showed the slight gap between her two front teeth. "Well, I suppose for our visitor from up North, I could clear a *little* time." She quirked an eye toward Fantine. "But you're gonna have to finish Allison Wells' wedding dress before she comes in here at five thirty for the final fitting."

Fantine's expression made it pretty clear that she'd rather not deal with Allison Wells or her wedding dress. "Lord, that child is so particular," she muttered under her breath. "But I'll get it done."

"Thank you," Erica said, stretching her hand toward the woman, but to her surprise, Gladys pulled her into her arms and hugged her like a long-lost sister.

"My little great-nephew got himself killed in that Iraq," she muttered into Erica's shoulder. "Seems like we've lost a lot of local boys. I'm glad you're doing what you're doing. And it'll be a pleasure to make your dress."

"Oh for the love of God," Bitsi muttered impatiently. "Why can't you just pick a dress off the rack? It's not like this is Oscar night and you're up for Best Actress."

Erica ignored her, focusing all her attention on the two older women.

"I promise it won't be too complicated. Did you see the NAACP Image Awards this year?"

"Girl," Gladys gave Erica's arm a playful slap. "I never miss that. Did you see what that Beyonce had on?"

"I'm not going there." Erica laughed. "Don't have the assets, if you know what I mean. I was thinking more of Victoria Rowell? You know who she is? She's on a soap opera. I think it's—"

"*The Young and the Restless*. But I liked her better on *Diagnosis Murder*. Don't have much time for soap operas, but I like mystery shows, and that one was pretty good."

"Do you remember her dress?" Erica asked. "Simple little black thing."

Gladys eyed her with a frown. "It ain't so simple, child. What makes a dress like that is the fit and the fabric."

"I have a specific fabric in mind for the bodice," Erica told her. "But I want to be a little more, uh . . . " She hesitated. "*Creative* with the skirt.

Gladys perched her glasses on the broad bridge of her nose and stared at Erica like she was reading the lines of her genetic code. "Creative, huh? You sure we're going to have what you're looking for here in Billingham?" she asked at last, squinting at Erica. "Milan, this ain't."

Erica nodded. "Oh, I'm sure," she said calmly. "Positive."

Gladys paused for just a second, eyeing Erica coolly. Erica held her breath, hoping the woman hadn't completely read her mind—or if she had, that she wouldn't call her out here and now in front of Bitsi and ruin everything.

She must have decided to keep it confidential, because at the end of her consideration Gladys said, "Then that leaves the fit. Strip!"

"What?"

"You heard me. Take off that T-shirt and those jeans, girl," she barked, sounding more like a drill sergeant than a seamstress. She pulled a tape measure and a small notepad from an apron pocket. "Let's measure what you're working with, so I know how much material to buy."

Erica hesitated. The idea of stripping down to skin under the judging eyes of Bitsi didn't feel right. And then, of course, there was the strawberry-shaped hickey strategically placed right at the base of her neck. The memory of how it had gotten there made a warm flush of desire rise to her throat.

It was a one-time thing, she reminded herself. *After all, I'm just another woman he supposes to be "in love" with him. Which is about what I should have expected from that neo-fascist pig. He's in league with the devil. He's first cousin to the Antichrist. He's . . .*

One hell of a kisser.

And just like that, her mind took her body back to the pleasure that was an evening in Mark Newman's arms, Mark Newman's lips, Mark Newman's long, hard—

"Take it off, *now*," Gladys demanded, recalling her to the moment before her underwear could get too moist. "I need to see the shape of your body. The dress you're talking about fits close to the bust." And when Erica still blinked at her nervously, she laughed. "You ain't got nothing I ain't seen before anyway. C'mon, now."

Erica sighed, lifted her shirt and pulled it over her head, hoping no one would notice anything unusual at all.

When she looked at them, the older women were already busy with their tape measures, assessing her with calmly professional eyes. If they'd seen the hickey—and there wasn't much of a way they could miss it, considering the fact that she was standing in only her panties in the middle of the room—they had tactfully decided not to comment. Bitsi had apparently become uncomfortable enough to wander away, and now stood before a rack of dresses in sizes that would fit only the tiniest of flower girls, pretending to be engrossed.

"Does the fabric store have kente cloth?"

Gladys shook her head. "Not usually. I know where to find it, but I'll tell you right now, you can't make a ball gown out of kente cloth."

"I was thinking of using it to wrap my hair."

Gladys shook her head. "I'll design you something out of the same thing we use for the dress. It'll be afrocentric, if that's what you want. But a little more elegant. You'll see. I've done a lot of them," she said, raising her eyebrows toward her own turban.

"Whoa, whoa." Bitsi interjected herself back into the conversation. "Turbans, kente cloth?" She shook her head. "I'm not going to let you embarrass him like you did last night with all that crazy peacenik singing. You'll embarrass him again over my dead body, you hear?"

"I didn't embarrass him," Erica shot back.

"Did too."

"Well Mark didn't seem to think so."

Bitsi's lips were clamped tight with suppressed rage. "This is so ridiculous," she muttered when she'd calmed herself enough to speak again. "I can't believe you're still here at all. Mark's just too kind, too good-hearted and too distracted by your boobs and your butt and your big brown eyes to see that everything about you is calculated to destroy him. But I see it. I know what you're trying to do, and believe me, I won't let you!"

"You really *are* in love with him."

Erica released the words calmly, as matter-of-fact as the weather report. Immediately a crimson flush suffused Bitsi's face.

"Absolutely not," she huffed. "It's—it's—it's just my job to protect him. And that's all!"

Erica glanced at the two older women who had ceased their ministrations to listen to the exchange. She read in their faces that they were buying Bitsi's denials about as much as Erica was.

"Look, Bitsi. For the last time, I'm not trying to embarrass him, but I'm not turning into some big-haired pageant queen for him, either." She shot a quick glance of forgiveness toward Fantine. "No offense." The woman nodded her on, and Erica continued. "I'm more than willing to skip the whole thing all together. Why don't you buy *yourself* a dress and go with him?"

"No," Bitsi said abruptly, the red flush in her pale skin deepening to the color of her jacket. "He's made it very clear. He wants to go with you. God only knows why," she added under her breath. "You have absolutely nothing in common. Nothing to offer him, except—"

"Except?" Erica slipped her T-shirt back over head and slid her jeans up over her hips, and then turned toward the woman.

A nasty smirk creased the woman's face. "Well, you know how oversexed you people are."

Erica's hand went up in a flash, the vision of her palm print on the woman's sickly pale skin already crystal clear in her mind. But it didn't happen. Something stayed her hand, kept her arm from its follow through. Erica looked up to find Gladys, holding on to her upper arm for dear life.

"Now, now," she muttered, though she stared at Bitsi with eyes hard with dislike. "We ain't gonna let it come to that."

"No, we certainly are not!" Fantine exclaimed. "Bitsi Barr, you ought to be ashamed. I've known you your whole life—your mother, too. Your grandmother is one of my dearest friends. I know full well they didn't raise you to say such things. Especially not" —she cut her eyes in Erica's direction—"to a guest here in Billingham. What must she think of us?"

I think this is a town full of racists. I think this is a state full of racists. I think this is the most backwater, hostile, awful place I've ever been, and I can't wait to get the hell out of here and as far from Mark Newman as I can get! The words were on the tip of Erica's tongue, but she tamped them down and mastered herself, letting her hand and arm drop back to where they belonged.

"I'm sorry," Bitsi said, sounding sorry only for having been called on her bullshit, but not for letting it fly free in the first place. "I only meant . . ." she shrugged. "Well, you see she doesn't even wear a bra! What kind of woman goes around without a bra?"

"Plenty of 'em," Gladys replied, chuckling. "White or black don't have nothing to do with it."

"Amen," agreed Fantine. "Why back in the seventies, I went around without one a few times myself. Remember, Gladys?" she elbowed the other woman, a girlish grin on her pink lips. "We marched with Dr.

King in the sixties, then burned our bras in the seventies?"

"Sure did." Gladys nodded. "Those were the days, girl."

Bitsi stared at them in unadulterated horror and then grimaced. "Well, things are different now. Thank God."

"Too bad," Fantine muttered. "Anyway, she won't be wearing a bra underneath that dress, so she'd only have had to take it off for us to measure anyway." She inhaled, drawing herself up in righteous indignation. "I didn't march with Dr. King down the streets of Billingham for *your* generation to say things like that. I think you owe Ms. Johnson here an apology."

Bitsi glared at Erica like the whole thing was her fault and curled her lips in an expression that made it perfectly clear these would be among the hardest words she had ever spoken. Swallowing like she had a mouthful of cod liver oil, she murmured, "I'm very sorry."

Erica just stared at her. A thousand responses filled her brain, but not one of them was gracious enough to be spoken out loud. Finally, Gladys stepped into the silence with, "That's all right. She understands. We're all a little in love with that Mark Newman. Shoot, if I was a few years younger . . ." and she ended the sentence with a whooping chuckle that settled over them all like a soothing balm.

"Besides," Fantine picked up the last hanging edge of discourse and yanked it neatly into place. "He's such a gentleman. It's appropriate that he invite his guest with him to the fund-raiser, and I'm sure Ms. Johnson here has no intention of embarrassing him— or herself—in any way. Isn't that right, dear?"

Erica felt all their eyes turn toward her again, inquiring, waiting for the reassurance.

"I have no intention of embarrassing him," Erica said loudly and slowly, feeling a little like a little girl with her fingers crossed behind her back. "And, for the record, I'm not trying to seduce him, I'm not out to destroy his career and I'm not in love with Mark Newman, either."

In love with Mark Newman.

Mad as she was at Bitsi and the whole damn situation, mad as she was at him and scared as she was knowing that X-rated picture was floating around in the world, waiting to be used for no good purpose, she couldn't help feeling that same little quiver she'd felt from the very first moment she looked into Mark Newman's eyes.

It didn't make any kind of sense. Quivering and shivering over Mark just made her like the woman in one of Aretha Franklin's old songs. Added to a chain of fools.

And now the three women were looking at her with equally revealing expressions on their faces: Gladys and Fantine with frustratingly knowing smiles on their faces, and Bitsi with a cold and certain jealousy.

"I'm serious," Erica said, struggling with her face, but it didn't seem to want to cooperate. "I'm not in love with Mark Newman! He's not my type! He believes in all the wrong things. I mean, he shoots animals, for the love of God! And—and—and—there's that annoying little smirk he gets on his face. Like he thinks he's some kind of—of—sex god. God's gift to women, I mean," she corrected, afraid of the possible admission the use of the word *sex* might betray. "Surely, you've seen it. That look he gets? That frustrating, I-think-I'm-so-good-looking look?"

But the other women just stared at her like she'd sprouted three heads. Mark Newman danced in the air around her, invisible to all but her. He seemed to be almost laughing at her.

Oh go away, you big show-off, she told him in her mind. *Some creep is about to make me a porn star, and it's all your fault.*

"Never mind," Erica grumbled aloud, feeling the heat that had warmed her insides now warming her cheeks and ears. "I'm ready to go the fabric store now."

"Yeah, we'd better git. It's gonna take all afternoon to stitch your dress together." She eyed Bitsi. "I'm guessing you got better things to do."

"Yeah. Much better things," Bitsi grumbled. She shot Erica a final parting glance of war. Then, without another word, she turned away from them and stomped out of the store.

"I'm ready," Erica told the women.

"No, you're not." Gladys jotted the last of Erica's measurements into a little spiral notebook and then looked up, frowning disapproval.

"I'm not?" Erica repeated.

"No, you're not." Gladys stepped close to her and lay her two hands heavily on Erica's shoulders. "You got something up your sleeve with this dress, young lady. And before I sew a stitch, I promise you, I'm gonna know *exactly* what it is."

Dissent IS patriotic.
—Peace slogan

Chapter 20

◇◇

He noticed her eyes first.

As Erica slid into the limousine, he took one look into their deep brown depths and knew: she'd been sent the picture, too.

The second thing he noticed was the dress—a smoking hot, Foxy Brown short, sun gold, silky swish of material, trimmed with black and gold swatches in a pattern that looked like words. He couldn't read them, but he felt a smile curving his lips anyway: It was like her to take advantage of every opportunity to protest. Mark might have laughed aloud if his head hadn't been pounding with a headache that felt like a jackhammer in his skull.

"You look beautiful," he said in a low voice as she settled in beside him.

And she did. Compared to Bitsi's long, black skirt and rhinestone jacket, it was a movie-star kind of dress, the kind of dress that would raise eyebrows of jealousy at a stuffy old fund-raiser like this, and now that she was sitting beside him, he could clearly make out the words "peace" "Iraq" and "troops" in the black border of the dress.

If he'd had the leisure to think about it, he might have been worried about that. But for once, it wasn't that lusciously curvaceous body—or what she was wearing on it—that held his mind.

"We have some unfinished business," she whispered into his ear, and he knew from the tone of her voice and the look on her face that she wasn't talking about the business of unwrapping the package he knew lay beneath those strategically placed bits of gold cloth.

"I know," he said softly. "But not here."

Bitsi must have heard the exchange. She shifted a little in her seat on Mark's left but said nothing.

Angelique squeezed into the limousine next in a shimmery gown Mark would have called "white," but he supposed the women around him might have termed bisque or ecru. Chase followed, talking animatedly about something that had happened at some rally he'd coordinated today in one of the many places Mark had been since leaving Erica's arms that morning.

Mark closed his eyes. His head ached, his stomach churned. After the late start and the early-morning tussle with Malloy, he'd been too keyed up to eat. After arriving in Harpersville and beginning his long day of campaigning, he'd been too busy to do more than grab a drink here and a snack there. The best meal he'd had all day was a handful of corn chips and an ice-cold bottle of Dickey Joe's while he changed into his tux.

Usually the beer helped, but today it just made him feel queasy, tired and sick.

Just gotta get through this last event, he told himself. *Get through the meet and greet, make some remarks, sneak out before the dancing starts.*

Chase interrupted his thoughts with a brisk, "Mark, you listening?"

Mark looked over at him sharply. In his tuxedo, his friend managed to look dapper and neat, his extra pounds concealed by pressed black fabric. He held a folder in his hands from which he had been reading something Mark was supposed to be listening to.

"Sorry," he muttered, rubbing his eyes. He cut another quick glance at Erica, but she was staring out the limo's tinted windows, weighed down by her own thoughts.

Waiting for the other shoe to drop. That's what we're doing. Waiting.

They needed to be alone. They needed to talk. They needed to try to figure out what that photo meant and what, if anything, to do next. Almost without realizing it, he let his hand crawl across the leather and find hers, squeezing her fingers briefly in reassurance.

Her answering squeeze brought a strange sense of peace to him and he inhaled deeply. But the exhale made his stomach cramp so violently, he winced.

Mark focused his attention back on Chase and Bitsi. He wasn't surprised to find Chase staring at the space where their hands were entwined. Even Angelique had cast a glance in that direction . . . but at least she was smiling about it.

"Sorry," he repeated, nodding toward Chase's folder. "I'm listening now. Read it to me again."

Chase shook his head and answered him with a sigh of his own. "What's with you today? You tired or something?"

"Tired." Mark seized on the word like a life line. "Yeah, I'm double-dog tired, Chase." He quirked an eyebrow at his friend. "Any way we can get out of this thing?"

Chase shook his head. "You shouldn't want to get out of this thing, Mark. This is your fund-raiser. People paid from five hundred to a thousand dollars a plate to come. The least you could do is be interested in knowing who they are." He nodded at the folder, and Mark remembered Chase had been reading the attendee list for the night's event: names he needed to remember, names he needed to be certain he knew.

"Sorry," Mark murmured for the third time, wishing he meant it. The truth was he wasn't sorry. He felt like crap, his mind was awhirl with confusion and questions—most of them concentrated in the person of the woman sitting beside him, calmly holding his hand but avoiding his gaze. He closed his eyes again and imagined himself alone with Erica Johnson in the fluffy, white four-poster bed at Dickson's Inn.

The sound of Chase tossing the folder aside brought him back to reality again. Chase fixed those sharp brown eyes on him, searching for answers Mark wasn't yet ready to give. He put on his best poker face and stared back, meeting the man's eyes levelly.

"You all right?" Chase asked him, frowning concern.

Erica shifted toward him, big brown eyes locked on his face.

"Stomach hurts," Mark responded, deciding not to deny it. "Probably just hungry."

"They were fully briefed on your dietary preferences," Bitsi said crisply. "You'll be having filet mignon."

"I think I'm going to skip the dinner, Bits," Mark announced, since just the mention of food made his stomach flip with nausea. "Think I might be coming down with something."

"You need me to call the doctor?" Bitsi asked. "I can have him meet you at your house tonight."

"What's going on?" Chase asked at last. "Didn't you sleep well last night?"

Mark opened his mouth to reply, when to his surprise, Erica's friend made her first appearance in the conversation.

"You know he didn't, Chase," she said in a voice of pure mischief.

"Oh hush, Angelique," Erica whispered.

"What? It's not like everybody in this car doesn't know what's going on. Mark—" She leaned toward him and patted his knee. "I can call you 'Mark' now, right? I mean now that you're my best girl's man?" Then without waiting for him to answer she continued, "Mark and Erica have decided to make love, not war. Literally. They're taking all that energy they wasted in disagreement to a whole 'nother level, if you know what I'm saying."

"That's enough, Angie," Chase said, and to Mark's surprise he touched the woman's forearm with an intimacy Mark had never seen him display toward any woman. "As much as I respect the power of love, right now we've got to do the politics. Mark's got to be on his game. People don't pay a thousand dollars a plate to have the senator forget their names. If that happens, it's gonna take this campaign, if I may borrow your phrase, to a whole 'nother level. And not a good one."

Bitsi glared at Angelique. "Love? I don't think so. They had sex." Bitsi rolled her eyes. "This is a case of lust, at best. Apparently Mark is indulging in a taste of the exotic."

Before Mark could react, Erica was leaning over him looking like she was about two seconds from wringing Bitsi's neck.

"You know what?" she said in a menacing voice. "I'm just about sick of you."

"Ditto!" Bitsi shouted back.

"Ladies! Ladies!" Mark interjected, but then another cramp attacked his stomach and he couldn't speak for the pain. He concentrated on breathing through it and let the conversation go on without him.

"Let's just stick to the issue at hand," Angelique said calmly. "Mark and Erica are a couple."

"We are not, Angelique," Erica muttered, pulling her hand out of Mark's.

"Yes, you are," her friend continued, ignoring the objection. "It's time for everyone in this car to stop denying what we all know to be true and start dealing it with. Politically, of course. And personally. I'm no expert on relationships, but—"

"Then you really should shut up," Erica muttered.

"Amen," Bitsi seconded.

"I'm no expert on relationships," Angelique repeated a little louder than before, "or politics, but it seems to me in both realms, the truth will set you free." Her eyes locked on Mark's face and then Erica's. "And the truth is, this could be long term. If the two of them can get over their stubbornness and try to be happy." Her braids caressed her elegant neck as she turned back to Chase. "Now, Mr. Politics D.C., them's the facts. The only real question is how you're going to play that with your constituents so that Mark here can marry my girl and still keep his Senate seat in a state still known for lynchings and the Confederate flag."

Mark wanted to cheer the woman's plainspokenness, despite a few inaccuracies in her assumptions. He wanted to fully appreciate the embarrassed blush in Erica's cheeks and the creeping flush of annoyance in Bitsi's. He wanted to hear Chase's reply to Angie's frank question.

But the car was too hot and the air was too close. He pulled at the bow tie that was throttling him and took another deep breath and then another, trying to fill his lungs.

Just get through this event, he told himself. *Just get through this event . . .*

Then the driver was announcing their arrival and he realized the limo had stopped.

"Bitsi," he heard himself saying, and his voice almost sounded normal. "Would you go on ahead and . . . "

"Of course," she murmured, already yanking on the door in her haste to escape the car. "I'll make sure they're ready."

"We'll go on, too," Chase offered, opening the car door. The lighted driveway and the bright lights of the mansion suddenly illuminated the dim car. "Come on, Angie. Walk with me."

Angie? He wanted to speak, wanted to ask Chase a million questions, but the breath wouldn't come. Instead, he nodded, quirked his lips into a grim smile and raised his hand in a salute.

Just . . . get through . . . this event . . .

The car door slammed and they were in darkness again. He closed his eyes, concentrated on the warmth of Erica's hand and the effort of breathing.

When he opened them again, she was staring at him, all gentleness and care. As rotten as he felt, Mark was conscious of his heart skipping a couple of beats in his chest. He wanted to grab her and hold on with his all his strength.

Her lips were moving, but all he could hear was a rush of sounds skimming past his ears, undecipherable and unfamiliar. He gasped, struggling to force the air through his body, but his chest felt as heavy as lead. He tried to focus, but Erica's face was fading, going fuzzy around the edges as though she were being consumed by darkness.

Like a scene in a surreal movie, he watched her face change, the soft expression morphing into concern and then fear. He read his name on her lips, but now he couldn't hear at all. A rush of heat filled his ears and stole his vision in a cushion of velvety darkness. He felt her arms go around his waist. Then consciousness departed and he couldn't even feel her anymore.

Our poll indicates the margin between the two Republican candidates, incumbent Mark Newman and state representative Peter Malloy, has narrowed in a few short weeks to a statistical dead heat.

—The *Billingham News*

Chapter 21

He was only out for a second—just long enough for Erica to start screaming. She pounded on the glass window separating them from the driver and when the man lowered the window, she shouted, "Something's wrong! He can't breathe!"

And instantly, the man threw the car into gear and yanked it onto the street, tires squealing.

"No . . ." The sound was a wheeze more than word, a weak, out-of-it-sounding attempt at communication. He waved back toward the mansion like he wanted to go back there. "Get . . . through . . ."

"Don't 'no' me, Mark Newman," Erica told him. She pressed him against the seat and clawed at the buttons of his dress shirt and fancy tie, determined to help him get more air. "Lie still, Mark. Lie still."

Those piercing eyes locked on her for a long second, and Erica steeled herself for his resistance. But he must have felt pretty badly, because he lay back and closed his eyes, still gasping raggedly for air.

"What happened? Can you tell me what happened?" the driver demanded. Erica noticed he'd pulled off the billed cap and now held a cell phone in his hand. For an instant he seemed familiar, but Erica couldn't place how or why.

"I don't know," she told him. "He's having trouble breathing . . . and then he just slumped over . . ."

As if he could hear her talking about him, Mark's eyes fluttered open. There was a sweaty sheen to his forehead, slick and unnatural. His lips twisted into a funny little grimace and once again he lurched upwards with a sudden burst of strength.

"Be still," Erica told him and Mark nodded, panting. He was the color of a piece of chalk and just as cold.

"Be . . . okay . . ." he managed, and then vomited in a hard, gut-wrenching splash onto floor before losing consciousness.

"Mark!" Erica cried. She pled with the driver: "You've got to hurry! Something terrible is happening! Something—"

The driver was muttering into the cell phone in a low voice, and Erica thought she heard the words "police escort" and "ETA" before the man's eyes found hers in the rearview mirror.

"We'll be at a hospital in three minutes," he told her in an authoritative voice, and Erica heard sirens closing in around them. "Describe his symptoms," he commanded, jerking the wheel of the limo to the right and then accelerating through a red light, simultaneously pounding on his horn.

"He can't breathe," she told the man. "He was complaining about his stomach. Actually, he's been complaining about it for days."

The driver narrated the information into his phone.

"You're a cop, too, aren't you?"

The driver didn't answer, simply settled his hat back on his head and concentrated on his driving. But in that instant, Erica had a flash of a baseball-capped man on an airplane ride.

"You're the bodyguard!" she exclaimed. "You were on the plane . . . and in the pizza restaurant. That was even you on the Mall that night. The homeless man!"

But the man simply drove, seeming to gather more and more speed with every passing second, and neither confirmed nor denied her.

A few moments later he brought the limo to a brake-squealing stop in front of the ER. Instantly Mark was surrounded by medical personnel and whisked away on a gurney, an oxygen mask strapped to his face. The driver was gone, disappearing into the crowd of police, nurses and doctors like the chameleon that he was.

Bewildered, Erica started after the phalanx of medical personnel racing toward the entrance.

"Ms. Johnson?" a kind-faced male nurse took her by the elbow and guided her into the building. "Come on with me."

"I don't know who you *think* you are," Bitsi hissed at her when she arrived, reeking of cigarette smoke and looking positively pink with fury. "But let me tell you, you are *not* who you *think* you are."

Erica rolled her eyes. Whatever the woman *thought* she was saying wasn't what she was saying at all.

The nurse had led her to a small, brightly lit room, complete with a couple of comfortable chairs, a television, coffeemaker and a bed.

"The staff uses it," he explained. "Our media-relations person expects this place to be crawling with press when the word gets out. She thought you'd be more comfortable waiting here."

And she had been . . . or at least as comfortable as she could be, as worried as she was.

Until now.

Bitsi, Chase and Angelique had arrived in a noisy clamor of concern. Or at least Chase appeared concerned, and Angie's face was crumpled into a worried frown. Bitchy—Bitsi—on the other hand, had launched into this ridiculous tirade.

"Look, Bitsi," Erica said, struggling to keep the ragged edges of her self-control. The woman was working her nerves, had been working them all day, and was now in overdrive. "I'm sorry he happened to get sick when you weren't in the car to hold his hand. But I thought it was more important to get him *here*, where they could do something for him, than to run inside the building and get *you*!"

"You could have called me. I had to hear it from one of the officers, who heard it over the scanner!" Bitsi continued in her same "scorned woman" vein. "I mean the *scanner*! Do you know how it makes me look—not to have any idea what's happening to him? And at an event like *that*?"

Erica ignored her, but Chase patted the woman on the shoulder with an almost brotherly affection. "You handled it like a champ, though, Bits. Mark would have appreciated the announcement you made, and the way you went around to thank everyone individually for their support."

"She really was good, Erica," Angelique added, like now, all of the sudden, she was on "Bitchy's" side, even though it was Chase she stood closest to, looking almost as though she'd been fused to his side. They made something of an odd couple: Angelique, tall, thin and dark; Chase short, round and white. Erica looked the two of them over carefully and was a little surprised to find Chase holding Angie's hand.

What on earth was going on between these two? she wondered, as Angelique continued to sing Bitsi's praises.

"Really tactful, really reassuring," her friend continued, as though she were the one sleeping with the enemy and not Erica herself. "'Just a bit of the flu.' That's what she told them. 'He's been working two jobs, remember. Representing us in the Senate and running for reelection.'"

"Well, isn't that great," Erica muttered.

Bitsi scowled at her.

"You're not who you're acting like. You're not Katharine. You're not important enough to him to even be here, and you know it," she continued with a maniacal energy in her voice. "No. You're just some woman he wanted to sleep with. And now that he has, it's over. You're just—just some kind of fling. Some kind of jungle-fever fling."

"And that eats you up inside, doesn't it, Bitsi?" Erica said, feeling her anger burning through her resolve to stay calm. "That he prefers me to you just burns you up inside. That's why you've been sending me those awful little missives."

"Missives?" Bitsi rolled her eyes. "Not this again. What missives? I don't know what you're talking about. I haven't sent you anything."

Erica stood, pacing the little room for what felt like the ten thousandth time in the hour since she'd been parked here. In that time, no one had come—not even the young nurse who'd been so kind at first. No one.

Mark could be dead for all I know, she thought, and then pushed the very notion aside. No one as annoying as Mark Newman could just . . . die. It was impossible.

She focused every bit of her attention on Bitsi, trying to erase the image of Mark as anything less than his usual arrogant self. "If we're going to start telling the truth, like Angelique suggests, let's just tell all of it, okay?" She crossed the room, narrowing the space between herself and Bitsi. "So here's a truth for you: I *know* you're the one doing it. It's all too sneaky, too carefully orchestrated, too thoroughly planned. Those letters have your stink all over them."

"And I told you: I haven't sent you anything!" Bitsi's voice rose with the vehemence of her denial. "I don't know who's been following you—taking pictures of the two of you in various compromising positions—but I can assure you that it's *not* me."

"Then how do you know someone's been following us taking pictures?" Erica demanded. "I didn't say anything about pictures. I said letters."

"Mark told Chase," Bitsi offered quickly, but the two spots of color highlighting her otherwise pale cheeks flamed from pink to ruby red. "Chase must have told me."

Chase shook his head. "Wasn't me. I didn't know anything about the pictures until Angie told me two days ago. You know how Mark is. Plays personal things close, sometimes."

"Well, then it must have been Mark himself," Bitsi corrected nervously. "There are no secrets between us."

"There was one." Erica narrowed her eyes and stared hard at the woman until she looked away. "I insisted Mark not tell you—or Chase. Because I knew it was you all along. And just now, you proved me right when you said *pictures*."

"I just happened to guess," Bitsi attempted, but Erica shook her head.

"Admit your shit, Bits," she said, using Mark's nickname for the woman, and feeling a fresh pang of worry for him. She saw his face as she'd seen it last: ashen, forehead damp with cold sweat, his chest working with the effort of every gasping breath. Erica shuddered.

Please God. Let him be okay. I won't war with him no more . . . I promise . . .

"Admit your shit," she repeated when her prayer was through. "You said 'pictures' because you knew they were pictures. You know all about it, because you're the one who got those pictures. Didn't you?" Erica demanded. "Didn't you? You and your ex-CIA spy, master-of-disguise—"

"So? What if I did?" Bitsi's chin rose in defiance. "What if I did?"

"There's no 'what if.' You did. Of course you did," Erica continued. "It's quite impressive, really. How did he do it? Some kind of telephoto lens for the night at Mama Tia's? Was he hiding in the ladies' room stall? Or did he disguise himself as the attendant? He's good, that one. And I'm guessing you knew Mark would take me to Mrs. Dickson's place, so you must have planted a camera and waited for your opportunity."

A slight smile snaked across Bitsi's face. "Something like that," she said, with not a little pride. "I asked my man to do a little surveillance from the beginning, ever since Mark insisted on inviting you on this trip. I mean, really, he knew full well Malloy would use this to try to narrow the gap during the primary. Sometimes, I don't understand what Mark is thinking . . . "

Angelique grunted her disbelief. "Honestly, girl, that's some serious mess. Maybe he's thinking about what would make him happy. Maybe you ought to start thinking less about him and more about your own self."

Bitsi ignored the part of Angelique's words she didn't want to hear and rolled her eyes. "Like she could make him happy. Please. These two can't agree on the time of day." She shook her head and said to

Erica, "But he *is* a man. He finds you attractive—
though for the life of me I'm not sure why. True, you
have big boobs and you insist on wearing those tight
T-shirts, but from where I'm standing, that's hardly
enough for all of this hoopla. And the photographs
are my way of convincing him of that."

Chase frowned.

"How? What were you going to do? Sell them
to the media? Give them to Malloy?" He shook his
head. "How could you do something like this, Bitsi?
You call yourself his friend—"

"I had his best interests at heart!" Bitsi practically
shrieked, jabbing a finger in Erica's direction. "She's
political poison and he's squiring her around town
like she's the First Lady or something! I wanted him to
understand how dangerous this could be—and what
better way than to illustrate it for him in living color.
Because if I could do it, Malloy could do it. Or even
that dumbass Democrat he'll face in November! And
then what happens to his presidential aspirations,
huh?" She forgot herself and pulled a cigarette from
the little beaded bag on her shoulder and popped it
in her mouth before recalling her location. "See how
she's eroded his support since she got here! The latest
poll numbers show he's losing ground to Malloy, and
his career is—"

"I don't want to hear another word from you about
his career, do you understand me?" Erica hissed,
blinking back the tears stinging her eyes. "They don't
even know what's wrong with him yet, Bitsi! Don't
you get this? He might die and you're plotting his
stupid *career*!"

Bitsi studied her for a second and barked out a nasty, nervous laugh.

"Oh God. Don't tell me you really *are* in love with
him?" Bitsi cackled again. "Are you? Oh come on, Er-

ica. You've got to realize it would never work. I mean politics is his life. He needs a wife who agrees with his basic beliefs and agendas."

"He needs a wife who loves him, warts and all," Erica snapped before she thought about it. "He needs a wife who will help keep that ego in check and remind him that he's no better than the rest of us. I think I fit that job description pretty damn well!"

"Bravo!" Angelique started clapping like she was watching a theater piece for one. "You go, Erica! You fight for your man!"

"And I suppose you really believe that," Bitsi challenged. "Even though you two are complete opposites."

"We're not complete opposites," Erica said, her voice shaking with the suppressed fury this woman engendered. She curled her hands into fists to keep from reaching for that lank curtain of hair and yanking on it until the other woman's scalp bled. "There's more criteria in a successful relationship than what political party you belong to, or what color you are. There's another whole list of characteristics and qualifications. Things like trust and loyalty, having passion for people. A passion for life. It doesn't matter how it's directed. It matters that you both have it, and that you both know that, when it's all said and done, you're willing to work together, to fight together, and to serve the common good together . . . " Erica stopped short, realizing she had just paraphrased the speech Angelique had given her days ago.

And damn if for once, girlfriend hadn't turned out to be right, Erica realized with a sudden rush of emotion that might have been gratitude and might have annoyance, she couldn't say for certain.

Bitsi was staring at her like she'd sprouted horns, but before she could say anything, the door to the little suite opened. Two figures—one male, one female, both clad in green scrubs and white coats—entered the room.

"I'm Dr. Cortez," the woman said, her dark hair bobbing briskly in its bun, "and this is Dr. Penwatha." The man nodded his head in a curt little bow. "We have news about Senator Newman . . . and I think you all better brace yourselves."

Erica felt her breath catch in her throat.

"What is it?" she asked. "Is he all right?"

"He'll be all right," Dr. Penwatha said, his voice lightly accented and reassuring. "But—"

"The senator was poisoned," Dr. Cortez announced abruptly.

"Poisoned!"

The word was repeated by every voice as Erica, Angie, Chase and Bitsi each registered its shock in turn.

"Poisoned?" Erica repeated, shaking her head.

It was unbelievable, outrageous and horrible beyond anything Erica could have ever prepared herself for. The room reeled a little and she reached out for the solidness of the wall behind her, taking a deep, steadying breath.

"We have to run a few more tests, but yes. We believe Senator Newman has been poisoned," Dr. Penwatha repeated in his gentle, soothing way. "Cyanide poisoning, to be exact."

Cyanide poisoning? Erica shook her head as if the motion would clear her ears and help make sense of what the doctor had just said. The past several weeks replayed in her mind like a silent movie: the queasiness that he'd complained of so frequently, the sudden sweaty clamminess . . . but *poison*? *Cyanide*?

"B—but how can that be?" Bitsi stammered, her white face even paler than usual. She sank onto the arm of the chair Angelique sat in, looking as sick as Erica felt. Erica thought she saw the woman's pale eyes fill with tears as she turned her unlit cigarette again and again in her fingers. "Wouldn't it kill him?"

"Not in small-enough doses," Chase said, stroking Bitsi's back in a calming, friendly gesture.

"You're right, Mr. Alexander." Dr. Cortez turned toward him and Erica noticed for the first time how really young she was: she was like a dark-haired, bespectacled, female Doogie Howser. "Cyanide is contained in certain foods, like apricot pits, and lots of everyday chemicals like nail-polish removers, photo developing fluid, metal cleaners. Very small doses aren't lethal . . . at least not immediately lethal. Over time, they can ultimately kill." She paused, letting the information she was dispensing sink in. "It appears that, somehow, the senator has been exposed to cyanide—and in greater doses than one would be exposed to just by eating apricot pits or using developing fluid." She paused, looking first in Chase's face and then Erica's—then Bitsi's, and then Angelique's, as though weighing in on the drama of this revelation. "I've already notified the police; they'll be here shortly. But they'll want to know what he's been exposed to that might have been tampered with. Cyanide sometimes has a nutty smell. Like almonds. But other times it can be completely odorless. For the patient man or woman, it can be the perfect poison."

Bitsi's face crumpled. "Someone's trying to kill him?" she whispered.

The doctor nodded. "It appears that way."

"Oh God," she moaned. Then her eyelids fluttered and she did the last thing Erica ever would have expected of the tiny powerhouse: She fainted. Slumped right into the arms of a surprised and uncertain Angelique.

Dr. Penwatha glanced at Dr. Cortez. "Told you: your bedside manner needs some work," he muttered, helping Chase and Angelique lay her out on the bed. He glanced over at Erica. "You're Ms. Johnson, right?" he asked, searching her features for confirmation. "I saw you on the news with the senator a while back. Funny how two people can be on different sides of something and both be right." He jerked his head toward the recesses of the ER. "He's doing better. We should be able to transfer him to a private room in a bit. But he's asking for you. If you want, I can take you to him right now."

Later, she would realize how her face changed at these words, know how quickly she'd stood up to follow the doctor. In that moment, though, all Erica heard was "I can take you to him" and she was on her feet.

She wasn't sure what she'd expected: something out of a bad hospital drama, a haggard-looking patient in a hospital gown, hooked up to machines of every size and kind. What she found instead was Mark Newman, handsome as ever, still in his pants and open tuxedo shirt, propped up on the bed and smirking at her like he'd just said something obnoxious and was feeling particularly pleased with himself for it. In fact, the only hints of the ordeal he'd been through were the tubes in his nostrils and the IV tubing taped to the back of his left hand.

Erica had to work to suppress a smile of relief, had to work even harder to keep herself from rushing into his arms and sobbing out her fears.

I'm cool, I'm cool, she told herself as her heart leaped and quivered and danced in her chest. *It's just been a scary experience, that's all.*

He surveyed her like he was reading her mind,

smiling and silent and completely frustrating.

"You look a mess," he gasped in a gravelly, jagged sounding voice, even while those cerulean eyes did a jig in their sockets. "Your hair is wild, you've lost your headband, and your makeup's smeared. What have you been doing with yourself, woman?"

It appears this campaign has turned ugly—seriously ugly. Senator Newman has been poisoned slowly over several weeks—perhaps months, and at this point, we have to assume political motivations.

—Sergeant Andrew McAfee, Capitol police

Chapter 22

◇◇

"Don't you wish you knew?" she quipped without missing a beat.

No hysterics, no histrionics. Just her usual classy, sassy, self.

Thank God, Mark thought, taking what felt like his first deep, slow breath in a long time. He winked at her, trying to let her know he was okay by rubbing a spot on the gurney beside him with a hand that felt like lead. He inhaled, intending to launch into a long-winded commentary about what had happened, about how he was fine—too tough to be down for the count. But instead, all he had the strength for was a wheezy-sounding, "Sit with me."

It was enough. She smoothed the white sheet covering the gurney with her slender brown fingers, hopped up on the offered space beside him and entwined her hand in his own.

"You okay?" she asked gently, those lovely eyes probing his face.

He nodded, wanting to elaborate, but the words wouldn't come. There were things he needed to say—

would say—and it was probably better to conserve his energy for those.

"They said," she began carefully. "You'll feel better in a couple of days. They said you're lucky—they're able to treat cyanide poisoning so well you'll be good as new."

He nodded again, watching her face. Something flickered in her eyes and he had the sense of something omitted, something unsaid.

"I know . . ." he began, his voice like sandpaper in his throat. In spite of the antidote dripping into his body through the IV and the oxygen assistance, breathing was still an unpleasant effort. That's what cyanide did, they'd told him: deprived the body of oxygen, making it harder and harder for it to get air until eventually the person went into convulsions or lost consciousness.

"Relax," she said, watching him struggle to find the breath to talk. "You rest. Whatever you have to say, I'll be happy to listen to it tomorrow."

Mark frowned, shook his head and inhaled again.

"Police . . ." he began.

"They're here," she said quickly, misunderstanding him. "At least the local police are. I've heard they've also contacted the Capitol police. Your Sergeant McAfee's probably on the way." She gave him a slight smile. "I guess right now we're all suspects: me, Chase, Angelique, Bitsi." A hardness came into her voice as she said the media director's name, and Mark knew instantly there'd been a confrontation in his absence that he'd have to hear about later. "Everyone who had access to your food and drink. That's how they think it might have been done, through something you ate or drank." She frowned. "The problem is your dietary regimen. You eat the same

things on the same days from the same places . . ."
She shook her head, and he knew she was going
easier on him that she would have if he hadn't been
connected to various machines. "Lots of suspects. It's
going to take a while to sort out who did this."

"No."

The word came out right: firm and forceful, meant
to be obeyed. Weak as he felt, he couldn't stop the
smile from creeping across his face at her expression.
She looked three-tenths surprised and seven-tenths
like she wanted to throttle him.

"No?" she asked. "What do you mean, no? No to
what? Which part?" She leaned closer to him, close
enough for him to feel her breath on his face. "Mark,"
she asked him sternly, busting him down to wayward
fourth grader in a blink of an eye. "Do you know who
did this?"

He shook his head, inhaled deeply and said slowly:
"I know . . . how to . . . find her . . ."

"Her?"

He nodded. "Poison . . . a woman's way."

"Bitsi," she muttered, and he noticed the seething
anger snaking through the words. "I wouldn't put
anything past that bitch."

He shook his head. "Not . . . Bitsi . . ."

"How do you know?" she demanded, mahogany
eyes a-flash. "How do you know what *else* she's ca-
pable of?"

Else? Mark frowned. He wanted to hear the story,
but his body wouldn't let him. He could feel the last
bit of his energy draining out of him. Even his eyelids
felt like they were weighted and thick.

"Don't know," he murmured. "But . . . I know how
to . . . flush 'em out—"

She slid off the bed. "Let me get one of the detectives . . ."

"A press conference . . ." he finished in a rapid wheezing breath. "Announce our . . ."

"Our?" she asked.

"Engagement."

Her eyebrows rose. "What?"

"Tell the world . . ." he began, but a sudden wave of fatigue was washing over him, making it harder to make himself clear. "She'll make herself known . . . if you . . . Get Bitsi . . . press conference . . . marry me . . ."

She said nothing, but he watched her face as she processed what he was saying, thinking it through. When he saw understanding glimmer in her eyes, he let the last of his energy drain from his body.

"Do it," he muttered. His eyelids fell, lifted, fell again. "Promise me. Promise . . . "

Still she said nothing, but he thought he saw something like resolve tighten her face. Then, exhaustion and medication overtook him and he surrendered to sleep.

"He wants us to call a press conference," Erica heard herself saying. "He's convinced that's the best way to flush out who did this."

Their numbers had increased substantially in the hours since Mark's collapse and the hospital had accommodated. Now that Chase, Bitsi, Erica and Angelique were joined by Detectives Alba and Malone of the state police, Sergeant McAfee of the Capitol police and a handful of uniformed officers, the little staff lounge where Erica had made herself comfortable in the first hour of waiting had been abandoned for larger digs. A large conference room, tucked in a distant corner far from the day-to-day operations of the hospital, had been outfitted as a sort of police comfort and command center.

The smell of strong coffee permeated the room.

Sergeant McAfee raised the space above his eye where an eyebrow would have been if he'd had one. But he didn't have one: His face was as smooth as a cue ball from the dome of his pale bald head to the point of his chin.

"A press conference?" he repeated.

Something about the man's shaved, albino appearance was a little unnerving, but Erica reminded herself that Mark trusted him completely.

"Yes. As soon as possible."

Bitsi swung incredulous eyes in Erica's direction. "Of course we're going to have a press conference," she said in her usual know-it-all voice. Apparently the brief fainting spell hadn't slowed her down much. "It's already scheduled for . . ." she glanced at her watch. "Forty-five minutes. In time for the local late-night news. We've already talked about all that. The doctors will speak, then the police . . ." She shrugged. "I don't see how that's going to help find out how Mark's been poisoned. Or by whom."

Chase scratched at the top of his head. "I have to agree. People who do stuff like this love to get that kind of media attention, but from everything I know about it, they rarely step forward as a result." He glanced over at the detectives. "Isn't that right?"

"Sometimes," Malone looked as Irish as her name, with thick red hair pulled into a ponytail swinging down her back. She wore her badge on a loop on her belt like Erica had seen on TV shows. "But we have gotten leads from releasing certain information to the media," she said, fixing a pair of sea green eyes on Erica. "What did you have in mind?"

Erica hesitated. Her next words—if they actually made it out of her mouth and into the realm of the real—would change everything. At least for a short while . . . and maybe forever.

Am I sure I want to do this? she asked herself. *What if he's wrong? What if—*

"Mark has a theory," she continued, and was glad her voice didn't betray the butterflies of nervousness fluttering around inside. "And I think he's probably right. He wants to make a very specific announcement at this press conference. One that he believes will cause the person responsible to make another move and ultimately reveal herself."

"Herself?" McAfee repeated, invisible eyebrows rising with his voice.

"I'm pretty sure it's a herself," Erica said firmly. "And Mark thinks so, too."

"My money's on that, too," Angelique muttered, as though her opinion had been solicited. "This is some jealous-woman shit. No doubt."

"Well, neither one of you are cops, so what do *you* know?" Bitsi thrust out her chin and put a couple of knobby fists on her hipbones like she was fighting for something. "What's this announcement? What exactly does he want to say?"

Erica inhaled.

It's just a ruse. . . . It's just to find out who did this.

But why couldn't she erase the image of herself in a long, white dress, standing at an altar with Mark Newman on her arm?

"He wants to announce our engagement," she said in the firmest voice she could muster. "We'll marry as soon as he's well enough."

Sorry, girls. He's now officially taken.
—Bitsi Barr

Chapter 23

×◇

"I knew you'd do it." Mark grinned like there was no tomorrow, and when her face turned down into that I-hate-that-you've-won look, he grinned that much harder. Victories—even the smallest ones—were always sweet with this woman. And a victory like this one was enough to send him into a diabetic coma.

"It's only to find out who's poisoning you," she declared, but he noticed that instead of sitting on the chair beside the bed, she settled herself on the edge of the bed beside him. "I'm not going to actually marry you or anything stupid like that."

"No, no, of course not." He chuckled. "Why on earth would you do that? Even though you can't keep yourself away from me, even though you love every second you spend in my presence, you wouldn't want to marry me or do anything foolish like that, now, would you?"

She rolled her eyes. "No, I wouldn't. And since you're going to act like that"—she scooted her luscious behind away from him and off the bed—"I only sat next to you because I thought it would make you feel better. You know, a little physical therapy?

But this booty doesn't need to be anywhere near your smug-ass self. So take that," she said, and before he could stop her, she had not only taken the chair, but also slid it a few feet away so that she was now officially out of his reach.

Damn, Mark thought, his smile flipping to a frown in less than a second. *Me and my big mouth!*

"And McAfee and the local police agreed?"

She nodded. "You've got a full security detail. Allegedly, I have what they call a 'discreet undercover' detail, too, but they must be very, very discreet, because I haven't seen 'em."

"If McAfee says you have it, you have it. He knows his job." He took a moment to stare at her: The wild curls were restrained by another colorful head wrap and she wore a light cotton skirt in a summery shade of blue with a plain tank, covered by what looked like a man's shirt, knotted at her waist. By her standards, her attire was downright conservative, and he knew she'd worn it to present the right look for the press. He appreciated the effort, but not the dark circles under her eyes or the tight lines of strain around her lips.

"All this is beginning to get to you, huh?" he asked.

"I'm fine," she lied, and he knew it from the way her eyes dropped from his face. It was a tell: When she was telling him the truth, those eyes always flashed fire right into his face.

He was a second from calling her on it, but something stopped him. A bit of inner wisdom? Either that, or he was finally beginning to understand the woman a little, he decided. He chose another tactic.

"Thanks."

And for this simple word, he got the eyes, brown and deep and lovely, liquid with unshed tears.

"What else could I do?" she asked, blinking a little fast. "I thought it through. This will probably work. And—and—you may be a Republican, but I don't want you to die or anything."

He bit back the quip and nodded. "I know. That's how you are. You don't like to see anyone suffer, no matter what. It's one of the many things I've come to admire about you."

She blinked a few times, pushing back those tears quivering on her eyelids, and Mark longed to reach over and brush them away. But he hesitated, trusting something deeper than his mind this time. Something with a timing all its own.

"You? Admire me?" she barked out a laugh that was as fake as Pete Malloy's brown hair. "Hello? Have we met? I know you're not actually saying something nice about me."

He had to fight with the impulse to give her the wry quirk of a smile, fight down a clever comment. It was always easy to toss off glib one-liners, always easier to turn the thing into one big sparring match. A verbal war. But he was beginning to understand he'd never win this woman that way. And he was beginning to realize how much it mattered to win this woman, even if the election was lost.

So instead of smart-mouthing back, he focused on keeping his face straight and his words honest.

"There are many, many things I admire about you, Erica Johnson," he said softly, and from the way his heart squeezed tight in his chest he knew it was the absolute truth. "I admire your passion, I admire your intelligence. I admire your compassion—the way you can put your own beliefs aside for the good of what another person needs. I admire your beautiful voice, and your sense of your own style. I love the way you hear your own drum and you march to it and you never, ever compromise." He paused a moment. "I even love that you're a Democrat. I love the way you keep me on my toes. Keep me honest. Prepared. I just . . . love you."

That made those tears quivering on her dark lashes fall at last. He stretched his hand out for hers, but instead of rushing into his arms as he had hoped, she turned away from him.

"Have you seen the paper?" she reached over and grabbed the thing from a little tray that still held the remains of his breakfast. "The polls say your lead has diminished from double digits to within the margin of error."

There was a scratch at the door and then it swung wide. Mark glanced over and saw the broad face of his long-time friend, Dickey Joe, and his daughter Mary. Mary held some kind of green thing—a potted plant with a big bow around it—in her hand.

Reluctantly, Mark let his hand fall back on the crisp white sheet.

"Hey buddy! We're not interrupting nothing, are we?" Dickey Joe bellowed as if he could cover his embarrassment by the sheer force of sound.

Mark immediately noticed two things.

When the door swung wide he saw the dark blue shadows of uniformed officers blocking the entrance to his room like a human gate. On a stool beside one of them he thought he saw what looked like a six-pack of beer in longneck bottles, with one of those longnecks gone AWOL. Mark frowned. What kind of security detail drank on the job? Didn't sound like the kind of thing Sergeant McAfee would have allowed on his worst day—

And Mary's lipstick.

A deep persimmon color that didn't exactly jibe with her fair skin and blonde hair. Mark knew he'd

seen that color before . . . but his memory failed him
and he couldn't be certain where or on whom.

"Hell yeah, you're interrupting," Mark grumbled,
not bothering to be gracious about it.

Mark watched his old friend's eyes flicker from
Mark to Erica and back to Mark with an expression
of jovial interest.

"Well," he drawled in his usual, unfazed, good-
ol-boy style. "From what I hear, you got the rest of
your lives to make goo-goo eyes and kissy face at
each other." He leaned forward to thrust out a thick-
veined hand, "Congratulations, buddy! And as for
you" —he scooped Erica into a sudden bear hug—
"Good luck, honey. You're gonna need it."

Erica's face got that reddish bloom Mark knew to
be a deep flush of embarrassment.

"We're not really . . ." she began.

"We're not really sure how this announcement is
gonna affect the election," Mark finished, overriding
her. He reached for her again, seized a few fingers
and pulled her onto the bed beside him, sending her
warnings with his eyes. "But as I was just saying to my
future bride here, there's nothing a like a brush with
the Reaper to make you rethink your priorities."

"Yep, I know that's right." Dickey Joe took the plant
from his daughter and set it on a counter across the
room, already loaded with flowers, fruit baskets and
cards—most from members of Congress who had
heard about his sudden collapse. "Just a little something. I told Mary all you probably wanted was some
beer, but she insisted on a little green. Said it would
brighten a drab, old hospital room. Looks like she
wasn't the only one with that idea."

Mark quirked a smile at both the man and his shy
daughter. "Still a good idea, though. Thank you,
Mary."

She blushed a little, raised her eyes just enough to nod at him and looked away again.

"Definitely a good idea," Dickey Joe agreed. "If it hadn't been for that plant, we'd be here empty-handed. The cops out there"—he jerked his head toward the door—"took your beer. Mary told me not to bring none, said you probably couldn't have it just yet, anyway. But I told her, Mark Newman's a creature of habits, and he's had two beers every evening he could get 'em since I been knowing him. And I don't believe any hospital stay is going to change that."

"They won't let him have any outside food or drink until they know where the poison came from," Mary offered the carpet, not raising her eyes.

"You're right," Erica said. Her eyes included them all, but he knew that her words were for Mary's ears and encouragement alone. "And I don't think it helps that everyone knows Mark's habits. It probably made it easier for whoever did this. Half the world knows about the eating schedule and the two beers, nine glasses of water, fish on Thursday and God know what else! So you were right to discourage your dad from bringing the beer today."

"Well, all I can say is if I'da wanted that joker right there dead, he'd been a goner a long time ago. How long have you been drinking my home brew? Ten years? Twelve?"

Mark nodded. "Something like that."

"Well, I told them cops that, but they took it, anyway. In fact," he said, chuckling a bit. "I think we're a couple of suspects now."

"You look very tired, Ms. Johnson."

Mary's voice was soft and clear. Dickey Joe fell silent, and Mark saw the devotion in his face. Mary was lucky. Shy as she was, Dickey Joe had always been her protector, her biggest fan. One look in the man's eyes and it was clear: He saw no handicap, saw nothing a little unusual, nothing "off." He simply saw his beautiful baby daughter and acted accordingly.

For the first time in a long time, something paternal stirred in Mark's heart. He imagined a little girl, with skin the color of coffee and cream, sprigs of curls like her mother's dancing like a halo around her head as she ran. "Daddy," he heard her say and had to stopper the emotion building in his throat. "Daddy." And in his eyes, she wasn't "mixed" but perfect, and he knew he'd have to do serious damage to anyone who ever made her cry.

Erica moved, pulling away from him and dragging him out of that fanciful daydream and back to the conversation.

"—but the inn is a mob scene," she was saying. "Almost as bad as the hospital."

"Surely they can make you a bed around here somewhere?" Dickey Joe asked. "A place where you can lay your head."

"I bought a new lipstick," Mary said as though the remark followed from the conversation naturally. "It's not quite the same as yours, but I couldn't find an exact match. What kind was it?"

Lipstick. Mark peered at the girl again. Sure enough, the plum color she wore was very similar to Erica's favored shade. That was where he had seen it before.

"Mary here has decided your fiancée is the epitome of style." Dickey Joe shook his head, the doleful father doing his best with his daughter's quest. "Why, last week, she had me all around town looking for fabric to make headbands! Turned out we can just order 'em on the Internet."

Erica laughed, but Mark couldn't quite get there. He stared at Mary, who, there was no doubt, was uncharacteristically animated in Erica's presence. Here she was, looking Erica dead in the face, without the hint of a blush or a stammer, asking questions.

Questions about how to dress like her, look like her . . .

"There are some really good shops on the Internet for African-inspired clothing, but the very best are in Washington, D.C. When you come to visit me—"

Mary shook her head and now her eyes lowered to the floor tiles again. "I'll never go to Washington again."

Erica's eyes swung to Mark and then Dickey Joe. "Not even to visit me?" she asked gently.

This time Mary raised her face and looked Mark fully in the eye for a long, calculating second that made the room suddenly seem colder.

"I'm not good with Washington. It's too . . . fast," she said slowly. "I'm not . . . fast."

"Fast is overrated," Erica said lightly, and to Mark's dismay, she slid off the bed and away from him altogether. "Tell you what. When all this is over, and Mark is reelected, you'll come to Washington and—"

"No." Dickey Joe's voice was suddenly hard and flat. The smile slid from Erica's face as though she'd been slapped. "It's just . . ." Dickey Joe continued, trying hard to bring his voice back to its earlier "'aw shucks" tone. "I miss you too much when you're gone away from me, Mary," he said. "We gotta look out for each other, right?"

It could have been his imagination, or did a look pass between father and daughter? A look that seemed part conspiracy, part warning, and part something that Mark neither understood nor could easily guess at.

But when he looked again, whatever he'd thought he'd seen was gone.

This whole thing's got me spooked enough to distrust one of my oldest friends and his shy daughter? He shook his head, trying to clear the nagging feeling of suspicion.

"Oh," Erica said, and he knew from her tone she'd picked up a little of what he had. "I only meant to help," she finished lamely.

"Of course, you did," Dickey Joe sighed, sounding 100 percent his usual self again. "And I certainly didn't mean to come in here and lay any of our problems on your doorstep. You've been real nice to Mary and I appreciate it. I just don't think she should travel anywhere right now. Especially not D.C. Not after how hard it was for her up there working in Mark's office last summer."

Mark read the questions in Erica's eyes, and he knew he'd have to tell her the rest of those stories another time. For now, she contented herself with simply saying, "Of course not," grabbing her purse off the foot of the bed and turning her attention back to the young woman. "I like that lipstick, but I think it's a little strong for you." She pawed through the bag, searching. "I had a sample, a shade that was just a little too light on me. You can try it. If it works you can have it."

Mary's eyes sparkled with delight. "Really, Ms. Johnson. I could have it?"

"Sure." Erica grinned and ducked back into the slouchy shoulder bag again, still looking for the elusive tube of lipstick. "If I can find it in all this junk. And call me Erica. Please. Aha!" She said at last, pulling a fire-engine red cylinder from the bottom of her sack. "I knew I had it." And handed the lipstick to Mary.

The girl stared at it like it had magic powers, and then smiled at Erica. "Will you help me put it on?"

"Sure." Erica shouldered her bag again. "I'm sure I could use a little freshening up myself."

"There's a ladies' room right down the hall."

"No," Dickey Joe said in that same warning tone, just as Mark said, "Use the one in here."

Dickey Joe's eyes locked on Mark's face with an expression Mark couldn't fathom. He looked almost panicked. Mark heard warning bells going off in his mind again. Something here was wrong. Very wrong.

"I mean, Mark's right," Dickey Joe said in that same fake-sounding jolly voice he'd used only a few moments before. "Why walk all the way down the hall when there's a bathroom right here?"

Mary turned slowly toward her dad like she'd never seen him before.

"There's more room. And it's brighter," she said simply. Her eyes found the floor again. "And . . . if it doesn't look good, you and . . . he . . ."—she jerked her head toward Mark—"won't have to see."

"It's okay," Erica offered, putting her hand on the girl's shoulder. "I promise I'll take good care of her. We'll be back in ten minutes, looking absolutely lovely. You'll see."

"Erica—" Mark began, but she shot him a look he understood to mean *shut up* and led the girl out the door.

The second the door closed behind them, Mark leveled his hardest gaze on Dickey Joe.

"I always thought you were my friend, Dickey Joe."

"I am your friend, Mark," Dickey Joe said but there was an edge in his voice.

"Then you better tell me what's going on," he demanded. "Why don't you want Erica to spend any time with her? Why the sudden paternal care and concern? I thought you liked Erica."

"I like her fine, it's just—"

But he didn't get a chance to finish. The door of Mark's hospital room swung back so suddenly it slammed against the wall, and immediately the room was filled with uniformed and heavily armed officers—Capitol police, local forces and even a couple of FBI.

"Hands up! Put your hands up!" a voice screamed as the barrel of every weapon spun toward Dickey Joe.

"Look, I can explain it all. Or at least I think I can . . ." Dickey Joe began, slowly raising his hands to his ears.

"Down on the ground!" And now Mark recognized the voice as that of Sergeant McAfee.

"What the—?" Mark bellowed.

"Senator, we identified the source of the cyanide," McAfee said. "It was concealed in the beer, sir. Dickey Joe's home brew. The lab found small amounts in the seven bottles left in your office, the two at your home and in the empties at your condo on Capitol Hill."

Mark stared at Dickey Joe who now sat on the floor with his hands locked in handcuffs behind his back.

"Is this true?" he asked, even as he prayed it was a mistake. Had to be a mistake. A terrible, awful . . .

"Yeah." Dickey Joe sighed. "It's true. I'm awful sorry Mark. I swear I didn't know . . . not until just yesterday when all hell broke loose . . . "

"How could you not know you were lacing the brew with cyanide?" Mark shouted, giving his fury and hurt its head.

"Because I didn't do it!" Dickey Joe shot back. "It's Mary. Mary's been doing it!"

Mark stared at him, stunned beyond speech. An officer hovered over his longtime friend reading him his rights, but Dickey Joe waved him away. "I plan on tellin' you everythin', sir," he told the cop. "I owe my friend Mark that much."

Sergeant McAfee waved the uniforms out of the room with, "Get the girl back in here," and closed the door, leaving only Mark, Dickey Joe, the two detectives and himself inside.

"Speak," he commanded in a field voice Mark himself would have been proud of.

"I noticed it as soon as she got back from D.C.," Dickey Joe began, keeping his attention fixed on Mark. "She's always liked you, had a schoolgirl crush on you, like a girl does on a teacher sometimes. But since she got back from D.C., since things went so bad for her up there, she hasn't been right. She's been obsessed by you. Everything about you. Talks about you all the time, things you did, things you're gonna do. How smart you are, how handsome, how she's gonna help with the campaign . . . on and on . . ." His voice broke. "When she said she wanted to bottle the last case of beer herself, just for you, I didn't think anything of it other than it was just part of this crush. Until I heard about the poison. Then I knew."

"Shit, Dickey Joe," Mark muttered.

"I couldn't turn her in, Mark. She's my daughter. She needs help. Especially now that she knows you're in love with someone else. When she found out about Erica . . ." he shook his head. "It's creepy. Like she wants to *be* her, or something."

Erica.

Mark lunged off the bed, his bare feet on the floor, wearing nothing but the hospital gown. He glanced around for his cane, didn't see it and kept moving in painful uneven strides as McAfee barked, "Where?" and pulled his weapon out of its shoulder holster.

"Ladies' room." Mark shoved the man aside in his haste and led the way out into the hallway before the phalanx of uniforms raced past him, storming up the carpeted concourse toward the waiting area and the restrooms near there.

He was slow, too damned slow! He thought, hating the injury, hating wars and crimes and violence. Katharine floated to the top of his mind and he felt the crushing feeling of loss.

I won't lose Erica, too. I won't. I won't—

By the time he reached it, the officers had already burst into the place and searched. One look in McAfee's face and he knew. His worst fears had come to fruition.

"They're gone," the sergeant said.

Heav'n has no rage like love to hatred turn'd
Nor Hell a fury, like a woman scorn'd.
—William Congreve, *The Mourning Bride*

Chapter 24

The first thing she became aware of was the sharp pain at the back of her head, right at the spot where the neck met the skull. It hurt . . . and made everything else hurt: blinking, thinking, opening her eyes . . .

Mary, she remembered, trying to reach up to touch the sore spot. But she couldn't: her arms were tied together at the wrists and stretched in front of her, bound to a thick girder post that looked almost as wide around as Erica herself.

Mary.

They'd gone into the ladies' room and, expecting nothing more than a makeup lesson, Erica had bopped up to the mirror . . .

And Mary had whacked her from behind with something hard and heavy that had turned out all the lights.

She looked around.

If the girl was here, she was invisible.

She couldn't decipher where she'd been taken, exactly, but it looked like one of those dank, dark undercover spaces that every public complex had. The place where the heating and the cooling systems shook hands with the plumbing. A place filled with the roar of engines working overtime to make others comfortable. A place where the invisible things—the things most people took for granted—got done.

But there was no one here with her. No one she could see.

"Help!" Erica hollered over the whir of machinery, ignoring the throb of pain that started pounding in the back of her head. The hospital was crawling with cops. And hadn't Sergeant McAfee promised her she'd have an undercover detail, someone with her at all times? They had to be looking for her, searching the building for her. "Somebody! Anybody!"

"Be quiet." The girl's voice was very calm, very low, very sweet, but its owner was still unseen. "I'm not quite ready."

Ready? Ready for what? Erica was on the verge of repeating the words out loud when the girl appeared.

She was dressed almost identically to Erica: a long bohemian-style skirt and huarache sandals, tank top, and oversized shirt knotted at her waist. She'd done something to her hair—curled it somehow—so that it approximated Erica's own tousled 'do, and she'd tied a colorful kente band around it so that the excess fabric hung limply on her shoulders. Erica's bag was draped over her arm.

Mary strutted between the concrete pillars like she was working the Paris runway, turned and pirouetted back.

"I did it," she said proudly. "I look just like you now. Don't I?" And when Erica didn't answer, she repeated the words in a firmer voice than Erica had ever heard her use. "Don't I?"

"You look . . . nice," Erica said carefully. She pulled at the thick rope binding her hands, but it was no use. The bonds were tied tight.

"I don't look *nice*," Mary corrected, a flush of annoyance coming to her cheeks. "I look like *you*."

"Right. Just like me," Erica agreed, deciding it was probably best not to antagonize the girl. Obviously, she'd come unglued, lost some critical facility for reason. And since she'd already taken a pipe to the side of her head, Erica decided arguing with Mary really wasn't in her best interest.

"We look like sisters," Mary pronounced, swirling in the skirt. "We would pass for sisters on the street. Don't you think he'll think we're sisters?"

Erica frowned. "Who?"

"The senator," Mary breathed, using the man's title with a reverence that was creepier than anything else she'd said or done up to that point. "Only he won't be a senator much longer. He's sick now. He doesn't need to go back to that awful old Washington. Now he'll have to stay here. With me and Daddy. So we can take care of him."

Dread churned in the pit of Erica's stomach.

"You poisoned him," she said, understanding instantly. "Oh, Mary . . . you could have killed him."

"No," the girl shook her head so vehemently the head wrap slid down over her eye. "It wasn't enough for that. Just enough to make him sick. Sick enough to withdraw from the election and come home. Only . . ." She frowned. "Now he wants to marry you. He won't be happy unless he has you. But," she gave another quick turn making the full-bottomed skirt swing in a wide arc. "Now that I look like you, he'll never know the difference."

It was a crazy-person thing to say, the most clearly crazy thing Erica had ever heard anyone say. The throbbing bump on the back of her head, this dank and desolate spot, her hands slowly losing their feeling with the tightness of the cords around them, the matching clothes—all of those things pointed to jealousy. But to say that Mark wouldn't know the difference between Erica and Mary? The girl had turned around some bend from which there was no outlet, no return.

"Mary," Erica said gently, "I'm not sure that's going to work."

"Of course it will work!" The girl snapped, her eyes wild. "You just said we look alike."

"We're *dressed* alike."

"Exactly," Mary exclaimed, triumphant. "Exactly."

"But we *look* totally different."

Mary shook her head. "How? I don't see it."

"Well," Erica said slowly. "To start with, I'm black."

"I was raised to believe color doesn't matter," Mary sniffed, resting on her superior moral fiber. "That's what they teach us in school—not to see people as colors. Color doesn't matter. So I don't see what difference *that* makes."

Erica processed this information in silence. The girl had so warped the lessons of tolerance in her mind, Erica knew she would be unable to dissuade her. Instead she took another tack.

"What about the way I talk to him? The way I—"

"You're the most arrogant man alive, Mark Newman." Mary's head bobbled on her neck and her finger waved into space. "You're nothing but a warmongering, cold-hearted Republican!"

Do I really sound like that? Erica frowned. *I'm sorry Mark,* she told him in her mind. *If I ever get out of here, I'm laying off the name-calling. I promise.*

Mark.

Just thinking of him renewed her courage. They had to be searching this hospital for her. They had to be.

"Well . . . they'll be finding us soon," Mary said, looking around the place like she fully expected to be surrounded by S.W.A.T. officers within moments. "It's time for us to finish the switch," she said and ducked behind one of the massive pillars again. Erica heard noises, as though she were chipping at a section of the concrete. When she emerged a moment later, she held in her hands one seriously large-barreled revolver.

"I hid this weeks ago, when I was here doing some volunteer work," she said cheerfully. "I think that shows a lot of foresight, don't you? I'd never have been able to get this in here now." She grimaced. "Too many cops."

Erica's stomach did a slow roll.

"Wh—what are you going to do with that?"

Mary laughed. "I'm not going to do anything. I'm Erica Johnson. I'm the princess in the story and I'm going to marry Mark Newman and live happily ever after. But"—she heaved a sad sigh—"poor Mary. She's going to kill herself. Unrequited love. So sad."

The ending Mary was writing flashed through Erica's mind like a movie. It wouldn't work, it couldn't work. But in Mary's deranged mind, they were identical. Somehow, she really believed that she could kill Erica, make it look like suicide and escape to live her life in Erica's place.

"Mary," she said softly. "Mary."

"No, I'm Erica now," she said cheerfully, bending back to the concrete bunker where she'd stored her weapon. Erica watched her carefully load a single bullet in the chamber, snap the barrel shut and pace the short distance between them, leveling the gun at

Erica's temple. "You're really going to have to help me do this, Mary," she said in what Erica supposed was her best approximation of Erica's voice. "I really *hate* guns."

Two seconds from death.

Erica felt the knowledge of her own imminent demise sweep over her like a cold wave. In the time it took for this sad, sick little girl to twitch her finger, her life could be over.

Unless . . .

"Wait!" Erica said quickly. "If you're going to be *me* now, there's a few things you've got to know!"

Mary paused, and Erica felt the gun move. The cold steel left the side of her head and hovered somewhere in the space between Erica and Mary.

"Like what?" Mary asked. She sounded confused, uncertain.

"Like how to tie a head wrap, African style, for one thing," Erica said quickly. "If you walk up to Mark with that thing hanging half off your head like you've got it right now, he'll know you're not me." Erica nodded her certainty. "He'll know. I'm sure of it."

Mary frowned. With her gunless hand, she reached up and touched the lank fabric, hanging loosely over her forehead and shoulders. "Y—you think so?" she asked uncertainly.

"Yes. See, you have to pinch it around the top of your head—then bring the edges around themselves," she explained, knowing full well the description would make no sense. Tying African head wraps—like so many things in life—was something you did or you didn't do. It wasn't something you could explain. "I'll have to show you," Erica said quickly. "Untie me. It'll only take a second."

"No." Mary's voice was hard and flat.

"But you *have* to," Erica insisted. "If you don't, he's

sure to be suspicious. And if he's suspicious, you might get caught! He's watched me tie my hair a dozen times. Finds it fascinating," Erica lied, giving her desperation its head. "You have to let me show you. You want to live happily ever after, don't you?"

Hesitation and uncertainty flickered in the girl's pale face. She touched the kente cloth again. "I thought I might have done it wrong," she admitted in a soft voice.

"A little," Erica agreed. "We can fix it in a jiffy, though. You untie me, I'll show you. Then you can shoot me. Or even better, you can give me the gun and I can shoot myself."

"Would you?" Mary said, looking genuinely relieved. "I was a little worried about the killing part. If you really would shoot yourself, that would help. Help so much."

I cannot believe I'm having this conversation, Erica thought. It was like the script to one of those really bad television movies. The kind that come on late at night when only the least picky of insomniacs was still awake.

"Glad to help," Erica said as cheerfully as she could manage.

"All right," Mary said brightly, bending to loosen the bonds. "Thank you! Thank you so much."

A few moments later, Erica was rubbing life back into her numb fingers and wrists.

"Show me!" Mary said, practically jumping up and down in her eagerness. "Show me! Show me! Show me!"

She might have been cute—a kind of overgrown girl-child who didn't know any better—if Erica hadn't known how deadly this fractured young woman's mind was. Still, she tried to smile as she said, "You'll have to hold still."

The bouncing ceased instantly. Mary held herself as still as a statue and let Erica work.

"You twist this here . . ." she said, tucking and twisting the ends of the fabric around Mary's head, all the while watching the girl's gun hand grow more and more relaxed. She was going to have to make a grab for it. There wasn't any other option. "Then tuck, then twist, tuck, then twist . . ."

"I wish we had a mirror," Mary murmured. "I can't see how you're doing it."

"There was one in my purse," Erica said easily, as if they were just a couple of girlfriends playing "hair salon." "You want me to check or—"

"I'll look," Mary said, and in the instant she bent toward the slouchy old bag, Erica made her move: She grabbed for Mary's wrist and screamed out "HELP!" as loud as she'd ever screamed in her life.

She felt the rebound of the gun as it barked its report. She jumped away from the thing, cowering against the ricocheting bullet. With the only bullet gone, Erica had expected Mary to run, to flee against imminent discovery.

But the woman stood over her, gun aimed directly at her heart, finger on the trigger.

"That was very stupid, Mary," she said angrily. "But then, you always were stupid. Stupid and slow and stupid, stupid, stupid!" She repeated, letting her voice rise to a shriek. "Good-bye, Mary!" and her finger curled around the trigger.

Erica's life flashed before her eyes: her childhood in D.C. Working at Mama Tia's. Her days at Howard, where she'd first met Angelique on the Delta Sigma Theta line. All the faces of every kid she'd ever taught at Bramble Heights. Mark Newman . . .

She closed her eyes, thanking God for every second of it. Then she heard the sharp report of the gun.

And felt nothing.

She opened her eyes, feeling her body for the wound, but there was nothing. Nothing at all.

She looked up. Mary stood in front of her, a strange, transfixed expression on her face. Almost as Erica watched, a spot of blood bloomed, flowered, spread across her white tank. Then she crumpled to the ground in front of her.

"Oh my God," Erica mumbled, sinking to the ground beside the girl. Her eyes were open and blood trickled from her mouth, but she wasn't moving. Not even a little bit. "Oh my God . . ." Erica repeated, feeling sobs of panic, relief, fear and anger bubble down her cheeks. "Oh my God . . . "

A man appeared out of the darkness, thin to the point of rangy, with nondescript brown hair, eyeglasses and holding a serious-looking black semi-automatic out in front of him.

It was the fourth time she'd seen him—that she knew of—and yet she still didn't know who he was until he pulled a baseball cap out of his pocket and settled it on his head.

"I could have had a clean shot a long time ago, if you hadn't spent all that time playing with her hair," he complained.

"Did you have to kill her?" Erica screamed at him, tears rolling down her face. "She didn't know what she was doing. You had to have heard the crazy stuff she was saying—she didn't know what she was doing!" Erica gestured toward the gun. "The gun went off—she didn't have any more bullets. It was just that one! Did you have to—"

The man bent, pulling the gun from Mary's cold, dead hand. He opened the chamber, and even Erica could see.

The chamber was fully loaded, loaded enough to kill Erica several times over.

"Yep," the guy said calmly. "I had to."

They heard voices, the sounds of a search. "Over here! I've got her. She's okay!" He sighed. "Looks like my cover's blown this time," he said, as if they weren't kneeling over the body of a desperately troubled girl. "Too bad. I liked this gig."

In two days, the people of this state will make their choice about who they want to represent the Republican party as the candidate for the Senate. I hope they choose me again. But whatever decision they make, I sure as hell hope it's based on the candidates—and not who they work with, talk with or sleep with.

—Mark Newman

Chapter 25

❯❯❯

"Are you sure you're up to this?"

Angelique was staring at her with a frown on her face.

"Yeah," Erica agreed. "If Mark can do it, I'm sure I can. All I have to do is sit in the audience and listen."

Nothing in her bags had seemed appropriate for tonight's debate, not after the tragedy of Mary's death. Not with the whole state—if not the nation—looking at her not just as Erica Johnson, but also as Mark Newman's intended bride. Shopping was out of the question: She'd attained a kind of bizarre celebrity status, and might have been mobbed with well-wishers and curiosity seekers. With her now was a very visible security detail.

Angelique had been dispatched with instructions: Find something that suited the event, Erica and her mood. Her purchases now lay spread across the bed: a long, full skirt in deep purple, matched with a gold blouse and short jacket; a neat black suit with a short skirt and long tailored jacket over a zebra-print blouse; and a fitted navy blue dress with a dramatic colorful scarf belt.

Erica considered the collection, but it was impossible. She'd have to try them on. The idea made her head hurt—but then everything made her head hurt. There was a lump the size of a golf ball still sticking out behind her right ear.

Erica sighed and sank onto the bed, fingering the purple skirt. Angelique had spent too much—she could tell by the expensive fabric, but the skirt looked comfortable and elegant. The kind of skirt that would lift around her knees when she moved.

She saw Mary, twirling in her skirt before she could stop the memory. She shuddered.

"I know," Angelique murmured, sitting down beside her. "It's been a hell of a week."

"You can say that again." Erica pushed the purple away. There was no way she could wear it. Not tonight. She could still hear Dickey Joe's sobs when he'd been told what had happened. *I shoulda gotten her some help. I shoulda gotten her some help . . .*

It seemed weird to be sitting here, on the edge of the fluffy bed back at Mrs. Dickson's Bed and Breakfast with Angelique. So much had happened since they'd arrived, and so much was still ahead of them, too. She concentrated on Mark, imagining what he must be feeling, knowing that in few short hours he would face a packed auditorium, a panel of questioners and his opponent in a final debate before the primary election. The rest of his state would have the privilege of watching it on television, or reading about it in the next day's papers.

Thanks to the doctors at Mercy Hospital, he was on the mend physically, the effects of the cyanide having been treated. Dr. Cortez had argued for at least another couple of days of bed rest, but Mark had refused. "After the election, I'll rest all you want," he'd told her, sounding like the old soldier he was. "The debate's just a few hours. I'll be okay."

But emotionally Erica knew he wasn't okay. He was hurting, even though he seemed determined to cover everything over with a little more arrogance than usual, with a "can do" mask.

"I wouldn't give Malloy the satisfaction," he grumbled when Bitsi suggested canceling the debate. "The people of this state need to see what a buffoon he is. We're doing it."

"We could shorten it, though," Bitsi proposed, and Erica noticed she sounded far more timid, far more deferential than normal. Like she knew exactly how much trouble she was in with the boss, and didn't want to further annoy him.

No sale.

"No changes," Mark snapped at her and Bitsi nodded and backed away. For the first time, Erica had almost felt sorry for her. Almost.

"Your man is tough," Angelique was saying now, calling her back to the present. She held up first one finger, and then another, and another. "Shot, poisoned—God only knows what else—and he's back on the campaign trail in a matter of hours." She shook her braids. "Talk about taking a lickin' and keepin' on ticking. He's like—like—the Six Million Dollar Man." She cocked an eyebrow at Erica. "You remember that show?"

Erica wanted to smile. She tried to picture Mark as Steve Austin ("We can rebuild him, make him better than he was") but it was hard. Every time she blinked she saw Mary's crumpled form, the bright head scarf still wrapped around her blonde curls.

She shook her head, pushing the memory away. She looked down at the bed. The blue dress with its bright scarf was too great of a reminder of yesterday's ordeal.

That left the black suit.

I hope it fits, she thought, pulling it toward her and removing it from its hanger. She stood up and slipped out of her shorts and pulled off her "Be the change you want to see" T-shirt.

"So," she said stepping into the skirt and shifting the attention to her friend with a cheerful brightness she didn't feel. "It looks like *you've* got some new developments. Don't tell me. Chase Alexander is 'Mr. Politics.' The guy you started chatting with on the Internet. Right?"

Angelique flushed. Now that the topic of conversation was her own business, her sassy, know-it-all certainty evaporated into a girlish giggle. "Can you believe that?"

"It's absolutely incredible." Erica pulled on the jacket and buttoned it. "When did you figure it out?"

"On the plane. He took out his laptop and I took out mine and we started talking and it turned out we already knew each other!" she exclaimed. "Or at least sort of." She sobered a little, her face growing serious. "You know, he's not the kind of man I would normally have even considered. You know: short, fat, white. But in the chats, I got to know him. How funny he is. How smart. So it didn't bother me as much that he looks the way he looks. He's actually kind of cute. Think about it."

Chase Alexander? Cute? It wasn't something Erica wanted to think about, but she kept that observation to herself.

"Sounds like you're seeing him through the eyes of love."

Angelique didn't deny it. Instead, she considered for a long moment before stating simply, "Maybe. It's only been a week." Then she added, after another pause, "But sometimes, you meet someone and you just *know* there's something between you. You know there's something there. You understand what I'm saying."

Erica nodded. "Unfinished business," she said. "That's what Mark calls it."

Angelique nodded, too. "And you? Now that . . . everything's over," she continued diplomatically, "you still getting hitched?"

Erica's heart gave a painful squeeze, but she managed to fake a smile along with her shoulder shrug. "I doubt it."

"You doubt it," Angelique repeated. "Why?"

"It was a ruse, Angelique. Remember? Just to catch . . . to find out who was poisoning him," she finished, not wanting to have to say Mary's name.

Angelique's expression made it clear she wasn't interested in discussing Mary right now, anyway. "I know you're not going to tell me you don't want to marry him. Because it's written all over your face that you do."

"How can you want to marry someone you've only known a few days?" Erica shook her head. "You might be that crazy, but I'm not."

"Well, can you at least admit that you're crazy in love with him?" Erica opened her mouth, but Angelique raised a finger in warning: "And remember who you're talking to and don't bother to lie to me, girl."

Erica sighed. "Suppose . . . just suppose . . ." she said slowly, "suppose I was. So what? How is this ever going to work? I mean, look at the kind of trouble I caused in his world in a couple of weeks."

"Hey, that poison stuff had nothing to do with you. That girl started that stuff long before she knew you existed," Angelique pointed out. "In a way, your being in the picture might have saved his life!"

"Maybe. But what about the election? What about the fact that, technically, I'm rooting for the other guy? Well, not Malloy. He looks like an even bigger jerk than Mark. The Democrat. Nanke, or whatever his name is."

"Honestly, Erica," Angelique said. "Can't you lay aside the politics for once? I asked you a simple question: Do—you—love—him?" She repeated, saying each word loudly and slowly as if Erica were a member of the "slow" class back at Bramble Heights. "It's a one-word answer. Yes or no."

"Oh fine," Erica retorted. "Yes. So what? That doesn't change the fact that this whole thing will never work."

Angelique's mouth opened for her next argument or objection, but Erica silenced her with an upturned palm. "I'm done, Angelique. I don't want to talk about him anymore. I just want to get through this debate and go home."

"Home?" Angelique frowned. "But we weren't scheduled to leave until Wednesday."

"My recent fame—or infamy—counts for something at the reservations desk, at least. They let me swap out my ticket. I'm leaving tonight."

"But Erica—"

"Not a word," Erica repeated, showing her the palm again. "Now." She nodded toward her attire. "What do you think?"

Angelique sighed. She cast an appraising eye over the tailored folds of the black suit and frowned. "It fits fine, but it's a little plain. It needs something."

"I know just the thing," Erica said, disappearing into the closet and pulling out her suitcase. She rummaged around inside it, displacing underwear, skirts, jeans, until she found what she was looking for.

"Erica . . . you're not going to—"

"Oh, yes I am."

Angelique's brown face crunched into genuine concern. "Erica, you already said you were leaving. I don't see why you have to—"

"That's the point, Angelique. I don't want to hurt him, but *this* is who I am. *This* is why it would never work between us. And I can't think of a better way to tell him that than *this*."

"I'll tender my resignation tonight if you like." Bitsi stood before him, reeking of smoke, her eyes red-rimmed as though she'd been crying. "I wanted to make sure the debate went well"—her red lips quirked upward into the tiniest smile Mark had ever seen—"and it did. You were great. I'm not even worried about tomorrow anymore. Hell, I'm not worried about November. The people of this state are standing right with you, Mark."

Mark rubbed his forehead. He was tired—exhausted, really. His chest hurt, his leg hurt, his throat hurt. It had taken everything he had to appear normal, to appear his usual self. Now, sitting on the old leather sofa in the den of his home, he should have felt better. Should have felt relief. Except there was still Bitsi Barr to deal with, and . . .

He craned his neck toward the window.

Where was she?

His handlers had strict instructions to bring her back here, to his home, after the debate. So where was she?

"I'd say your reelection is assured," Bitsi was saying when he tuned back into her. "Except—"

Mark waited, but she pursed her lips.

"Except?" he prompted.

"Well, you've seen the numbers. Support for the war is definitely eroding across the nation. Here's no exception. They're with you now, but . . ." She shrugged her shoulders. "Erica Johnson and her stupid T-shirts might just have a point." She rolled her eyes. "I can't believe she actually pulled that crap again. Ripping off her jacket when you introduced her. Once is fine, twice means you don't have any better ideas."

Mark might have laughed two days ago . . . but today it wasn't funny. Not considering the things Bitsi had done. He let her ramble on for a few more minutes about Erica and her T-shirts and her war sentiments before he manhandled her back to the subject of her own transgression.

"I just want to know one thing." He lifted his leg up onto a nearby hassock, whipped off his tie and tossed it toward the desk, watching it land and drape over the lamp shade. "Why? Why did you do it, Bits?"

She inhaled, long and hard and deep and her fingers twitched in a way that he knew meant she needed a cigarette. "You *will* be president one day, Mark," she said at last in a low voice. "You will be the leader of the free world."

He opened his mouth to object to so dramatic a characterization of his possible future, but she shook her head and held up her hand.

"Let me finish before you say anything, Mark. Otherwise, I might not get it all out." She hesitated for a moment then barreled on. "You know how I feel about you."

"C'mon, Bitsi," he began, but she ignored him.

"I love you. I've always loved you. But you were married to Katharine and I loved her, too. When Katharine died . . ." Her eyes found his. "I'll admit it. I hoped. But you've always seen me as a buddy—a sister, I guess. And I got over it. Especially since there wasn't anyone else in your life. Sure there were the staff members and the interns and the female members of the Senate and their staff members and interns." She shook her blonde hair until it bounced. "But they weren't any competition. For all the attention they paid you, you never looked at a single one of them, until Erica Johnson walked into that hearing room, with her hippy-dippy ideas, her outlandish slogans, that wild hair, and suddenly you were grinning like a schoolboy and rearranging schedules and running after her like—"

"I know how I feel about Erica," Mark snapped. "What I don't know is how you could stoop so low as to have some—some—CIA mole following me around taking pictures! I don't see what made you frighten and embarrass her—and me—like that," he growled. "Did you know I almost punched Malloy's lights out over those pictures? Did you know that?"

"No," Bitsi said calmly. "But I had to do it, Mark. And I'd do it again. Even if you're mad at me for it."

"You'd better believe I'm mad."

"Even if you fire me—"

"That could happen, too."

"I had to know what kind of woman she was. After all, she's more than a candidate for 'wife,' Mark. She's a candidate for First Lady of the United States."

"So." Mark leaned forward, pinioning her with his gaze. "Are you telling me the pictures were some kind of test?"

Bitsi nodded. "I had to know what kind of woman she was. I had to see if she'd sell them, try to exploit them . . . try to exploit you. I had to know how she dealt with the press. I had to know whether she could be discreet and keep your counsel. I had to see what kind of judgment she had, and how she behaved under stress." Her eyes found his again. "In short, I had to know if she was worthy of you, Mark. And I suppose she is. My only wish is that she were a Republican, but hey, I guess you can't have everything, right?"

The joke fell sour and flat. Mark frowned at her, shaking his head. "Aw, come off it, Bitsi. You're trying to make this sound all grand and important, when the truth is, you just didn't like her. You were jealous and you wanted her gone, plain and simple."

Bitsi flushed pink, an odd expression of pride and pleading on her face, but when she spoke, her voice stayed even and relaxed. "You're right. That, too. So. Do you accept my resignation, or my apology?"

Mark considered the woman, his emotions churning inside him. What she'd done was awful. Underhanded. Potentially harmful and extremely hurtful. It showed a nasty side that Mark didn't want to have a thing to do with.

But on the other hand, she was a longtime friend, a woman who believed in him more than any other. And she'd been the first to know that something was more than a little off about Mary. Bitsi's instincts had sent the girl packing, sent her back home. Too bad that once she'd gotten there, she'd spent her energy on a twisted kind of revenge.

He didn't know what to do, and, it wasn't just his decision, he realized. Erica had a right to weigh in on Bitsi's fate.

"I don't know yet," Mark announced, grabbing his cane, pulling himself to his feet and stumping toward the window. "Where the hell is she?" he asked the night sky. "She should have been here *before* me, not after."

Bitsi frowned. "They didn't tell you?" she asked.

Mark froze. He turned away from the window slowly, every nerve in his body strained and taut.

"Tell me what?"

"She's gone," Bitsi said. "She caught a plane back

to Washington, right after the debate. I thought you knew."

"Hell no, I didn't know!" Mark shouted, pushing past her out of the room and through the kitchen toward the front door. "What time was the flight? What time is it now?" he demanded, snatching his keys up off the counter. "Is she still in the airport or is she already in the air?"

"I—I don't know," Bitsi stammered. "It must be the last flight out . . ."

Mark whirled on her. "You're going to have to do better than that, Bitsi. If you want to stay on the team."

It took her a second to fully appreciate his meaning. For an instant he thought she was going to jump on him, swing her arms around her neck. But instead, she whipped out her cell phone and cigarette and dialed.

"This is Bitsi Barr, calling for Senator Mark Newman. What's the last flight to Washington, D.C.?" She cut a glance at Mark. "Boarding now."

"Stop her from getting on it," he said already moving for the front porch. The two security guards that McAfee had now assigned to him full-time moved into place beside him and he almost barked at them. But he knew it wouldn't do any good. They were soldiers: They had their orders. They'd do their duty whether Mark Newman liked it or not. It was just going to take some getting used to.

"Stop her!" Mark repeated.

"How?" Bitsi called after him.

He tossed her a grin. "You've got a devious mind. Think of something." He gestured to his security team. "Come on, boys, you're with me."

"Ms. Johnson?" The man had a dark uniform with a badge that read AIRPORT SECURITY, and was accompanied by two other uniformed men with grim looks on their faces.

"Yes?" Erica replied. She'd just taken her seat, fastened the seat belt securely around her midsection and locked herself into the upright position. She'd just looked out of the window at the tarmac and seen the cornfields swaying under the night sky and felt the first pinch of longing for things that might have been.

You've changed my life. You've changed the way I see the world, Mark Newman, she thought blinking away a tear. *Damn you.*

But before the full force of her sadness could sweep her away, these uniformed and unsmiling men had surrounded her.

"Will you come with us, please?"

Will you come with us, please? The words were ominous, commanding and more than a little creepy. Erica had a flash of a movie she'd seen once—a political thriller—where people had been captured, brainwashed and reprogrammed by dark uniformed, unsmiling men.

"I—is there a problem?" she asked, trying not to sound nervous. She glanced around her, looking for a friendly face, or at least someone who might remember seeing her if she were suddenly to vanish from the face of the earth. If only she'd been able to persuade Angelique to leave tonight! But no, her best girl, her wingman, her backup, had turned her down to fly back to D.C. tomorrow with her new man, Chase. "What is it? What's wrong?"

All the passengers nearby were looking at her as though she were some kind of criminal.

And of course the T-shirt didn't help.

"Come with us, please, ma'am," was the only reply she got.

"Should I get my—"

There was no need to finish. One of the unsmiling uniforms had already retrieved her bag from the overhead compartment.

She followed the dude in the security uniform up the aisle and off the plane, while the two others followed behind.

"This way," he said when they'd ascended the jetway, nodding her toward one of those doors labeled ACCESS ONLY. He swiped a card key, typed in some numbers and then yanked on the handle.

Warily, Erica stepped inside. It was a small room that had the look of an interrogation cell, with its long bunk of a seat, a small table, and bright fluorescent lights. But instead of a police questioner, Mark Newman sat on the bench, his hands folded over the crook of his cane, looking as sweaty and irritable as if he'd been the one yanked off a hot airplane for no good reason.

"I should have known you were behind this," she snapped at him as soon as the officers closed the door, leaving the two of them alone in the little room. "This time, Mark, you've gone too far."

"It was Bitsi's idea."

"Don't blame her. I know Bitsi Barr would have been only too happy to see me get on a plane and get away from you forever."

"That's very true," he said and for the first time in a long time, that corn-pone grin stretched across his face. "She's still very much in love with me, you know. Probably always will be. Maybe we should try to set her up with somebody. You got a couple of friends you think she'd like?"

Erica stared at him, too stunned to speak. The man had just had her removed from an airplane under heavy police escort . . . and for what? To talk about Bitsi Barr's love life?

It was outrageous, obnoxious, irresponsible and annoying.

Classic Mark Newman.

"You pulled me off an airplane to get me to help you find Bitsi a date? You really are too much, Mark," Erica chuckled in spite of herself. "Thanks for that. I needed a good laugh. I hope the taxpayer's find it as funny."

Mock confusion crinkled his brow. "What? I think you'd want to help me find Bitsi a steady fella. If she's got someone of her own, she'll leave us alone." He hesitated, frowning. "It's gonna be hard, though. Finding her a man who can measure up to me."

"You're unbelievable, you know that?" Erica shook her head. "I just have to know one thing, Senator. How do you get your head through the door, as big as it is?"

Irritation ignited in his eyes, found fuel and started to burn.

"But it's true," he asserted.

"You're unbelievable," she repeated. "A legend in your own shower." She glanced back at the door. "I suppose I'm locked in here?"

He shook his head. "You can go. Anytime you want."

"Good," she said. "Maybe I can still catch the plane."

"I doubt it. I just barely caught you as it is. Had them race one of them little motorized cars down to the gate so I could pull you off there before push-back." He shrugged. "They're in the air by now."

Erica sighed, turning away from him. This is what she'd wanted to avoid. This scene. These words. But she should have known he would insist on hearing it. He didn't like unfinished business.

"Okay, Mark," she said, turning back to him and

squaring her shoulders in determination. "You want to hear it, I'll say it. It's been . . . " She paused, struggling for the right words. "Frustrating and fascinating. It's been scary and exciting and passionate and painful . . . and . . ." She swallowed down the emotions rising in her throat. "Unforgettable," she said softly, knowing that of all the words, that one was the most true. "But it's over now. It's time for us to go back to our lives." She shook her head. "I'm not going to bother to tell you I'm not attracted to you. Or that I don't care for you." Her voice shook a little and she had to struggle to keep it even, composed. "But this can't work for the long haul. And we both know it."

He stared at her a long time, long enough for her heart to start beating in that wild nervous thump. Long enough for her to start remembering what it felt like to be in his arms. Long enough for her to want to feel his lips on hers.

Finally, when she thought she'd die of anticipation, he stood up slowly, unfolding every long, lean, handsome inch of himself and limped over to her.

"Really?" he murmured, coming close enough for her to smell him, close enough for an embrace.

"R—really," Erica stammered, fighting the impulse to back away from him. Instead, she raised her face to his and put on her biggest, baddest, I'm-not-afraid-of-you-mask.

But being close to him like this crumbled her resolve, like kryptonite weakens Superman.

He knew it, too, the big, arrogant so-and-so.

"You sure?" he asked again. "Because, here I was," he sputtered in a tight voice, "thinking you ought to marry me. For real."

Down, fool, Erica told her heart, when it had the nerve to start jumping for joy in her chest. "No," she said, finding the strength to shake her head. "I think that's a really bad idea."

He didn't like that answer much. She could tell by the irritation that flashed in his eyes. "What's the matter with you, woman? Do you have any idea how many women want to hear those words from me?"

There it was again: that absolutely shocking sense of himself. Erica couldn't help but laugh, which annoyed him that much more.

"All the more reason to turn your ass down," she said lightly. "If Bitsi's jealous enough to start snapping pictures of you doing the do with another woman, another one of your femmes might just be jealous enough to try to kill your sorry behind. Then where would I be? A good-looking widow, 'tis true, but a widow all the same." The thought of how close he'd come to death already drained the humor from the words. "That was a bad joke," she muttered. "But you get what I mean."

"I'm not joking. I'm serious."

"So am I!" Erica snapped. "Mark, someone *poisoned* you! Yeah, I know, I know, you're fine," Erica said quickly waving away the objections and insistences. "The point is, someone tried to do it, and what sane woman would buy into *that*? Just for the joy of being a senator's wife? For the hope of being the first black First Lady? Don't think so, buddy. Not on your life."

"A woman who loves me like I love her would buy into it," he grumbled, putting on a petulant expression. "But I guess . . ."

"Oh, I love you just fine," Erica replied. "I just don't want to die."

"Aha!" he roared, suddenly jubilant, and immediately began wheezing with the effort of the sudden shout. He paused a moment to take a deep breath, a happy expression in his eyes. "I got you to say it," he murmured. "I got you to say it. You *do* love me. I knew it."

Crap. Fate had stepped in and tipped her hand, and once again, he was in the driver's seat.

"Okay," she said, at last. "Let's take your premise and say I *do* love you."

"You do," he insisted. "You do."

"Okay, I do," Erica agreed, seeing victory dance in his eyes. "So I love you. So what? In the words of that song Tina Turner sang, 'What's love got to do with it?' Any of it."

"It's like Angelique was saying in the car. It's time to accept the long-term possibilities."

"Mark—"

"Erica. Good, we remember each other's names."

"Mark—"

"Again? They didn't tell me *you* had a medical attack, too. Sounds like it was something with memory. Well," he drawled, watching her face, "I'll save you the trouble of saying whatever you're trying to say by telling you this: I don't care. Yes, I'm a public servant. Yes, I've got a public life. But my private life is for me to conduct as I see fit."

She frowned. "That's not true, and you know it. First of all, you're running for office. Your life is an open book. Second of all, since you're a public servant, everyone in the world seems to feel like they can weigh in on how you conduct your private life. And"—Erica rolled her eyes—"in case you've forgotten, I'm black."

"No, really?" he asked, his eyes crinkling with mischief. "I thought that was just a really dark tan."

"And liberal."

"I'm willing to overlook that unfortunate fact."

"And you, Senator Newman, are a jerk."

He laughed, wheezed, choked and sobered. "Okay, let's *take* your premise," he countered in his best I'm-smarter-than-you tone he could muster. "But you love me."

"Oh stop it."

"You love me," he insisted, catching her by the arm and pulling her close to him. "You . . . love . . . me," he murmured, covering her mouth with his own.

She wanted to fight him, wanted to deny him. But it was impossible. Everything within her surrendered to the flame of desire the man ignited in her, everything within her abandoned its fight for the safety and security of being in his arms.

"I love you," she whispered when, breathless and spent, their lips broke apart. Erica pressed her head against his chest, feeling the necessity for separation but unwilling to let him go. "God help me . . . I love you. But, I have to leave, Mark. I just don't see how this can work."

"Did I ever tell you about Katharine?" His voice rumbled in his chest, filling her ear. "About how I asked her to marry me the first time we met?"

Erica shook her head. "Tell me."

"It's true. I just looked at her, and I knew." He chuckled. "Of course, she disagreed. See, you gotta understand. In high school, I was a slack-jawed, tobacco-spitting redneck who didn't care for much more than drinking beer with my buddies and getting into fights on Saturday nights. And she"—his voice grew wistful with the memory—"She was sophomore class president, on the varsity cheering squad and taking all honors classes." He chuckled a bit. "She was way out of my league. So far out of my league no one ever thought it would happen. Least of all her. I'll never forget it. I was smoking a cigarette with one of my buddies outside the school and she walked by with some of her cheerleader friends and I yelled out, 'Little Missy, you're gonna marry me one day!'"

"What did she say?"

He frowned a little, trying to recall. "I think it was either 'Drop dead' or 'Get lost.' Something like that." He chuckled again. "Took me five years and a lot of changes to make that happen. But she married me. And I like to think she was happy in the bargain." He pulled away, capturing her eyes in his own. "I knew from that first second—when we were staring each other down in that hearing room—you were the next woman in my life. And I'd like to think you'd be happy in the bargain, too. I'd work hard," he said earnestly. "I'd work hard to make sure of it."

Yes, her heart said. *Yes, oh yes, oh . . .*

"Will you still feel that way when you lose, Mark?" she asked in a strained voice, feeling the tears she'd been fighting for so long welling up in her eyes again. "Will you still love me? Or will you blame me?"

"So that's it," he said, looking suddenly relieved. To Erica's surprise, a smile spread across his face. "You're worried about the election."

"And you're not? What the hell are we here for if you don't plan on winning?"

"Did I tell you that I love your spirit? That I love the fight in you? Because—"

"Oh stop with the love sonnet," she snapped at him, slapping the tears from her face. "You can say you love me all you want to, but I know full well how much you hate to lose. All this admiration is going to go straight out the window if you lose this primary— if you're sitting at home next year with me—but without a job. This primary race has already gotten way too ugly because of me. Malloy's been taking advantage of the worst in people, spreading all kinds of ugly rumors and nasty innuendo."

"All of which turned out to be true," Mark interrupted with a chuckle. "If you recall a certain extremely intimate moment between us . . ."

"Laugh if you want. But I don't think it's particularly funny that someone tried to kill your white ass."

"Why? Would you miss my white ass?"

Yes, damn it, she almost shouted, but he had that self-satisfied smirk on his face already, like he was enjoying knowing just how much she cared for him. "That's beside the point," she said huffily at last. "The point is you're a good senator. You're good for this state. You really have your constituents' interests at heart and"—she swallowed like her throat hurt to admit it—"you're a decent man. You're . . . strong . . . and passionate . . . and when you want to be, you can be really"—another hard swallow—"gentle and tender and sweet." Her eyes met his again. "But you're ambitious, Mark. You want your seat in the Senate, and pursuing this crazy idea about our marriage is one sure way to lose it."

Mark shook his head. "I don't think so. First of all, I don't think the people of this state are either that racist or that stupid. I did some checking, Erica. Did you know that in the 2000 census, almost twenty percent of the population here classified itself as mixed? That means there's a lot of carrying on between people of different cultures—even here in the Deep South. And second of all, yeah, there's been some nastiness, but on the whole, you've been far more of an asset to this campaign than a hindrance. People who never voted before—and certainly wouldn't have considered voting for me—are interested, are coming to events and listening to speeches—all because of you. They like you. They like *us.* They like hearing me flesh out my positions with your objections. They like that you keep me on my toes. I predict that not only do I win the primary, but for all this bullshit about a 'close race,' we take it by a landslide. And after you marry me, we'll win the general election without breaking a sweat. That's what I predict."

"And if you're wrong?"

Mark bent toward her, laid a hand on either shoulder and pulled her close.

"I have lost many things," he murmured, staring hard into those deep brown eyes. "I have lost them and had to pick myself up off the ground and start again. And you're right, it isn't always easy. And sometimes it completely *sucks*." He paused a moment, searching her eyes as if to be sure she was really listening, to be sure she really understood. "I can tell you with absolute certainty that if I lose my Senate seat, the next day there will be other things I can do, other ways I can serve, other titles I can hold. But if I lose *you*"—he shook her shoulders gently—"it will be a long time before I find anyone—anyone—who will fill the void in my heart like you do." He shook her again. "All I'm asking is for you to follow your heart. Hell, read your T-shirt. And if it's really true, it won't matter who's what color, or what political party, or anything. Will it?"

"What about all those women who are in love with you?" she said softly. "What about them?"

"What do they matter, if I'm only in love with you?" He traced her cheekbone with a finger. "So, what about it? I can't promise it'll be easy and I'm pretty sure it's going to take a hell of a lot of patience—from both of us. But I want to try. I really want to try."

Erica looked down at her shirt, considering its message, the moment and her heart. A power beyond her own mind must have selected it, the words spoke so fully to this moment, this decision, and this war within her.

All blood is red.

"Let's try," she murmured, brushing her lips against his. "Let's try."

Senator Mark Newman married Erica Johnson today in a private ceremony here in Billingham. The couple, who had been engaged for the past year, exchanged vows at St. Matthew's Church.

"It's been a long time coming," said Angelique Dawson Alexander, one of the new Mrs. Newman's oldest friends. "These are two of the most stubborn people on the planet."

Mrs. Alexander, who is black, and her husband, Senator Newman's chief of staff Chase Alexander, who is white, say that the couple are a powerhouse in Washington because of their differences. "I think they fight it out at home," said Mr. Alexander, chuckling. "Then the senator comes in ready to work toward the best outcome. Marriage is all about compromise, and government is all about compromise. So it works for everyone."

According to media relations director Bitsi Barr, the couple will honeymoon in Baghdad, visiting with our servicemen and -women stationed there. "It's an unusual honeymoon, but they are both very committed to seeing our troops return home safely."

Political pundits speculate that Newman is still considering a presidential bid in 2012, but Barr neither confirmed nor denied the rumors. "Right now, he just wants to be a good senator and a good husband. Let's let the newlyweds have a bit of 'happily ever after' before we deal with all that."

—The *Billingham News*